Books by Va

INVASION AMERICA SERIES
Invasion: Alaska
Invasion: California
Invasion: Colorado
Invasion: New York
Invasion: China

DOOM STAR SERIES
Star Soldier
Bio Weapon
Battle Pod
Cyborg Assault
Planet Wrecker
Star Fortress

EXTINCTION WARS SERIES
Assault Troopers
Planet Strike
Star Viking

Visit www.Vaughnheppner.com for more information.

The Lost Starship

by
Vaughn Heppner

ISBN-13: 978-1500986193
ISBN-10: 1500986194
BISAC: Fiction / Science Fiction / Military

Wearing perfectly pressed trousers and shiny boots, Captain Maddox of Star Watch Intelligence flexed his bare chest. Muscles like strings of steel writhed upon his lean frame. He gripped a viper stick, swishing it back and forth, so the spectators murmured uneasily.

A mansion rose in the distance, a replica of the Hall of Mirrors in Versailles. It belonged to Octavian Nerva of Nerva Incorporated, a conglomerate specializing in warship construction. Through an extraordinarily long life, Octavian had clawed his way into becoming the richest man on Earth.

Caius Nerva—the founder's youngest son—stood on the opposite end of the meadow as Maddox. The thickly muscled man had glassy eyes, moving in a half stagger as he circled an area he'd already stomped flat. He, too, swished a viper stick.

"He's intoxicated, sir," one-eyed Sergeant Riker whispered. "But he's playacting the stumbling part. I believe he suspects your real intentions and wishes to kill you in order to cover his tracks. I doubt I'll leave this place alive, either, if that means anything to you, sir."

Captain Maddox glanced at his one-eyed aide. The Old Guard had thought to saddle him with a seasoned veteran, someone to hold his hand during the investigation.

"You've gathered enough evidence tonight, sir," Riker told him with pleading in his eye. "You were right about Caius' involvement in the fraud. You've solved another case. Isn't that enough?"

"Go away," Maddox said.

Sergeant Riker showed his well-known stubborn streak. "Sir, I've been thinking about the card games—the last ones in particular. I believe...well, sir, it seems obvious you did cheat. You deliberately pricked Nerva's infamous pride."

Captain Maddox raised a single finger. He'd spread his jacket on the dewy grass with his tunic on top. Beside the garment was an open bottle of wine with a goblet keeping it company. Maddox bent low, scooped up the glass and swirled the liquid. He inhaled the aroma, sipped, swallowed, nodded in satisfaction and set the goblet back beside the bottle.

Sergeant Riker scowled. "Sir, Caius has taken the Methuselah Treatment. He looks as if he's twenty, but he's really sixty-three." When Maddox didn't reply, the sergeant added, "Must I remind you, sir? The cure makes a man stronger, quicker and tougher than a regular person."

Maddox glanced at the sergeant. "Yes. I suppose that's true."

"Then, may I ask why you're doing this, sir?" the sergeant whispered. "The brigadier will be upset if you duel. And the others...they'll see this as deliberate provocation."

As Captain Maddox regarded Caius, he decided to concede a point to his aide. "Let us call this a test, Sergeant."

Riker blanched. "Sir, I'm not sure you're hearing me. Do you realize how dangerous viper sticks are?"

"Hmm," Maddox said.

"A touch against the spine can paralyze a man," the sergeant said. "A brush across the forehead can take away the ability to speak. Prolonged exposure to the face kills."

"I shall keep that mind, Sergeant. Thank you."

"Sir...what could you possibly be testing by provoking a duel with one of the Methuselah People?"

A truth about me, Maddox thought, the words like a gleam of steel in his soul.

Caius Nerva shoved his chief security officer, who had been whispering in his ear. The push caused the other to stumble away. That was no mean feat. The officer was a seven-foot clone, specialized for size and strength.

Turning, Caius Nerva pointed his viper stick at Maddox. "The only way you can back out with a shred of dignity is to declare yourself a cheater. Make your decision, sir. What will it be?"

"Step back, Sergeant," Maddox said.

"I don't understand why you're doing this," Riker whispered. "Both our lives are in jeopardy."

Maddox didn't plan on telling anyone his reason for doing this. He had a secret, something he had come to suspect about himself. Not even the chiefs of Star Watch Intelligence knew about it. If he were correct, his shame would be intense. This morning, he would test himself against one of the Methuselah People. It would be difficult to find a more dangerous opponent for viper stick dueling.

"You deliberately provoked him by cheating at cards," Riker whispered. "You *let* him catch you, didn't you?"

Maddox said nothing.

"This is your last opportunity," Caius Nerva shouted. His eyes were just as bloodshot as before, but he didn't look drunk anymore.

Nerva acted like a pompous ass, which proved to be an excellent cover. In reality, the man was a ruthless killer.

Maddox turned sideways, facing the heir. Putting his left hand on his hip, the captain lifted the viper stick. As a fencer, right foot forward, he approached the other.

Several watching women screamed. The sound was full of anticipation.

Nerva gave an ugly laugh. "You've sealed your fate, sir. Whatever happens is now on your head."

Maddox felt heat rise in him. He stuffed it down with icy calm. Viper stick dueling was no place for wild charges. It called for speed, daring and perfect timing.

The sergeant was right. The brigadier had given him an assignment, which he'd gladly accepted. The price for this little change in operational plans might give his enemies in the service a way to bring him down.

Maddox gave another of his apparently uninterested shrugs. He would worry about the consequences later. Now, he narrowed his focus to the present battle.

Maybe Nerva took the shrug for a nervous tic. The man grinned with malice and his dark eyes held a predator's delight. The heir to the company fortune had killed before, always during a duel. The government frowned on the practice, and it forbade service personnel to take part. Still, duels had come back into fashion with the Laumer Drive that allowed humanity to settle distant worlds. On many colony planets, law and order was hard to come by. Duels became a substitute. Perhaps as important, honor meant something again. Unfortunately, a person like Nerva exploited the concept to indulge a murderous passion.

Maddox studied his opponent. In truth, he'd been gauging the man all night during the billiards games, the brandy sipping, cigar smoking and the intense contests of five-card stud, blackjack and Altair shuffle.

The two warily approached each other. According to custom, Nerva thrust his viper stick high and forward. Maddox did the same. The tips *clacked* together, causing a sizzling proton discharge.

Maddox felt the vibration buzz in his handle.

Both men crouched slightly and began to circle each other.

The viper sticks were long, a little over six feet and highly flexible. Some duelists used the whip-about. A defender might parry a slash, but the tip would whip across the opposing stick to thrash against a dueler's shoulder, numbing it, leaving him or her defenseless. Often, such a tactic ended a duel, leaving the victim with a slowly deteriorating deltoid muscle.

Many considered viper stick dueling to be the height of folly, preferring to keep to swords or force blades. Some viper stick conventions allowed the practitioners to wear helmets and padded armor. This time, at Nerva's insistence, they had stripped to the waist.

As Caius Nerva circled, he showed his teeth and slashed with a speed that shocked all who witnessed it.

Maddox had seen Nerva show the same grin all night, always signaling that the man was about to display something he considered spectacular. It barely gave the captain enough warning. He dropped his right arm so his viper stick avoided the other and shifted to the left. Nerva's tip swished past, missing by a bare inch.

The spectators *oohed* with delight.

Nerva had already glided away and his eyes narrowed, perhaps with surprise.

Maddox gave him a cool smile.

Did that goad Nerva? Possibly. Caius launched an assault. The viper stick swished with feral sound. Each of Maddox's parries brought a sizzling proton discharge and a vibration to the handle. After the seventh shock, his hand tingled with semi-numbness. He wanted to set the stick aside and shake his fingers, flexing them, before resuming the duel. Viper stickers often allowed each other such intermissions. Nerva had insisted on a constant fight, he said, to test their mettle. Maddox hadn't had any reason to disagree. Now he wondered. Caius Nerva kept a tight grip of his stick, a feat of some accomplishment.

How does he do that?

Even as Maddox wondered, he shifted his fingers before re-gripping. His sweaty hold had become slippery. With speed, he parried, and the viper sticks sizzled once again. Nerva's nose twitched. Maddox smelled it too. The air between them stank from the proton discharges.

Both men stepped back. Maddox switched hands, flexing his right as he held the viper stick with his left. Quickly, he rubbed his sweaty palm against his trousers.

"I am better than you," Nerva declared.

Although Maddox's face remained the same, a silent determination filled his breast. He couldn't believe the man was doing so well. He had thought...

"You are a dog," Nerva said. "If you will admit that, I will permit you to crouch like a beast. Then, at my command, you will pull down your trousers, and I will swat you a single time on the bum. In such a way, you will survive this meeting."

"If you played cards half as well as you boast," Maddox said in a causal tone, "you wouldn't have lost quite so often."

Anger flushed across Caius Nerva's face. He strode toward Maddox, and the tempo of his attacks quickened. It was faster than a man should have been able to achieve. That astounded the captain as he strove to defend himself. Could he have been wrong about his secret? Was he normal like everyone else?

Perhaps even more surprising than Nerva's performance was that Captain Maddox fended off the assaults. He did it through perfect footwork, strenuous exertion and nearly continuous retreat. Sweat dripped from his lean frame, and his muscles writhed with intoxicating interest—the women couldn't tear their gazes from him.

Nerva had bulk and greater strength. A faint sheen of perspiration made his thick pectorals and bulging biceps gleam.

"You're a dead man, Captain," Nerva said in an even voice, as if he wasn't winded in the slightest.

5

A rigid grin was Maddox's only answer. He'd never fenced with someone possessing such speed. Clearly, Sergeant Riker had been right about the Methuselah Treatment granting more than extended life. Well, that wasn't certain, was it? There were other possibilities as to why Nerva fenced so well.

Then Maddox heard it. The faintest of whines came from Nerva. The captain's right eyebrow lifted as the shock of understanding struck him. He had badly miscalculated indeed.

Nerva must have noticed the eyebrow. He laughed in a mocking way.

Given the possibilities, Maddox stuck with more zeal than seemed wise. He had to know the truth. It was a dangerous and complex maneuver: a thrust, stop, thrust and reverse whip-around. The fact that the attack caught Nerva by surprise likely gave Maddox the microsecond's edge he needed to pull it off.

Their viper sticks sizzled, and the tip of Maddox's weapon caressed the top of Nerva's dueling hand.

The spectators gasped with astonishment. Until now, the fight had completely gone Nerva's way.

Maddox jumped back, and his gaze lifted as he watched Nerva's face. The man's mouth opened, but there didn't seem to be any facial tightening due to exquisite pain.

I can't believe this. The implications are absurd.

Instead of agony, surprise filled Nerva's orbs, the disbelief that Maddox could have touched him. Their gazes locked. With a sickening realization, Maddox knew the truth. Nerva must have a prosthetic arm, one of the new Japanese models from Tojo 5.

It appeared as if Nerva came to a decision: he would play this out as if he were normal. The man bellowed: a nearly perfect imitation of agony. He dropped his viper stick, and he pulled his seemingly injured hand against his chest, cradling it.

A prosthetic arm, no wonder Nerva had been able to grip the weapon throughout the fight. It was also possible the man had *dead skin* at strategic locations on his person: his shoulders, chest, maybe his thighs. The dead skin would act as armor, although he would lack feeling at those places. In order to maintain his gentlemanly reputation, Nerva now pretended injury. The man was clever.

Before anyone could congratulate Maddox, or before Nerva could admit defeat, the sound of air-cars caused everyone to glance

6

west. This was a restricted area, guarded by Nerva Conglomerate anti-air lasers. Who could have broken through the cordon?

Maddox turned toward the sound just as everyone else did. He spied three marine air-cars. Ah. They must have gained security clearance. The combat vehicles were obvious, with their camouflage paint and the gun turrets on either end. A loudspeaker clicked on.

"I REQUEST THE IMMEDIATE PRESENCE OF CAPTAIN MADDOX OF THE STAR WATCH!"

A woman standing some ways behind Maddox screamed. It had the shrill distinctive sound of someone witnessing something horrible.

The captain felt the small hairs rise on the back of his neck. He sensed the attack before he turned.

I shouldn't have taken my eyes off Nerva.

The duel hadn't officially ended. In that regard, the air-cars meant nothing. As quick as a cat Maddox twisted around to face Nerva.

The captain took in the scene faster than his body could react to defend himself. Nerva had already picked up the dropped viper stick. The man didn't bother to pretend anymore. He used his right hand, the supposedly numbed one. It certainly meant that Nerva had a specially treated prosthetic right arm, one immune to a viper stick's discharge. Nerva began a slash. There was no way Maddox could lift his own weapon in time or dodge the blow.

Instead of taking the full brunt of a viper stick discharge—ending up permanently paralyzed at best, killed by proton shock at worst—Maddox heard a stunner fire. A blot of nearly invisible force struck Nerva in the chest. Because of the stunner's high setting, the blast knocked the man backward. His viper stick still slashed, but higher than it would have, several inches back and with less force and speed. The combination allowed Maddox to twist out of the way.

Then, Nerva was down on the trampled grass, panting. The shock of the stunner's blast must have disoriented him. It certainly stole his concentration. His arms continued to move downward toward him. The right hand pulled the viper stick directly onto his prone body.

A security officer roared with outrage, likely at the stunner shot.

As Maddox stumbled backward from the inertia of dodging the viper stick, he watched fate handing out its verdict.

7

Nerva's viper stick fell on top of him, striking his chest, neck, chin and face. It discharged with double force. Caius Nerva groaned and went rigid. Then, he exhaled a final time, dying from proton shock.

A marine air-car lowered, its antigravity pods humming as it turned toward the spectators. "CAPTAIN MADDOX, THE BRIGADIER REQUESTS YOUR IMMEDIATE PRESENCE!"

Ignoring the vehicle, Maddox glanced to his left. Sergeant Riker, his aide, held the offending stunner in his gnarled fist. The old man had just saved his life. The sergeant had also legally ended his own. The man was Maddox's second. For killing the enemy duelist, any jury would demand the sergeant's immediate transfer to a prison planet.

Dropping his viper stick so it hissed and writhed against the ground, Maddox approached the sergeant. He didn't worry about Nerva's security personnel, not with the marines landing.

"Sir?" the old man said helplessly. "I didn't mean for his viper stick to strike him. I was just trying to stop him from crippling you. Anyone could see there was a pause in the duel. He took unfair advantage of the air-cars."

"I'll get you out of this, Sergeant. Not to worry."

Riker reversed the grip of the stunner, handing it to Maddox. Tired resignation filled the sergeant's voice. "I don't know how you could possibly help me, sir. I just killed Octavian Nerva's heir. I'm doomed."

Riker was right. The sergeant *was* doomed. But Maddox refused to leave Riker to his fate. The problem was that he had no idea how to save the man.

8

-2-

Captain Maddox fought the urge to shift uncomfortably on his chair. He had been sitting here, anticipating the worst, for what felt like hours. Instead, he maintained his rigid posture before the large desk.

He was in Star Watch Headquarters in Geneva, Switzerland. The air-car had rushed him here. All the Star Watch marines knew was that the so-called New Men had struck again, hard. The Fleet was on high alert.

Maddox frowned. The marines had taken Sergeant Riker to a detention center deep underground. Likely, that was for Riker's immediate protection.

The Nerva security personnel would have already informed Octavian Nerva about his son's death. The tycoon might demand a trial. It was more likely his magnificence would want a bloodier solution.

The Methuselah Treatment was greatly extending the age of those who took it. Some recipients had already reached three hundred years of age. Such elders were rare, as the process was ongoing and incredibly expensive. The treatment had its drawbacks, as well, at least according to certain psychologists.

Those who reached such extended ages often experienced stagnation and magnification of character traits and behaviors. In Octavian Nerva's case, he'd been punishing those who angered him for so long that nothing short of torture satisfied him. Thus, to avenge his son's murder, he would undoubtedly hire man-hunters to kidnap Sergeant Riker, and the magnate would probably come after Maddox, as well.

He and the sergeant could conceivably face a prolonged existence on a hidden habitat orbiting Saturn or Neptune. Certainly, Octavian Nerva would visit them to test new forms of agony against their persons.

Because of this, Sergeant Riker was in the deepest cell possible. The marine guards were supposedly incorruptible, but Nerva might go to considerable lengths to investigate the truth of this belief.

Captain Maddox could not afford to consider these details as he waited before the desk. Instead, his mind had fixated upon the update concerning the New Men.

Behind the large synthi-wood furniture, Brigadier Mary O'Hara of Star Watch Intelligence massaged her forehead. Many called her the Iron Lady. She had gray hair, a matronly image and never lost her temper. It was possible Maddox's duel had tested her famous calm. A sigh escaped from her compressed lips.

Believing it was time to explain, Maddox cleared his throat.

Brigadier O'Hara looked up sharply, her glare like whips.

The words died on Maddox's lips.

She blinked several times. Each flicker of her eyelids seemed to lessen the intensity of her stare. Finally, she appeared to have regained the composure of the Iron Lady.

"This is a fine mess you've dumped into my lap," she said.

Maddox nodded, saying, "I take full responsibility for it, ma'am."

"First, Captain, let me say that your words are meaningless. Like it or not, Sergeant Riker will soon be leaving for Loki Prime."

The extreme jungle world was the worst of the prison planets. Sentencing to such a habitat had replaced the old-fashioned death penalty.

"Given that," the brigadier continued, "I fail to see how your so-called *responsibility* comes into play."

"Sent into exile? Ma'am, that is ridiculous."

"Is it, Captain?"

"Quite," Maddox said. "Caius Nerva had a prosthetic arm."

"No," the brigadier said. "Now, you're being ridiculous."

Maddox appeared not to hear. "During the duel, I struck the top of his right hand with the viper stick, ma'am. The discharge had no visible effect."

"Captain, I expect my people to maintain greater awareness during a mission. I would also appreciate more mental acuity than you're currently showing."

The faintest of frowns appeared on Maddox's face.

"Caius Nerva had huge muscles," the brigadier said, "did he not?"

"He did indeed, ma'am. In truth, that surprised me. Nerva didn't seem like the type to train rigorously. It's clear he ingested muscle-enhancers, but he would have still needed to lift several hours a day."

"Those taking the Methuselah Treatment do not have their limbs lopped off to attach bionic appendages," the brigadier said. "They have regrows...like a lizard developing a new tail."

"The top of his hand—"

"Captain," the brigadier said in a warning tone.

Maddox fell silent.

"I expect my people to listen when I speak," she said.

He stared at her.

"Caius Nerva had big muscles. You admit as much." When the captain refrained from commenting, the brigadier said, "Look at this." She lifted a clicker from the desk and pressed a switch.

A holoimage appeared between them. It showed Caius Nerva in a swimsuit at what must have been a beach party.

Maddox frowned. The man looked much slimmer than he remembered. He glanced around the image at the brigadier.

"For your duel," O'Hara said, "for the entire night, he more a bodysuit."

Maddox's frown deepened.

"If you look closely enough," she said, "there are certain telltale signs."

"But—"

The brigadier held up a single hand.

Maddox ignored it. "Ma'am, I've seen bodysuits. He wasn't wearing one."

11

"I don't believe you've seen the newest model from Tojo 5, the Samurai Deluxe. It hasn't hit the market yet. It is totally lifelike, as you can attest."

"The stunner shot proves you wrong, ma'am. Such a bodysuit as you're implying would protect the wearer from the stun."

"It did," she said.

"I saw the man fall."

"Yes, because Sergeant Riker wisely set his weapon at the kill setting. The stunner hit didn't injure Caius Nerva. The *force* of it knocked him down. The viper stick did the rest when it struck his face."

"Why would Sergeant Riker set his stunner for kill?"

"For the best of reasons," the brigadier said. "He suspected that Nerva wore a bodysuit. Realizing that, the sergeant knew the stun wouldn't harm your opponent. Your man was trying to *knock* Nerva away from you. Rest assured, none of this is conjecture. I've already spoken to Riker. He has admitted everything."

Captain Maddox drummed his fingers on the armrests. "The sergeant didn't say anything to me about this."

"Don't blame him for that. Your man deduced it during the duel. Your impetuousness uncovered that much, I suppose."

"The suit sweated," Maddox said.

Brigadier O'Hara sighed.

"Ah," Maddox said, realizing that was part of the deception. He turned his head, staring at a model starship inside a glass case. "The sweat fooled me, as it was meant to do. The designers intentionally made a skin-perfect bodysuit."

"That it fooled you, Captain, is a testament to the designers. Usually, you are more observant. This time, your emotions blinded you."

Squinting, Maddox continued to stare at the starship model.

"Despite your youth, I expect much more from you, Captain," she said.

Maddox appeared not to hear.

"The part I don't understand," the brigadier added, "is how you managed to fend off Nerva's attacks. I watched a rerun of the duel. Your sergeant's bionic eye under his patch recorded everything. I had a specialist study Nerva's reaction times. In his bodysuit, Caius

12

Nerva's speed was beyond phenomenal. You should not have been able to parry every strike."

Maddox stopped breathing. He had tested himself because of his possible secret, to see if it could be true. Here was conclusive proof, was it not?

No, no, this cannot be. There must be another explanation. Disguising his unease, Maddox spoke casually, "I practice, ma'am."

"Please," she said. "Do not insult my intelligence."

"I have a dueling bot at home. Extended bouts help keep me toned."

She studied him.

Inwardly, Maddox readied himself for the accusation. Outwardly, he appeared serene.

The brigadier pursed her lips before pressing the control, making the holoimage disappear. Opening her desk, she deposited the unit in a drawer and shut it with a click.

"I imagine Octavian Nerva's man-hunters will be coming for you as well," the brigadier said. "You uncovered the fraud and helped to kill his son. Octavian's money and influence gives him reach into the Star Watch, perhaps even into Intelligence. You must leave Earth, leave the Solar System."

"Not without Sergeant Riker," Maddox said.

"That is out of your hands, I'm afraid."

Maddox hesitated. He couldn't believe the brigadier had dropped her inquiry about his ability to defend himself against Caius Nerva. Why had she said anything then? He would need to think about this, but not right now.

"Why did you send the combat cars for me, ma'am?" he asked.

She put both hands on the desk as if to brace herself. A diamond wedding ring glittered on a finger, reminding Maddox that the Iron Lady was married. The ring was her only indulgence, a huge diamond, almost garishly so. Rumor said she was deeply in love with her husband of many years.

"There's been another attack," she said.

"You mean the New Men?"

She scraped back her chair as she stood. "I'm attending an emergency meeting of the Admiralty. You will accompany me, Captain, as my aide. I will desire your input afterward."

"You flatter me, ma'am."

"I do no such thing," the brigadier said. "The Commonwealth and the entire breadth of Human Space will require every advantage we can muster in this emergency. Under normal circumstances, I appreciate your unique outlook, and I wish to make use of it. However, this last indulgence with the viper sticks doesn't do you any credit, Captain."

He'd stood when she did. "When does the meeting begin?" he asked.

"In fifteen minutes."

"Will Admiral Fletcher be there?"

"I don't want you to *talk*, Captain. Stay in the background. Listen. There's no need for Fletcher to notice you. You're in enough trouble as it is. So am I for this mess you've given me."

Maddox said nothing.

"Now, follow me," she said. "We're taking a combat car so we can get there on time."

-3-

Captain Maddox mingled among those standing against the back walls of the spacious chamber. He positioned himself in such a way that Admiral Fletcher or one of his people couldn't spy him.

The massive conference table seated over fifty admirals, commodores, commanders and marine generals. Behind them was twice that number in aides. Everyone here belonged to the Star Watch except for three envoys in the center area.

One of the representatives wore a long robe and a scarlet headscarf, a sheik-superior from the Wahhabi Caliphate, a Muslim star empire. The second envoy, with a great handlebar mustache, represented the Windsor League, a combination of British, Canadian, Australian and Indian colony worlds. The last was a Spacer, a small woman with dark features and short hair. She symbolized the confederation of traders and industrialists with no fixed abode other than their starships.

There were other human worlds without a representative here, but they were in the minority. The men and women seated at the great table had at their disposal—if one counted the envoys—three-quarters of the military strength in what people commonly referred to as the *Oikumene* or Human Space. Over two centuries since the discovery of the Laumer Drive, mankind had colonized many star systems with an Earth normal or terraformed planet. The number grew if one counted every star system with a mining colony or scientific research center.

The majority of those worlds belonged to the Commonwealth of Planets. Before the advent of the New Men, there had been

15

interplanetary wars, revolutions, coups, rebellions, insurrections, all the old ills of the Pre-Interstellar Age. Before the creation of the Commonwealth of Planets fifty years ago, the nations on Terra had fought each other, often using colony world strength. After a space bombardment with hell-burners smashing Greenland out of existence, the surviving nations started a process that led to the stabilizing Commonwealth, a union of sovereign star systems. A few years later, to give the Commonwealth teeth, they created the Star Watch to patrol the space lanes and protect the frontier worlds.

In all that time, no one had encountered aliens, although explorers had discovered several non-human artifacts. According to the best guesses, the alien societies had guttered out when humanity first mixed tin with copper to produce bronze.

The Oikumene was civilized space. Once one traveled farther, he entered the Beyond. Many voyagers had done just that: explorers, locators, Laumer technicians, bounty hunters in search of lost men or treasures and those wanting to begin again. There were known colonies in the Beyond and those hidden from sight. Fanatics of all stripes had left civilization, traveling in every direction. What grew to fruition on those hidden worlds? A few worriers fretted about it. Most people shrugged.

As a great philosopher had once said, "People are most concerned about the pebble in their shoe." They fretted about their mundane worries instead of troubling themselves on cosmic matters.

In such a way, events had matured as the Oikumene or Civilized Human Space slowly expanded. Now, the New Men had appeared from the Beyond. Two still shots showed they looked human enough, if a little taller and thinner than the norm, with golden skin. No one who had encountered one of their warships had survived.

Already, Odin, Horace and Parthia had fallen before the New Men. Each was an independent star system. No one had heard a word from those planets since. The Commonwealth had sent envoys. They had yet to return. Maddox knew that several months ago the Star Watch had sent various battle groups to strategic systems, guarding the direct path from those conquered regions into Commonwealth territory.

It was one thing to smash an independent system's handful of ships. It was another to face the might of the Star Watch.

As an Intelligence officer, Captain Maddox was privy to more knowledge than the average person about the New Men. The golden-skinned invaders had uttered only three words to the Odin fleet before its destruction and to the planet Parthia before its conquest. Presumably, the New Men had said the same thing to the others, too, but no one else had managed to get out a recording of those encounters.

Those three words were, "Surrender or die."

Had the invaders slain everyone on Odin, Horace and Parthia? That seemed inconceivably barbaric. No one had practiced such planetary genocide before. Yet, what did anyone know about the New Men? Almost nothing. Were they Homo Sapiens or did they simply *look* humanoid enough to fool everyone? No one had interviewed one of the invaders regarding their philosophy or religion.

"Surrender or die." No linguist had been able to detect an accent in those words to give a clue as to possible origins. What spaceship of colonists could have produced the New Men one hundred and fifty years ago, say, after disappearing into the Beyond? How large of an empire or star union did they possess in the Beyond? Or, were the New Men like the ancient Huns, perhaps, who moved en masse as nomads from one place to another? What technology made their starships so effective?

A few strategists had speculated advanced aliens as being behind the New Men. The theory was simple. Aliens had bred these New Men as assault troops for a larger invasion into Human Space. It was as good an idea as the rest, given the number of facts was the same as any other concept: zero.

There were many questions about the golden-skinned invaders, but no concrete answers.

The coinage of the phrase *New Men* had come from an Odin newscast showing the only known footage, which had been several seconds long. A tall golden-skinned man with dark hair wearing a silver bodysuit had bounded with incredible speed at elite space marines in the spaceport of Garm. The defending squad occupied a building. They wore exo-powered armor and fired shock rifles.

Due to the brevity of the footage, it had been difficult to get an accurate idea of the battle. Seen in extreme slow motion, two shock rounds passed the invader. Some experts believed the silver suit had interfered with the targeting computers in the rifles and the homing devices in the ammunition. While the Odin military had been small, they had used the latest export technology.

For a fraction of a second, one could see the New Man's face. It had *not* been screwed up with controlled fear or even rage. Instead, he looked calm.

The brief recording also showed his weapon. Pistol-sized, it shot an energy blot. In a fast jerk, the recording had switched directions. The energy hit caused blue web-lines to short-circuit heavy armor and fry the Odin marine inside.

Then the footage ended. No one knew if the surviving marines had won that round or if the lone New Man had slain them.

Afterward, the Odin newswoman's voice had trembled as she spoke about the *New Man*, an innovative breed of human who had invaded civilization from the Beyond. Her observation had stuck.

"Surrender or die." No one knew what had happened to the defeated populations. That by itself had given rise to the worst fears. Surely, though, New Men would practice advanced forms of mercy toward the defeated. Or, would they believe themselves so superior to old-style humans that the losers needed extermination?

Whatever the case, until someone thought up a better name or the invaders gave humanity one of their own, they were the New Men, and their initial assault had sent a shockwave through every government in Human Space.

In the large conference chamber, Captain Maddox looked up as the whispering died away.

Lord High Admiral Cook in his white uniform and rows of medals walked in. A young lieutenant trailed him. Cook was large and red-faced. The woman behind him was beautiful, with brunette hair. She had athletic grace but appeared tired and nervous.

The Lord High Admiral came to the front of the conference table, placing his thick fingertips on the glossy top. He scanned the assembled throng, and he didn't seem to be in any hurry to sit down. The lieutenant standing to his left and a little behind wore her officer's cap. Cook didn't. He had a thick wave of white hair and a seamed face.

"We face a grave challenge," Lord High Admiral Cook said in his deep voice. "Because of its intensity, I will come straight to the

18

point. As many of you know, we have moved seven battle groups into these various star systems."

He pointed at the center of the table. A holoimage snapped on. It showed the battle groups in red, guarding the strategic routes from Odin, Horace and Parthia into Commonwealth space.

"What most of you don't know," the Lord High Admiral continued, "is that we sent another battle group into the Beyond. It was a fast-moving, hard-hitting group under Admiral von Gunther. The plan was to slip in through the back door, as it were, entering the Odin System from the Beyond. Von Gunther had orders to face down the invaders or destroy them if they proved hostile. He was also instructed to see what these New Men had done to the population and learn the fate of our envoys."

Cook breathed heavily. Then he indicated the woman to his left. "I have been speaking with Lieutenant Noonan. She commanded a *Galen* class escort. I would like to tell you she returned in it to us." The Lord High Admiral shook his head. "Her lifeboat was the only craft to survive von Gunther's encounter with the New Men."

People gasped, glancing at one another. An entire battle group destroyed? It was difficult to envision. The New Men must have moved an armada to the Odin System. Did they plan a massed invasion against the Commonwealth then?

Like everyone else, Captain Maddox reexamined the pretty woman. She took a step back, as if the combined stares physically shoved her. Then, a subtle change came over her, a hardening of her features. She stood straighter. It was difficult to interpret the emotions behind her stoic mask.

"We sent a powerful force to investigate the Odin System," the Lord High Admiral said. "It was composed of fourteen capital ships, four of them *Bismarck*-class battleships, two motherships and the rest varying types of cruisers. It also included accompanying destroyers, missile boats and escort vessels, along with ancillary repair ships and three troop transports."

The Lord High Admiral cleared his throat. "We called it a battle group for security purposes. But, as you can see, it had twice the usual numbers."

Cook's features stiffened as he raised an arm to indicate Lieutenant Noonan.

"I want you to hear her story." The Lord High Admiral turned to the woman, and he seemed to become fatherly. "Lieutenant Noonan, if you would please relate your first meeting with the enemy, the battle and your eventual escape, I would appreciate it."

Maddox arched his neck to get a better look at her face. Her eyes seemed haunted.

Lord High Admiral Cook stepped aside.

She moved into his vacated spot, holding her arms rigidly at her sides like a cadet in training. Maddox noticed that she clenched her hands into fists. This must be difficult for her.

Noonan inhaled. Then, she began to speak fast.

"Admiral von Gunther took us into the Pan System," she said. "We had jumped from Aphrodite Five. As most of you must realize, we had to go deep into the Beyond to get to Aphrodite Five."

Faster than light travel involved the Laumer Drive, with Laumer-Points and tramlines. Many stars possessed these wormholes that connected systems. Delicate ship instruments found the precise entrance location. The drive then allowed a ship to jump almost instantaneously between the two points, moving many light years along the tramline in the blink of an eye. Coming out of a Laumer-Point often strained the passengers. People varied on the effects. Some felt shaky as if with the flu and recovered in minutes. Some vomited and trembled uncontrollably, taking several hours to recuperate. A few died, usually from heart failure. As important, most computer system—electrical, bio or phase—often shut down after a jump and took precious time to reboot. It meant that most warships coming out of a Laumer-Point were vulnerable to a swift enemy attack—if the enemy vessels were close enough.

Crossing a star system to reach the next Laumer-Point often took weeks of travel. It meant that some jump routes were strategically more important than others.

"From the Pan System," Noonan said, "the battle group meant to go to the Larson and then into the Odin System to confront the New Men."

She shook her head.

"We had moved fast, trying to leave as little evidence as possible of our passage. The admiral had decided to go to combat conditions once we attempted the jump from the Pan to the Larson System.

That meant we hadn't launched any nukes into the Pan System preceding our arrival from Aphrodite Five."

Maddox ingested the information. Because most starships and their crews were vulnerable until they recovered from Jump Lag, standard combat procedure called for thermonuclear-armed drones to jump first. Simple timers ignited them on the other side. Thermonuclear blasts would clear any nearby enemy ships waiting to ambush them. The small lieutenant was saying the battle group had failed to take that standard conflict procedure.

"As it turned out," Noonan said, "the New Men were waiting for us. They struck soon after we appeared. Our sensors were still down. Everything was, except for our shields. We had barely made it out of jump.

"I'd heard rumors that Admiral von Gunther had a picked crew of fast-recovering personnel. By what happened next, I believe it. He must have realized our peril sooner than anyone else did. Before his laser batteries could charge, he drove the *Scharnhorst* straight at the enemy. He must have known his vessel didn't have a chance. Two of our heavy cruisers were already drifting hulks."

Noonan frowned. "I don't know what type of energy the New Men hit von Gunther with, but their beams burned through armor faster than I would have believed possible."

"What about his shields?" Admiral Fletcher asked. He was a big man with a permanent scowl.

Noonan shook her head. "The enemy beams appeared to have cut right through von Gunther's shields."

The shock of the information broke the spell. Officers began whispering to each other.

"Attention!" Lord High Admiral Cook said in a commanding voice.

The room quickly grew quiet again.

Cook bowed his head to Noonan for her to continue.

She moistened her lips. "I don't know how it all happened. We couldn't record yet. I recall raising my head. The viewer had just come back online. I saw the *Scharnhorst* making its death ride. Von Gunther took his ship straight down their throats. The enemy beams scored direct hits on his armor. I saw it with my own eyes. The armor plates blackened as the beams bored into them. I remember scooting forward on my chair, wondering why von Gunther had

21

failed to raise his shields. Then I saw the telltale shimmer, and I knew he *had* raised them. The enemy beams simply ignored the electromagnetic deflectors, hitting the *Scharnhorst* again and again.

"My people finally began stirring. I've always come out of Jump Lag quicker than others could." Noonan shrugged. "I remember hearing von Gunther on the comm. He ordered us to retreat. He ordered us to race back to Earth and report on the New Men. He tried to say something else. I believe he had learned something important. Before he could finish his thought the *Scharnhorst* broke apart under the enemy beams."

Maddox noted the widening eyes, the stir of those around him. Once more, Lieutenant Noonan's tale had surprised everyone.

Admiral Fletcher spoke up. "How many ships did the New Men have?"

"Three, I believe," Noonan said.

Instead of whispering, men and women began to talk aloud to each other. *Three* enemy ships had done this to the *Scharnhorst*? By the swiftness of the battleship's destruction, it should have been twenty.

"Silence in the hall!" Lord High Admiral Cook roared. "I will have silence in my hall."

"I know what you're wondering," Noonan said. "How could three vessels do this so quickly to the *Scharnhorst*? The *Bismarck*-class battleships have incredibly powerful shields. It would take four equally great craft pouring their lasers against a shield for at least fifteen minutes to begin to make it buckle. Even then, it should last another ten minutes. Afterward, the armor plating could take a hell of a pounding."

She shook her head. "The enemy didn't outnumber us. It was the opposite. We had far more vessels than they did. And they didn't have monster craft, either. If I had to guess, each of their ships had the tonnage of a heavy cruiser. The *Scharnhorst* was bigger than each of her three tormenters. What's more, by its ramming attack, the *Scharnhorst* had forced the New Men to concentrate on her. I think von Gunther would have smashed one of their vessels if he could have reached them.

"As the admiral's flagship broke apart, our three surviving battleships began to unlimber their heavy lasers. The strike cruisers launched drones. Many of the destroyers together with the missile boats began flanking maneuvers. The New Men had hurt us, but we still had far more ships than they did. What's more, von Gunther's charge had given us time to recover from Jump Lag so that operating systems began coming online enough to begin fighting.

"I wanted to join the assault. The destruction of our ships enraged me. Yet, I had heard the admiral's last orders. He had almost told us something critical. I believed that then, and I still do. Something crawled down my spine. It wasn't fear of our destruction. It…"

Lieutenant Noonan's mouth moved silently before she said, "I think I sensed the historic pregnancy of the moment. As the others began firing, I reversed course and began an emergency evacuation for the Laumer-Point. As we entered the jump, I watched the rest of the fleet—"

"You fled the battle," Fletcher said, sounding surprised and outraged.

"Yes, sir," Noonan said, flinching. "You can say it like that if you wish. I prefer to say that I followed Admiral von Gunther's last orders. I did more than simply retreat. I also shouted orders for everyone to evacuate ship."

Admiral Fletcher struck the table with his fist.

Noonan took a step back as everyone stared at her with disbelief. Maybe it was too much. She lowered her gaze.

"You may find this hard to believe," she said.

Like the others around him, Maddox leaned toward her, as her voice had grown softer.

Noonan touched her chest. "In my heart, I felt the New Men would annihilate our battle group and come after us. What I had just seen—it terrified me. Their technology was far superior to ours. I felt a duty to return home and report that. It turned out I wasn't the only one who obeyed Admiral von Gunther. One of the motherships along with a strike cruiser and four destroyers made it through. After they recovered from Jump Lag, the others began to race for the next Laumer-Point. It would take them a week of hard acceleration to reach it. As they began the journey, all hands aboard my escort ejected in the lifeboats. I'd left the ship on automated, setting it to follow the mothership."

"This is gross cowardice in the face of the enemy," Admiral Fletcher declared.

"No," Noonan said, staring straight ahead. "I had a hunch. I believed the New Men would be coming. I took my lifeboat and raced behind a nearby asteroid. We barely made it. I began recording with passive sensors. This is what I discovered. Three enemy vessels of heavy cruiser size came through the jump point. It indicated to me that none of the enemy had sustained any damage from us. I learned something else, too. Their ships began functioning within thirty seconds of appearing in the new system.

"Jump Lag clearly didn't distress them like it does us, nor did it seem to bother their computer systems. Their sensors locked on the fleeing warships. The enemy beams fired within minutes of their arrival. It wasn't a laser beam. My instrumentation was clear on that. The fleeing cruiser and destroyers turned around to fight. The mothership launched several squadrons of strikefighters and bombers. And that's when things became weird."

Noonan bit her lower lip. "I heard several of our bombers hailing the New Men. Answering pulses returned from the enemy craft."

"What's this?" Fletcher asked. "You're suggesting those bombers were in communication with the New Men?"

"I suggest nothing, Admiral," Noonan said. "I'm just reporting what I saw. I watched a squadron of bombers detach from the wave of strikefighters heading at the enemy vessels. That squadron moved away even as Commodore Franks on Mothership *Constellation* gave them orders to attack. I'm not sure, but I think Franks trained his lasers on the errant bombers."

"What do you mean, *think*?" Fletcher asked, his features contorted with rage.

"*Constellation* gained sensor lock on the wayward bombers," Noonan said. "Then, I heard Franks accuse Commander Miles of treachery. Before the mothership's lasers could fire, the New Men destroyed the giant carrier under a combined barrage. Afterward, they demolished the attacking strikefighters. Within forty minutes of their arrival in the system, the New Men had annihilated the remaining ships of our battle group."

Noonan looked up, scanning those gathered in the chamber. "Three enemy vessels demolished a greater number of our ships without suffering any harm in turn. They annihilated us with an ease I wouldn't have believed unless I was part of it."

"Wait, wait," Fletcher said. "You must back up. What happened to the other lifeboats and to Commander Miles' bombers?"

Noonan cocked her head and stared into the distance. "The New Men beamed every lifeboat but mine. The last bombers...they approached the enemy vessels and landed in a docking bay. Afterward, the three ships left, heading back to the Pan System."

"Did the New Men order the bombers to land?" Fletcher asked.

"If they did, I didn't hear it," Noonan said. "In my opinion, Commander Miles went willingly."

Lord High Admiral Cook stepped near as he indicated an empty chair.

Noonan stared at him for a moment before sitting down in it.

The Lord High Admiral glowered at the others. "All right, then. You've heard what I've heard. There are several troubling elements to the story. I'm sure each of you has reached the same conclusion I have, but I will enumerate the problems. Compared to us, the invaders have seriously advanced weaponry. It allowed three of their ships to destroy masses of ours: a fleet composed of fourteen capital ships. I am inclined to pull our other groups back. I fear trying to beat the enemy in a battle of maneuver. In every way, the New Men are better than us at recovering from Jump Lag. Yet, the worst problem is this: we clearly have spies in our midst, traitors helping the New Men. How else did the enemy know to guard the Pan-Aphrodite route? It would appear that Commander Miles on Mothership *Constellation* communicated with them in some fashion. That the New Men were able to corrupt Star Watch combat officers would seem to mean they have an active secret service among us. It would also appear that they have full knowledge about Earth. In return, except for the color of their skin, we know nothing about them."

Lord High Admiral Cook rapped his knuckles against the table. "This is a dire situation, people. Before we move against them again, we will have to come up with a plan on how to defeat vastly superior ships. What's more, we must figure out a way to keep them from learning our secrets."

Silence filled the chamber as his words sank in.

Finally, Admiral Fletcher stirred. "Sir," he said.

"Go head, Admiral."

"What if the New Men don't wait for us to move, but they invade Commonwealth territory first?"

"Exactly," Cook said. He looked from right to left, taking his time doing it as he stared at each person in turn. Finally, he said, "I'm open to suggestions, people. Because if the New Men invade us, I don't know what we can do to stop them."

-4-

That night, Maddox lay in bed unable to sleep. He kept staring up at the ceiling, thinking about the past twenty-four hours.

Caius Nerva, Sergeant Riker, Admiral von Gunther, Commander Miles and the New Men—what did it all mean? The golden-skinned invaders from the Beyond had a secret service organization operating on Earth. That seemed clear from the lieutenant's story. The traitorous commander in the bomber had landed on an enemy warship. The three enemy cruisers had been waiting at the right entry point into the Pan System.

After the meeting, Maddox had checked a star chart. There were three jump points in the Pan System, all widely divergent from each other in location. The New Men had been waiting at the Aphrodite Five-Pan route. In order for von Gunther to reach Aphrodite Five, he would have first taken a long journey through the Beyond. That journey had taken at least two months. Maddox had confirmed the route with Brigadier O'Hara. By their ready presence and quick attack, the New Men had logically known a Star Watch battle group was on its way and nearby.

With his hands behind his head on the pillow, Maddox thought about that. *I doubt their sensors are so superior to ours that they can see down tramlines or light years away into a different star system. If their sensors were that good, the New Men would have spotted Noonan in her lifeboat while she hid behind the asteroid. The easier answer is that traitors in the battle group were sending secret messages to the enemy.*

If the New Men had agents in the Star Watch and the Commonwealth governments, that meant enemy case officers had been here awhile. It took time to set up a good spy ring and to solidify a hold onto traitors who would willingly see their comrades die because of their treachery.

How long have the New Men been among us? It was a chilling question for more than one reason.

Maddox swiftly rose to his feet, padding down the hall to the liquor cabinet in his living room. He wore briefs, exposing his lean frame.

In moments, he held a tumbler with ice and Scotch whiskey. He sipped, closed his eyes and felt the fiery liquid go down.

He knew himself to be unusual in several ways. Swirling the ice, he poured himself another and slammed it down this time. With a gasp, he clunked the tumbler onto the liquor cabinet.

He'd never really been drunk before. His body burned up alcohol far too quickly for him to stay intoxicated. He had tested himself, and it turned out he had a fast metabolism. What's more, his core temperature wasn't 98.6 but 99.4 on average. Dueling came easier to him than for others because his reflexes were abnormally quick. He was also stronger than he looked, benching fifty percent more than someone his size should have been able to do.

I'm different—not a lot different, just enough to help me win most of the time.

As the tumbler sat on the cabinet, Maddox rotated it. A numbing swirl struck his brain, the whiskey doing its damage. The feeling would go away soon.

Why don't I swig from the bottle? See how much I can guzzle.

He'd defeated Caius Nerva while the other wore a Tojo bodysuit with advanced speed settings. The brigadier recognized that he shouldn't have been able to parry every stroke. Yet he had. Even so, he would have lost the match except that Sergeant Riker understood what had been going on.

My aide set the stunner to kill. That wasn't the first time Riker had surprised him.

Frowning, Maddox began to pace like a caged leopard. Why was he different? He wished he knew.

The Parker family had raised him. Maddox still remembered the day when his "mom" had told him the horrible truth: "You're adopted."

Four years ago, using the full extent of his skills, Maddox had hunted down his real mother's identity. There had been precious little to discover. She had arrived on Earth just in time to deliver him. She'd come on a Spacer packet from New Poland. He went there, and after two weeks of detective work, he found she had come from Brisbane. The trail had iced up on the small Windsor League planet. He hadn't been able to find out anything more there.

Nancy Halifax, his mother—he believed the name an alias—had taken the interstellar voyage a little over two decades ago. She came to Earth, delivered him and died. From her sparse records, she'd appeared normal enough.

But I'm not. The first time Maddox had seen the footage of the New Man attacking the Odin marines, it had shocked him. That's when he had started to wonder.

That was his terrible secret. He wondered if his mother had met a New Man, an invading rapist perhaps. The implications…

That would have happened over two decades ago. Did the New Men know then they were going to invade the Oikumene? Did they begin to infiltrate the Commonwealth back then?

The inferences were horrible. The evidence pointed to a long-term infiltration. There were traitors among them, people who had sided with the invaders.

Maddox laughed bleakly. Lieutenant Noonan's tale would unleash a witch-hunt among the military. How long would he last under that kind of scrutiny with a burning mentality for vengeance? If High Command came to a similar conclusion about him…would the Intelligence people torture him for information he didn't have? If the New Men were that superior in technology and ability—

I have to run. But where will I go? Will my father's people take me in? Wouldn't genetically superior people look down on a half-breed?

Maddox stared at the melting cubes in the tumbler. He laughed again, a hopeless sound. He wasn't used to making those. This was all a theory, nothing more. Surely, there were other explanations for his enhanced physical abilities.

Maybe I'm just gifted. Maybe I'm a sport, a mutant. Don't those appear in a population from time to time?

He cocked his head, realizing he'd just heard a quiet click from outside. Slowly, he lowered himself until he crouched on the rug and concentrated, listening. His eyes widened. He heard the soft hum of antigravity pods outside his apartment.

Yes, something was outside his window. The drapes were shut. He'd have to crawl over to the window and peer out to see what it was. He lived on the fortieth floor. That meant—

A crash sounded. The living room window blew inward. Because he crouched low, the spray of shards that shredded his curtains flew over him except for one. That sliver of glass grazed the top of his shoulder, drawing blood.

Maddox hadn't turned on the lights. That was a piece of good fortune because he wasn't spotlighted now. He looked up from his position. A sleek air-van lifted into sight about thirty meters away. A side door slid open on the van, and two operatives readied themselves for a leap. They wore repulse-packs, body armor and helmets with masks. Each of them carried a stubby shotgun-type weapon.

Tanglers! They're man-hunters. Did Octavian Nerva send them?

Maddox had no way of knowing. He also lacked a weapon. Simply running seemed like a poor idea. He had to upset their timing.

As the van closed the distance, sliding nearer to the window, Maddox reached up to the liquor cabinet. His fingers curled around the tumbler. The two hunters jumped, gliding toward his smashed window. Beyond them hovered the air-van with the open side door. Through that, Maddox spied the driver at the controls. It was a narrow opening.

With a snarl, Maddox stood, cocked his arm and hurled the tumbler. It paid to do the unexpected. His glass would bounce off body armor and mask alike, so hurling it at the approaching hunters seemed futile.

The tumbler sped past the two, reached the open van and shot through the narrow opening. It failed to connect with the driver's head. Instead, the glass struck his armored window and shattered. A shard struck the driver's face. His arms shot out and, likely, his foot didn't remain in the right place. The air-van lifted, accelerating fast.

30

One of the hunters must have noticed something amiss. He glanced back.

Maddox was already moving away from them.

The second hunter cocked his head as if listening to an earbud. Then their repulse-packs brought them through the window and into Maddox's living room. One of them struck the back of the couch with his shins. That upset his balance. The hunter slammed onto his chest against the rug. The other landed smoothly, his legs churning as he ran.

Already moving, Maddox thought fast, gauging his options. They must have struck in the living room because someone in the van had radar and knew his precise location. Now, for as long as it took the driver to recover and bring the air-van back into place, he would be on equal footing with these two.

Neither of them shouted his name or took a shot. Likely, they scanned with their helmet HUDs in the darkness.

Maddox glided through the hall. His normal coolness evaporated. The senior Nerva had acted with speed, sending hunters after him. Did that mean the tycoon had already struck at Sergeant Riker?

New Men, Methuselah People—how much corruption could a planet take? With all these bribes changing hands, everyone should be rich.

Panic thrummed in Maddox's brain. He wasn't sure who he was anymore. Did he belong in Star Watch Intelligence or not? This was like the day his mother had told him they'd adopted him.

"What?" he'd asked her. "You mean I'm not your son?"

"Of course you are, dear. I love you. Your father loves you."

His world had turned upside down. "Do you mean my real father?" he'd asked.

A hurt look had crossed his adopted mother's face. He remembered that. It had helped him realize she did love him. He also knew that something had departed his heart that day. His famous cool had begun to assert itself from that time forward. Maybe he'd had to operate that way to protect himself.

Behind him, armored footfalls told Maddox the man-hunters knew where he was. A repulse-packed whined. It would push the hunter, giving the man speed. Maddox knew he wasn't going to reach the heavy rifle in his bedroom in time.

31

He darted into the bathroom since he was already at the door. With a lunge, he lifted the porcelain cover off the toilet's water tank. Whirling, he charged back.

The first hunter poked in his tangler barrel and helmeted head. Maddox swung. The porcelain cover smashed into pieces against the helmet. The tangler made a *popping* sound. A golf ball-sized capsule struck the wall, exploding into strands, immediately tightening. If the capsule had hit him, he'd have been tangled in an unbreakable web. At the same time as the shot hit the wall, the hunter catapulted backward, striking his partner with his repulse-pack. The two hit the far hall wall, bouncing off and tumbling forward.

Like a lynx, Maddox was on the first attacker, his legs straddling the fallen man's shoulders. The captain clutched the head with one hand under the chin, the other on the back of the helmet. With a savage twist, Maddox snapped the vertebrae, killing the man.

The other must not have realized what had happened yet. The man shouted, and a knockout mist hissed from a small cylinder on his chest.

Maddox recognized the danger. They had masks. He didn't. Holding his breath, he squirmed away, rolled on the tiled floor with his shoulders and slithered around the corner into his bedroom. Another *pop* sounded. Another capsule splatted against a wall, this time in his bedroom.

"Claude!" the hunter said.

Frenchmen or French Canadians, Maddox thought.

"I kill you," the hunter shouted.

Maddox didn't think so. Reaching into the closet, he pulled down a heavy rifle, a Khislack .370. A flick of a switch turned on the targeting computer. On silent feet, Maddox backed up, climbing over his bed and moving onto the far side. He aimed at the wall. The computer gave him an image of a man in body armor tiptoeing toward the bedroom door, holding a tangler in one hand and a force blade in the other.

With the barrel aimed at the wall, Maddox fired three times, each shot making the Khislack buck in his hands. The targeting computer told him the story as the heavy bullets blew through the wall. The home invader staggered, made a gurgling sound and slumped onto the tiles. They were both dead now.

What about the driver in his van?

Had Octavian Nerva just sent Maddox a message with this attack?

The panic in Maddox's brain changed to rage. If he'd been thinking with his normal coolness, he might have reconsidered his actions. The captain sprinted for the living room. A frozen snarl spoke of his resolve. The Khislack felt good in his hands. He'd taken down the hunters with it. Now it was time to finish the job. As he rounded the corner, he remembered the van's radar.

The driver must know I'm coming.

His momentum was too much for him to stop in time. So Maddox dropped, lying down on the floor. As he did, the air-van's machine guns blazed. Heavy rounds shattered the walls, breaking plaster, vases, the couch, paintings, a piano and various mementos from past missions.

With his head down, with dust, pieces of plaster and piano splinters striking his hair, Maddox fired blindly at the van. A second later, he realized how seriously outgunned he was. He could only believe he was still alive because the other had forgotten to link the machine guns with the radar.

Maddox slithered backward.

Machine gun bullets now began chewing the floor where he'd been. Spouts of destruction raced at him as the rounds tore synthi-wood flooring and the concrete underneath. He rolled frantically to the left. The flooring splintered beside him where he'd just been, slivers pelting his ribs, sticking in his skin.

Some of his famous cool began to reassert itself. *I'm dead if I don't think.*

With deliberation, Maddox lifted the Khislack, using the targeting computer. He fixed on the van and fired three rapid shots. The titanium-jacketed rounds would easily slice through the walls, striking the van's armored windshield. Likely, the rounds couldn't penetrate that immediately. He would have to hammer his way in. Maddox knew he didn't have the luxury of time to do that. Those three shots were only an attempt to rattle the driver. He'd done it once already tonight with the tumbler. Maybe this would give him the margin he needed to escape.

After the third trigger-pull, Maddox was up and running. The machine-gun rounds had already shattered his main door. Lowering a shoulder, Maddox smashed through the remains, cutting his naked skin.

That didn't matter. Getting deeper into the building did. How badly did the hunter want him? The driver must realize he had broken all kinds of alarms. If the driver waited around too long, the police would catch him or worse, Star Watch Intelligence.

There's only one person I can speak to about this.

As Maddox reached the inner stairwell, he knew what he had to do.

After making a report of the attack to the police and Star Watch Intelligence, Maddox hurried to headquarters. He slept fitfully that night in an extra room, showered in the morning and ate a light meal of nuts, cheese and orange juice.

By 9:10 AM, he stood before Brigadier O'Hara's desk.

"I just heard about the attack," the Iron Lady said. "Nerva moved faster than I anticipated."

Maddox stood at attention, nodding slightly, wearing a spare uniform he kept in his locker here.

"Sit," O'Hara said. "You're straining my neck making me look up at you."

"Ma'am, I prefer to stand telling you this."

"Tell me what?"

Maddox hesitated. This was harder than he thought. He didn't care for extended introspection. He saved his logic for solving cases, for beating the competition. As he stood before the brigadier, he realized the Star Watch had become his family. His first family had proven to be a sham. He believed in the Star Watch, in protecting people through his actions. He was good at what he did. It gave him a purpose, something larger than himself. By speaking now, he jeopardized that. Yet, by staying silent, he possibly aided the enemy, keeping needed information to himself instead of passing it along to help the Star Watch defeat the New Men.

"Ma'am, this is…this is difficult for me."

"Do sit down, Captain, and dispense with the dramatics. If you have something to say, simply say it."

35

Maddox hesitated before sitting on the edge of the chair with his back stiff.

"Ma'am, I'm not sure you should trust me."

Her eyebrows lifted. "Well, well, this is a surprise. What have you done now, Captain?"

"I have done nothing. It's what was done to me."

"Do you mean this latest attack?"

"No. I mean—" His lips grew numb, and he found it impossible to utter the words.

This is ridiculous. Why can't I just come out and say it? Because I'm afraid, he realized. *That's funny. I've spent my entire life ignoring fear, showing others it is a foreign emotion to me. Yet, now I can't tell the brigadier the truth because I'm afraid of what she'll say.*

"If you're quite through..." she said. "We have important matters to discuss."

"Ma'am, I have been compromised."

"You have?" she asked. "When?"

He actually felt lightheaded. No. This wasn't going to happen to him. With a scowl, he concentrated before speaking slowly. "I was compromised at my conception."

He expected her to make a soft snort of derision, to wave her hand in dismissal. Instead, her eyes seemed to light up. He wasn't sure, but the corners of her mouth twitched as if she attempted to contain a smile. That didn't make sense.

"Can you be more precise?" she asked.

"I was adopted, ma'am."

"Oh, I see."

"I don't think you do. My mother barely made it to Earth on a Spacer liner."

"You're adopted, you say. I'm assuming you searched for your real mother."

Maddox told O'Hara about his search, how it led to Brisbane in the Windsor League. There, his mother's trail had dead-ended.

"I wonder if I should inform you," the brigadier said, "but you're not the only person with adopted parents."

"Right," he said. "But I am the only one with a New Man for a father."

All humor, hidden or otherwise, evaporated from the brigadier's face. The light in her eyes became hardened intensity. She sat forward, studying him.

"Why do you say such a thing?" the brigadier asked.

"Ma'am, you wondered yesterday how I could parry Caius Nerva's viper stick stokes. I believe the answer lies in my heightened abilities."

"I see. You're quite proud of yourself, are you?"

"No, ma'am."

"You're not a proud man, Captain Maddox?"

He considered the question. "You are correct. I am proud to a degree. I think a good Star Watch officer should be."

"Do you believe—?"

"Brigadier, I haven't come here lightly. I might even say this is painful to me. I have found certain differences in myself. They are not startling, but they have given me an edge at times."

"Why tell me this, and why tell me now?" she asked.

"It should be obvious," he said. "The New Men have infiltrated our domain. After Lieutenant Noonan's report yesterday, someone with their blood will become suspect. Before Intelligence runs me down like a dog, I thought to tell you my suspicions."

"Given your allegations to be true," the brigadier said, "we might lock you away."

"Yes," he said. "I realize that."

O'Hara leaned back in her chair, steepling her fingers as she studied him. "You're certain you're a New Man? There are no doubts?"

"I'm not one hundred percent certain, no. It's simply that, given the evidence, it seems like the most logical possibility."

"Yes, I suppose it might, at that." O'Hara put her hands on the desk. "Sit back, if you would. You're making me nervous perching on your chair like that."

Maddox slid back, placing his forearms on the rests as if he expected cuffs to appear and lock him down.

"Captain Maddox, since you feel so inclined to share your suppositions with me, I will tell you a secret few know. It has weighed heavily on me and a few others for many years now."

37

She rocked slightly. "Starting twenty-five years ago or so, certain events began to take place that troubled a few of those in the highest ranks of the Star Watch. How old do you think I am, Captain?"

"I wouldn't care to guess."

"Nevertheless, do so, please."

"Hmm, you must be in your fifties, ma'am."

"Which means you believe I'm in my sixties," she said. "If you add several decades to that number, it would be right."

The answered surprised him. "You've taken the Methuselah Treatment?"

"Just the initial procedure," she said. "The Star Watch cannot afford more. Besides, there are serious drawbacks to those who become too old. I am nearing my retirement age. We have decided that ninety-five should be the cutoff point."

"I had no idea."

"Good. That means few others will have either."

"I also don't understand why you would tell someone like me."

"I'm getting to that," O'Hara said. "I've been around for some time. That's my point. I've seen these reports gather."

"What reports?" Maddox asked.

"The special ones that have made us uneasy for the last two decades," she said. "At first, they appeared random. Then, they coalesced into a pattern. We couldn't see the pattern at the time, mind you, just feel it tightening around us."

"Us," Maddox said, "as in the Commonwealth of Planets?"

"No. Us as in the Oikumene. I have spoken with the top Windsor League Intelligence people, although I haven't had those conversations with my Wahhabi or Spacer counterparts. We now believe these hidden maneuvers were the work of the New Men. It is my belief that they were laying their groundwork."

"For an invasion?" asked Maddox.

"We don't know that part yet, but it's possible. Let me rephrase. After the lieutenant's story, I'd say it's likely."

"By 'we,' you mean Star Watch Intelligence?"

"No," O'Hara said. "Several Windsor League officers, the highest ranks here and a few people above us."

"Clearly, the New Men have invaded the Oikumene," Maddox said.

"Are they invading? Are you sure?"

38

"What do you call the conquest of Odin, Horace and Parthia?" Maddox asked.

"It could be conquest. It could be extermination. It could be assimilation."

"What does the last part mean?"

"Let me lay my cards on the table," the brigadier said. "After much research, we believe the New Men are the result of genetic experiments. Nearly one hundred and sixty years ago, some colony ships from the Thomas Moore Society headed for deep space. They were peopled with utopians, those certain they could perfect humanity. Now, we can't be sure, but the majority of us in the know believe the Thomas Moore Society colonists were the genesis to the New Men. Among the utopians was a group who wrote that the easiest way to achieve their dream was to modify man. Could they have gained the ascendency out there in the Beyond? Did they practice simple genetic selection or experiment with gene-splicing? Did they use the scientific techniques we have to produce better tomatoes or hybrid wheat and transform people?"

"I have no idea," Maddox said. "Why do the New Men have golden skin?"

"Maybe as a mark of their superiority?" the brigadier said, "maybe because they settled a world with a hot star. I don't know."

"What did you mean when you said assimilation earlier?"

"Taking the conquered people and selecting those with superior genes for breeding. That is one idea. There are others more repugnant."

"Such as?" Maddox asked.

O'Hara fixed her gaze on him. "Maybe they place a fertilized gene-modified egg into a captive woman's uterus. The captive becomes a breeder for the New Men, a brood mother, if you will."

Maddox's eyes widened. "Do you think that's what happened to my mother?"

The brigadier shrugged.

"How can you be so calm about this?" he asked.

"Please, Captain, use your intellect. Even though you're our youngest, you're also our best operative. Lately, however, you have become far too emotional. I want my former star officer to reappear for duty."

39

Maddox and the brigadier stared at each other for a long moment. She looked away first. Slowly, the truth dawned on him.

"You've known about my mother for some time," he said. "In fact, it's likely you covered her trail in Brisbane."

"Likely?" the brigadier asked.

"You did cover it."

She nodded. "Why did we do so?"

"Because the trail led into the Beyond," he said. "You wanted time to figure this out. That meant you couldn't have people going about it half-cocked, giving away the game that you knew."

"Good. You're thinking again. It's about time."

"Where in the Beyond did the trail lead?" Maddox asked.

"*That* we don't know," she said.

"What do you know?"

"After listening to Lieutenant Noonan's story, it appears we didn't prepare well enough. Oh, we have a far larger Fleet, given the level of peace before the invasion. It's possible our enemy recognized our awareness. In fact, now I believe that is a certainty. We have battled their agents in secret, but they are impossibly clever. Yes, we've won a round or two, but they have outmaneuvered us time and again. Their abilities are terrifying. Some of us have begun to wonder if there's any hope for humanity."

"I have two questions," Maddox said. "Why have you let me run free until now, and why are you telling me this?"

The brigadier smiled. "I've known about you a long time, Captain. I have championed your cause against some who seriously distrust you. We haven't told you any of this because some among us fear you. Some doubt your loyalty, after yesterday's story, more than ever. But this should be made clear to you. Until we actually capture a New Man and test his DNA, and then compare it to yours, we can't know for certain that you have their blood."

"But—"

"Your skin isn't golden," the brigadier said. "You have Caucasoid pigmentation and features. Yes, you have some heightened abilities. Does that mean you're one of them?"

"It means I'm a half-breed."

"I don't like the term, Captain."

"Nevertheless—"

40

"Don't mistake a possibility for an actuality," O'Hara said. "And even if you have half of their genetics, so what? Why does that make such a difference as far as your loyalty goes?"

Maddox digested her words. "Tell me this then. Why did my mother's trail lead into the Beyond? What was she running from?"

"At this point, we simply don't know. Therefore, you shouldn't let possibilities bother you."

He wanted to grab at this hope. *Maybe I'm not part New Man.* Then reality, at least as he saw it, resettled in his heart. *Yet, what other explanation is there? What has the highest probability? That I'm a half-breed: a genetic experiment that got away from the New Men.*

"You must put this behind you," the brigadier said. "In reality, your origins don't matter. It's who you are now that counts."

Yes, who am I? Maddox decided to shelf the probing for the moment. Still, a cynical smile touched his lips as he looked at the brigadier. "On to the second question then," he said. "Why tell these things now?"

"My dear boy, isn't it obvious? Yes, some will think you're merely being clever, thinking four or five moves ahead of us. You're telling me this to hide your tracks, taking a gamble with me."

Maddox felt his heart go cold. Despite her earlier words, it sounded as if O'Hara believed he really had New Men genetics.

"I know you have a good heart and good intentions," O'Hara said, "but more importantly, so does he."

"He?" asked Maddox. "Who is *he*?"

A secret door slid open, startling Maddox. A large man with a red face and a white uniform stepped into the room.

"Me," Lord High Admiral Cook said. "I don't think you're a plant or a sleeper. I believe you're just the man we need to give us an edge against the New Men before they begin their invasion in earnest."

41

-6-

Maddox stared at the Lord High Admiral. He hadn't expected this.

The brigadier rose and began to move from her desk.

"Stay seated," Cook told her. "You, too, young man."

Maddox had belatedly shot to his feet. He paused for a second and then sat back down.

The big man moved stiffly, as if he had bad knees. He probably did. Maddox wondered how old the Lord High Admiral was. Probably older than the brigadier.

With a grunt and the creak of his chair, Cook settled himself. Apparently satisfied with his position, the Lord High Admiral turned to him.

"You've made this much easier for us, my boy. I appreciate that. I admit I had a reservation or two about you. Not anymore. You have my complete trust."

"Thank you, sir," Maddox said.

"No, no. I thank you. The New Men situation baffles me. How could three ships demolish an entire strengthened battle group like that? Oh, I grant you, the New Men had several edges. They caught von Gunther's people gripped in Jump Lag. And that beam of theirs that cuts through shields is a real killer. It was all too brisk against armor too."

"May I ask a question, sir?" Maddox asked.

"Son," Cook said, "you can ask me all the questions you want, if you do it during the next half hour. That's all the time I can spare—

that you can spare. If we're going to make this work, you're going to have to leave fast."

The accelerated tempo and scope of these events shook Maddox. He needed time to adjust. No. He had run out of time, hadn't he? He'd have to do his deep thinking later. Right now, he had to go with this and see where it led. The Lord High Admiral had said he could ask anything he wanted. Well, all right then.

"Sir," Maddox said, "do we have any idea of the number of starships the New Men possess."

"No idea at all," Cook said. "Logically, though, we should have more vessels than they do. They started with a tinier base and can't have anything close to our population levels. However, Admiral Fletcher's suggestion of compiling one giant armada and rushing them seems too risky. They would surely learn of such a massive gathering. They might also take the opportunity to target our unprotected industrial planets and bomb us back into a primeval age.

"My boy, because the stakes are so high, we've decided to use caution and approach this like an interstellar war. That means blocking key jump routes, guarding our most important systems and attacking their strategic lines and industrial bases. If you're captured, you can tell them all this."

"I don't plan on getting caught," Maddox said.

"Glad to hear it," the Lord High Admiral said. "Naturally, we've sent Patrol scouts into the Beyond."

The Patrol arm of Star Watch went on the deep recon missions. They were the risk takers and they often traveled years at a time, searching new star systems, expanding the Commonwealth's knowledge of the Beyond.

"We have to learn more about the New Men," Cook said. "I mean, actually learn something concrete about them. I don't have much faith in those missions, though. Likely, we'll never see those Patrol scouts again, which is a shame."

The Lord High Admiral's jawline tightened. "Son, let me tell you, it's no fun sending volunteers to their deaths. I don't like it one bit. This isn't a cold game to me, where people become counters to move across a board. This is a death struggle of competing races, winner take all. I believe that with all my heart."

The Lord High Admiral glanced at the brigadier. Then, he refocused on Maddox.

43

The captain could feel the man's force of will. The Lord High Admiral must have hooded some of it during the meeting yesterday. Not now. Those green eyes studied him with fierce intensity.

"I've felt for some time that our enemy believes he's superior to normal humans," Cook said. "The people he uses as agents—" The Lord High Admiral waved his big hands. "We don't have time for a history lesson. They didn't have to move at this precise moment if they didn't want to. That they did invade the Oikumene seems to indicate they feel they have enough resources to defeat us."

From her desk, O'Hara cleared her throat.

"Not now, Brigadier," Cook said. He focused on Maddox again. "We don't know their politics. That's her point. We don't know their situation. Maybe they're like the ancient Ostrogoths who fled before Attila the Hun's grandfather. Maybe some truly wicked aliens are out there pushing the New Men into us. I doubt it, but we don't know. We're clueless about far too much. One thing we have an eyewitness to—Noonan and her lifeboat crew told us how three cruisers slaughtered a Star Watch battle group."

"Could they have planted that?" Maddox asked. "Could they have captured Noonan and given her false memories about what really happened?"

"Sure they could have," Cook said. "We have experts trying to deduce just that. Some believe that's the actual case. It's too hard for most of us to accept three ships doing what they did. Maybe in reality the battle was a slugfest with nearly even sides. The New Men won, captured Noonan and brainwashed her into thinking what she told us. There aren't any mental marks or other evidence pointing to that, but anything is possible, I suppose."

Cook shrugged. "If that's the case, though, we have much less to worry about. Then, when our main fleets engage, we'll do much better than we thought we would. We're fools if we hope Noonan's evidence is wrong. These New Men are a menace beyond anything we expected. And that's where you come in, Captain."

"I can't see how one man can make much of a difference in this," Maddox said.

"Firstly," Cook said. "You won't be one man. You'll be part of a team, a very unusual team, to be sure."

Maddox noticed the Lord High Admiral and the Iron Lady trading glances. Okay then.

"How can one team make a difference in such a broad war?" he asked.

"Right. That's the question." The Lord High Admiral's nostrils flared. "You're about to leave on a quixotic quest, Captain, maybe the craziest assignment anyone has ever gone on. We're desperate. It's more than possible that humanity is facing extinction. The New Men strike me as arrogant beyond anything we've faced before. The trouble is that their arrogance seems to be entirely backed by real ability. I think they *are* better than us at waging war and waging a secret spy contest. I think they're doing unspeakable things to the populations on Odin, Horace and Parthia. I hope to the Lord in Heaven I'm wrong, but I have a bad feeling in my gut that I'm right."

"Begging your pardon, sir," Maddox said. "That doesn't answer the question, and my half hour is fast running out."

"You're right." Cook glanced at the brigadier. "You want *me* to tell him, don't you?"

"I couldn't do it, sir," she said.

Maddox was surprised at the tone of her voice. The Iron Lady sounded weary, sad, as if... *This will be a supremely difficult operation. That's what they're hinting at. She can't give me the orders to do this because she fears for my life.*

For the first time, Captain Maddox felt himself blush. It was a strange sensation. Did Brigadier O'Hara have a motherly concern for him? Did she look at him as more than her star officer? She'd been aware of him since his birth, watching, maybe wondering about him.

Lord High Admiral Cook cleared his throat.

Maddox looked up.

"I'm going to tell you a story," Cook said. "It's an old one. You may have heard rumors about it before. There is supposed to be a star system far out in the Beyond. It's a smashed system, all the planets long ago turned into rubble. Whoever fought that ancient war used planet busters of unimaginable strength. According to the tale, hundreds, thousands of wrecked starships drift as useless hulks. Some believe that aliens battled there while our ancestors chased cave bears from their dens. We'll probably never know the reasons for the conflict or what drove them to such desperate measures."

Cook leaned a little closer. "Among the asteroidal debris and dead ships is a working sentinel. It's a huge vessel still seeking its

45

ancient enemies. Even more importantly, this automated sentinel, this primeval Guardship, contains advanced weaponry beyond anything we have. If the Star Watch could gain this craft, and if it was better than the New Men's starships, then maybe we could win the coming battles."

Maddox watched the old man as he spoke. Yes, during his many assignments he'd heard rumors of this sort. The story had wandered through the star lanes for a long time. He also knew that a few prospectors had searched for the destroyed system. The legend went that no one who hunted for the alien super-ship was ever heard from again.

"If this star system is real and the sentinel is there," Maddox said, "anyone attempting to board it would die."

"Not if the team doing it had the right personnel," Cook said.

"Who would these people be?" Maddox asked. "I don't see how I possess any of the needed qualities."

"You would bring several elements to the table. First, you would be the team leader, guiding and prodding the others. Second, you're a specialist at intrigue and subterfuge. Anyone able to pull this off would need such talents. Third, you're a lethal survivalist. Fourth, if you win your way onto the sentinel, the brigadier and I believe you would be trustworthy as its commander. Lastly, we both think you would make an excellent starship captain."

"That's a lot to carry on my shoulders," Maddox said.

"Come, come, my boy," Brigadier O'Hara said. "You're just the man to do it. If you can't, I don't know who can."

"Break onto an alien sentinel from a war six thousand years ago?" Maddox asked.

"Yes," Cook said. "It sounds mad. That we're down to something like this shows the desperation of the hour. There's something else you should know, too."

Maddox felt the back of his neck prickle. He had felt such stirrings before. It warned him that the old man had saved the worst for last.

The Lord High Admiral scooted his chair around, bringing it closer so their knees almost touched. "Captain, this will be a dangerous mission for more reasons than its objective. After listening to Lieutenant Noonan's tale, it seems our enemy has infiltrated our various organizations even more deeply than I'd believed. It's taken me a long time to admit this." He glanced at the brigadier before staring back at Maddox. "How can one accept such a bitter truth until the reality of it stares one in the face? It's good the Iron Lady has been at the helm of Star Watch Intelligence all this time. She's seen more clearly than any of us have."

"That's all past us now," she said. "We're finally on the same page. That's what counts."

Cook stared at his big hands.

"Sir..." Maddox said.

The Lord High Admiral raised his head. "Son, no one on our side can know what you're doing. That's another reason you're the perfect candidate."

"By no one," Maddox said, "you mean no one other than the brigadier and you."

The Lord High Admiral's features grew even graver. With his eyes fixed on Maddox, the old man nodded.

The captain felt a stir in his heart. Maybe he should have felt betrayed at their suggestion. Instead, a thrill raced through him. Perhaps he had been born for this very purpose. The Lord High Admiral was saying that he wanted him—Captain Maddox—to save the human race. That was an impossible burden. Yet, that was also a goal to fire a man's imagination. It meant that what he did was vital. It meant that he was important. He mattered in the grand scheme of things. Cook and O'Hara trusted him. In a way, they were like his parents, asking him to save the family.

"Yes," Maddox said. "I accept the challenge."

"I haven't told you the rest," Cook said.

"I think I already know, sir. You mean to fool the New Men, or their operatives here. That means I will have to act as a fugitive from justice. I will be on the run. In Intelligence parlance, I will be out in the cold."

"I told you he's sharp," O'Hara said proudly.

"One thing troubles me," Maddox said.

"Yes?" Cook asked.

"You can't just be sending me out there on a rumor. The operation is too important. That means you have facts about this system, not just old stories."

"You're right," Cook said. "Son...there's a crazy genius out there, half mad explorer and half compiler of ancient secrets. His

47

name is Professor Ludendorff, and we have some of his notes. Ludendorff claims to have made it to the star system in question. Even more importantly, he says he saw the sentinel and measured a few of its abilities. He says it isn't just big, but claims the vessel is three times the size of a *Gettysburg*-class battleship."

"That's massive," Maddox said.

"There's more. Ludendorff says he studied a few of the wrecked hulks. By examining areas of damage, he claims the sentinel fired some sort of neutron beam. I don't know if you're aware, Captain, but our scientists say such a weapon is impossible. If one could develop it, though, that beam would quickly overload our present shields. It couldn't slice through them like the New Men's weapon. What the neutron beam would likely do, however, is bypass regular armor. It would hit the inner systems with devastating power. If that wasn't enough, the professor claims a shield flickered into place over the sentinel on two occasions. The second time, he had his instruments running. The shield must have used dampeners, increasing its strength compared to our shields and changing its complexion. There are reasons to believe this shield would hold up against the New Men's beam. That would give the sentinel a deadly advantage against our enemies, giving us a tactical edge, maybe enough to win fleet actions."

"I'd like to talk to this professor," Maddox said. "Where is he now?"

Cook shook his head. "We wish we knew."

"Do the New Men have him?"

The Lord High Admiral raised his hands. "He's lost. That's all that matters for now. We have a thick book of his notes. We have also located one of his former assistants."

"Where?"

"On the prison planet Loki Prime," Cook said. "It turns out she's amassed quite a criminal record."

"What's the assistant's name?"

"Doctor Dana Rich," Cook said. "Among her many talents, she's a clone thief and computer systems specialist."

"This is slim evidence to use, some madman's notes and a criminal's testimony."

"The truth, son, is that we haven't spoken to her. At this point, we're going off Professor Ludendorff's notes alone. We also have reasons to believe he's not as mad as advertised."

"If Ludendorff was there, why didn't he board the sentinel himself?" Maddox asked.

"He didn't have those on his crew who he considered as the right people."

"What is *that* supposed to mean?"

The Lord High Admiral reached down, taking a briefcase from beside his chair. He set it on his knees, clicked it open and extracted a folder.

That's quaint, Maddox thought. *Why isn't he handing me a reader?*

"I'm told you have an excellent memory," Cook said.

"Nearly photographic, sir," Maddox said.

"Read these files. Because of our fear of being compromised, it's better if you gather these people on the run than if we send them to you. I suspect you'll find they are an unusual group. There's a reason for that. Each of them mentally matches the professor's requirements."

Maddox looked up.

"Let me rephrase," Cook said. "Ludendorff believed the sentinel will only *accept* certain types of individuals."

"How did he reach such a conclusion?"

Instead of answering, Cook checked his wrist chronometer. "We're almost out of time, I'm afraid. You should know that your sergeant is already on a penal ship heading for Loki Prime. He will be sent down by pod in the area where Dana Rich is believed to live."

"Believed?" Maddox asked.

"If we searched her out ourselves, we're afraid the New Men would learn too much about our plan. They might beat us to her. That cannot be allowed to happen."

"I'm supposed to break her and Riker out on my own?" Maddox asked.

The Lord High Admiral nodded.

"Sir," Maddox said. "No one escapes off a Commonwealth prison planet, particularly not Loki Prime."

49

"There's a first time for everything," Cook said. He put his meaty fingers into a pocket, taking out a small disk. He handed it to Maddox. "Those are the codes you'll need to the prison planet orbitals, Loki System satellites and the location of a fast Patrol scout orbiting the moon. I think you'll find it's a unique little vessel."

Maddox nodded instead of laughing in their faces. Then he flipped open the folder and began to read the first file. He didn't like what he found. Keith Maker, an ex-strikefighter ace with a serious drinking problem. How did a pilot like that have the right mental qualities? Maddox decided not to worry about it now. Instead, he kept reading. He would remember the facts and mull them over later.

"By the way," Cook said. "You'll need a topflight navigator who knows her way around in deep space."

"Yes, sir," Maddox said.

"I'm giving you Lieutenant Noonan."

Maddox looked up. Hadn't the woman been through enough already? During the meeting, she'd looked worn down. Despite his gut feeling that this was a bad idea, he kept his opinion to himself.

"The lieutenant's career is in ruins," Cook said. Perhaps the Lord High Admiral sensed Maddox's unease about the woman. "By her quick thinking and actions, she gave us a rare window of opportunity. Even so, too many Star Watch officers view her retreat through the Laumer-Point as cowardice in the face of the enemy. This will give her a chance to redeem herself. I think she's earned that."

Maddox couldn't very well refuse the Lord High Admiral. Clearing his throat, the captain asked, "Did she request this assignment?"

"After she learned that her brainwave patterns matched our needs, yes, she did," Cook said.

Maddox kept his frown inward. This was getting stranger by the moment. "I suspect that means you told her some of the broader picture."

"Will that be a problem?" Cook asked.

The Lord High Admiral's question surprised Maddox. He took the opening. "She's not an Intelligence officer, sir. She may have already compromised the operation with her bold recounting of the battle."

The older, bigger man leaned forward and his eyes radiated intensity. "Then we'd better get started, Captain, before the competition catches on."

Maddox realized he didn't have a choice in the matter. Nodding, he looked back down at his folder and continued to read.

-7-

Lieutenant Noonan burned with resentment. Usually, she kept that part of herself cordoned off from the rest. She did not have an axe to grind, but many of them lined up in a row.

She stood beside a gargantuan foundation inside Paris' largest mall, the Le Monde. Thousands of shoppers passed her. Most chattered to each other in French, a few must have spoken German.

"Mademoiselle," someone said from behind, his voice barely audible over the splashing water and buzz of the crowd.

She turned. A man in a black leather jacket with a shaven scalp gripped a single rose. He looked dangerous, holding himself loosely like a knife-fighter. As he extended the red flower to her, a chain jangled on his wrist. He didn't smile but watched her closely.

Valerie Noonan had lived with this all of her life. She attracted unwanted attention because men liked the way she looked. Her beauty should have been a blessing. Because of her circumstances, it had simply been one of the many hurdles to jump.

Valerie shook her head. She didn't want his stinking flower.

He continued to speak in a low voice while still extending the rose.

"I don't know French," she said.

"English," the man said, speaking it better than he had the French. "You look lonely, and you're lovely. Please, take this as a gift—from me to you."

"I don't know you," she said.

His lips parted. "We can change that easily enough."

She turned her back to him. In these matters, some men only understood rudeness.

With a shock, she felt the weight of his hand on her left shoulder. The man had just violated her space. He must think he could intimidate her into doing what he wanted. He was about to get a surprise.

Valerie reached up, grabbing his fingers. They were rough-skinned, indicating manual labor or close combat training. She whirled around, twisting his hand and arm. He cried out in pain, his body spun around so he bent low, facing the mall's tiles, with his arm half way up behind him.

"You don't hear very well, do you?" she asked.

"Let go," he said in a flat voice.

Something about that warned her—this man was more dangerous than she'd first suspected. Instead of releasing him and trying to run, she kept twisting.

That's when the heel of his boot crashed against her shin. It exploded with pain, and it made her angry. She twisted his fingers even harder than before. His other arm reached up and slapped her wrist. A buzz of pain shocked her, a sizzling jolt through her entire arm. On their own accord, her traitorous fingers loosened their hold.

The man with the shaven scalp and black leather jacket straightened, facing her. He hadn't smiled before. He frowned now, an ugly thing. There was evil in his eyes.

"That was a mistake," he told her in a low voice.

Valerie Noonan had grown up in the Prosperity Atoll of Greater Detroit in the old United States. In this case, what *prosperity* meant were survival credits from the government, what people had once called welfare. The *atoll* was its own world, surrounded by those who worked for a living, paid taxes and therefore had the right to vote.

Valerie's father had fought in his youth as a Beck & Loch corporate soldier. He'd lost his legs to a land mine and had been psychologically unable to take prosthetics. The corporation gave him a lump sum discharge and left him to his fate. Her dear old dad had gambled that away and soon found himself with a three-year-old daughter and very little to live on. He moved into Greater Detroit, accepting the government stipend and the lowering of status.

Valerie's mother had died in a car accident when she was ten. Her dad drank too much and didn't have any ambition for himself. He became her drill instructor, making her study and often wheeling beside her as he guarded her way to school. The man had arms like no one could believe and an attitude and a knife that had cut anyone foolish enough to take on the crazy cripple. Most of the time, the gang members that prowled everywhere in Detroit left Valerie alone. The few times they'd tried something when her dad wasn't around, his training had seen her through.

She studied hard and aced everything. Finally, her dad's endless filling out of forms got her admitted to a VA high school on the edge of the city. She went there, and discovered that the Prosperity schools had been a joke. She would have been better off reading fiction all the time.

Instead of wilting, she worked overtime to catch up. By graduation, her marks had become sterling. Even so, she barely made it into the North American Space Academy. There, she busted her tail once more. Despite her beauty and good grades, she was from Detroit. She'd lived on welfare and therefore was a second-class citizen. Her fellow cadets looked down on her. As compensation, she worked even harder and almost ended up as the class valedictorian.

Had that won her an ensign position on a battleship or maybe even a strike cruiser? No. They didn't even send her to a destroyer. She found herself the navigator on a lousy escort, the smallest combat ship there was. Even there, the others had snubbed her...until the day the commander had an accident in the reactor room.

She had been the right person to become escort commander, but the reviewing board hadn't agreed with the obvious assessment. That had happened during the journey into the Beyond. Her first piece of good fortune struck then. Admiral von Gunther had reviewed the board's finding. He had personally vetoed their recommendation and instead placed her in charge of the escort.

In her mind after that, von Gunther could do no wrong. It was the critical reason she had obeyed his last order. She would have done anything for him. During her three weeks on top, she had commanded a Star Watch escort. Then, the battle with the New Men took place. Now, all her hard work had evaporated into nothing. The others with their privilege had closed ranks against her, calling her devotion to the admiral, who had always treated her fairly, cowardice in face of the enemy.

That plain made her angry. Yeah, she had gladly volunteered for the Lord High Admiral's insane plan. The old man had some of the same grit as von Gunther. He had listened to her story and thanked her for what she'd done. The others yesterday in the conference room…she knew what those hostile stares had meant.

As she stood beside the giant fountain in the huge Paris mall, Lieutenant Valerie Noonan's wrist throbbed from the shock of a buzzer. Her shin hurt where this goon had kicked her with his iron boot heel. What a bastard.

Now he acted tough, as if he could do something bad to her. Well, there had been gang members in Detroit who had tried to rape her before. Two of them would never walk right again.

The thug with his rattling wrist chain reached into his jacket. Valerie had a good idea he meant to draw a knife. She'd seen her dad make a similar grab. With those eyes, she knew this thug liked to cut people.

Knives were bad mojo. Vid shows often had a hero kicking a knife out of a cutter's hand. She knew it didn't quite work like that in real life. Her dad had taught her how to use a knife, and she had wielded one on those wannabe rapists back in the day.

Therefore, Valerie didn't wait for Mr. Tough Guy to pull out his blade. Despite her throbbing shin, she stepped forward and rotated her waist fast. At the same time, she smoothly swung an arm, closing her fingers into a fist. She shot a right cross against his nose. If she could break it and make his eyes water, he wasn't going to be able to see so well.

It all happened to script. She heard bones crunch. His head rocked back and tears of pain automatically began to well. Valerie kept stepping forward. The man's hands went to his nose. That was a bad mistake. She drove a knee against his groin.

He grunted, *oofing* his bad breath into her face. Valerie reached up, put her hands on his shoulder, and shoved. Mr. Black Jacket toppled, striking the back of his skull against the tiles as he hit the floor.

People had stopped to watch. A few of the women began clapping.

55

Valerie grinned at them. Then she realized that she was supposed to keep a low profile. What was the best way to deal with this now? Okay. She had an idea. She bowed at the waist, first in one direction and then in another.

A few people laughed.

Afterward, Valerie turned around and began walking away. Some of her burning resentment had departed. Security would be here any moment to take care of the man. She didn't want to answer any questions. It was time to fade into the crowds. She had done that in Detroit too.

"Impressive," another man said quietly.

She glanced to her left. This man also wore a black leather jacket and had a shaven scalp. The sight of him made her stomach tighten. What was going on? This wasn't good.

"Clancy failed," the man said. "I assure you, I won't."

Valerie saw that he had a shock wand hidden in his grip, most of it up his leather sleeve. She reached out, trying to block the hand that held the wand. The man's other hand chopped her wrist. He obviously knew close combat techniques. Her wrist exploded with pain. She jerked her arm away. Then he brought the wand closer. If it touched her—

A third man now got into the action. This one was tall and lean. From behind, he hit the thug's elbow. The shock wand slipped out of the numbed grip and clattered onto the mall floor. The taller man kicked the shock wand away into a crowd of people.

"What the—" Black Leather Jacket said.

He never had the chance to finish his question. The taller man grabbed the back of the man's belt and positioned his other hand on the man's shoulders. The taller man strode briskly, and he must have been stronger than he looked. He drove Black Leather Jacket headfirst against a mall column. The man struck it with considerable force.

Valerie winced at the brutal sound.

The man simply collapsed at the base of the granite-looking column.

Someone in the crowd screamed.

The taller man gripped one of Valerie's elbows. "My name is Captain Maddox," he said in a cool voice. "I believe the Lord High Admiral spoke about me."

Valerie could only nod.

Captain Maddox led her away from the brutality, quickly merging into the crowd. Behind them, people stopped and stared at the fallen man. Valerie knew enough to realize the thug had been an expert at what he did. He could have been a professional hitman.

"Who were they?" she asked breathlessly.

"The enemy," Maddox said.

"What enemy?"

He didn't glance down at her. He kept moving his head unobtrusively, no doubt scanning the crowd.

"For now," Maddox said, "we shall call the enemy *them*."

"You can't mean the New Men," she said.

Maddox winced slightly. "None of that please. *Them.* That's what we'll call the enemy in public."

"You can't be serious."

"Ah. I didn't know you had a sense of humor. Thank you for informing me."

She frowned at him. "Are you making fun of me?" She didn't let anyone make fun of her.

"Lieutenant Noonan, I am not making fun of you. This is simply my way when I'm nervous."

She gave him a more careful study. He didn't look nervous in the slightest.

"This way," he said.

She didn't need to ask. He had powerful fingers, and his grip hurt her elbow. There was a sense of urgency to him, too. Normally, no one guided her. It began to dawn on Valerie, however, that she had stepped into a seriously dangerous assignment. The Lord High Admiral had hinted in that regard. He had tried to warn her away from doing this. Well, he had pretended to. Valerie knew enough about dares to realize he had been goading her into going.

I'm as good as any taxpayer. I am *a taxpayer now. I didn't run away from the New Men. I followed the orders of the best officer in our fleet. The Lord High Admiral asked me to do this because this is finally my chance to shine in the line of duty. I'm going to show them. I'm going to show them all what Tank Noonan's daughter can do.*

"Do you see any more of the black leather jacket gang?" she asked.

"No," Maddox said. "They've dropped away. They're watching us, though. They wonder what I'm doing here with you. They're curious about what we're going to do next."

"What are we going to do?" Valerie asked.

Captain Maddox glanced down at her. He was handsome and maybe even younger than she was, and there a feeling of extreme competence in his bearing.

"We're going to do the unexpected," he said.

"Okay. What is that?"

"Do you see that door over there?" Maddox asked, inclining his head to the right.

She glanced at it, a utility door it seemed to her. "I see it."

"Good. Then turn around one hundred and eighty degrees from it and *run*," he said, releasing her elbow as he broke into a sprint into the direction he'd just told her to go.

While panting, Lieutenant Noonan glared at Captain Maddox. She sat in the passenger seat of his flitter, a fast sportster with a bubble canopy. Below, the mall and the greater metropolis of Paris quickly faded from view as they climbed with unbelievable speed. She couldn't even see the Eiffel Tower anymore.

The engine hummed, but there was hardly any vibration. This was some craft, clearly a specialty machine approaching combat efficiency.

After that harrowing sprint, Valerie was still sucking down air. Sweat prickled her face and neck.

Maddox glanced at her and flicked yet another switch. A conditioning vent poured cooling air against her skin. She repositioned, opening a top button. Ah, the blowing air felt good.

Valerie liked to stay in shape. Compared to Maddox, though, she was an out of shape slob. The captain seemed placid as he kept checking his instrument panel. He'd sprinted like a cheetah back there. Only as Valerie broke out of the mall, struggling to catch up to him in the parking lot, had she realized a sniper fired at them—not that she'd heard anything. The captain had thrown himself to the paving, and she'd seen something glittery break apart on the hard surface. Maddox had produced a long-barreled gun, snapping off several shots. Then he'd sprinted back, grabbed her and forced her to bend low as they wove through parked vehicles.

She would have asked what was going on, but it was all she could do to keep her legs churning as he propelled her along. Finally, he'd holstered the weapon and pulled out a black unit, pressing

59

buttons. She'd yelped when a flitter literally dropped out of the sky in front of them.

Another of those glittery things broke apart against the machine's canopy. Then they'd piled in. The flitter lifted before she clicked on her buckles. Now they headed north.

"Who shot at us back there?" she said between gasps.

"That's a good question," Maddox said. "I wish I knew."

"You must have an idea."

He glanced at her. "There are several possibilities."

She frowned at him. "I'd guess it was the same people who came for me in the mall."

"That's loose thinking at best," he said.

"What do you mean?" she asked, stung. "That makes perfect sense. They tried to kidnap me in the mall. I saw what the sniper fired at you. It wasn't bullets. Steel-jacketed rounds don't break apart on paving or against armored glass. He shot darts. Something with knockout drugs would be my guess."

Maddox gave her another glance, this one more quizzical.

"Did I say something stupid?" she asked, exasperated.

"I didn't expect someone like you to be so observant in these kinds of situations," Maddox said.

"What's that supposed to mean?"

He raised an eyebrow. "A Star Watch lieutenant. What did you think I meant?"

She said nothing.

"Someone from Detroit perhaps?" he asked.

Her face stiffened. "You listen to me—"

"Save yourself the indignity," Maddox said. "I meant no insult. I'm letting you know that I've read your file."

"Yeah?" she asked. "What does it say?"

"For the most part it speaks about your competence in your chosen area of expertise."

"And the rest?"

He grinned. "None of us are perfect, are we?"

"If you think because my family lived on welfare that you're better than us, you have another thing coming. "

"That's an interesting word."

She scowled. "What is? What are you talking about now?"

"Better," he said.

60

"What about it?"

"You asked if I think I'm better than you. That's too broad of a question. I run faster, so that makes me a better runner. As a navigator in space, you would be better. You have to add a qualifier to your statement for it to make sense."

She debated remaining angry with him, but he *had* helped her in the mall. The thugs with the black leather jackets...who knew what they would have done to her.

"You're a slick operator," she said. "I can see that."

"And you revert to your upbringing in times of stress," Maddox said.

"Maybe I do. Is that going to be a problem for you?"

"Negative," he said. "It makes your selection more reasonable."

"That still doesn't answer my question. Who do you think shot at us back there?"

"I've narrowed it down to two possibilities," he said. "One, maybe the sniper belonged to the men trying to kidnap you. But then, why did they shoot at me?"

"Who were they anyway?"

"Yes. That's a good question. Could our enemy have moved this quickly? I don't like what that implies."

"What does it imply?" Valerie asked.

"That they have operatives within the Star Watch," Maddox said.

"So, who shot at you?"

"It could be the same people or one of the Methuselah People, a tycoon."

"Why would he or she come after you?"

"He no doubt believes I caused the death of his son. He wants revenge. Octavian Nerva has the money to hire the best."

"Octavian Nerva of Nerva Conglomerate?" she asked in shock.

"The same," Maddox said.

"You have powerful enemies."

"Not half as powerful as those after you," he replied.

Valerie turned away, staring out of the canopy. They shot through clouds as they continued to fly north. *This man helped me. Maybe he saved my life. I have to quit getting so mad so easily.*

Valerie realized her upbringing had made her ultra-competitive. One of her few friends had said she was prickly like a porcupine. "Make people like you," her friend had suggested. "That will make

61

things a lot easier for you. Besides, you're beautiful. You should learn to use that to your advantage."

Well, life hadn't been easy. Smiling at problems hadn't helped her any. She'd had to lower her head and charge through her problems. Stubborn pride and hard work had been her secrets.

"So what's the plan now?" Valerie asked.

"First. I need to know how much you know."

"Sure. We're off on the wildest goose chase in the galaxy. We have to find a place that doesn't exist and commandeer a warship that can do the impossible. Is that the same mission you're on?"

"If you feel that way, why did you agree to do this?"

"Why did you?" she shot back.

Maddox studied her before saying, "I believed your story about the battle with the three starships."

"And?" she asked.

"And we need that alien sentinel if we're going to defeat the invaders."

"You think the ancient ship exists?" Valerie asked.

"Don't you?" he asked.

Valerie shrugged. "I don't know. It's possible, I suppose. It doesn't seem very probable, though."

"If it doesn't exist, how do we defeat the New Men?"

"Oh, so we're done calling them *them*?"

"We're in private, not in public."

Valerie closed the button she'd undone. "In my opinion, the New Men can't be invincible. I don't think anyone is. All you have to do is find their weak point and exploit it."

"I've heard worse theories. But what if our point turns out to be weaker than theirs?"

She frowned. "They have a deadly beam. We should start researching like crazy, using what I recorded from the battle. In time, we'll probably duplicate that beam. That will give us a weapon to bypass *their* shields. Until then, we play for time in order to do our research."

"And if they invade en masse before we're ready?" Maddox asked.

"Then that's how we stop them," Valerie said. "We hit them with mass, trading ten ships for one of theirs."

"What if they have too many ships to make the formula sustainable?"

"I doubt they do. We must have a far larger population and industrial base."

"Hang on," Maddox said.

She glanced at him, not getting it.

"Hang on," he repeated. "We're going to turn."

Oh. She grabbed an armrest and hunkered lower.

Maddox banked the flitter, and he took them down fast.

"Where are we headed?" she asked.

"Scotland."

"Any particular reason?"

Maddox nodded. "We have to get our pilot."

"Who is he?"

"Keith Maker."

"Where in Scotland is he?" she asked.

"At this time of the day," Maddox said, cocking his head. He seemed to be thinking. "He should be in a pub in Glasgow, beginning his afternoon beer. He likes to take his time with those. Later in the evening, he'll start on the whiskey shots."

"What kind of pilot is he?" Valerie asked. "The man sounds like a drunk."

"Indeed," Maddox said.

She gave him a dubious look. "You're kidding me, right? We're not really going to recruit a drunk for the mission."

"By recruit, you mean get him to voluntarily join us?"

"What else would I mean?" she asked.

"Ah. I see. No, we're not going to recruit him."

"Well, that's a relief. Then what are we going to do with a drunken pilot in a Glasgow pub?"

"Kidnap him," Maddox said.

-9-

Maddox let the flitter drop toward Glasgow. He'd taken himself off the traffic control net as they'd lifted from Paris. Because of an advanced anti-tracking device, the machine would be incognito for an hour, maybe two hours if he was lucky.

Given enough flight time, there would be an anomaly somewhere. That would alert the planetary tracing system. A clock would begin ticking then: the countdown. At that point, it would only be a matter of time before the tracing system cracked his invisibility. He had to be gone from Earth before that happened, or it would jeopardize the entire mission.

The kidnapping attack against Lieutenant Noonan troubled him. The brigadier had suggested the New Men had infiltrated the Star Watch with agents. The strike against Noonan would seem to prove the enemy had burrowed much farther than he'd believed possible after leaving the Lord High Admiral. It made more sense now why Cook and O'Hara had set up the operation the way they had.

Humanity was up against a deadly enemy. If the New Men were smarter than people, as regular humans were compared to chimpanzees, what chance did humanity have?

Is humanity the old breed, the obsolete model? How do you defeat a superior foe? The New Men know us, but we don't know them. Right now, our advantage appears to be numbers. Are they using the women on Odin, Horace and Parthia to breed vastly more soldiers? Will they outnumber us in twenty years?

Maddox scowled. He needed to concentrate on the task before him. He'd read the personnel files in the brigadier's office. It gave

64

him a rundown on the candidates. He didn't really know them yet. Their files helped him to know what to look for.

Lieutenant Valerie Noonan clearly had issues. Who didn't, though? He'd observed her in the mall dealing with the first kidnapper and the second. The woman knew how to handle herself in a tough spot, although she wasn't a professional in that department. He had begun to take her measure during their conversation during the short flight.

In his opinion, Lieutenant Noonan wanted acceptance. She keenly felt herself as the outsider. She also carried a two-ton chip on her shoulder. Maddox found it telling that she didn't rely on her beauty. It told him she likely didn't believe herself to be beautiful. The concept was preposterous, but there it was, blinking like a neon sign.

From what he'd read, observed and heard from her own lips, he believed she must be an excellent navigator. She might prove to be a difficult companion in the scout, though. Valerie had not liked his running speed or his competence. It threatened her. He was certain anyone who could do something better than Valerie Noonan threatened her. Like most things in life, that had its good sides and its bad. She would not quit easily. Good. The mission would likely prove to be extraordinarily difficult. Quitters were not welcome.

That brought him to Keith Maker. By the file, the drunkard *was* a quitter. He found the ace's inclusion on the mission as highly questionable. The man's brain patterns seemed as if they were the only qualifier.

"Don't crash us," Valerie said, sounding worried.

Maddox leaned to his left, looking down at the city. Individual buildings rapidly grew in size. It was one thing to fly a spaceship and another to pilot a flitter about to wreck.

For Valerie's sake, Maddox eased the rate of their descent. Then he continued to think.

A few years ago, a painfully young Keith Maker had shot down six enemy strikefighters and five bombers, one more than he'd needed to become an ace. He'd fought in the Tau Ceti Conflict, a system-wide civil war. The Star Watch had quarantined the fighting to Tau Ceti. The split on Earth, and on many colony worlds, as whom to back had threatened a larger rift in the Oikumene. Because of that, the Commonwealth Council had decided to let those on Tau Ceti settle the issue there.

Before the quarantine, Keith Maker had joined the gas and asteroid miners rebelling against the Wallace Corporation. He'd been on the losing side. Not that Keith had been around at the end. Before that, the miner chiefs had grounded him. The reason was that he'd endangered his squadron with his drinking. The dividing line in Keith's combat career had been his brother's death, a fellow pilot and his wingman.

Until that dreadful day, no one had flown better than Keith Maker could. Afterward, he became sloppy in every way.

Before leaving the brigadier's office, Maddox had commented negatively on the man, saying, "He strikes me as useless."

"No," O'Hara said. "That's not what our profilers say. You're going to need a daredevil, likely in more places than we can estimate. If you can get Keith Maker working again, there will be no one better."

"And if I can't get him *working*?"

"Then you're the wrong man for the mission," O'Hara had told him.

Maybe I am, at that, Maddox told himself. *Just how many broken or cracked tools can this mission absorb?*

"What are you grinning about?" Valerie asked him.

"Excuse me?"

"You're looking all serious as you plunge us to our deaths. Then you start grinning. What are you thinking?"

That I'm as cracked as the rest of you.

"The grin is the realization of how much I'm enjoying your company," he said.

"Ha-ha," she said, "very funny."

Maddox braked, and he brought the flitter down onto a rundown parking pad. There was the good side of Glasgow and the bad. They were definitely in the latter. Most of the parked air-vehicles here were police cruisers and corporation meat-wagons that carried security personnel.

"We're going to move fast while we're in Glasgow," Maddox said.

Frowning, Valerie stared outside at the dingy buildings.

"Worried?" Maddox asked her.

"This place looks worse than where I used to live in Detroit." She scowled at him. "No. I'm not worried. Why, are you?"

"A little," Maddox admitted. "The gun laws are enforced in Scotland. So, I can't give you one."

"What about that long-barrel under your coat?" she asked.

"I'm licensed to carry, at least for a little while longer."

"What does that mean?" she asked.

"Didn't the Lord High Admiral tell you how this was going to go?"

"Maybe I forgot," she said.

Maddox examined Valerie, deciding against telling her that soon he would be a hunted ex-Star Watch Intelligence officer. He would be in the cold, outside any legal aid.

"We have to go in and out," he said.

"With a struggling man between us?" she asked. When Maddox climbed out of the flitter without answering, she said, "I'm not sure I can help you with that."

He looked back at her. "You have scruples against kidnapping?"

"As a matter of fact," she said, "yes. I don't believe in making anyone doing anything against their will."

"That's a noble sentiment, and it does you credit. Would you prefer to wait here, then?" That's what he'd wanted from the beginning, but he wanted it to be her idea.

She glanced around. "How safe is this city?"

If he said worse than Detroit, she would probably join him to prove she wasn't afraid.

Before he answered, she asked, "Is the parking pad dangerous?"

Maddox shrugged to indicate *maybe*.

"You don't think I can look after myself?" she asked.

"It's your funeral if you stay," he said.

A hint of worry entered her eyes, and Maddox wondered if he'd miscalculated.

"I'll wait here," she said. "Give me the keys to your flitter. If it gets too rough, I'll take it up."

"Have you ever flown one of these before?" he asked.

"How hard can it be?"

Maddox hesitated before tossing her the control unit. "If you see that light flash," he said, pointing at the instrument panel. "Take it up and come and get me."

67

"You're kidding, right?" Valerie asked.

"No."

She hesitated before saying, "Sure thing. No problem."

Maddox nodded once. He wasn't sure about this. Yet he didn't want her along in the pub. If she had cold feet about forcing Maker to join the team, he didn't want her around.

"I'll be back soon," he said.

"Whatever," she said, pressing a switch, making the canopy slid back into place.

Maddox strode to the tollbooth, swiping a false ID credit card through the slot. Afterward, he moved down the rundown streets. It was the middle of the afternoon, and the city creatures had begun to stir. The workers would leave their shifts soon, heading home. That meant the night people had begun to wake up. Already, the first gang members leaned outside their chosen residences. At least, he took them for crawlies.

Humanity had gone to the stars. That hadn't eradicated poverty, overpopulation and sloth. Some people didn't like to work. Some weren't any good at it. Many preferred illegal trades, preying upon their fellow man, or woman as the case might be. Glasgow had its slums, congregated in its welfare island. Instead of an entire city given over to welfare, only half of the population accepted the dole.

Earth was unlike any other world in the alliance. It had a teeming population twenty times the size of the next three largest planets. Humanity had begun here, and it showed in countless ways. Seventy years ago, there had been enforced emigration. That hadn't worked out so well and had eventually been discontinued. Now, the only involuntary emigrants were those leaving for a prison planet, in other words, the murders, rapists and other notorious criminals.

I wonder where Sergeant Riker is now. I'm going to have to free him from Loki Prime along with this Doctor Dana Rich.

Loki Prime was considered as the worst of the penal colonies.

Maddox zipped up his jacket, turned up his collar and used his right hand to mess up his hair. He still didn't blend in. He knew eyes watched him, judging whether he would be worth robbing. The predators of this concrete jungle had finely tuned senses. Just like the lions on the Serengeti Plains, they could sniff out weakness. A strong person had little to fear this time of day.

68

A prickle touched between Maddox's shoulders. Someone else watched him now, someone dangerous.

Long ago, he had learned to trust his senses. He resisted the impulse to look around. This type of predator wouldn't scare off easily. He would—

Ah. The feeling evaporated. Whatever greater beast had zeroed in on him, had decided this wasn't the time or place to attack.

As Maddox hurried to his destination, he realized there were too many gaps in his knowledge. He was beginning to believe that neither the Lord High Admiral nor the Iron Lady had told him enough.

How had the enemy known to go after Lieutenant Noonan in the mall? That indicated there had been enemy agents in yesterday's meeting when Noonan had told her tale. It might even mean the agents knew about his mission. Maybe they wouldn't know the exact parameters, but they would have learned by now that something was brewing. That might mean killers beyond anything he'd faced before were after him. Octavian Nerva's hitmen would be like Sunday school teachers in comparison.

Maddox's gut squeezed. It hit him here, as it hadn't before, the stakes involved. He was up against the toughest enemy he'd ever faced. Worse, he only had bits and pieces of the real picture.

I'm more out in the cold than I realized.

It might even be possible the Lord High Admiral had sent him on a red herring in order to lure the New Men agents in the wrong direction.

The thought threatened to bring Maddox to a halt. He shook his head. He was letting the enemy rattle him. The New Men weren't gods. They were beings of flesh and blood. Stick a knife in one and the man would bleed.

Another thought occurred to him. The best place to stop something was in its infancy. If the New Men had an inkling of his prize, they would logically attempt to kill him now.

Maddox flexed his fingers, letting his legs eat up one city block after another. Finally, he reached Danny's Pub. It was an ancient brick building. There were bars over the windows and garish neon signs of Budweiser and Lagers beer. He pushed through the door into an atmosphere of smoke and beer fumes.

With the defeat of cancer one hundred years ago, the old antismoking laws had changed. People could smoke inside again. Maddox had seen a history show or two on the subject. Some of these drinking establishments looked just as they'd been in the early twenty-first century. It seemed Danny's Pub was one of those places.

To the side, a man stood throwing darts. He thunked a red one into the "6" area. Other beefy individuals sat at the wooden bar, talking and sipping from their pint glasses.

A small man sat at a table, sucking on a stim stick, making the end glow as he carefully examined his cards. He wore a suit and tie as if it was his uniform, and he looked to be in his mid-twenties. He had sandy hair, a ready grin and mischievous blue eyes. On a right hand finger, he wore a ring with an onyx stone. He sucked the stim stick again, lowered his cards onto the table and grabbed the handle of his pint glass. He sipped golden beer, and for a moment, the merry eyes became hooded.

"Are you in or out, Keith?" a man at the table asked.

The other three card players were bigger and heavily muscled. Maddox took them for debt collectors, experts at breaking bones.

"What will you have?" the bartender asked.

Maddox turned away from the game and moved to the bar, putting a shoe on the foot railing. "Give me your house beer," he said.

The bartender filled a pint, put a napkin before Maddox and clunked the glass before him. The captain sipped, glanced at the bartender and nodded.

"Haven't seen you here before," the bartender said. He was a thick man with a shiny dome. "Have a sense about people, I do," the bartender said, stroking the side of his nose. "You're trouble."

"Oh?"

"You watched the card game too closely. Took a keen interest in it."

The talking at the table stopped. Maddox glanced at the players. All four men stared back at him, Keith Maker having twisted around to do so.

Maddox might render the debt collectors, the dart player, the men at the bar and the bartender unconscious. It would take some doing, though. The easier method would be to shoot them dead,

70

maybe drug Keith Maker and guide the stumbling man to the flitter. Maddox did not intend to kill innocent people, however.

He mentally shuffled through his options. The number of people in the bar at this hour surprised him. After a moment, Maddox decided on his approach and picked up his beer, beginning to guzzle. When he finished the glass, he gasped and clunked the container onto the bar.

"Now give me a whiskey," Maddox said. "No. On second thought, line up three shot glasses."

"Do you have the credits?" the bartender asked.

Maddox took out his credit card and slid it to the man. The bartender ran it through a device and slid it back. With his thick fingers, the bartender plucked three shot glasses, pressing them from the inside. He grabbed a bottle, uncorked it and poured until the liquid brimmed to the top of each glass.

The card players still watched, saying nothing.

Maddox grinned, nodded to them and picked up the first shot glass. He made certain not to spill a drop. With a practiced flip of his wrist, he tossed the contents down his throat. It was fiery going down, and the sensation exploded into his brain. In quick succession, he did the same with the other two glasses. His eyes bulged for a moment on the last gulp.

"That's quite a thirst you have," Keith said.

With a single finger, Maddox indicated for the bartender to approach. The man complied and opened his mouth to ask something. Before the bartender could get out the words, Maddox poked an index finger into the man's mouth, rubbing the tip against the fellow's teeth.

The bartender jerked back, outraged. Maddox caught the big man by the shoulder, dragged him closer and wiped the wet finger against his shirt.

"Next time," Maddox said, "keep your fingers out of my shot glasses." He pushed, making the bigger man stumble away.

As Maddox turned, two of the debt collectors stood up angrily. He pretended not to notice, grabbing a chair, bringing it to the card table.

"What do you think you're doing?" one of the standing men asked.

Maddox laughed good-naturedly, and he lightly punched Keith Maker on the shoulder. "Just making a point, you know. I believe in doing things in a sanitary fashion."

"You okay, Bernie?" Keith asked the bartender.

The man glowered and spit on the floor. "I say we beat the tar out of him. He's trouble, Mr. Maker. I can feel it."

This is Danny's Pub. Danny was the name of Keith's brother. He must own this place. Why wasn't that in the file?

Keith seemed to consider the bartender's suggestion, finally shaking his head.

The two enforcers sat back down, sliding their chairs to make room for Maddox. He scraped his a bit farther away from Keith.

The small pilot in his suit and tie squinted one-eyed at Maddox. Keith took the stim stick out of his mouth and mashed it against an ashtray.

"Bernie's right," Keith said. "You stink of death. Maybe you should move along."

"Want us to *make* him move?" one of the bone breakers asked.

Keith kept looking at Maddox as he shook his head. "He's carrying, Pete. This bloke is a tiger, and you're a junkyard dog. He'd eat the three of you like that." The pilot snapped his fingers.

Maddox's estimation of Keith rose.

"Why are you here?" the man asked.

Maddox reevaluated his plan, and changed it on the spot. "Could I have a word with you in private?"

"Did the Wallace Corporation send you?" Keith asked.

Maddox shook his head.

Keith squinted, peering more deeply into Maddox's eyes. "That's quite a trick," he said thoughtfully.

"What's wrong, Mr. Maker," one of the bone breakers asked.

Maddox had the feeling Keith understood that whatever the whiskey had done to him was quickly dissipating.

"Okay," Keith told Maddox. "I'll talk." He stood, picked up his pint and moved toward a back booth. "Don't touch the cards," he told the others.

Maddox followed the small man, listening as the three enforcers muttered among themselves. He slid onto the other side of the booth as Keith.

"Let's make this quick," the ace said.

72

Maddox spread his hands palms up onto the table as if he was laying down his cards. "Have you ever heard of the New Men?"

"Do you think I'm an imbecile?"

"Not in the slightest," Maddox said. "What you might not know was that there was a battle near the Odin System, near in terms of jump routes. The actual fight happened in the Pan System. Star Watch had a battle group. The New Men had three cruisers. The three destroyed everything and lost nothing."

"If that's true, how do you know about it?"

Maddox wondered if the other files were as wrong about the rest of the candidates as the one had been about Maker. "A lieutenant escaped in a lifeboat and hid behind an asteroid. After the New Men left, she made it back to Earth."

Keith ticked off his fingers as his lips mouthed soundlessly. Then he looked up. "That would have happened at least a month ago."

"Yes."

"Just saying," Keith muttered. "Well, supposing all this is true, why tell me? Why would that bring you here?"

Maddox grinned because now he knew how he was going to do this. "We can't beat their ships."

"By 'we' you mean…?"

"The Commonwealth, the Windsor League—humanity," Maddox said.

"The New Men aren't human?" Keith asked.

"Great Danes are dogs, but they probably wouldn't treat Fox Terriers as equals."

"No," Keith said. "I suppose not. Yet, that doesn't answer the question."

Maddox leaned closer and told the ace about the destroyed star system and its last alien sentinel.

"I've heard a similar story somewhere," Keith said. "Not with quite the same details, but I'm aware it means nothing."

"I'm from Star Watch Intelligence," Maddox said quietly. "I'm going after the sentinel because Earth needs the ship in order to face the New Men on better footing. There's a professor who has been to the system, and he took notes on his observations of the sentinel."

"Have you seen those notes?"

"Some," Maddox said.

Keith pursed his lips, looking thoughtful.

73

"The professor believes that certain types of individuals have a better chance at breaking into the alien vessel than others do."

"How would he know that?" Keith asked.

"You were supposed to be a great pilot," Maddox said, hedging.

"I got by."

Maddox grinned. "That's not what your file says. You were something of a miracle worker when it came to strikefighter combat."

Keith said nothing.

"My point is that some men are fantastic pilots. Some are fools at the controls. If the fool asked you, 'How do you fly so well?' What would you tell him?"

"Don't know that I could tell the fool much that would help him," Keith said.

"Compared to the professor, we're all fools when it comes to the alien sentinel."

"In other words, you don't know how he knows," Keith said.

"That's right."

"I see," Keith said. He appeared wistful. "I remember taking some tests in high school. They found I had an incredible aptitude for flying. Went into a special combat program, I was going to join. Then the Tau Ceti thing broke out. Had uncles living there. Anyway, I went AWOL, took a liner to Tau Ceti and told them about my specialty. They let me teach my brother, thinking he must have been as good as me. He wasn't, but Danny could fly rings around most others."

Keith adjusted his tie, blinked himself out of his reverie and studied Maddox. "You think I'm one of those the professor spoke about?"

"Yes."

"That means you're here to recruit me."

"I hadn't planned on it," Maddox said.

"No?" Keith asked, frowning.

"I was going to kidnap you."

"Oh. I see. What changed your mind?"

"You did," Maddox said.

"How did I do that?"

"You called me a tiger earlier. I see you're one, too. Even if I could kidnap you, it wouldn't help the cause. Either you'll come freely, or you won't be any use to me."

"Why do you want me on this?" Keith said. "What's my specific task supposed to be?"

"Pilot," Maddox said. "You also have the right brain patterns."

"Do you think I do?"

"I have no idea. I'm taking the brigadier's word for brain patterns being important, and she's taking this professor's word."

"I've already fought in one war," Keith said. "I don't relish the opportunity to join another."

"I understand. Yet, I should point out two important features you'd do well to consider before you say no."

Keith picked up his beer, sipping. "Go on. I'm listening."

"The New Men have agents on Earth. If you elect to stay behind, they're going to be calling on you. Don't ask me how, but they'll know I talked to you. One way or another, they will make you talk to them."

Keith's eyes tightened. He nodded. "What's your second point?"

"You once fought to help miners gain their freedom from corporate injustice. This time, you'd be in a fight for the survival of the human race."

"Do I look like an idealist to you?" Keith asked.

"Not anymore," Maddox admitted.

"Thank you."

"You should think about it in practical terms," Maddox said.

"How so?" asked Keith.

"If the New Men can win as easily as I think they can, you're done here. We all are. That might take them three years. It might take ten. A practical man, one owning property, no less, would want to stop that."

Keith made a fist, and he rubbed the onyx against the sleeve of his suit. Then he aimed the ring at Maddox.

The captain almost ducked, wondering if the ring was a hidden weapon. He decided that no, it was just a ring. Keith was attempting to make a point.

"Do you see this?" Keith asked.

Maddox nodded.

"I was never an idealist, but I wanted adventure. There were tons of Scots miners at Tau Ceti. Anyway, my kid brother tagged along, and now he's dead. I think you're trying to get me to tag along with you."

Maddox could see he wasn't going to talk the man into anything… Either Keith Maker would join or not.

First clearing his throat, Maddox said, "I'm officially asking you. Will you join me on the search for the alien sentinel?"

The smaller man sat back, his gaze fixed on Maddox. "You're a bloody bastard. If I stay in Glasgow, you've made sure I'm a dead man."

"If you believe what I'm saying is true," Maddox said.

"So, in your own devious way, you actually *are* kidnapping me. You're using force to twist my arm."

"The force of persuasion only," Maddox said.

"You've boxed me in so I can only make one move. You would have made a deadly fighter pilot." Keith picked up the pint glass, draining the rest of the beer and belching as he put it down. "You must believe I'm crazy, though. I'm supposed to get up and go with you now, right?"

Maddox nodded.

Keith looked away. He snorted, shaking his head. "Do you know what I'm feeling right now?"

"No."

"I'm stupidly excited. I'm feeling…*alive*. I want to drink to celebrate. But that's what I yearn to escape. At first, I drank to drown out Danny's death. Now, the alcohol has become my dark abyss. I'm falling deeper into the abyss every day, Mr. Star Watch Intelligence officer. You're throwing me a rope and shouting for me to grab hold. You'll drag me out of the abyss. I like the booze too much, though. I'm not the man I was."

"I'm leaving in a minute," Maddox said. "Either you come with me, or we'll have to do this without you."

"You are a bloody bastard. I've never told anyone what I just said. You simply ignore it."

"I heard you," Maddox said. "I understand what you're saying. We'll have months ahead of us for you to explain your pain in detail. You can tell me everything you want to confess. But there's one other thing. If you join, you have to agree to take orders from me."

76

"Getting cold feet about taking me, are you?" Keith asked.

"No. I'm in a hurry. As I said, I believe I have hunters on my tail. We have to move fast to stay ahead of them."

"Okay," Keith said. "So where's the next stop?"

"Up there," Maddox said, glancing at the ceiling.

"In orbit?" Keith asked.

Maddox stared at the ace.

Keith began to slide out of the booth. After a half-second, Maddox did likewise.

The small man in the suit and tie turned to the waiting card players. "I have to run an errand. It'll take me around twenty minutes."

"Should we leave the cards on the table?" one of them asked.

"Bernie," Keith told the bartender. "Make sure none of them looks at my hand."

"Yes, Mr Maker," the bartender said. "Can I ask where you're going?"

"You can ask all you want, Bernie, just make sure you keep a vigilant eye on those cards."

Bernie the bartender nodded. He wouldn't look at Maddox.

"Let's make this quick," Keith told Maddox.

"Yes, Mr. Maker," Maddox said.

The words seemed to relax the bone breakers and made the bartender smirk. Then Maddox and Keith Maker exited the pub and hurried onto the street.

-10-

Halfway to the flitter, Maddox felt a chilly sensation between his shoulder blades again. Was this the same predator from earlier or someone else?

What did it mean if it was the same person? Could the New Men have put an operative into Glasgow before he set down? Could Octavian Nerva's hitmen have done that? That seemed almost too incredible to believe. The likelier explanation was that someone else had read the Lord High Admiral's candidate list. Keith Maker's name was on it. If that was true, though, why hadn't whoever else knew this already picked up the ace?

How much of a head start do I have? It may be less than an hour. I know so little. Just how good are the New Men? How good are those working for the oldest Methuselah People?

Keith glanced at him. "What's wrong?" the ace asked.

That's what made him an excellent strikefighter pilot. The man pays attention.

"If I go down," Maddox said. "Leave Glasgow and bury yourself in whatever bolt-hole you've made for yourself."

"Do you think what I do is illegal?"

"Not on the surface," Maddox said. "You own a bar. But the company you keep—the bone breakers—tells me you might have other activities."

After several strides, Keith sighed. "You know what the trouble is with the world?"

"I imagine you'll tell me."

"Too many people prefer to live in the moment. They'll sell the future for another few credits today. My problem is that I see too clearly. Once I understood that simple truth, I realized the loan business would be extremely profitable."

"I believe you mean loan-*sharking*," Maddox said.

"I didn't call it that at first. I thought about the Wallace Corporation. They won in Tau Ceti. You know why?"

"Because they had bigger muscles," Maddox said.

"You're a clever chap. You see that money talks louder than anything else does. I'd lost my brother to idealism—" Keith grinned— "to adventure. I decided it was time to cash in, to do things the easy way. I began to make money the way I'd shot down enemy pilots."

"We're being watched," Maddox said, as his neck hair rose. "I feel it. Try to act normal."

After a moment's hesitation, Keith shoved his hands into his suit pockets and began to whistle.

The sensation grew until it became too much for Maddox. "*Duck*," he hissed. Reaching in his jacket, he gripped his long barrel, spun around, scanned the buildings and barely saw a glitter flashing toward him in time. By flinging himself to the side, rolling on paving, he avoided the dart. It shattered against the nearby wall. Getting up, Maddox sensed as much as saw motion up on a roof two blocks away. He lifted his weapon and deliberately fired twice in that direction. The sniper ducked, and two tiny fountains of masonry blew upward where he'd been.

People on the street didn't shout or panic at the shots. They were too busy disappearing.

Maddox turned and sprinted along the sidewalk. Keith Maker was already halfway down the block. The kid could travel. As Maddox ran after the ace, he took out a call unit and pressed a switch. Would Lieutenant Noonan know what to do?

"Cross the street!" Maddox shouted. Intuition told him to duck again. He did, and another dart hissed past his head, lifting hairs.

Then Maddox ran across the street. He fired at the same building. Afterward, he tucked his gun away, sprinting onto the other side. Keith panted, wiping sweat out of his eyes.

They converged on a cross street, with an intervening building blocking the sniper's line-of-sight.

"I'm out of shape," Keith said, breathing hard.

With his forearm, Maddox pushed the smaller man against the brick wall, the one facing the direction of the sniper.

"He'll be moving into a new location," Keith said. "It's what I'd do."

Maddox looked up into the sky. Where was Lieutenant Noonan? He took out the call unit and pressed it again.

"Reinforcements?" asked Keith.

A flitter appeared. It moved smoothly over the buildings by about one hundred feet.

"That's illegal," Keith said, noticing the car. "You'll have the Air Patrol on us in no time."

The flitter changed directions, and it came down fast, screeching as the bottom struck the middle of the cross street.

"Second-rate pilot," Keith observed.

Maddox was already moving. The bubble canopy slid open.

Lieutenant Noonan had a disheveled look. "I told you I could do it." She took in Keith Maker, and then gave Maddox a questioning look.

"A slight change in plans," Maddox said. "Scoot over."

"I can drive," she said. "I already proved that."

"This isn't a debating society, Lieutenant," Maddox said in a crisp voice.

She became stiff-lipped and slid into the passenger side.

In theory, there was a backseat, but it didn't really seem big enough for anyone but a child. As Maddox ran around the front of the flitter, Keith approached the passenger side.

"Tight fit," he said, "but I've been in worse." He climbed into the back, sitting sideways with his feet on the upholstery.

"Wedge yourself in tight," Maddox said, climbing behind the controls. "We're going fast, and we have a lot of distance to travel."

"Where's the next stop?" Keith asked.

Maddox began tapping controls. The canopy closed and the flitter lifted. "Whoever shot at us must be tracking the vehicle. Now hang on, and belt in."

"Don't know that I can do that back here," Keith said, looking around.

Lieutenant Noonan clicked her buckles into place.

Maddox first gained some height. Then he aimed the flitter's nose toward the clouds, and he gunned it. The Gs pressed him backward into the cushioned seat.

"I'll ask again," Keith said. "Where are we headed in such a hurry?"

"Luna orbit," Maddox said.

"You must be bloody kidding," Keith said. "We're going orbital in this little thing?"

"He said into Luna orbit," Noonan said.

"What?" Keith asked. "This machine is too small to get us to the moon."

"You're right," Maddox said. "Fortunately, we only have to go part way. Our scout will home in on my beacon."

"That's bloody clever," Keith said. "But what if the competition homes in on the same beacon?"

"Are you a praying man?" Maddox asked.

"What?" Keith asked. "No. Don't be ridiculous."

"What about you?" Maddox asked Noonan.

"Sometimes," she said. "Should I start?"

"Please."

***

One thing helped them tremendously. Supply shuttles, heavy lifters and plain old-fashioned laser-launched rockets boiled from the surface in bewildering numbers up into orbit.

The many cargo-haulers carried munitions, spare parts and personnel to the waiting naval vessels parked in Earth orbit. The bigger shuttles headed for the even greater number of military craft around Luna Base. News of the golden-skinned invaders had radiated everywhere. The Commonwealth Council had decided that humanity's homeworld would remain as secure as possible from enemy assaults. It meant that at least one quarter of the Star Watch had permanent patrol duty in the Solar System.

The masses of cargo-haulers lifting from Earth brought hairy traffic control problems. On the way up, Maddox answered four different calls asking for identification and clearance. His still held, but for how much longer? Once, a traffic control officer yelled at him, telling him he was in the wrong zone. He apologized and did his best to reroute. A rocket roared several kilometers away, the laser-ignited flames leaving a smoking trail.

The sheer volume of space traffic shielded them from greater scrutiny. Besides, the flitter was tiny compared to the vessels around it, a mouse skittering across a pasture full of cattle.

"Someone will notice if we drift," Noonan said.

"Given time," Maddox answered.

"Does this machine have vacuum maneuverability?" Keith asked.

"How could it?" Noonan asked. "It isn't big enough."

"What are you planning, mate?" Keith asked.

"I call it velocity," Maddox said. The flitter sped for orbital space, using the antigravity pods at full strength and its fuel at a prodigious rate.

***

Later, they drifted as the flitter left the Earth behind. The blue-green planet had stretched from horizon to horizon a half hour ago. With the naked eye, they'd seen several shuttles docking with a massive battleship, no doubt unloading supplies. Now, the planet was three times the size of the moon as seen from Earth on a clear evening.

The antigravity pods had reversed, giving them weight. Air kept recycling as it hissed through the conditioner vents.

"When this is over," Keith said, "I would like to purchase one of these flitters. I imagine the Commonwealth Council will want to heavily reward us for what we've done."

"This craft is a beaut," Maddox agreed, "one of the service's specialty craft."

Lieutenant Noonan shook her head. "I can't believe we're doing it like this. This is a crazy stunt."

"To tell you the truth," Keith said in wistful tone, "this reminds me of Tau Ceti. Our strikefighters had a bit more elbow room. There was a little cubicle in back for calls of nature. We did a lot of patrolling in those machines." He put a hand before a vent. "I've been in a stalled strikefighter a time or two. You had to wait for the repair ship to come and pick you up. It could get awful lonely. Made a bloke think, it did."

"What are you thinking now?" Noonan asked.

"Eh?" Keith said.

"Never mind," she said.

"That could be our ride over there," Maddox said. A red light appeared on his panel. It was the third one to come this close. The other blips had been a mail rocket and a satellite making its orbit. For the last ten minutes, Maddox began to wonder if Keith was right about the New Men homing in on their beacon."

As if reading his mind, Noonan said, "I don't know why your brigadier didn't make this easier for us."

"The brigadier is terrified of leaks," Maddox said. *Really, O'Hara is terrified of the New Men's ability.* "Otherwise, she would never have made me get the two of you like this. Yes, our exit from Earth is outrageous. It may be all that's keeping us a step ahead of the enemy. My guess is they'll start to expect the unusual from us. They'll adjust."

"Once we leave the Solar System, how will they find us again?" Noonan asked.

"There," Maddox said, ignoring her question. "I think that's our ship."

Lieutenant Noonan looked where he pointed while Keith poked up his head, peering between the two of them. A point of light the size of a star appeared in the darkness. After a time, the star grew until finally the scout's main engine nozzle became distinct.

The scout looked like a late twentieth-century shuttlecraft, only five times larger. It had a fusion reactor, a Laumer Drive and space for twelve crewmembers.

"How are we going to exit the flitter and get aboard the scout?" Noonan asked. "I don't see any vacc-suits in here."

"We're taking the flitter with us," Maddox said.

The lieutenant gave him a dubious glance.

Keith must have noticed. He put a hand on her shoulder. "It will be a snap, love."

She glared back at him.

"Sorry," he said, removing his hand, "meant nothing by it. We're going to be mates, so we might as well get along."

"Mates?" she asked, bristling.

"He means friends," Maddox said.

Lieutenant Noonan blinked several times until her brow smoothed out. "Oh. *Mates*. I'm sorry. It's been…trying the last few years."

Keith chuckled. "Not to worry, love. I won't try to be familiar."

She turned around, facing him. Then she stuck out her hand. "Mates it is. I'm Valerie."

"Keith," he said.

They shook hands.

"Glad to make your acquaintance, love," Keith said.

Maddox was pleased that Lieutenant Noonan—*Valerie*—could bend a little. If his crew were at each other's throats the entire journey, this would never work. Eventually, they had to come together, learning to be a team in name as well as in deed.

"We'll use repulse power," Maddox said. He checked the panel. "I still have a little in the batteries." The flitter hummed as he tapped a control, and the craft began to slide toward the scout.

The bigger vessel had a rakish appearance. It had two gun emplacements, one under each of its stubby wings. The guns would fire a limited number of cannon shells. The scout lacked real armor. Nor did it possess a shield generator, making it nearly worthless in a space fight. The ship's primary function was to explore, often going down into a planet's atmosphere to land.

Patrol duty in the scout was dangerous, and in naval terms, provided cramped quarters. It was better than flying an unarmed yacht, though.

Maddox pressed a remote control, and a large bay door in the scout opened. Even so, squeezing the flitter through that opening would be a tight fit. Switching on headlights, he eased the craft through without scraping anything and brought the flitter to a gentle landing. Magnetic clamps took hold, and the bay door began to close.

"Nicely done," Keith said.

Nodding, Maddox used a control unit. As soon as the bay door shut, large vents hissed an atmosphere into the holding chamber. Soon, the bubble canopy slid away. The scout air was cold with a metallic tang. Valerie shivered. But the air proved breathable.

"We made it," Maddox said. "Now we have to scoot. I don't know what kind of assets their people have. But I don't doubt they have something that can defeat a scout."

"Our enemy has military vessels they'd dare to use this close to Earth?" Valerie asked.

"Not marked as New Men ships," Maddox said.

"What will they be marked as then?" she asked.

"My guess would be corporation ships. Maybe even Nerva Conglomerate vessels."

"Why them?" she asked.

"Because that's who hailing our scout," Maddox said, staring at his call unit. "Come on. Let's get to the control room. I have a feeling we're going to have to see how fast this thing can really fly."

-11-

The control room was small with three seats facing instrument panels. One was for the pilot, and one controlled weapons and navigation. The last panel controlled everything else.

"No," Maddox said, as Valerie slid into the pilot's seat. "That's why we have him along."

Without a word, she moved to the weapons/navigation position.

Keith Maker plopped onto the pilot's seat. After buckling in, he examined his controls. "Just to let you know, I've never flown one of these before. Maybe Valerie should pilot us until I have a chance to familiarize myself with the ship in detail."

"Negative," Maddox said. "Lieutenant, start explaining whatever he needs to hear."

"How do I know what that is?" she complained.

"He'll ask you," Maddox said. Without waiting to hear her compliance, he switched on his panel. The Nerva vessel was on an intercept course with them, although it was still far away. It had clearly launched from Earth sometime after they did. It had the size and shape of a *Ventra*-class shuttle, the most common workhorse out here.

Through the comm unit, a gravelly-voiced man demanded to speak to the scout's owner.

Maddox's fingers flew over the controls. He turned on a voice scrambler, and he kept his video image off, so the other ship wouldn't see his face. His plate showed a fleshy individual with a fresh scar across his nose.

"This is the SWS Scout *Geronimo*," Maddox said.

"I want to speak to the captain," Scar Face said.

"Give me a minute," Maddox said. "I'll get him." He muted his end, watching Keith. The ace gingerly began testing switches.

"I still think I should pilot us," Valerie said in a querulous tone.

"*Lieutenant*," Maddox said. "When I desire an opinion from you, I'll ask for it. Otherwise, during a situation, you will immediately follow orders."

She stiffened, and it appeared as if she couldn't let it go. "This isn't a naval operation. It's an Intelligence venture."

Maddox swung around to face her. "Don't be fooled, Lieutenant. During the entirety of this mission, we will be operating under standard Star Watch regulations."

"Okay. So what's his rank?" she asked, jerking a thumb at Keith.

"Ensign Maker," Maddox said.

"Reporting for duty," Keith said, grinning.

Valerie glowered before she turned away.

Military protocol would become vital later. They attempted to find a super-ship. If the Star Watch were going to beat the New Men, they'd have to run the alien sentinel along proper lines. That meant instilling discipline from the beginning. If they were going to run a combat vessel, they would have to act like a combat crew, no matter how few those crewmembers turned out to be.

"Are you plotting our course?" Maddox asked her.

She hesitated before answering. "Where are we headed?"

"Sir," he said.

It took her several beats. "Sir," she added.

"Eventually, we're going to the Loki System," Maddox said. "What's the best route there?"

"That depends on several factors...sir," she said. "If we use the regular route, sovereign naval personnel will question us every jump. Unless we have authorization, I don't see how they're going to let us jump into the Loki System."

The lieutenant was sharp, and she remembered the details he'd given her. Despite the two-ton chip on her shoulder, Valerie struck him as capable.

Maddox considered her information. Meanwhile, Keith kept pouring over his panel, shooting Valerie questions.

Finally, Maddox took a disc out of his pocket. The Lord High Admiral had given it to him this morning. He slid his disc into a computer slot. After entering his security code, he opened a document, finding the relevant section, speed-reading as much as he could.

The comm-operator in the Nerva shuttle became more insistent.

Maddox checked the time. He'd already stretched how long it should have taken a crewmember to inform the captain of a call. He opened channels again, keeping on the voice-scrambler.

"This is Captain Lewis," Maddox said. "How can I be of assistance?"

Valerie gave him a questioning glance.

"I don't think this is no Captain Lewis," the Nerva operator said. "I'm talking to Captain Maddox of Star Watch Intelligence. Do you know there are suspicious reports about you?"

"Who is this Maddox?" Maddox asked.

"Prepare for boarding," Scar Face said.

"We have guns," Maddox said.

"So do we. And we have an armored hull. We'll destroy your dinky scout."

With a tap, Maddox checked the nearby area. The closest ship was an SWS destroyer. He kept looking. Ah, he spied a cruiser and then a battleship. Between the various vessels were more shuttles and supply rockets. It was a regular convention of spacecraft out here.

"Attack us, and the SWS *Saint Petersburg* will retaliate." Maddox said, talking about the destroyer.

"Call them if you want," Scar Face said. "Let them impound you, Maddox."

"I don't get it," Valerie said. "Why does he think the destroyer will work against you?"

Maybe he was already out in the cold as Brigadier O'Hara had predicted would happen. Had someone already fabricated a lie about him? If so, was that someone Octavian Nerva or an agent for the New Men? At this point, did it matter whom?

"Let me consider your information," Maddox said into the comm.

The Nerva operator laughed sourly. "You have less than five minutes. We'll be rendezvousing with you in that time."

Maddox turned off his microphone. He studied the threatening shuttle. It had a warfare pod attached under its belly. That meant the shuffle could likely make good on its threat.

"We have to leave now," Maddox told the others.

"Understood, mate," Keith said.

"You will refer to me as 'captain' or as 'sir,'" Maddox said.

"Aye-aye, I understand, Captain," Keith said. "Where are we headed?"

"Lieutenant," Maddox said, recalling what he'd just read on the Lord High Admiral's disc. "We're going to use a Class 3 tramline."

"Sir," she said, "the scout is too big for one of those."

A normal Star Watch commander didn't like taking unnecessary risks, especially those that might damage his or her vessel. Maddox realized that, so he understood why she would say what she just had.

"Your objection is noted and will go into my log," Maddox said. He'd have to start a ship's log now. "Nevertheless," he said, "we will use a Class 3 tramline. I don't think the approaching shuttle can enter a class three route, if it even has a Laumer Drive, which I very much doubt."

Lieutenant Noonan appeared as if she wanted to say more. Finally, she muttered, "Yes, sir."

The many tramlines or wormholes varied in size. Class 1 was the biggest and could accommodate the largest vessels. Battleships, motherships and some of the bigger cruisers could not enter a Class 2 tramline. Class 3 was even smaller. They were seldom used by anyone but explorers and Patrol people. Wormholes smaller than Class 3 were unusable by anything except for small packets. A ship using a Class 3 tramline could go to some star systems more directly than a battleship, which could only use a Class 1 jump route.

"Do you want the quickest route to Loki, sir?" Valerie asked, as she studied her computer.

"No," Maddox said. "I want to use the least traveled systems. The fewer records of our passage, the easier it will be to throw off any hunters."

Many systems parked monitors near the most used jump route. They kept careful record of what ship went where. It was part of what made life safer in the Oikumene compared to the Beyond.

"That will take me more time to calculate," she said.

"This is your last chance to survive," the Nerva operator said, interrupting their conversation.

"Let's go," Maddox told the other two.

Newly ranked Ensign Maker tapped his screen. The fusion engine vibrated with power, making the bulkheads shake.

"Sorry about that," Keith said. "But by our friend's words, it's time to leave in a hurry. Engaging…now." Keith tapped the screen again.

It wasn't a slow acceleration. One moment, the *Geronimo* was at relative rest. The next, five Gs of force slammed each of them against their cushions and restraints.

Lieutenant Noonan's head snapped back against the upper rest of her chair. She lay there, panting.

The force of the acceleration caused Maddox to lose his breath. It was all he could do to blink.

For Ensign Keith Maker, this was obviously a delight. With five Gs of acceleration, the small man shouted with joy.

"We're on a rocket ride tonight, my love!" Keith sang in an off-key voice. "From Orion to the Pleiades, we'll shoot into the galaxy of star delight. Oh, fire the works, sweetie, plunge us into the whirlpool of moonbeam divine."

At last, Maddox sucked down air. "Turn on the antigravity pods."

Keith kept singing.

"Ensign Maker!" Maddox shouted.

"Yes, sir," Keith said, glancing his way.

"This isn't a strikefighter. We have antigravity dampeners. Use them."

"Oh," Keith said, "my mistake, mate, I mean, Captain, sir."

"Check your records for the nearest tramlines," Maddox told Valerie.

"Ah. Found it," Keith said. He tapped a control. Immediately, the pressing Gs lessened to something more bearable.

"Oh no," Valerie whispered.

"What's wrong?" Maddox asked her.

"Sir," she said. "The Nerva craft has launched a missile. It's heading straight for our scout. He means to destroy us."

As *Geronimo* kept accelerating, Maddox opened channels with the Nerva shuttle. "You know traffic control has seen that," he said. "Your missile's signature has become huge."

"Ain't that a shame," the Nerva operator said. "And do you know what happens next?"

"The destroyer or the cruiser will target your missile and beam it down," Maddox said.

"I call that step one," the operator said.

Maddox understood then. Step two would be an investigation all the way around. The destroyer would act, boarding both ships as a matter of protocol. Those in the shuttle might already have assurances by Nerva that he would free them from captivity. What would happen to the mission, though, if he—Maddox—found himself impounded with the shuttle? No. He had to survive and escape now.

"Captain," Valerie said. "The missile is bearing down on us. It's accelerating at fifteen gravities, three times faster than we're going."

"I heard that," the operator said.

"How much time until the missile reaches us?" Maddox asked.

"Give me a second," Valerie said.

"You should have already computed it."

"I know! I'm not used to running navigating, weapons and radar all at once."

"You'd better start, Lieutenant."

"I know!" she shouted. "Sir!"

The Nerva operator chuckled. "Time's running out for you, Captain Maddox."

"Thirty seconds," Valerie said. "Thirty seconds to impact."

"What's the shuttle doing?" Maddox asked. "And why isn't the destroyer knocking the missile down for us?"

"I'll tell you what I'm doing," the operator said. "I'm dropping back down to Earth. See you around—never."

The comm clicked off.

"Twenty seconds to impact," Valerie said. "Captain, why hasn't the destroyer beamed the missile down? I don't understand their delay."

A terrible thought struck Maddox. Just how deep did Nerva's bribery go? Could the Methuselah Man have corrupted a Star Watch destroyer crew near Earth orbit? Did the New Men back Octavian

Nerva? Maybe the industrialist fronted for the New Men secret service.

Maddox had no doubt the brigadier had been monitoring the situation the entire time. Likely, the other side was burning agents to do what they did. Yet if the Lord High Admiral was correct, humanity would never have a chance at survival if they didn't acquire the alien sentinel.

"I'll show you how we used to take care of missiles," Keith said. "Get ready, Lieutenant." The pilot cut acceleration. Then, he rotated the scout so the cannons aimed at the missile.

"I see it," Maddox whispered. He meant a visual contact. The missile's long exhaust made it a bright object, and it headed straight for them.

"Engage the cannons," Keith said.

Lieutenant Noonan shook her head. "The missile is using advanced ECM. I can't get a targeting lock on it."

"Switch the guns over to me, love," Keith said.

She didn't hesitate, but tapped a screen.

"Yes, you little crawly, come to poppa." Ensign Maker tapped a control. Each time a cannon fired, the scout trembled slightly.

Maddox watched his screen for what seemed like an interminably long time until finally, a bloom appeared.

"Bingo," Keith said. "The boggy is eliminated."

Maddox studied his panel. He couldn't believe it, but the ace was right.

"Good work, Ensign," Valerie said. "I'm never going to doubt you again."

"Thank you, thank you," Keith said. "All donations to my party fund will be appreciated." He began tapping the panel.

The scout rotated once again. "I'm going to use five dampened Gs, mates, we're about to accelerate."

"This is SWS Destroyer *Saint Petersburg* calling SWS *Geronimo*," a woman said. "Respond *Geronimo*."

"Have you plotted our course yet, Lieutenant?" Maddox asked, ignoring the new message.

Valerie waited a beat before saying, "I'm working on it, Captain."

"The sooner I have that the better," he said.

"Yes, sir," she said.

"Will the destroyer laser us if we don't comply with their orders?" Keith asked.

"I plan to prolong the procedure," Maddox said. "By the way, you have my congratulations on expert firing. That was well done."

"Thank you, sir," Keith said.

Maddox went back to his instruments, talking to the destroyer's comm officer.

"I'm going to have to report you for firing weapons in Earth orbit without proper authorization," the destroyer's comm officer said.

"Do what you must," Maddox said. He had no doubts now that someone had compromised the destroyer commander. The rot was definitely deeper than he expected.

"You will desist from accelerating," the comm officer said. "My captain wants me to inform you, he will be shooting out your engines otherwise."

"Tramline in three minutes," Valerie said.

"Class three?" Maddox asked.

"Yes, sir," she said, "although, it will be a roundabout way to our destination."

"At least it will get us out of this mess," he said.

"It will, at that, sir," Valerie said.

"Do you copy my last message, *Geronimo*?" the destroyer officer asked.

Maddox began an argument with her. As he started to work himself into a supposed rant, Lieutenant Noonan shouted:

"Get ready for jump!"

The Laumer-Point was invisible to human eyes. Even so, an opening to a small wormhole appeared several kilometers from the accelerating *Geronimo*.

"This is SWS *Saint Petersburg*," the destroyer comm officer said. "We have our main laser locked onto you. You must immediately shut down the scout's Laumer Drive or we won't be responsible for your destruction when our beam takes out your engine."

Keith's fingers flew over his controls. "Expelling chaff and an emitter," he said. "Get ready." He tapped controls. Even with the dampeners, massive acceleration struck. The scout fairly leaped away.

93

At the same time, loud beeps emanated from Valerie's panel. The destroyer had lock-on. A beam flashed, and it would have hit but for Keith's fast actions in changing their estimated position.

"They're retargeting!" Valerie shouted.

Another beam flashed. It stabbed into the chaff, annihilating the emitter.

"I knew they'd fall for it," Keith whooped with delight. "Now, hang on. I'm going to hit the entrance faster than I should."

"SWS *Geronimo*, comply with our orders. You must remain in the Solar System or face destruction."

Maddox leaned low to the microphone. "Yes, *Saint Petersburg*, we agree. We're shutting down our drive now."

"Clever," Keith said. "That should give us the seconds we need."

"*Geronimo*," the destroyer comm officer said, "your engine is still online. You must comply with our orders or face immediate destruction."

"We're shutting down now," Maddox told her.

"This will be a little tricky," Keith said, as he squinted at his controls. "We could miss the opening. According to procedures, we should do this gently."

Despite the ship's velocity, Keith flew them perfectly. The SWS Scout *Geronimo* entered the wormhole. That broke the targeting lock from *Saint Petersburg*. At the same time, a laser flashed. Since it lacked mass, the beam swept past the wormhole opening, missing the *Geronimo*. Because the scout *had* mass, it entered the wormhole and left the Solar System, heading along the tramline for the New Panama System.

-12-

Tramlines granted humanity faster than light travel. This meant that news spread at the speed of starships, no faster. Like the old colonial days of wooden sailing ships, packet liners brought information that might be days, weeks or even months old. That meant a fast ship could out-distance the news, at least for a while.

As the SWS Scout *Geronimo* accelerated through the empty Karakas System, heading for the next jump point, Ensign Keith Maker tried to focus on that.

He told himself his shakiness was a case of nerves. He clicked a reader, studying yet another scout function manual. His gaze roved over text, but he forgot the words the second he looked at the next one.

Lifting a hand, he watched it quiver.

I need a drink. There has to be something aboard this speedster I can guzzle.

Like the other two, Keith now wore a Star Watch uniform. The captain had insisted each of them don one. Maddox must believe the clothes made a person. What horse manure. Yet...Keith felt different wearing his regs. It reminded him of Tau Ceti, and that was both good and bad.

He recalled the duty rules. That he was in a military again. It also reminded him of Danny Maker, his younger brother.

I miss you, boyo. I wish...

Keith made a fist, wanting to smash the reader. His throat convulsed, it was so dry. He needed to oil it with a beer, or preferably, several shots of whiskey.

They were two days out from the Solar System, from Earth, and this was the first time the scout ran on automated, without someone in the control room. Maddox slept, and who knew what the pretty lass did. Valerie could read three times faster than he could and pored over the scout's manuals. The woman was a stickler for rules, and it was obvious she felt better in uniform.

Each of them had already spent considerable time learning the scout's functions. It made better sense to Keith how they had escaped the destroyer. The *Geronimo* could boost like the devil. There at the end of the confrontation, that's exactly what they had done. Maybe even as important, the ship had an impressive cloaking device and was constructed of antisensor material. After Valerie explained how the device worked, he had finally started to believe they could sneak into the Loki System without the monitor detecting them and blasting them to atoms. It would be tricky, but with Maddox and him—

Keith slapped the reader onto the table. He sat in the wardroom. It could comfortably hold six people, nine if everyone squeezed together. He'd forgotten how much he hated tight places. It was different in the cockpit of a strikefighter. Then it felt as if the universe was his home. He could go anywhere in the fighter. But sitting inside a vessel with the bulkheads squeezing around him, without a wide-angle view of the stars…

I definitely need a sip of something. How is a man supposed to live in this tin coffin? It's not as if I'm on the clock. It's downtime, matey.

He stood, cracked his knuckles and stepped to the hatch.

A short walk down the corridor into the storeroom, that's all it will take. Then I can rummage me a beer maybe find a bottle of good Scotch. The captain can't deny me that, can he? Ha! I remember him guzzling in my bar. The chap can drink with the best of them. He'll understand.

Keith opened the hatch. The scout thrummed softly all around him, a smooth ship for its small size. Still, he could hear the air recycling through the vents. It was cooler than he liked and there were hints of something off in the ship's atmosphere.

He took several steps down the main corridor. The captain's hatch was closed and probably locked. Maddox didn't seem trustful of anyone. Behind the engine-room hatch, Keith could hear Valerie testing machinery. Did the lieutenant think she could repair damage if it came to that?

A tremor washed across Keith's shoulders. He looked around. In strikefighter combat, he used to feel the same thing when an enemy snuck up behind him. Checking all around, he failed to spy any cameras. Soon, he chuckled. No one watched him. Yet, he wondered why it felt as if someone did.

I know why. I need a drink worse than I realized.

He reached for the storeroom hatch, but hesitated. He ached to open the door. His hands trembled, and he wanted to taste beer. Even more, he wanted that numbing to his mind. He needed to feel the intoxication begin to take hold. Then everything would be better with the world. Just a good buzz was all he wanted. That wasn't too much to ask a man.

I saved their arses back there from the destroyer. They owe it to me, this little throat-wetter.

His hand inched closer to the hatch, and he stopped it again. Keith wondered on the wisdom of a drink.

He was on the adventure of his life. This was greater than going to Tau Ceti. A terrible threat menaced humanity. Blokes with god-complexes with heightened abilities and racist theories of their superiority told regular Joes to surrender or die. The enemy acted with fierce arrogance, taking on entire battle groups with three warships, and winning those fights.

If I start drinking again, I might endanger the mission. I need to think this through.

Keith stood like that for ten seconds, then twenty, then thirty. He grimaced and made a fist. He wanted a drink, but he also wanted to escape the need for whiskey. He'd been falling into a deeper abyss for some time now. He remembered looking down at that hole when he'd still been standing on the ledge.

He would sit on the edge of his bed, holding a whiskey bottle, knowing that if he started drinking, things would only get worse. A few times, he had set the bottle on his nightstand and had gone and done something else. A different part of his brain had told him to pour the liquor down the sink, get rid of the stuff. He had done that once, watching the amber fluid drain away. Then he had berated himself for a week afterward about wasting good booze. That stuff cost money.

For a time, fear of the abyss, of going down into drunkenness, had halted his mad binges. Then a day came—he wasn't sure of the exact date—when he'd finally given in and plunged into the abyss. He'd been falling ever since, wondering when he would hit rock bottom.

No, no, he told himself. *I'm free of drink now. That's why I left my pub. I have to save the Earth. To do that, I have to stay sober.*

Keith closed his eyes and willed himself to leave. He wanted to walk away, but he stood there instead, battling against his better judgment. When he opened his eyes, he found that his hands were on the storeroom hatch.

With a terrible feeling of resignation, he turned the wheel and opened the hatch. He climbed through into the storeroom. A quick study showed him a carton that looked as if it might contain drink.

Clicking the carton's locks, he opened it, and a Danny-boy grin spread across Keith's face. Look at those green bottles. Saliva moistened his mouth, and his thirst raged.

With trembling hands, he reached in, removed one of the lovely bottles and worked out the cork. A last moment of doubt filled him. Guilt made him lower the flagon.

"I'll just take one sip," he said quietly. "How can a sip, a mere taste, hurt anyone?"

Keith shook his head. It couldn't hurt. That meant it would be okay. As he brought the bottle to his lips, he knew that he was lying to himself. He had waged such interior arguments many times. In his heart, he wanted to drink, so he didn't mind lying to himself. That helped ease his conscience just enough to get the opening to his lips. Then it wouldn't matter anymore. His need for booze would take over.

He upended the bottle, and precious whiskey filled his mouth. He allowed sip after sip of the fiery substance to slide down his throat. Oh, but that was good. The warmth going down his throat, and then the heat in his stomach—there was nothing better in the world.

Soon, the buzz would hit his mind, and everything would be cozy. Keith laughed, a bubbly sound, and lifted the flagon again.

He noticed a slight movement to his left. Then, something hard struck, and the green bottle shattered in his hand. Glass flew everywhere. Some gashed his hand. One piece cut his lip. Whiskey soaked the front of his uniform, and the rest rained onto the floor.

Blinking in shock, Keith turned.

Captain Maddox stood there with a baton in his grip.

Keith opened his mouth, too stunned to speak. He wanted to curse the man. Blood dripped from his hand. A look into the captain's eyes killed any accusation.

"Ensign Maker," Maddox said, speaking calmly as if nothing had happened. "Several days ago, you suggested I was tossing you a rope and hauling you out of the abyss. Am I correct in saying that?"

Keith licked his lips, and tasted blood. His brain throbbed with indignation.

"I'm addressing you, Ensign. I'm asking you a question. I expect an answer."

Keith touched his lip. He stared at the blood on his fingers. Then he looked at Maddox again.

"I am your rope, Ensign. I *am* going to help you break the habit. I need a pilot with a clear mind and perfect reflexes."

"Are you going to beat me with your baton?" Keith asked.

"Negative. I respect you too much to thrash you as if you're a convict."

Keith raised his hand, the one with the gash where blood dripped. "This is some way of showing your respect, mate."

"That is incorrect," Maddox said. "My respect compels me to act. If I didn't respect you, I would let you drink to your heart's delight and leave you on one of the planets we're passing."

"Leave me with what I know about the mission?" Keith asked.

"Yes."

Keith couldn't help it. He believed the man. This Captain Maddox was as hard as nails. He meant to defeat the New Men. Keith liked that about Maddox. In fact, he realized he respected the man, and he felt shame for this encounter.

"I want you to pay attention to me," Maddox said.

Keith nodded.

Maddox set the baton aside. Then he held out his hand. In the middle of the palm sat a dull black pill.

"The mission is everything," Maddox said. "We don't have time to rehabilitate you the old way. I need you now, Ensign. I wondered if you had the willpower to desist for the length of the operation. I'm afraid the allure of intoxication has a stronger grip on you than you

99

realize. Therefore, it's time for stronger medicine. This time, literally."

"You mean that pill?" Keith asked.

"Take it," Maddox said.

With his left hand, Keith plucked the pill out of the captain's palm.

"You have a choice," Maddox said. "This pill, the first of several, will begin to react inside you. After a few days, it will have reconditioned your body. If you drink alcohol after that, you will become very sick, as in vomiting."

"What," Keith said. "Are you crazy? I'm not taking this." He held up the pill.

"Ah. Well, then you leave me no choice. Good-bye, Mr. Maker." Maddox turned and headed for the hatch.

"That's it?" Keith asked. "That's the end of your talk?"

Maddox halted, but he didn't turn around. "I believe I made myself clear some time ago."

"About what, sir?"

"Ship discipline," Maddox said.

Keith scowled. He needed to get his hand bandaged, maybe even have it stitched. "So where does this leave us?"

"Once you clean up, you can leave your uniform on your cot. You won't need it anymore."

"Wait a minute. You're saying I'm finished here?"

"Precisely," Maddox said.

"But you need me. You need a fantastic pilot. You said so yourself."

"True," Maddox said. "Yet, the rest of us can't rely on a crewmember that won't follow orders. We must function as a team, or this won't work."

"So if I want to stay on this crazy mission, I have to take your bloody pill?"

Maddox stood silently with his back to Keith.

The small ace weighed the black pill in his hand. He shook his head. Part of him hated Maddox. Part of him didn't want to let the man down. He'd seen the officer in operation. If anyone could see this mission through to the end—

100

"I don't believe this," Keith said. He popped the pill into his mouth and forced himself to swallow it. When he looked up, Captain Maddox was facing him.

"We should attend to your hand," Maddox said. "If you'll follow me into medical, I'll have the robo-doctor stitch it."

Keith held his ground. Now that he'd taken the bloody pill—

"Why do it this way, sir?" Keith asked.

"Lack of time," Maddox said.

"Did you have bottles in here to test me, sir?"

Maddox hesitated before saying, "You're an elite pilot, Ensign. But, like most of us, you have weaknesses. We must steel ourselves for the great venture. Humanity's survival depends on it."

"You have a weakness?" Keith asked.

"You can count on it. I'm human, after all."

Keith was beginning to have his doubts.

"Come with me," Maddox said. "Let's attend to your hand."

Keith smelled the whiskey in his uniform, and a touch of nausea hit. Could the pill have worked that fast on him? He couldn't believe this—no liquor in his immediate future. The thought made him tremble. Another part of him wondered if this was the best thing that had happened to him in the last several years.

Can I stop drinking? As Keith followed the captain, a real ray of hope rose up. Yet, he knew the thirst for alcohol would return. What if Captain Maddox wasn't there to stop him next time?

Keith didn't want to let the man down. He'd take the rest of the pills, too, but he didn't see how a little vomiting could stop him for good. He put it from his mind as he hurried after Maddox to the robo-doctor.

-13-

Lieutenant Noonan hesitated before the cargo bay hatch. She could hear Captain Maddox working on his flitter.

Four busy days ago, they had escaped down the Class 3 tramline, fleeing the attacking destroyer. Since then, she'd pored over the scout's manuals, soaking up information, checking everything she could think of about the *Geronimo*. By her review, the ship was in excellent condition. She wondered if the captain had been as thorough in his examination of the craft. In her opinion, he cut too many corners. A good ship's commander followed the procedures. Regulations were there to ensure a properly run vessel.

Valerie tugged her uniform straight, swung open the hatch and ducked through.

Theoretically, the cargo bay was the largest area in the ship. All kinds of stacked and secured containers in here meant that Maddox only had a little room for his flyer. The machine looked bigger than she remembered. Probably, that was a matter of perspective.

Litter lay strewn about the craft: the rear seat in sections, metal panels and pads. The captain ducked out of sight. He stood inside the flitter. A second later, an unseen drill *whirred* with sound.

Valerie eyed the pieces on the floor. What was the captain doing now? She wished he wasn't so secretive. He kept everything to himself, telling them what to do at the last minute. She liked more information and a heads up so she could do a task well, not just a rush-job.

The drill *whirred* longer. Then hammering sounds started from the back. A moment later, metal screeched against metal. There was further drilling and an oath of what might have been frustration from Maddox.

Finally, the captain reappeared in the canopy area, with an electric drill in his hand. He had removed the clear bubble.

"Lieutenant," Maddox said. "Can I help you?"

"Uh...sir, we're approaching the next Laumer-Point. It will take us into Remington Three, which connects with the Loki System."

"Excellent."

She nodded and finally blurted, "What are you doing, sir?"

He raised an eyebrow. "Enlarging the flitter's carrying capacity," he said.

"May I ask why, sir?"

"I plan to take the ensign with me down onto the prison planet."

"I see."

"Excellent," Maddox said. "Now, if you'll excuse me..."

Valerie held her spot.

Maddox didn't move as he watched her.

He should let us know what he expects. He should do that well before an operation so we can prepare.

The captain set down the drill. "What's on your mind, Lieutenant?"

"Sir," she said, coming to attention, looking up at the ceiling so she wouldn't have to keep staring into his eyes. "I request permission to speak freely."

"By all means, please do so."

"Thank you, sir. I, uh, do not want to presume upon your authority. You are the senior officer. Yet, as the second-in-command, it is my duty to address the issue. Article 12, Section 3 demands I speak up."

He waited.

Valerie's shoulder muscles tightened. "Sir, you broke regulations when you struck Ensign Maker two days ago."

Maddox still said nothing.

"Regulations forbid striking a fellow officer except in cases of self-defense," she said.

"Technically, I struck the bottle out of his hand."

"With a baton, sir," she said. "The glass cut him. It might have taken out an eye."

Maddox became quiet again.

103

That caused Valerie's stomach to squirm. She would have preferred anger. Unable to take the silence, more words squeezed out of her. "I-I know some people believe I'm a stickler for the rules. Those are their words, not mine. My point, sir, is that the regulations protect all of us. Without them, what are we?"

Nothing changed about Maddox, but he seemed to come to a decision. "You have character, Lieutenant. I appreciate that. It's likely we view our roles from divergent positions. One of the reasons Lord High Admiral Cook and Brigadier O'Hara chose me for this assignment was my ability to adjust as needed. For many situations, we won't have a rulebook addressing the exact problem. In others, the rules stand in the way. In compensation, we have our judgment. I used mine in tackling the delicate situation with Ensign Maker."

"Yes, sir," she said, and she made ready with her next argument.

Maddox spoke again. "I'm going to finish up here," he said. "It will take me a few hours more. In time, we'll have a briefing in the wardroom."

Realizing he was dismissing her, Valerie saluted. She wanted to dig deeper. Without rules, chaos reigned. Anyone could see that was true. But she knew how to follow orders. She turned and headed for the hatch.

✳✳✳

Twelve hours later, Valerie sat in the wardroom with Ensign Maker. The ship hurdled through Remington Three toward the next Laumer-Point, which would take them into the Loki System.

The two of them waited on Captain Maddox. Keith's lip was healing quickly, but the back of his right hand still looked bad. How dare the captain strike the man or the bottle he had been holding? An inch the other way and Maddox might have broken bones.

The hatch opened, and the captain ducked through. He looked striking in his uniform and cap, and he wore a regulation sidearm.

Valerie stood at attention while Keith kept sitting. The captain waited. Belatedly, the pilot rose to his feet, although he didn't come to full attention. The man lacked military manners.

"Please," Maddox said. "Sit down."

Keith practically dropped into his chair. Valerie sat with decorum, putting her folded hands on the table. She knew that bad manners drove out good, and she was determined that wouldn't happen to her.

Maddox strode to the head of the table, sitting, regarding them. "I'll make this brief. Until we reach the alien sentinel, entering the Loki System is going to be the most dangerous aspect of our mission. As you know, no one has ever managed to escape off Loki Prime. There's a reason for that. An SWS monitor guards the main jump point while heavily armed orbitals watch the surface for any technological activity. If they detect a problem, they launch missiles onto the planet. Because of its thick cloud cover, lasers can't penetrate from space to the surface. A few of the orbitals do have laser cannons, though. Those are for shuttles or other vehicles attempting to land on the surface or trying to leave.

"Now, the Lord High Admiral has provided me with security clearance codes for the orbitals. I doubt any other ship has arrived from Earth to program a new security system into place. Even so, this is going to be tricky, and it could take expert flying. Any questions so far?"

"I have one," Keith said, raising his hand.

"Go ahead."

"Are we taking the scout down onto the surface?"

"Negative," Maddox said. "We'll use the flitter."

"Your speedster isn't rated for vacuum flight, sir," Valerie said. "I looked it up on the ship's computer."

"This is a modified flitter," Maddox told her.

"While you're on the surface, what are my duties here, sir?" Valerie asked.

"To wait by the controls for my signal," Maddox said. "It's unlikely, but you may have to enter the atmosphere to pick us up."

"May I ask why you think that, sir?" she said.

"How far I can climb out of the atmosphere will depend on the weight of my passengers."

"Do you expect any danger while on the planet, sir?"

"Considerable danger," Maddox said. "Murderers, rapists and other criminals are all serving life sentences on Loki Prime. The flitter will represent their only chance of escape. We don't know the conditions down there, but I expect trouble."

"I checked the regulations, sir," Valerie said. "I found that it's forbidden to take firearms down onto the planet."

105

Maddox scrutinized her. "You do realize that we're headed to Loki Prime in order to break people out of a prison planet? Technically, that's unlawful. I'm proceeding upon the direct orders of Lord High Admiral Cook. One could argue that he has no right to order me into a seemingly lawless action. Yet, he has because of the enemy's infiltration into our organizations. You do see that, yes?"

"I-I suppose so, sir," Valerie stammered.

"Your answer is evasive," Maddox said. "As an officer that follows the regulations, is it yes, or is it no?"

Valerie tried to squirm away from answering. "The Lord High Admiral is trying to save us," she said.

"By breaking the law?" asked Maddox.

Valerie opened her mouth to answer but found that she didn't know what to say.

"Lieutenant," Maddox said, "I believe you're now experiencing a common failing among all of us. To wit, that our theories have a terrible tendency to crash against reality. In such an instance, one should employ judgment to make a calculated choice. The trouble is that, at times, your judgment will fail you, just as it has me in several instances. Then you must dust yourself off and begin anew, attempting to learn from the experience."

"Are these new procedures, sir?"

"We can speak about procedures later," Maddox said. "Right now, we shall concentrate on the mission. The rescue of Doctor Dana Rich takes priority. Without her, it's doubtful we can reach the alien star system or have any real chance of gaining entrance onto the sentinel. Here is the last known picture of her."

Maddox aimed a hand-unit at a wall. A photo appeared of a dark-haired woman. The hair shined with conditioner and reached well beyond her shoulders. She had dark eyes and a deep brown complexion, giving her an exotic appearance. Her smile indicated cynicism, while her brow showed high intelligence.

"She has an Indian and Cherokee background," Maddox said.

"I thought Cherokees were Indians," Keith said.

"Not that kind," Maddox said. "I mean a citizen of India."

"Doctor Rich was born on Earth?" Valerie asked.

"Yes, in Bombay," Maddox said. "She hasn't been to Earth for over twenty years, however. She emigrated to Brahma."

"How old is she?" Valerie asked.

"The file didn't say. She's highly intelligent, capable and considered very dangerous. She's a clone thief, having broken into Rigel's Social Syndicate highest-level holding cells."

"They must have been important clones," Valerie said.

"Of the ruling syndic himself," Maddox said. "He and his cronies control the Social Syndicate."

Valerie shook her head. She'd never heard of them.

"It doesn't matter now," the captain said. "I have a locator—"

Valerie laughed. "I don't see how this will be difficult, then. Oh. Please excuse my interruption, sir."

"Finish your thought, Lieutenant."

Valerie fidgeted before saying, "Can't you fix Doctor Rich's location, fly down, spray the area with a knockout gas and pick up her inert form?"

"I'm afraid not," Maddox said.

Valerie glanced at Keith before turning back to Maddox. "Am I missing something, sir?"

"As I was going to say," Maddox told her, "I have a locator to help me find Sergeant Riker. He's my assistant in Star Watch Intelligence. He has already been sent to Loki Prime with the task of finding the good doctor. After picking him up, I hope to proceed quickly on the ground to her."

"Your sergeant, sir?" Valerie asked.

"Yes. He's a good man."

"Brave, too," she said. "He agreed to drop alone onto the prison planet?"

"No. He was sentenced to Loki Prime for killing Caius Nerva, Octavian Nerva's heir."

"Why would your sergeant kill the heir to the richest man on Earth?" Valerie asked.

"I'm sure he'll enjoy telling you the story, provided we make it back alive." Maddox checked a chronometer. "We have forty minutes until we reach the jump point. This time, we'll use our cloaking device and go in with silent running. We must be ready for any eventuality."

He eyed them before picking up the clicker, bringing up another picture. This one had a timetable on it. "Let's go over our operational details," Maddox said.

107

They did for some time. As the captain neared the conclusion, and despite her reluctance to do so, Valerie found herself impressed with him. Maddox made excellent plans.

Soon, the captain stood. "That's it, then. We're about to make history—the first to break anyone out from the deadliest prison planet in the Commonwealth."

-14-

SWS Scout *Geronimo* moved silently through the Loki System. The cloak kept the ship hidden from the masses of sensors sweeping the areas between the planets. Each satellite-beacon did so with automated regularity.

Since exiting their Laumer-Point, they'd drifted, using their initial velocity to move. There was a reason for tiptoeing through the void—complications—even more than Maddox had anticipated.

There were four planets in the system. At the center was an F spectral class star, a blue-white fireball twenty percent larger than the Sun. The nearest world was a rare chthonian planet. It was odd for several reasons. Firstly, once it had been a gas giant like Jupiter, which made it strange because the planet was in the inner system. It was rare for Jovian worlds to be so close to a star. Usually, gas giants were in the outer part of a system. Secondly, the proximity to the star had a drastic effect on the Jovian planet. Through time and gravity, the star had stripped away the gas giant's atmosphere and outer planetary layers. All that remained was the world's rocky core. In many respects, the chthonian planet now resembled a terrestrial one.

A Class 1 Laumer-Point existed between the star and the chthonian planet. It was the main entrance into the Loki System— the *Geronimo* had entered elsewhere. A Star Watch monitor waited to guard the jump point.

Monitors were slow ships, designed to slug it out toe-to-toe with other heavies, using powerful beams. Their deflector shields were

109

often as strong as a battleship's. Some, like the *Archangel* out there, had warfare pods attached.

Upon spying the monitor with passive sensors, Lieutenant Noonan had spotted the *Archangel's* pod. A quick computer match had told her it contained drones. That gave the monitor the ability to launch missiles. The heavy would likely use that tactic against any starship able to outrun it, staying out of beam range.

Of course, because the monitor remained near the Class 1 Laumer-Point, it could strike other vessels while their crews experienced Jump Lag coming through, making unwanted starships easy targets.

The SWS monitor had a distinct shape: perfectly round except for the attached warfare pod. Every inch of space on that vessel was devoted to its massive engines to supply the beam power and deflector shields. If *Geronimo* tried to fight *Archangel*, the monitor would swat it out of existence within the first minute. The trick was keeping far away from the monitor and its long-range beams. The scout was a flea compared to the giant fighting ship.

Archangel's beam range was almost one hundred thousand kilometers. Because of laser dissipation, the closer one approached the warship, the stronger the beams burned. Fortunately, for the crew, according to the operational plan, *Geronimo* wouldn't remotely approach the monitor.

The system's second planet was Loki Prime, the prison world and target for their venture. It orbited the star at a greater range than Earth did the Sun. Because this star was larger and hotter, it made the prison planet a sauna, carpeted with dense and dangerous plant-life.

Geronimo had entered the system through a Class 3 tramline, the backdoor so to speak. The chthonian planet orbited the star at a Venus-like range. The Class 3 tramline was close to the system's third plant, a gas giant in a Jupiter-like orbit. That meant over one billion kilometers had originally separated the scout from the monitor.

The distance gave them a wide margin of safety from the monitor. It was a slow ship. That meant *Archangel* would have to accelerate for days to reach the gas giant. *Geronimo* could be long gone by then, as it was faster than the monitor. However, if the slugger-ship launched seeker drones…that would be a different matter. The scout would have to retreat fast to the outer system Laumer-Point if it saw the monitor launching drones.

The star system's fourth planet was a distant Pluto-like object, of no apparent worth or interest to the present venture.

Even so, if *Archangel* or its heavy missiles didn't unduly trouble Maddox—he had been briefed on the monitor and its Laumer-Point guarding mission—the dark beacons littered throughout the inner system most certainly did. One could as easily call the beacons satellites. Even though they orbited the F-class star, the sensor satellites were small, little bigger than Maddox's flitter. The appellation "dark" meant they were constructed of stealth material, making them difficult to spot. There were over one hundred satellite-beacons orbiting the void between Loki Prime and the other planets on either side of it.

The danger was this: if a beacon registered the *Geronimo,* and the scout failed to give the correct security clearance, the sensor satellite would activate the nearest drones.

Like the star-orbiting satellites, masses of drones moved around the nuclear fireball. These weren't heavy drones as *Archangel* carried, and that was a relief. These were smaller but carried nuclear warheads just the same.

If a beacon's automated sequences decided the scout was an intruder, it would send a radio signal to the drones nearest the *Geronimo.* The missiles would thereupon accelerate at their ship, attempting to destroy it.

In essence, the Commonwealth of Planets had turned the majority of the void around Loki Prime into a mobile minefield, constantly searching and seeking to destroy the unwanted.

Still, all those factors—the SWS monitor and the space minefield—didn't trouble Maddox too much. The Lord High Admiral's computer disc had explained the exact situation. The real trouble was the extra destroyer on patrol around Loki Prime. The starship and its designation clinched it.

Fifteen hours ago, the lieutenant had turned to Maddox in shock. "Sir, that's the *Saint Petersburg* out there."

A week ago, in the Solar System near Earth, the same destroyer had tried to beam them out of existence. What was it doing here, and maybe as importantly, how had it beaten them to the Loki System?

Maddox had brought up the destroyer's specs. The warship had two medium laser batteries and fifteen point-defense cannons. Each of those cannons fired bigger shells than the *Geronimo's* two guns. The vessel had reflective armor plates, and at a moment's notice, it could raise a deflector shield. The destroyer had a regular crew of forty-seven officers and ratings. It also happened to be one of the new fast models able to outrun the *Geronimo*. Unlike the massively round monitor, the destroyer was long like the proverbial cigar-shaped starship. It also contained sensor pods to strengthen its ability to sniff out hidden foes.

The *Saint Petersburg* could outpace and outfight the scout. First, despite its extra sensor pod, it had to find *Geronimo*. And that might not be as easy as the destroyer commander believed.

As Maddox sat in the wardroom thinking, he watched an image slaved to the scout's sensors. The destroyer presently slid behind Loki Prime. The opposing vessel wasn't in Low Loki Orbit, but it could reach there quickly enough.

Drumming his fingers on the table, Maddox wondered if he should attempt sending a computer virus against the satellite-beacons. Maybe he could capture several, force them to fire drones at the destroyer. Of course, that might alert the *Archangel's* commander. Still…

Which of *Geronimo's* crew had the knowledge to attempt such a delicate task? If Doctor Dana Rich were aboard, maybe she could try it with a high chance of success. The Commonwealth authorities must have known desperate people trying to free their friends from the prison planet would try something like that someday. There would be rigorous safety precautions and security clearances to overcome.

Maddox shook his head. Trying to capture satellite-beacons through computer viruses would likely backfire on them. He had to slip onto the planet and sneak away with his volunteers. He had to do that while *Saint Petersburg* patrolled the area.

The destroyer's officers and crew must believe they were doing their duty. It was the orders from above that would be suspect. The New Men must have infiltrated someone into Star Watch High Command.

How do we defeat an enemy with better ships and a superior intelligence service? What's their weakness?

112

If they were still human, they had weaknesses, right?

An intercom buzzed. Valerie spoke through it. "Captain, if you could come to the bridge please."

Maddox headed there. The lieutenant liked to refer to the control room as the bridge. She was pure navy.

Entering the chamber, Maddox asked, "What seems to be the problem, Lieutenant?"

"Sir," she said. "It's time to make a course correction. *Saint Petersburg* is behind Loki Prime, and we're soon exiting our optimum time of opportunity."

She meant their velocity and heading. It was easier in terms of fuel and likelihood of remaining hidden to make corrections out here rather than when they were close to the planet. It would take them longer to reach Loki Prime if they braked now, but that couldn't be helped.

"Ensign?" asked Maddox. "Are you ready?"

"Do you really think this will work?" Keith asked.

"There's only one way to find out," Maddox said. "Engage."

Keith glanced at Valerie before he turned on the special system. Instead of braking normally with fusion-generated thrust, he turned on the stealth system, dumping gravity waves.

The vessel shook, enough so Maddox grabbed his instrument panel. The others did likewise. A strained sound came from the engine room, where the massive gravity generator worked.

"How much longer are we going to do this?" Keith asked. "It's shaking our scout apart."

"Thirty seconds longer," Valerie answered, studying her board.

The shaking worsened and so did the noise.

"I don't know how this will fool anyone out there?" Keith shouted.

"Steady as she goes," Maddox said, even as his body trembled from the ship-wide vibration.

"Get ready to shut down the stealth propulsion system," Valerie said. "Three, two, one...shut it down."

Keith tapped the controls. The shaking quit and the noise rapidly dwindled to normal. The pilot looked up with a grin on his face. "Nothing to it," he said.

A light flashed on Valerie's board. She studied it, tapped some controls and swallowed uneasily. "A beacon noticed us, sir," she said.

"Is it demanding our security clearance?" Maddox asked.

"Yes," she said, looking up troubled. "What do I do, sir?"

"Give it our code," Maddox said. "Let's find out if the *Saint Petersburg* had the authorization to change the Loki security systems."

"Begging your pardon, sir," Valerie said, "but you might want to reconsider that. Even if we pass the security clearance, the beacon will alert *Archangel*. That's standard operating procedure."

"I see," Maddox said. That hadn't been on the Lord High Admiral's disc. Maybe Cook believed he would have already known such a thing. He hadn't. Maybe a rules stickler had her uses.

Valerie glanced at her board. "The beacon is demanding recognition clearance now, sir. It will alert *Archangel* any moment."

"Answer it," Maddox snapped. "Give it our clearance. Then type in SSA-452-B75-Alpha afterward."

"What is that, sir?" she asked, as she tapped in the information required by the beacon.

"I'd hoped to only have to use that last code on the orbitals," Maddox said. "It's a Star Watch Intelligence clearance, demanding a three day delay on procedures."

"You mean the beacon won't alert the monitor for another seventy-two hours?" Valerie asked.

"Exactly," Maddox said.

Lines appeared on the lieutenant's forehead as she considered this. Then her head lifted sharply. "Seventy-two hours delay won't be long enough, sir. I mean long enough for us to reach the prison planet, insert, lift with the personnel and leave the star system."

"Hmm, yes," Maddox said. "That could prove troublesome for us three days from now."

"What?" Keith said. "Am I hearing you right—Captain? We're going in, but we're not getting back out?"

"Nonsense," Maddox said. "We'll think of something in three days."

Keith mulled that over, soon shrugging and returning to studying his instruments.

"Begging your pardon, sir," Valerie said. "But that would make this a suicide run. A three day delay isn't long enough."

"What do you suggest we do, Lieutenant?" Maddox asked. "I'm more than open to suggestions."

"I'm not sure there is a way to do this," she said. "We must turn back and rethink our plan."

"Negative, Lieutenant. We're heading in."

"But sir—"

"Lieutenant Noonan," Maddox said. "I will go down onto Loki Prime and rescue my sergeant. I will then find Doctor Dana Rich and bring her back to *Geronimo*. Afterward, we are going to find the alien star system. Anything else is a defeat for Earth."

"We need a plan for getting out of the Loki System," she said, "a chance for victory."

"Agreed," he said.

"You have a plan, sir?"

"What do the regulations say about questioning the commander of his ship?" Maddox asked.

Valerie opened her mouth and squirmed in her seat. Finally, she closed her mouth without another word.

"For your conscience's sake, Lieutenant, I prefer not to tell you what we're going to do later."

She stared at him.

If Maddox had to guess, she didn't believe he had an idea. The lieutenant must think he was lying to her. Well, he did have a plan. It was risky at best. But at this point, he didn't know what else to do. He'd worry about it when the time came.

A half-hour later, there wasn't any change to the SWS monitor many hundreds of millions kilometers away. If *Archangel* had begun accelerating for Loki Prime, it would have meant the beacon had reported them, but it hadn't.

"The beacon honored your secret code, sir," Valerie said.

Maddox stood. "You have first watch, Lieutenant. Ensign, I want you to get as much sleep as you can. It will be some time before we have to brake again."

"Sir?" asked Valerie. "Do you think the people in the *Saint Petersburg* know we're here in the system, sir?"

"Absolutely," he said.

"Our cover is blown, then?"

"It was from the start," Maddox said. "But we're going to beat them anyway. And do you know why we will?"

"Because we must, sir?" she asked.

"No," he said. "Because we're the best at what we do and we have the latest in stealth technology."

"I'll drink to that!" Keith shouted.

Maddox and Valerie both turned to stare at him.

"Uh, a turn of phrase," Keith said. "Maybe it was in poor taste. Sometimes my excitement gets the better of me. I just mean to agree with you, Captain. We're the bloody best at what we do."

"Get some sleep, Ensign," Maddox said. "You're going to need it."

"Aye-aye, sir," Keith said, exiting the control room.

Maddox waited until he heard Ensign Maker's hatch clang shut. Then he turned to Valerie. "You're doing well, Lieutenant. I appreciate your steady nerves."

She was silent for several seconds, finally saying, "I grew up in a tough neighborhood, sir. It takes a lot to rattle me. Uh, sir, I've been thinking. You don't want to tell me your idea of dealing with the beacon because your plan is highly illegal, isn't it?"

"Why, Lieutenant, what a suspicious mind you have." With that, Maddox left the chamber. He still had a few modifications he needed to make to the flitter.

***

During the next forty-eight hours, they made two more course corrections, slowing their velocity each time. Thus, it took two days after the incident with the beacon for the scout to enter Loki Prime's orbit. They had another twenty-four hours until the beacon reported their presence to the distant monitor. They were far behind schedule for clearing the Loki System.

Because the *Saint Petersburg* was so close, the fusion generator was presently offline. *Geronimo* used the cloaking device, a heavy drain on its batteries. As a nearly invisible object to Commonwealth scanners, they had avoided the destroyer as it continued to circle the planet from a far orbit.

Because of Maddox's orders, the scout entered Low Loki Orbit as *Saint Petersburg* moved across the other side of the world. Even though there were only two ships close to Loki, it was difficult to spot a vessel doing its best to hide. Orbital space around the Earth-sized world was vast compared to a scout. It was one of the reasons they had a chance of pulling this off.

Maddox sat in the control room, watching Valerie monitor her instruments. He no longer wore his uniform but camouflage gear and cap.

"This place is crawling with detection satellites," she said. "I don't see why you think your flitter will make it down undetected, sir."

"I trust the Lord High Admiral's codes to see me through," Maddox said.

She turned around, facing him. "That's an awfully slender thread, sir."

"Agreed," he said. "In the event I fail to return, I want you to slip away. On all accounts, don't let the *Saint Petersburg* capture you."

"Sir, if you fail, I'm never going to make it out of the Loki System alive."

"You have the cloaking device—"

"Begging your pardon, sir, but it won't run much longer on the batteries. It will need fusion power."

"Turn on the engine and keep the cloaking device running. Then sneak out the best you can. Once they detect the scout, flee at full speed. Get back to Earth. Tell the Lord High Admiral I failed. On no account can you let them capture you."

"I'll try, sir."

"Do more than that. The New Men mustn't learn about the sentinel. If I fail, tell the Lord High Admiral to come with a fleet. At that point, he'll have to openly try for the alien vessel."

"That would alert the New Men, sir. Out in the Beyond, they will intercept the Lord High Admiral's fleet and destroy it."

"Maybe, maybe not," Maddox said. "There's a reason the New Men haven't kept attacking since their conquest of Odin and Horace."

"I suppose that makes sense." She looked away, and she seemed embarrassed. "Uh, good luck, sir."

"Why thank you, Lieutenant. I wish you the same."

"Thank you, sir. I could use it."

"Well, let's get to work," Maddox said. "We're under the clock and time is ticking."

117

-15-

"You're flying us down," Maddox said.

Keith climbed into the flitter, taking the controls. He wore similar camouflage gear as Maddox. On their belts, the two of them carried force blades and pistols that fired explosive pellets. Packs were in the flitter's back area.

Maddox glanced behind. He'd torn out the rear seat, pulled off the back plate to the trunk and laid down foam. In a pinch, they could fit two people back there by having them lie down.

"We'll be cutting communications in a minute," Valerie said over the cargo bay intercom. "Do you remember the sequence to alert me that you're coming back up?"

Keith glanced at Maddox.

"Go ahead," the captain told him.

"We hear you, love, and we remember the procedure. Keep a tight hold of the barn. We'll be coming back sooner than you realize."

Valerie might have muttered something. It was indistinct over the intercom.

"Ready, Captain?" Keith asked.

Maddox nodded.

With a flick of a switch, the pilot closed the canopy. Next, he unlocked the magnetic clamps holding them to the deck. The engine hummed into life and he turned on the interior vents. Lastly, the flitter gently lifted.

Even though the Scotsman had never flown the flitter before, he already handled it better than Maddox could.

118

He's a natural at this. It's no wonder the Tau Ceti mining chiefs allowed him to teach his brother to fly strikefighters.

The seconds ticked by. Outside the flitter in the cargo bay, the atmosphere hissed away. It wouldn't do for the outer door to open and have the departing atmosphere hurl them against the side of the opening. Soon, they floated in a vacuum.

Finally, a crack appeared in a bulkhead. The sliver grew as the two halves slid apart. Maddox shifted in his seat in anticipation of the next few hours. Everything should work just fine. If it didn't, at least he had an ace for a pilot. The bulkheads shuddered as the doors clanged as far apart as they could. Brilliant stars dotted the void outside.

"Here we go, Captain," Keith said.

The flitter glided smoothly, exiting the cargo bay. Maddox twisted around. Loki Prime spread out below them. It was a mass of cloud cover, a fleecy wonderland with a rotten core.

It would have been good to remain in contact with Lieutenant Noonan. *Geronimo* had better sensors than the tiny flitter. But too many detection devices scanned the area. Radio waves would give them away.

Taking a deep breath, Maddox turned on the flitter's computer. He entered the security code, and knew the machine would begin emitting it to the various sensors.

"Repulse power," Keith said, nudging them toward the distant clouds.

Time slipped by as Loki Prime grew larger. It felt strange falling toward the seemingly expanding clouds.

"It's so serene out here," Keith said.

Maddox turned to him. "It is," he replied.

"Feels as if everything is right with the world," Keith added.

"It does, at that."

Keith turned suddenly, and he raised his healing hand, showing it to Maddox. "No hard feelings, Captain. You did what you had to."

"Glad you feel that way."

Keith returned to monitoring the controls. "At first, I wanted to pay you back. Then I got to thinking. You're only doing your job, right?"

"Yes."

"You didn't take any pleasure in it?"

"Not a bit."

"Didn't think so," Keith said. "You don't strike me as a crawly, Captain. You're tough. I'm not saying you're not. The way you handled my bartender with the enforcers sitting there—I knew then you would be a bad bloke to tangle with."

Maddox said nothing.

"Going to be some tough customers down there, aren't there?" Keith said.

"There are."

"I notice you have a case in back, sir. Do you mind if I ask what you're carrying?"

"An arm," Maddox said.

Keith cast him a dubious look. Maddox didn't elaborate.

"Don't want me to ask, eh?" Keith said.

Maddox still didn't reply.

"I understand, sir. You're in charge. Ah, did you feel that bump?"

"I did," Maddox admitted.

"We're in the top layer," Keith said, tapping a control. "Shutting off repulse power and engaging the main engine and antigravity pods—now. Here we go. Let the party begin."

The machine hummed, shivering almost as if with delight. To Maddox, it was odd. The last time he'd rode in the flyer they had been on Earth. Now, he was thirty-six light years away on an alien planet, well, coming down on one. This hardly seemed like the right way to it.

He thought about that. Down there was a jungle world in two ways at least, vast trees and terrible predators. He shook his head, putting that into his hindbrain. It was a time to concentrate on the essentials.

Several minutes later, the clouds engulfed them in a world of dirty gray wool.

"We're heading almost straight down," Keith said.

Maddox liked the pilot's confidence. He wondered about mountains, as in: were they about to crash down onto one? They didn't dare turn on the radar to find out.

"This stuff is thick," Keith said.

"I've seen thicker on Earth."

"Not this high in the atmosphere, you haven't."

Maddox digested that. He wondered how Sergeant Riker had felt plunging down through this substance. Riker wouldn't have seen anything. The penal authorities used modified marine drop pods. The prisoner went down in a one-way capsule, blind to the sights. He or she was never coming back. Had anyone in authority been down onto the surface to report on the conditions there? The Lord High Admiral hadn't given him anything concrete. That would seem to imply no. Maybe every convict died twenty-four hours after landing. With the present situation, that would be disastrous for Earth.

"The clouds are thinning out," Keith said.

Maddox reexamined them. They looked just as thick as ever. What did the pilot notice that he didn't?

Then, the flitter broke though the high cover, entering clear air. Above was the dense ceiling of clouds. Below them spread out a vast expanse of green. It went as far as he could see.

Keith whistled in admiration. "What is that, sir? From up here, I can't tell if its grasslands or forests."

"Jungle," Maddox said, "a jungle world."

Keith adjusted the flitter. Their nose aimed lower and they slid downward as if riding a giant slide. "The planet is Earth normal then, sir?"

"Reasonably so," Maddox said.

"That's doesn't make sense. Why use an Earth-habitable planet for housing criminals? These types of worlds—breathable, I mean—are rare."

"You're right on that score."

"So...what am I missing, sir?"

Maddox had read early survey reports of the planet. Giant trees and nasty poisonous growths underneath their leaves with grim insect life meant this was a hell-world indeed. It lacked metals on the surface, and the plants, spores and funguses meant the only livable areas were in the mountainous regions, which were sparse. In time, colonists would likely settle here—once they filled up the better worlds. It would take less than planet-wide terraforming to ready Loki Prime for civilized life, but it would need vast chemical sprays and biological tampering on a continental scale. According to the reports, Loki fauna was incredibly tough. Tests showed it would demolish with ridiculous ease any non-native plant or bacterial life.

That was the kicker. Loki Prime bacteria ate into human flesh as if they were pigs devouring pizza.

Maddox explained a little of this to Keith. Then a noise alerted them.

"What's that?" Keith asked.

"The locator," Maddox said. "We're low enough to begin searching for Sergeant Riker."

Maddox had received information from Brigadier O'Hara concerning the general area of Riker's drop. If he'd had to search the entire world for the man, Maddox likely would never leave the planet within the twenty-four hour limit. The captain didn't want to think about the endgame, the beacon waiting up there to make its report to the monitor. It was going to be hard enough down here as it was.

First things first, Maddox thought. *Concentrate on today, on now. Tomorrow will bring enough troubles.*

He watched the locator—nothing. So why had it beeped? Maddox checked the drop pod's coordinates and their position on the planet. This was the right place. The locator used a passive system with a limited range. How far could a man travel down there in three days? Riker hadn't been on the surface that long, more like two and a half days. Maddox felt he should have spotted the sergeant on the locator by now.

"Are we going to land?" Keith asked.

"Not yet. We want to stay high in order to sweep as wide an area as possible."

"You don't see him on that gizmo yet?" Keith asked.

Maddox adjusted controls. The locator seemed to be working. "Head west," he suggested.

Keith turned the flitter, and they headed in a different direction, west. They traveled for fifteen minutes.

"North," Maddox said. "Go north."

Without a word, Keith turned north.

Maddox watched the locator, willing it to show him Riker. The sergeant was a good man, if overly quarrelsome at times. The old man was resourceful. That's what Maddox appreciated about him the most.

He almost told the ensign to try east when a faint beep sounded.

Keith glanced at the locator. "Is that him?"

Maddox flexed his fingers. He'd been fearing that Riker was dead. Yet, the signal should be stronger. The bug inside the sergeant was powered by a person's body heat.

"Go lower," Maddox said.

Keith tapped controls, and the flitter began to sink.

Until Maddox exhaled, he hadn't realized he'd been holding his breath. The signal came in louder than before. Sergeant Riker was alive.

"We have him," Maddox said, triumphantly.

Keith grinned.

"Down," Maddox said. "Go down. We don't know what kind of trouble he's gotten himself into."

"Aye-aye, sir," the pilot said.

Maddox kept studying the locator. Soon, the jungle became visible as one. The treetops showed billions of shimmering leaves with swooping bat-like creatures plowing through dense swarms of hovering gnats, or the Loki equivalent of them.

Maddox frowned and shook the locator.

"Is something wrong, sir?" Keith asked.

"I don't understand. The sergeant is moving fast down there. Do they have cars, horses, what?"

Keith checked his controls. "We'll reach the trees in thirty seconds, sir. What do you want me to do?"

Maddox nodded. That was a good question. Why, and how, did Sergeant Riker move so fast across the landscape?

-16-

Sergeant Treggason Riker, formerly of Star Watch Intelligence, coughed explosively as he gripped a steering oar under his sole armpit. He only had one arm, and he negotiated a dirty dugout canoe as it shot down whitewater rapids. His head wove this way and that as he dodged dipping branches. Going this fast, they acted like slicers.

Riker's lungs hurt every time he inhaled. He'd contracted Loki Prime spores, what the Scorpions so colorfully had called *red rot*.

The sergeant hated the prison planet with its foul insects, funguses and infested inmates. Oh yes, he'd had a short discussion with the brigadier back on Earth about the mission. She'd told him Captain Maddox would be on his way to break him out of Loki Prime. O'Hara wanted to use Caius Nerva's premature death as a path onto yet another preposterous operation.

Why did I ever agree to this? The duel with Caius Nerva—Maddox went too far. I should have just let him...

Riker grunted as a branch slashed his left check. He'd missed seeing it because his bionic eye had short-circuited twelve hours ago. Something in the atmosphere—a lousy spore or germ—had infected who knew what inside the eye. This place devoured technical equipment, rendering it inoperable better than cyber-warriors could dream. No wonder no colonists had committed to settling this hellhole. Or if they had, the unlucky sods were long dead, fertilizing the gloomy abode.

Of course, the penal authorities had taken his bionic arm. Then they'd dropped him from orbit before departing to their cozy quarters. The Scorpions found him several hours later. The beginning of a long and painful initiation into Loki society had begun soon thereafter.

The prisoners, the Scorpions as they called themselves, had flintlocks—wooden barrels firing hard knots of wood. They had primitive huts and a brutal pecking order. The worst offenders were the ones who used poisons, both natural and concocted. Those criminals possessed blow darts and "claws" affixed to their fingers, the tips glistening with killing toxins.

The Scorpions were on the bottom of the giant mountain, the lowest strata of criminals. The little time he'd been with them, Riker had learned they mostly thought of ways to invade higher country. The higher one went here, the less funguses and hot bacterium there was. The Scorpions were too diseased, though, to fight on equal footing against the higher tribes. The lower one went on Loki Prime, the more deadly everything became to human existence.

Yet that's where Riker went: down. Behind him, Scorpions shrieked their war cries.

Riker glanced back. He saw them, ravaged individuals wearing cloth masks. Many had open sores on their bodies. The masks were wet with foul toxins, helping to keep out things like red rot. The toxins in the mouth-cloths made the wearers high and extra-savage. It was the trade-off for protection.

I would have stayed in their compound, but I think they planned cannibalism. These scoundrels knew I wasn't one of them. They kept calling me a weasel, a snitch.

Riker dearly wanted to blame Captain Maddox for his fix. The youngster seldom stayed on script with anything. Yet, the captain had great instincts for making the right moves. Brigadier O'Hara had told him the tech boys were putting a bug in him, the safe technical kind. Captain Maddox would use a locator to find and retrieve him on Loki Prime.

The youngsters will find me if I can stay free long enough. Riker had to believe that. It was the only thing giving him hope to continue.

Behind him, a musket boomed. Something hard and fast slashed leaves inches above Riker's head. A second musket fired, and a waterspout appeared beside the dugout, splashing his check.

Riker snarled with frustration. He wasn't going to outdistance them on the river. He had a steering arm. They had paddles, plunging their crafts faster.

I'm too old for these games. My lungs are on fire and I'm tired. I wish I'd stolen a flintlock.

Riker twisted his body to move his steering oar, aiming the dugout for the nearest shore. The whitewater shoved his craft, and he failed to spy a hidden rock in his path. Wood splintered as the dugout struck the river stone. Rushing water shoved hard. It lifted the back end of the boat, catapulting Riker over the rock, hurling him into the air and against the shore. He hit, grunting, with his legs dangling in the water. The raging current began to tug him in.

Making a mewling noise, Riker scrambled, slithering higher. Mud stained his overalls. Branches scratched his face and gray hair. Insects whirled around him. He hated their squishy forms.

"There, boys!" a Scorpion shouted. "The weasel is running onto land. We almost have him."

Riker's lips peeled back. His body felt aflame with aches and pains. He wheezed, as his lungs seemed to fill with fluid.

Keep moving. Trust the captain to produce another miracle. He needs me. I know he does. No one else has ever kept him grounded to reality as I do. The man believes he can do anything that he sets his mind to. He's quite mad.

The sergeant slipped and slid on wet moss. From the river behind him, another flintlock boomed. The wooden pellet slashed his side, ripping the fabric of his overall and spilling blood.

That would stir the insects.

Riker snarled again. He lowered his head and recklessly plunged through the growth. He was so tired, so spent, that it was impossible to think. At this point, it would be good to simply lie down and go to sleep.

They'll eat your flesh, Treggason. Think about that, my boy.

Riker widened his good eye and wheezed. That proved to be too much. He coughed explosively, spitting red gunk onto nearby fronds. He bent over and continued to cough.

"Hear him, boys! There's a crawly that can't run far. I say we cut off his arm and legs and eat his flesh while he's watching. That's always good for a few laughs."

Riker made a fist, and rage washed through him. He had more sense than Captain Maddox, though. Fighting the gang one to six would lead to his quick defeat. He had to keep running. He had to spin this out for as long as he could.

The sergeant began to walk, easing past branches and over-stepping rotted wood that would have made enough noise to give him away. Refusing to cough, he made grunting sounds as his chest heaved. Let them earn his flesh. Let them become infested with lowlander spores to make them puke.

Soon, pain and effort merged into a confused blur. With everything in him, Riker tried to concentrate. For a second, he halted and looked up. He could have sworn he just heard the hum of a flitter.

Captain Maddox?

No. He must have started to hallucinate. Riker turned back. He could hear the others beating the bushes for him. They were angry.

The sergeant managed a painful smile. A slimy substance had already begun to attach to his teeth. Given time, the gunk would rot them right out of his gums. Using a forefinger, he wiped away slime, brushing the substance on a leaf. He kept moving, but now he staggered.

"Do you hear that?" a Scorpion shouted.

Riker shivered. The red rot had taken hold. He must have a higher fever than before.

"He's close, boys. I can feel it in my gut. Do you hear my stomach rumble with desire?"

Scorpions laughed, sounding more like hyenas than men.

Now Riker ran. It was like that of a wounded moose plunging into the forest. Behind him, a chorus of shouts and wild whoops told him they had found his trail again.

Once again, the flitter sound filled Riker with wild hope. Had he run long enough to give the captain time?

Sergeant Riker silently jeered himself as a hopeless romantic. He must believe in impossible causes just as the captain did. The young officer had infected him with his insane optimism. They had worked together for a year. It had been the most eventful time of Riker's life. He was sorry to die on this Godforsaken planet. Without him as a tether to reality, Captain Maddox would take matters too far and kill himself in the line of duty.

127

"Run, Weasel!" a Scorpion shouted.

Riker glanced back. He saw a native in a loincloth, with a wet rag over his face like an old-time Western outlaw. The man carried a long-barreled flintlock in one hand. He had a pack on his back, while oil glistened on his skin. The oil helped to keep vile lowlander spores off his body.

The man knelt, raised the flintlock and let the hammer fall.

Time seemed to slow down for Sergeant Riker. The striking of flint against the pan produced an explosion of gunpowder. Where on this plant had they found the needed substances?

It didn't matter. A hard knot of wood struck Riker's back. It pitched him forward off his feet, so he crashed face-first against the soil. Pain made him writhe on the ground. He tried to get up, but failed. His limbs were refusing to move.

The snap and crunch of branches told him Scorpions approached. He heard their mocking laughter. No, no, he couldn't let them feast on his flesh.

"Maddox," he wheezed. "Can you hear me?"

"He's praying," a Scorpion said.

"Let's drag him to that rock. We can use it to hack off his legs easier."

"Are we going to eat him here?"

"I'm not dragging his carcass upstream."

"Sheds will be angry with you."

"What are you saying? You want to carry him?"

"No."

"So why are you talking about Sheds?"

"You know why. Don't pretend you don't."

Riker had almost lost consciousness. He knew about Sheds too. The man was huge and strong, and he ruled the Scorpions with savage brutality. The others feared Sheds' wrath. The chief had a grim garden of planted people festering with horrible diseases. Sheds liked to wander through his garden, taunting the inmates of his own private hell.

"Should we carry this crawly back then?"

No one spoke.

"Or should we eat him here?"

Again no one spoke.

128

"Hey, you," a Scorpion said, prodding Riker in the side. "Can you walk?"

Riker tried to stand, but slid back onto his stomach.

"We'll eat him," the same Scorpion said. "Blue, you and Fetch drag him to the rock. I'm going to do the hacking."

Riker didn't fight as they dragged his body over the damp ground. They used his legs. He was trying to drum up enough strength to make a last fight of it. The wooden pellet in his back kept leeching the last of his willpower, though.

I never thought it would end like this. I wonder what happened to Captain Maddox. Why did I hear the hum of a flitter? I suppose I'll never know.

"Here we go," a Scorpion said. "Prop him up."

Men grabbed Riker's torso. They heaved, and Riker's back exploded with pain as they laid him on the rock.

His good eye opened, and he struck with everything he had, punching a Scorpion in the gut. It ended up being little more than a shove. The native stumbled back, though.

"That's going to cost you," the biggest Scorpion said. He held a long branch with a sharp obsidian edge. They were individual stones wedged into the wood.

"I'd think twice before you use that," a well-modulated voice said.

Riker couldn't believe it. That sounded exactly like Captain Maddox. The man had the attitude down perfectly.

"Who are you?" a Scorpion asked.

Riker could feel the tension build around him. Six Scorpions stood by the rock. No. The rearward man slipped away into the brush. Then another bled off. Riker wanted to warn Maddox. Was it really the captain?

"If those men don't return," Maddox said. "I'm shooting you first."

"With what?" the biggest Scorpion asked. "Oh. Hey! That's a regular gun. You never made that on Loki."

"You haven't recalled your wayward men," Maddox said.

A flintlock discharged. The wooden pellet slapped leaves.

"You missed him!" the leader shouted. "Hey! Where did he go?"

129

Shots rang out. Riker knew the sound well. Scorpions began to tumble around him. Some groaned. One screamed in agony. The leader slid to the damp soil, dead, shot through the forehead.

Confusion filled Riker as he closed his eye. He lay on the rock, clinging to consciousness. His lungs began to fill with fluid, making him wheeze horribly. He heard more shots in the distance. Another flintlock fired.

Did Captain Maddox live? These Scorpions were uncanny woodsmen. Those who refused to learn Loki's lessons had died a long time ago.

Finally, a gentle hand shook Riker. He peeled open an eyelid. Captain Maddox looked down on him. The officer seemed concerned.

Riker forced himself to think. "How…" He began to cough.

Maddox eased him up. Riker spat red gunk, coughed, spat and coughed more. Finally, he began to wheeze as a queasy feeling consumed him. He shivered uncontrollably.

"How many did you kill?" Riker whispered.

"Five of them," Maddox said.

"There were six," Riker whispered.

"The last one was running hard. I let him go."

"Don't let that fool you, sir. He'll double back. What you have, it's incredible wealth to them."

"I'll keep that in mind. Now you must save your strength, Sergeant. We don't have far to go, but it will take some effort."

"I'm done for, sir," Riker said.

"Nonsense, Sergeant. I didn't come all this way to have you die on me. Besides, I need what lies in your skull."

"I'm not very lucid, sir. My thinking is off. The last one is returning. Count on it."

"I've already told you I'll keep that in mind. Now stand up. There's a good fellow. Lean your weight on me."

"How did you make it down here, sir?"

"I have my flitter," Maddox said.

"I heard it earlier."

"Good. Now concentrate. Yes, keep walking."

Riker swam in and out of consciousness. A raging fever made him desperately cold. He would have crashed to the ground many times, but Maddox kept him up. Riker couldn't believe this was

130

happening. He wanted to weep with relief, but he would never do that before the captain. He wouldn't give Maddox the pleasure.

"I have red rot in my lungs, sir."

Maddox said nothing.

With a final supreme effort, Riker opened his eye. The last Scorpion stood before them. He aimed his flintlock at Maddox.

"Drop your gun," the man said.

"Is that barrel made of wood?" Maddox asked.

"Drop it!" the Scorpion shouted. Oil slicked his skin in most places. Some of it looked dry, though. That was bad luck for the criminal.

Maddox pitched his gun onto the ground.

"That's good," the Scorpion said, grinning. He only had a few teeth left, and they were all green. "Now, tell me who you are?"

"I'm with Intelligence," Maddox said, "Star Watch. I'm on Loki Prime looking for Doctor Dana Rich. Have you heard of her?"

The Scorpion cawed with laughter. "Of course I've heard of that bitch. She's two tribes up on the mountain."

"Ah," Maddox said.

The Scorpion cocked his head. The rag over his face was almost dry. Riker knew the man needed to re-soak it. "You don't know what that means," the Scorpion said. "Up the mountain. Did you just drop onto the surface?"

"In a manner of speaking, I did," Maddox said. "Now listen here, my good fellow. If you're interested in a reward, you'll tell me all you can about Dana Rich and her tribe."

"No," the Scorpion said. "I'm the one making the deals. You're—" The man cocked his head again, and he glanced around before staring at Maddox. "Do you hear that hum?"

"I do in fact," Maddox said.

"What is it?"

"My taxi out of here," Maddox said.

"You'd better explain that to me."

As Riker watched, he saw the flitter glide into position behind the man.

"Look behind you," Maddox suggested.

The Scorpion did.

"You see now that I have the ability to reward you," Maddox said.

In disbelief, with tears in his eyes, the Scorpion stared back at the captain. "That's your air-car up there?"

"Indeed."

As a tear slid down his face, the Scorpion grinned. "Do you know what a ransom is?"

"I'm aware of the concept," Maddox said.

"Good. Because you're going to communicate with your driver and tell him to land right here."

Maddox shook his head.

"Do you want to die?" the Scorpion shouted, his cloth fluttering before his lips.

"You misunderstand," Maddox said. "I wasn't shaking my head for your benefit, but for my driver's."

"What?" the Scorpion asked, his forehead furrowed.

On the nose of the flitter, Riker saw a slot move out of the way. A barrel poked out.

"Go ahead," Maddox told the criminal. "Take a look behind you. I'm sure you'll find this of interest."

Once more, the Scorpion glanced back. That's when a heavy slung from the flitter's weapon blew apart his chest. The bloody remains toppled onto the soil.

"I should have listened to you, Sergeant," Maddox said. "The man did indeed double back. Now we're going to have to get Doctor Rich with only a minimum of information to guide us. I'd planned to chase the convict down and interrogate him."

The captain said more, but Riker didn't hear the rest as he slipped into blessed unconsciousness.

-17-

Maddox opened the flitter's emergency kit. It had a small diagnostic compu-doctor, a round device a little heavier than his fist. The captain pressed it against the sergeant's chest.

The medikit flashed red—not a good sign. Then, it injected Riker with various antibiotics and painkillers. Afterward, it gave a medical readout on a tiny screen.

Maddox examined the report, slowly climbing to his feet afterward.

"How bad is it?" Keith asked.

"We have to get him up to *Geronimo* or he'll die."

"So...?"

Maddox took several steps away from the prone sergeant, thinking hard. Riker had a fever and debilitating funguses or spores mutating in his body. *Geronimo* had a larger and more advanced medikit than the one here. It might save the sergeant—if they left immediately. The longer he waited, the less chance Riker had for survival.

Maddox seethed inwardly, although nothing showed on his face. Sergeant Riker was a good man, if too tepid on too many occasions. Still, the sergeant was good with a gun, resourceful when it counted and levelheaded. Yet Maddox couldn't fly him up this instant. He had to find Doctor Rich first. The space beacon was ticking, and soon it wouldn't matter what happened. They had to leave the Loki System, sooner being better than later.

Maddox didn't want to admit it to himself, but he was going to have to risk Riker's life. He owed the sergeant his, but—

Is this how I repay him?

It had been a poor idea to send Riker to Loki Prime. O'Hara must have believed she was protecting the sergeant from Octavian Nerva. If the sergeant had remained on Earth, Nerva's hitmen would have slain Riker in retaliation for Caius Nerva's death.

"Sir," Keith said, sounding worried. "He's moaning."

Maddox stroke back to Riker. He bent on one knee, putting a hand on the man's shoulder. It radiated heat.

Riker opened a bleary eye. Slowly, he moistened his dry lips. "Doctor Rich...she's higher on the mountain, sir. She's tough. Stronger tribes live higher."

"Ah," Maddox said. "I think I understand. Lower on Loki Prime is swampier, meaning worse spores."

"Right," Riker whispered. "And, sir—"

"I'm listening, Sergeant."

"They're...excellent woodsmen. If not, they die." Riker tried to say more. His eye closed before he could speak. Shivering, he collapsed back into unconsciousness.

"What's that mean?" Keith asked. "What he said."

Maddox stood, and he tapped his chin with a forefinger. He raised his head, examining the trees and the gloomy light. He listened to the nearby river churn. Closer to them, insects hummed. He kept slapping his skin, killing them. The bugs were bigger here, more insistent than the mosquitoes on Earth. Fortunately, both Ensign Maker and he had taken shots before leaving the scout. Riker likely had, too, before ejection, but nothing helped against worse spores in the lowlands.

"What are we going to do, sir?" Keith asked.

Maddox turned around. He couldn't abandon Sergeant Riker to his fate and he couldn't let Doctor Rich slip through his fingers. In times like this, Maddox had found a bold front achieved the best results. He was dealing with the worst scoundrels of the Oikumene. The higher tribes of criminals were the tougher ones. That would also mean smarter. They had nothing to lose. No, that was wrong. One could always die. His flitter and weapons represented incredible wealth to these people.

Yes, yes, he would have to use their avarice against them. Greed blinded people. Scam-artists used greed against normal individuals. They offered the victim riches and ended up fleecing them instead.

134

The conditions down here were dreadful. The citizens of Loki Prime led awful lives. Yet he had to keep in mind that each of these inmates was a criminal of the lowest sort. Everything demanded speed. Therefore, he must take chances and he must practice ruthlessness.

"We should leave," Keith said. "These insects are eating me alive."

Maddox regarded the pilot. Keith wiped a gunk-stained palm on his pants.

An idea blossomed then. Maddox knew exactly how he would use the inmates' cupidity against them. It wasn't his first choice, but it might be his only one at this point. Failing on Loki Prime meant the New Men would win by default.

No, I'm not going to let that happen.

"Hurry, Ensign," Maddox said. "Help me stow the sergeant in the flitter, in the back."

"We're leaving the planet?" Keith asked.

"Not yet," Maddox said. "We're departing this spot. We're going higher up the mountain."

***

Soon enough, Maddox felt relief as the flitter's canopy slid shut. The flyer's air-conditioner hummed, taking away the humid, rotten-smelling atmosphere.

"We should have brought breathers," Maddox said.

"Our injections will see us through, right?" Keith asked.

Sergeant Riker groaned pitifully from the back.

Keith's eyes widened, and he massaged his chest. "Bloody spores are in our lungs, eh, mate? They're mutating. I can feel them."

"He's been here for days," Maddox said. "We'll go through a complete scrub once we're back on *Geronimo*. We'll be fine."

"Do you really believe that, Captain?"

Before Maddox could answer, red blips appeared on the flitter's screen in the dash. The captain's brow furrowed as he examined them more closely.

Keith snapped off the answer, "Missiles," he said. "They're coming down fast."

"We've been spotted?" Maddox asked.

Keith's finger roved over the controls. "I don't think so. There's no radar lock-on. Are they heat-seeking missiles or radar directed?"

"Compared to the land around us, how much heat are we giving off?"

Ensign Maker had been lifting, bringing them above the trees. Now he lowered back among the giant branches in a hurry.

"It should be harder for the missiles to hit us if we're almost on the ground." Keith brayed a sharp laugh. "That'll be the day, mate, they can knock me down so easily."

Perplexed, realizing the odds for success had plunged even more drastically, Maddox wondered what had given them away.

"What's your pleasure, Captain?"

Maddox glanced at the pilot, unsure what Keith meant.

"Where should we go, sir?"

"Head up the mountain," Maddox said.

"Jolly good, sir."

Maddox kept one eye on the screen and the other on the terrain. The flitter was small enough to weave among the branches of the giant trees. They glided through a gloomy world. Each insect cloud maintained its own flock of bat-things darting through them.

Soon, the trees became smaller, the branches closer together.

"I'm going to have to lift above the treetops, sir," Keith said. "This is too dense."

Maddox nodded, trying to keep a sense of futility at bay. What had he done wrong? Had the destroyer changed the security codes? That didn't seem right. A Commonwealth penal service ship would have done that, not a Star Watch vessel.

Keith hovered over a tree, and he glanced at Maddox. "What's it going to be, sir?"

"How far out are those missiles?"

"Two minutes from impact, Captain."

"Let's wait here a moment. We'll use the trees for cover at the last minute."

"Will the orbitals keep sending more if the first ones fail?"

That seemed likely. Maddox wondered if there was a way to simulate the flitter's destruction. There was no time for that. Was there any possibility now of leaving Loki Prime?

The seconds ticked too slowly. Waiting for death was always hard.

"I'll be prodded and poked, Bloke," Keith said. "Look! The missiles aren't heading for us."

"What?" Maddox asked. "Are you certain?"

"I know how to read a fighter screen, sir."

Maddox studied the small panel and didn't know what the ace saw that he didn't.

"Higher up the mountain, sir. That's where the missiles are headed?"

"Why?" asked Maddox.

"I have no idea, Captain. Why do the orbitals launch missiles in the first place?"

Maddox wrestled with the concept. Riker kept coughing and moaning in back. The man sounded terrible.

The flitter lifted. Maddox stared at the pilot.

"Want to see what's happening, sir," Keith said. "That's how you beat your enemy. Can't just sit in the dark and hope for luck. You have to see his tactic in order to conjure up a counter."

Enemy, Maddox said silently. *We have to defeat our enemy.* He snapped his fingers.

As he did, he saw a black object streak down. It headed for a place higher on the mountain. Keith had been right. Then the missile disappeared into the trees. A second later, light expanded, and a cloud billowed into view. A second missile streaked down. It too created light and debris, seemingly hitting the same spot.

"Those orbitals mean business," Keith said with a low whistle.

"None of the missiles were directed at us," Maddox said.

"If they were, it was piss poor targeting."

"In answer to your question," Maddox said. "The orbitals search for high tech, demolishing it. If we didn't have our clearance, we'd already be dead."

Keith engaged the flitter's controls, sliding toward the missile strike.

"The conditions here are not favorable for creating high technology in the first place," Maddox said. "Secondly, the strike came during our time on the planet. Is that a coincidence?"

"Wouldn't bet the farm on it, Captain," Keith said.

"Neither would I. In my line of work, there are few coincidences."

137

"So let's say the natives didn't build a high-tech toy the orbital programs objected to," Keith said. "What else would they launch at?"

A grim feeling spread across Maddox's chest. The *Saint Petersburg* had come to Loki Prime. Back in Earth orbit, the destroyer had failed to beam down a Nerva drone fired at the scout. Immediately upon Keith's destruction of the offending drone, the destroyer's comm officer had demanded the *Geronimo* stay where it was. Maddox had refused, and the destroyer fired a laser at them. Now the same destroyer was at Loki Prime. Orbitals watching for high technology had just barraged the area he—Maddox—was heading to. Why did the missiles hit there? What was there they would attack?

"Doctor Dana Rich," Maddox said.

"What's that, sir?"

"The *Saint Petersburg* must have sent down a landing party to grab Dana Rich. Remember, in Glasgow a sniper fired at us?"

"I hadn't run so fast for a long time," Keith said. "I remember the crawly piece of slime, all right."

"How did the sniper know ahead of time to be there in Glasgow?" Maddox asked. "Someone else must have the Lord High Admiral's list. You were on the list. And Dana Rich is on it, and she's partway up the mountain. That's why the missiles slammed down there."

"Do you think she's dead?" Keith asked. "Do you think they're trying to murder her, whoever *they* are?"

"There's only one way to find out," Maddox said. "You see the smoke? That's where we're going—now."

***

In retrospect, Maddox realized he should have reasoned things out a little more carefully. Maybe his need for speed blunted his judgment. Maybe the lowland spores attacking his immune system dulled his thinking. In any regard, he flew straight into an ambush.

Keith Maker glided low over the treetops, nearing the black smoke. Flames appeared ahead, licking skyward. Maddox checked his gun before holstering it. Leaning back, he saw that Sergeant Riker slept fitfully. Small spumes of red trickled from the sergeant's nose. That wasn't blood. It would have been better if it had been. What had Riker said, red rot? That was an apt name.

"For the love of Pete!" Keith shouted. "Will you look at that, matey. I mean Captain, sir."

Maddox saw it, and worry erupted in spades. A Star Watch shuttle—correction, a smoking wreck of a shuttle—had been blown onto its side. The vehicle had gaping holes and crumpled areas. It would never lift off again. The dead were strewn around it, many of them missing limbs, some in Star Watch uniforms, some not.

Huts crackled with flames, and people crawled or dragged themselves in the outer area of the tree-blasted ground. Some looked up at them. A few of those shook their fists. One woman raised a flintlock. A puff of smoke a second later indicated she shot at them.

What the—

Maddox froze, unwilling to believe what he saw. One of the dead on the ground was unlike the others. In life, he would have been taller than the average human. That wasn't what made Maddox's gut twist. It was the color of the skin—golden. A New Man lay dead on the ground down there.

Questions flooded Maddox's brain. How had the invader gotten here? The likeliest explanation was aboard a *Saint Petersburg* shuttle. If there was one invader, couldn't that mean there were more? Did the New Men command the Star Watch destroyer? If so, how had the enemy maneuvered that? Maddox wondered if he should land beside the New Man. He could take a sample, a slice of skin or clot up some blood on a rag. Later, he could test the DNA. Then, finally, he could learn if he was part New Man.

"Blimey!" Keith shouted. He banked away hard, turning from the burning village.

That threw Maddox against the flitter's canopy. He heard heavy gunfire from below. The flitter shuttered. Something starred the bubble on the pilot's side.

"What's happening?" Maddox shouted, who couldn't see because of his lousy angle.

"A woman's firing at us," Keith said. "I think she hit our underbelly."

"Firing a musket?"

"A heavy repeater, mate! Now for the love of Saint Francis, shut your yapper, Captain, sir. I'm taking us down for a controlled crash, and I'm going to need all my concentration to do it."

-18-

The flitter bucked like a wild horse. Maddox clung to his harness and managed to look back at Riker. The sergeant flew in disorder, banging his head, smashing his shins.

"This is it!" Keith shouted.

Maddox looked ahead again. A huge tree filled his view. They were going to crash head on. At the last second, Keith turned them sideways, dodging death as metal screeched. They must have shaved the underbelly of the flitter against tree bark. Clunking sounds emitted from the engine. Smoke poured from the panel.

"Come on, you filthy pimp," Keith said. "Keep it going just a little longer. You won't regret it, I promise."

The pilot dodged another tree and slowed the flyer. Then branches blurred around them, striking the bubble canopy. The tough dome held, and finally, the Tau Ceti strikefighter-ace brought them down against a giant crackly bush.

Keith brayed with triumphant laughter, and he stabbed a button. The canopy slid open, letting in the planet's jungle smells.

"I did it, sir. We're down in one piece."

Feelings of disaster pulsed through Maddox's heart. Oh, they were down all right, on Loki Prime, the prison planet no one had ever escaped.

You're still alive, Maddox told himself. *The scout is up there. Let's not quit until you're coughing up your final bit of blood.*

"Excellent work, Ensign," Maddox said. "I'm doubling your salary."

"You mean doubling my share of the prize money, sir."

"That's right. Now give me a hand. We have to move the sergeant."

The smile drained from Keith's round face. Realization of their predicament spread across his features.

"We just crash-landed on Loki Prime," the ensign said. "There's a woman with an automatic rifle down there. Do you think the people from the shuttle came to this place to arrest you?"

"No such luck, I'm afraid," Maddox said. "Now help me with him."

"Why?" Keith asked. "He's probably better off where he is. We can't dart around if he's weighing us down."

A harsh rebuke died on Maddox's lips. The ace had a point. He could hear people coming.

"It's time for a strategic retreat," Maddox said. "Grab a pack and follow me."

The two rummaged in back. Maddox avoided looking at the unconscious sergeant. It wasn't fair leaving him like this, but Maker was right, the sergeant would be safer in the flitter.

"I'll return," Maddox whispered. Then he jumped out of the flitter and faded into the undergrowth. Keith followed hard on his heels.

Maddox halted and studied the terrain around him. The trees lacked the immense height of those in the lowlands. The ground felt firmer, drier. There were fewer insects and less strange funguses sprouting from the soil and tree trunks. He needed the flitter. Its radio could reach the *Geronimo*. That was his only way off Loki Prime now. He wanted to double-back, hide and see who came to his flyer. Instead, he started racing downhill again. He needed to sneak up on his hunters when they weren't tracking him. He needed an edge.

"Wait a minute, will you?" Keith panted. "I can't keep up with you."

Maddox debated leaving the ace behind. *Ruthlessness, remember?* He couldn't do it. Leaving the sergeant had been hard enough. That had been the logical move. Abandoning his crew—no, he wouldn't do that. Without honor, winning didn't matter.

Indicating a place behind a tree, he showed the pilot where to crouch. Since the man's heavy breathing made listening difficult,

Maddox moved several feet away. The intervening growth muted the noise.

Maddox bent his head, straining to hear what he could. Indistinct voices spoke in the distance. He needed to see who it was. Without intelligence, he couldn't formulate a sound plan.

First slipping near Keith, he said, "I'm going to spy on the enemy."

Keith looked up with wide eyes, and he almost shouted with surprise. Finally, the small pilot nodded. "You're as silent as a cat, mate. I wish you wouldn't sneak up on me like that."

"Stay here," Maddox said. "Recover your strength."

"You're leaving me alone?"

"I'm going to scout the area. I'll be back."

Keith drew his gun. "Okay, sir. I'll wait." He coughed as if to add to this statement. A new alarm entered the man's eyes. "I got the bad spores, don't I, sir?"

"We'll leave this planet soon enough."

"You promise that, Captain? I didn't sign up to end my days in misery."

"There isn't a place in the galaxy that can hold me, Ensign. You can rely on that."

"I'm going to keep you to your promise, Captain,"

Still sensing the fear in Ensign Maker, Maddox said, "You did a fantastic job bringing us down in one piece."

"It's what I do, sir."

"Exactly my point," Maddox said. "This is the sort of thing I do."

A grin crept across Keith's face. "Right. I'm okay, sir. I have this." He indicated the gun.

"Keep quiet, though," Maddox said. "Let me concentrate."

The ace drew his knees up as he leaned back against the tree. Then he closed his eyes, and suppressed a second cough.

Maddox glided away toward the voices. The gloom was less dense here than lower down on the mountain. He heard fire crackle in the distance, and the smell of smoke became noticeable. The voices had stopped speaking, but he could hear footfalls.

He circled them. Sergeant Riker had told him the natives were expert woodsmen. If he came at them from a different direction, he might catch his trackers by surprise. Determination hardened in

143

Maddox's heart. He strained to move soundlessly and quickly. It was a good thing he wore his camouflage gear.

Then his nape hairs rose. Maddox froze, straining to sense what had alerted him. Danger flowed around him. He felt the threat grow. Holding his breath, the captain rotated his neck, looking in one direction and then another. He couldn't see anything except for foliage. He had to keep moving.

With infinite care, he stepped softly, avoiding anything that might crackle or snap. He suppressed the urgency to know, to stare. He had come to believe that people gave off an unknowable sensation that a few individuals could sense. It was how he'd found the sniper so quickly in Glasgow. Maddox let himself blend into his surroundings.

His throat caught. The fierce warning of danger resumed. Once more, he froze. Something—

Then Captain Maddox saw something out of the corner of his eye. A golden-skinned individual walked through a small clearing. The man did it with much of the care the captain had just been practicing. There was a sense of intense athleticism to the New Man, as if he were some great cat in human guise. He wore a dark garment, tight at the ankles, wrists and throat. Only the hands and face showed the golden color. A hat covered his head, hiding the hair. The invader held a flat pistol. The man's face—Maddox wanted to turn his head to get a better look.

He resisted the urge. The slightest movement would give him away. The combat video he'd seen from Odin made him extra cautious. There, on the invaded planet in a spaceport, a single New Man had seemingly successfully charged suited space marines. Maddox only had his gun.

The fleeting glimpse of the New Man's face allowed Maddox a snapshot of his enemy. He sensed anger from the invader, a desire to kill and arrogance. The golden-skinned human would stamp out anyone who got in his way.

After the momentary glimpse, Maddox doused his curiosity to mute any telltale emanations.

Maddox didn't know how he'd given himself away, but the New Man began turning his head toward the captain.

Before Maddox could discover the answer, the undergrowth creaked. The sound came from the other side of the clearing. A leaf shook over there.

The New Man moved like greased death. Four times, he fired, sending bullets into the undergrowth. Someone grunted painfully back there. An unseen body thudded onto the ground. Another person staggered, crashing through foliage. She burst into sight, clutching a flintlock against her chest. Blood poured from her throat. Her eyes were glazed with approaching death.

The New Man snapped off another shot, obliterating her head.

As the golden-skinned superman fired the last time, Maddox brought up his gun. He moved faster than he could ever remember doing. He'd been waiting for the chance to act while the other was occupied. Even so, the New Man proved uncanny in his abilities.

Maddox pulled the trigger. The gun bucked in his hand. A bullet exited the barrel. The New Man had already reacted, diving away. Maddox saw this, adjusted, pulled the trigger a second time. The gun bucked once more, sending a second round at what should have been an easy target.

By now, the New Man had rotated his body, bringing up his flat weapon to fire back.

Maddox shot a third time. His mind moved at hyper-speed. He shot where he judged the New Man would be as the invader dodged yet again.

Then the golden-skinned man fired his gun from around his torso at Maddox. It was a trick shot.

Time resumed its normal speed. Maddox's first bullet missed. The second grazed enemy skin. The third pitched the New Man off his feet, entering against the ribs. The invader slid across the ground. Bright red blood spurted from his side, staining his garment.

At the same time, a bullet flashed past Maddox's head. He could feel the burn of its passage, although it missed hitting flesh by the proverbial hair's width. The round made his left eye blink rapidly. That caused him to jerk away, duck and finally roll, as he figured the New Man must be sighting him for another shot.

An entire second ticked away as Maddox completed his roll. He was on his feet in a low crouch, scanning where the New Man should be. Instead of seeing the invader aim at him, or lying shot on the ground, Maddox caught a last glimpse. The golden-skinned invader fled, disappearing into the undergrowth. His running speed was incredible.

What just happened here?

Maddox had never seen anyone move so fast. And the man had made his decisions faster than lightning.

With a feeling of unreality, Maddox stood. He wasn't used to being dazed like this.

You don't have any time to waste. You have to act, and you have to do it now.

"Right," he whispered. Maddox hurried to the fallen weapon. He reached down for it—

"If you touch the gun, you're dead," a hidden woman said.

Maddox debated grabbing the gun anyway and rolling. The voice indicated a person with icy calm. He waited one second, two. Then he said, "The New Man will be back."

"You mean golden-boy?" the woman asked.

"They consider themselves superior to ordinary humans."

"Drop your gun," the woman said, "and don't try to touch his."

Maddox listened, trying to pinpoint the woman's exact position. At the same time, he let his weapon thud onto the soil.

"Straighten up," she said.

He followed orders.

"Face me," the woman said.

Maddox found himself staring at a medium-sized woman with brown clothes, a dark ponytail and darker skin. She aimed a flintlock at him, and her hands were perfectly steady.

"Doctor Dana Rich," Maddox said.

Suspicion flared across her features. "How do you know me?"

"I've come to take you off Loki Prime."

It took a half-beat. Then she said, "You're the second person to say that today. I want to know why."

"I'm here because of the golden-skinned man you just saw. His kind is invading the Oikumene."

"Good. I think I'll aid them. Your people stuck me on this filthy piece of sod. You think after that I want to help the Commonwealth or the Windsor League?"

"The New Men won't reward you for long, Dr. Rich."

"Wrong," she said. "Before your missiles smashed their shuttle and killed the leader, they offered me more than you possibly could."

"Oh, right," said Maddox. "That's why he killed those people." He indicated the headless woman prone on the ground. There must be more dead hidden in the undergrowth. "You're spinning fabrications, Doctor."

"I don't care for people calling me a liar."

"Then don't lie to me," Maddox told her.

From the undergrowth in the direction he'd come, Maddox heard a branch snap, leaves rustle and finally a muffled grunt of a pain.

"We have to flee," he told Dana. "The New Man must have doubled back."

"Don't be absurd," she said. "If he was here, we'd already be dead."

Maddox looked at her questioningly.

"I'm beyond caring whether I live or die," she said. "This planet has sucked the joy of life from me."

Dana Rich didn't look defeated as she squinted down the rifle barrel at him, more like icily determined to overcome anything thrown at her.

"On your knees," she said. "It's time you answered some questions."

A distinct hoot sounded from the undergrowth.

Doctor Rich cursed, and her fingers tightened around her weapon. "Mister, grab those guns by the barrels. You were right. He's coming back. We have to get out of here."

"Let's work together," Maddox suggested. "We'll kill him."

"Hurry!" she hissed. "Do it now, or I'm going to kill you. And if you don't care about your life, think about your friend."

With a nod of her head, Dana indicated leftward.

Maddox glanced in the direction he'd heard the crashing noise a second ago. A striking woman stepped into view. She had platinum-colored hair pulled into a knot behind her head. She wore bikini furs, showing a voluptuous figure a trifle heavier than Maddox liked. Unfortunately, she had one of Keith Maker's arms behind his back with her other hand around his mouth.

"Meta is pretty," Dana said. "She's also from a heavy G mining world. That means she's stronger than anyone I know. She can snap your man's neck like a twig."

The cavewoman stared with hostility at Maddox. She had Keith's force blade and gun tucked in her fur shorts. The ace squirmed. She shoved his back arm a little higher, causing him to lift up onto his toes. Yes, she must be strong.

A warning hoot sounded once more.

Because of it, Maddox made his decision of how to play this. He grabbed the two guns by the barrels, his and the New Man's. Then he hurried toward Meta, with Doctor Dana Rich following. It was clear she didn't want to be here when the golden-skinned invader returned.

-19-

Maddox halted at Doctor Rich's orders. They must have run a good two kilometers, entering even thicker growth. Then they'd ducked into an area of woven branches overhead, making this spot even gloomier than the surrounding terrain. There were covered holes here. Could this be a storage area or a hideaway for times of trouble?

"Sit," Dana said, waving his own gun at him. He'd given her both weapons earlier. She carried the long flintlock with a strap around her shoulder.

Maddox sat on damp soil. Yes. This definitely seemed like a hideaway. If the tribes raided each other, a wise leader would have places to regroup if an enemy overran the main compound.

Meta shoved Keith against Maddox so the ace sprawled onto the ground.

"They surprised me," Keith explained, his mouth finally freed of the woman's silencing hand.

"Quiet," Dana told him. "Unless I tell you otherwise, don't speak."

Maddox nodded to Keith that it was okay to listen to her in this.

"Meta," Dana said, holding up the flat gun.

The cavewoman accepted the New Man's weapon. She inspected it a moment. A grin spread across her wide features. Then Meta faded from view, backing out the entrance, no doubt to stand guard.

Doctor Dana Rich moved to the side, sitting on a tree stump, studying the two of them. She kept the gun trained on Maddox. She

149

lacked a perfect poker face. It was clear she was curious about something.

"Why did you come down onto Loki Prime for me?" she said.

"Does it matter?" Maddox asked.

"Oh yes."

"Are you that eager to remain on Loki Prime, then?" Maddox asked. "If we're going to leave, we have to act now."

"You have a point," she said. "I obviously wish to leave. The question is can you beat their offer?"

"I doubt they offered you anything," Maddox said.

"Oh?"

"You're on the run from them. I think you've been hiding the entire time the shuttle has been on the ground. Otherwise, you'd be dead, killed during the missile strike. They would have at least been interrogating you there."

"I see you like to make guesses," she said.

Maddox shook his head. "No. It's not a guess; it's what happened. The New Man would never bother hunting for you otherwise."

"You're spinning a web of suppositions, hoping I'm so eager to get off Loki Prime that I'll believe anything you tell me."

"Doctor," Maddox said. "The New Men have invaded the Oikumene. They have superior starships. Do you know that with three cruiser-class vessels, they annihilated what amounted to a double-strength Star Watch battle group?"

"Did you see the shuttle back there?" Dana asked. "Did you look at its markings? Did you happen to notice what uniform the woman wore who shot down your flitter?"

"I'm afraid I didn't see her."

"She wore a Star Watch uniform," Dana said, as if that ended the discussion.

"That doesn't surprise me in the least," Maddox said. "The New Men have secretly infiltrated the Oikumene and slipped people into high places among Commonwealth personnel. We believe they're genetic supermen. Given their actions to date, we're in a species battle, and so far, our side is losing."

Dana no longer seemed as triumphant as a second ago. "Suppose this is the truth," she said. "Why would that bring you down here?"

150

"The answer may surprise you. Their technology is decidedly superior to ours, particularly in terms of starships. We need an equalizer, a superior fighting vessel, if we're going to stop their invasion. According to our records, you were with Professor Ludendorff when he studied the alien sentinel in the shattered star system."

For the first time, shock crossed her features. "Are you insane? I know Professor Ludendorff was. If I hadn't—" She shut her mouth, pressing her lips together.

Maddox raised an eyebrow. What did that mean? What had happened during their expedition?

"You want the sentinel?" she asked in a sharp voice.

"Very much so," Maddox said.

"And you think I'm suicidal enough to go back there?"

"Given the alternative of spending the rest of your life here, yes," Maddox said.

Dana laughed, shaking her head. "Even if I believed your story—which I don't—I wouldn't do as you asked."

"Then you have two choices left. Rot on Loki Prime or become a genetic experiment for the New Men."

A hard grin twisted her lips. "I'll paint you another, mister. If there's some grand war obliterating worlds, I'll simply hijack a starship and leave the Oikumene. I'll head into the Beyond. The universe is full of planets. When faced with an invincible foe, the wise person relocates."

"What happens to the people who can't do that?" Maddox asked.

"Am I their guardian?" Dana asked. "No. The 'people' as you call them, support the ones who pod-dropped me here. I owe them nothing. Maybe you don't, but I plan to live a long, long life."

"Do you think Meta feels the same way about her mining world?" Maddox asked, raising his voice. "If you run from the New Men, her people die. Does she want that?"

Dana cocked her head, as if surprised at his questions. Then a snarl creased her features. Aiming the gun, she said, "Shut up."

"Why do you think you get to make everyone else's decisions for them?" Maddox asked.

Dana stood, still aiming the gun at him. "I know what you're doing. Meta isn't going to fall for that. It—"

151

Maddox could see the decision to kill him in her eyes. That she hadn't already done it meant she wasn't a hardened killer who could just blow a person away. She had to psyche herself up first.

She was as physically close as she was going to come. Using the palms of his hands, Maddox shoved against the ground, scooting himself closer toward her. Her trigger finger began to tighten. Maddox swept his left foot, connecting with her ankles. He kicked her feet out from under her. She fell hard and her finger yanked the trigger.

A loud *boom* crashed against Maddox's ears. The bullet smashed through leaves, thudding against a tree trunk. Then Dana's back smacked against the ground. She grunted, but she kept hold of the gun.

Maddox was already moving, diving at her. Grabbing the gun, he twisted. She yelled painfully, her forefinger wretched in the trigger guard. She tried to get up. With a twist, Maddox smashed an elbow against her face, making the back of her head slam against the ground.

Maddox tore the gun from her weakened grip, spun and aimed at the arch opening into the hideaway.

"Meta!" Dana shouted from the ground. "Run!"

At the same instant, Maddox fired, thinking he saw something darker than a shadow as a target.

"You wretch," Dana said. "If you killed her—"

Since he didn't hear anything to indicate a hit, Maddox switched tactics. He stood, grabbed Dana by the hair and heaved, lifting her to a standing position. Then he had the gun barrel pressed against her temple, backing away against a tree trunk, using her as a human shield against Meta.

"You'll never leave this place alive," Meta said, hidden by the undergrowth. "Let her go."

"I decline your suggestion," Maddox shouted. Looking at Keith, Maddox jerked his head to the side.

The pilot scrambled beside him.

"What now?" Dana asked. "Meta will wait all day to get a shot at you."

"That means we're at an impasse," Maddox whispered into Dana's ear. "I have a gun. Meta has a gun. Out there, the New Man is plotting to destroy us both. If we wait, we both die."

152

"Fine," Dana told him. "We'll join forces for the moment. What do we need to do?"

"What can we do?" Maddox asked. "My only transport up is the flitter. One of the *Saint Petersburg's* people shot the bottom of the craft."

"That's easy enough," Dana said. "We fix the flitter so we can fly out of here."

"You have such tools?"

"I bet the shuttle does," Dana said. "We'll take theirs."

"That means defeating the New Man and his remaining people. At least one of them has a repeater. It's possible another shuttle is on its way down."

As he spoke, Maddox heard quiet footfalls behind his tree. He understood that Dana knew Meta would try to rescue her. The doctor had kept him talking, likely to direct Meta. Now, the cavewoman would try to take him out from behind. This also meant Dana's agreement to work together was a lie. It was time to change the power dynamics.

First lifting his gun, Maddox brought it down hard against Dana's skull. It was a risk. He didn't want to give her a concussion, but he wasn't sure Keith would be able to guard her. Besides, that would mean giving his gun to Keith, and he needed it against Meta.

Dana crumpled face-first onto the ground.

The movement behind the tree stopped. Maddox waited, listening. Then he heard the faintest of footfalls again. A branch made a soft creak.

Because he didn't know what else to do, Maddox decided to use the oldest trick in a gunfight. Slipping his force-blade from Dana's inert form, he tossed it into the heavy undergrowth. He put it where he hoped was in front of Meta.

The handle of the force blade struck leaves. A gunshot rang out—Meta firing at it.

Maddox entered the undergrowth from the other side of the tree. He smashed past leaves and branches, and he reached Meta as she whirled around to face him. Another shot rang out. The round slammed into the soil.

Not wanting to kill her, Maddox refrained from shooting her in the stomach. Instead, he pistol-whipped her, using the bottom of his handle to strike her across the jaw in a right cross.

At that moment, it was obvious that Meta was from a heavy G mining world. The blow would have dropped most people. It barely caused her head to move. She must have strong neck muscles. With his left hand, Maddox punched her bare stomach. It was rock solid, like hitting a tree. She didn't even grunt.

Meta head-butted him, and if her forehead had connected with his nose, the fight would have been over. Maddox twisted his head aside in time. She staggered against him with her body. He let go of his gun and grabbed the wrist of her gun hand. She brought the flat weapon up anyway, just slower than otherwise. Her strength amazed him.

Fortunately, Maddox knew many forms of unarmed combat. Maybe Meta did too, but the blow to her jaw with the butt of his pistol might have dazed her just a little. With an intricate and fast move, he twisted her arm. He kicked her nearest foot, and he flipped her. She was denser than she looked.

Even so, she struck the ground with her back. Maddox stepped against her side as he held up her arm. He gripped her wrist with both hands and twisted hard enough so she let go of the gun. She groaned too, her first indication of pain.

Before she could recover, Maddox had the flat gun. He aimed it at her as he squatted and retrieved his own. Then he indicated that she proceed him into the hideaway.

Sullenly, rubbing her right wrist, Meta did as ordered, climbing to her feet and pushing through bushes. She gave a small cry of dismay as she saw Dana lying on the ground. The cavewoman knelt beside her, checking to see if the doctor was okay.

"Here," Maddox said. He gave Keith the flat pistol. "Check the ground back there. I dropped my force blade."

"Jolly good, Captain," Keith said. He headed there and paused. "I'm surprised you beat that viper. She's strong."

Maddox kept his gaze fixed on Meta.

With a shrug, Keith headed past the tree through the bushes.

On the ground, Dana groaned as her eyelids flickered open. With Meta's help, she sat up. Maddox noticed Meta squeezing Dana's arm as if signaling her. The doctor glanced slowly at Meta and then looked up at Maddox.

Pain swam in Dana's eyes, anger and surprise. "Who are you?" she asked.

154

"Captain Maddox of Star Watch Intelligence," he said.

"How did you defeat Meta?" the doctor asked. "You don't look strong enough."

"Don't let that fool you," Meta said. "He's tougher than he looks."

Despite the circumstances, Maddox found the cavewoman's voice intoxicatingly rich and sweet.

"Interesting," Dana said.

Maddox frowned. He didn't like the doctor's scrutiny. Something about it troubled him.

"You disarmed Meta," Dana said. "That was a dangerous thing to do. It would have been easier to kill her. Why didn't you?"

"Killing is distasteful," Maddox said. "I have no appetite for it, although when the necessity arises, I do what I must."

"Fair enough," Dana said. "Here's another question. What now, Captain?"

Indeed, Maddox thought. He fanned through options. His choices were limited, the situation worse than dire. Doctor Dana Rich did not wish to help him find or enter the sentinel. A New Man prowled nearby with heavily armed crewmembers. Sergeant Riker was dying. The *Saint Petersburg* waited up there, and orbitals too, with missiles and lasers. To make it even worse, the space beacon would report on *Geronimo* in twenty-three hours. If nothing else, he needed Doctor Rich's help to take over the beacon through computer chicanery.

"If you help me," Maddox said. "The chancellor of the Commonwealth Council will grant you a pardon for your crimes."

Dana hunched her shoulders.

Maddox waited for her to claim innocence. Most criminals did. It was one of the marks of their mentality: the idea that society or someone in particular had shafted them and thus everything they— the hurt individual—did wasn't really their fault but someone else's.

"Will the high and mighty chancellor pardon Meta as well?" Dana asked.

"To be honest," Maddox said, "I don't know. We can ask, and I can recommend, but that isn't a promise."

"Give me a gun," Dana said. "Then I'll know you bargain in good faith."

"For now, I'll keep the guns, thank you," Maddox said.

"You don't trust me?"

"Correct," Maddox said.

Dana scowled. "You know you're never leaving Loki Prime, don't you? You're as much a prisoner here as we are. Welcome to hell, Mr. Intelligence Officer."

"Doctor," Maddox said. "I know you aren't that simple-minded. Consider the evidence. Two warring factions have come down onto Loki Prime for you. You have become a valuable commodity. That won't stop until one side or the other has you."

"You don't need me," Dana said. "Let Professor Ludendorff help you board the murderous alien sentinel. He knows more about the vessel than I ever will."

"I respect your intelligence and cunning. Your statement means you want to know if we have Ludendorff or not. We do not, although we have his notes, or some of his notes. Star Watch Intelligence has also gathered a crack team to break into the sentinel. The last piece is you. Time is our enemy, Doctor. If you prefer to fester on this hell-world…"

"How do you propose we get off?" Dana asked.

"We need my flitter, its radio at least."

Dana studied him. "You're claiming to represent the Star Watch. Yet, your enemies came down in a Star Watch shuttle."

"I'll save you time from trying to pry the rest of the information from me. We're both operating in secrecy. The New Men have infiltrated spies and traitors into High Command, and we're no longer sure who to trust."

Dana was obviously processing his words. "Okay. At least that's logically consistent with my observable facts. I'll help you get off Loki Prime if you take us with you. After that, I make no promises."

"Done," said Maddox.

Dana became thoughtful again, finally saying, "I doubt we can capture the shuttle, though. Despite the missiles, they still have too many people and machine guns. We have our flintlocks."

"If we can reach the flitter, I can call for reinforcements."

"Help me up," Dana told Meta. When she was standing, with one arm over Meta's shoulders, the doctor gingerly touched the back of her head. "You hit me too hard. I'm feeling sick."

"You have my apologies," Maddox said. "Still, you'll have to lead the way. I should also let you know that if some of your people

156

try to sneak up and shoot me from concealment, you or Meta will be my first target."

"You mean Meta, then," Dana said, "because you're still hoping to convince me to help you with the sentinel."

"I think you'll find soon enough that I mean exactly what I say," Maddox told her. "Let us proceed on that understanding."

Dana stared at him as if she could divine his inner thoughts. Finally, she indicated to Meta to help her walk out of the hideaway.

In the distance, Maddox heard muffled flintlocks discharging. Once, a heavy assault rifle made sustained noise. Afterward, the number of flintlocks firing lessened.

"It sounds like a running fight," Meta said. "I hope one of them killed the torturer at least before dying."

Once more, the cavewoman's voice struck Maddox pleasantly. In another setting—*no, don't go there. You can't afford to have anything mar your judgment.*

"Torturer," Maddox said. "They must have grabbed some of your tribe before, doctor, to try to force them to reveal your location."

Dana glanced at Meta before saying, "You don't miss much, do you?"

"Sorry," Meta muttered.

Doctor Rich shrugged. "He has all the advantages. Don't worry about it." With Meta's help, she limped along. From time to time, Dana squeezed her eyes shut, and she groaned twice.

Maddox didn't think she was faking. It wasn't *if* the doctor had a concussion, but how badly.

Keith began breathing heavily, and he rubbed his chest several times.

After a while, Dana halted and shuffled around. Sweat slicked her face. "You seem to be playing fair with Meta and me. I ought to tell you then that we have even less time than you realize. The other tribes, both higher and lower, will be coming to investigate. They'll

158

know something catastrophic has happened. Each tribe will want to salvage what they can from us. We live like vultures down here."

"By all means, increase your pace," Maddox said.

They continued to move under the gloomy trees. The smell of smoke strengthened, and the sound of flames increased.

"The fire's growing," Dana said. "What do you know? No one figured that was possible. I've heard old-timers say tribes have tried to burn each other out with a forest fire. The soil and trees are too wet to make it work. When those missiles hit, they must have spread enough flammable substances to burn long enough to dry out nearby trees. It will be good to remember that—in case we're stuck here for the rest of our lives. Manufacture enough gunpowder and maybe we can burn out the Stone Dogs after all."

Maddox was only half listening. He kept analyzing their situation. Earlier, hidden scouts had paced them. Those scouts had hooted a warning, but they didn't seem to be there anymore. What had happened to them? Likely, once they'd seen Dana had made it to the hideaway, they must have run back to help against the shuttle crew. He bet each prisoner dreamed hours a day of ways off the planet. Even though the New Man was deadly, Dana's tribe kept trying to snipe him and the shuttle crew. They obviously wanted what was left of the shuttle.

Beside Maddox, Keith wheezed. The bubbling in his throat sounded worse than before. The pilot turned his head and spat red-stained saliva. Maddox wondered if Keith realized the significance of the color. He hoped not. He wanted the ace upbeat for as long as possible.

"This way," Dana said, indicating a faint trail.

Flintlock fire had intensified again, although it remained muffled in the distance. A heavy assault rifle opened up. A person screamed. It was a shrill and continuing noise.

Keith swore under his breath as he shifted his shoulders.

Dana noticed with seeming interest—Maddox watched her sidelong. He digested her awareness, trying to figure out what it meant. He didn't care for the screams either, although he could compartmentalize his unease so it didn't interfere with his present task. The point to remember was that this was Loki Prime. Here lived some of the most ruthless people in the Commonwealth. Many of those would use what they considered as squeamishness or weakness against a person. Dana was a hardened denizen of this place. Maddox knew it was important never to forget that.

Ahead of them through the undergrowth, a hidden man muttered incoherently between wheezing inhalations. With a sting of recognition, Maddox realized it was Sergeant Riker.

Dana must have heard him too. Her step slowed.

"Hurry," Maddox said.

She did, and in seconds, they came upon a gargantuan flattened bush and trampled ground. There were two crushed lines through the spider grass. Maddox frowned until he realized those were wheel marks.

The flitter—it was gone! How were they supposed to get out of here now?

Calm, stay calm—think. By the signs, someone had taken the flyer. They hadn't taken the sergeant, however. Maybe he knew what had happened.

Riker sat on his rear with his back to them. He fiddled with his arm, muttering, trying to—

The sergeant woke up. He found the package. Keith had asked him about the box earlier. The packet had held Riker's prosthetic arm. The sergeant had become lucid enough to fit the arm into his socket. Now, it appeared as if he was trying to turn it on, maybe make adjustments.

"Sergeant," Maddox said.

Riker's head lifted, but he didn't turn around.

"Keith," Maddox said. "Help him."

The pilot shoved his pistol through his belt and walked in front of Riker. The sergeant shouted in surprise, pressing his prosthetic arm. It hummed, and from the shoulder, it raised threateningly as Riker remained seated. The other arm moved. Riker grabbed a cloth and put it before his mouth.

"Walk around him please," Maddox told the women. "Keith. Back away. The sergeant doesn't remember who you are."

Dana and Meta complied until they walked before an even more astonished Sergeant Riker.

"Sit," Maddox told them.

Meta and Dana did. Maddox didn't think they would try anything now. They were too interested in getting off Loki Prime. Still, it paid to be cautious.

160

"Sergeant," Maddox said in a commanding voice.

Riker's head swayed. He kept his mouth covered, and the rag was red. The poor man's real eye was horribly red-rimmed and glazed. He must be running a high fever.

"It's Captain Maddox," Maddox told him.

"I know who you are, sir," Riker said in a wheezing voice.

"You found your arm, I see."

"Yes, sir, and I got it working. Who are these, these—" He began hacking, sounding wretched. He had to bend over and finally wheezed air down.

"It's no use for him," Dana said. "You need to—" She sliced a finger across her throat. "The swamp spores are deadly. They can spread fast."

"Ha-ha," Riker laughed drunkenly, staring at her. "Cunning witch, aren't you? Old Sergeant Riker isn't going to lie down to death so easily as that, though. Captain Maddox may be overly ambitious, but the lad needs a steadying hand like mind. He gets carried away otherwise. No, I'm not quits just like that. So, you can stop scheming. The young captain will see through your cunning, you can count on that."

"Never mind her, Sergeant," Maddox said. "Who took the flitter? Why didn't they shoot you?"

"Me?" Riker asked, sounding indignant. "Why not shoot me? Oh, no, sir," he said. "I woke up, I did. I took my arm and crawled out of the flitter. I hid because I heard them coming. I saw him too."

"Saw who?" Maddox asked.

"The golden-skinned killer, sir," Riker said. "He had people hooked up like oxen. A woman was with him. She had an assault rifle. They forced the others to lift the flitter onto the wagon. It was a big old cart, sir. I couldn't believe they lifted the flitter. It ain't light, you know?"

"Strange," Maddox said.

"Then I noticed their eyes, sir," Riker said. "The ones hooked to the cart like oxen. They looked drugged. Some of them cried out as they lifted the flitter. I think some of their muscles tore, or shoulders popped out of their sockets. The others kept right on lifting your flyer onto the cart. I wondered if they had super-strength."

161

"Or a New Man drug to give them such strength," Maddox said. "Hysterical strength, I believe it's called. I wonder if that's part of their secret."

"Sir?" Riker asked.

"Never mind," Maddox said. "What else? Do you have anything else to report?"

"I do indeed, sir. Old Sergeant Riker has been paying attention to your sly ways. I thought to myself, 'What would that young hothead do in a situation like mine?' Then it came to me, sir. I knew exactly what to do, and I did it on the spot."

"Do you care to tell me what that was?" Maddox asked.

Riker blinked his red eye, and he started coughing. Finally, after a twenty-second bout, he wheezed down air like a dying man.

"Sir," the sergeant said, "before the others reached the flitter I called upstairs."

"You used the flyer's radio?" Maddox asked.

"I did, sir."

Maddox went cold inside. Had Riker called the destroyer or the scout? "Who did you speak to?" he asked.

"Some pretty girl, sir. She sounded worried, though. She asked about you."

"Do you recall her name?"

"She wouldn't give it to me. Said something about the enemy able to hear over the radio, she did. And, sir, she's coming down to get us. She said regulations demanded she ignore your original orders in order to rescue the landing party."

Maddox had no doubt then. Lieutenant Noonan was going to bring the scout down into the prison planet's atmosphere. Perhaps she was already on her way. If Riker had used the flitter's radio, Valerie would likely home in on it. That meant she was flying down to the New Man, because he now had the flyer.

"How long ago did you send the message?" Maddox asked.

"It's hard for me to tell, sir. Some time ago."

Maddox's eyes widened. "She could be here right now." He took out his comm-unit.

"If your sergeant used the radio," Dana said. "It's possible the destroyer intercepted the signal."

Maddox nodded. "Come in, Lieutenant Noonan. This is Captain Maddox. Do you hear me? Come in, Lieutenant."

162

He feared jamming. If the enemy jammed, it would be clear the New Man understood that the scout descended. Maddox tried to fit the various pieces together, the *Saint Petersburg*, the New Man, the orbital missiles—

Valerie must have used my security code on the orbitals if she's taking the scout to the surface. It's a good thing I gave it to her. Otherwise, the orbitals would shoot her down. A new thought struck and Maddox wanted to curse. *The New Man has my flitter. Its computer has my security code embedded in it.*

His comm-unit came alive. "Come in, Captain Maddox, this is Lieutenant Noonan speaking."

Despite the burst of joy in his chest at hearing her voice, Maddox wondered if it was really her. What if the destroyer was homing in on his comm-signal? The heavy cloud cover meant the *Saint Petersburg* couldn't beam him. Yet they could launch missiles just as easily as the orbitals had done.

"Captain?" she said. "Are you there?"

"Who led the raid into the Odin System?" he asked.

"Sir?"

"Don't think," Maddox told her. "Just tell me."

"Do you mean Admiral von Gunther, sir?" she asked.

"Exactly," Maddox said.

"I don't see why that has any bearing—"

"Why shouldn't I punch an officer whenever I desire to do so?"

"What?" Valerie asked.

"Is there a reason I shouldn't do that?"

"Do you mean regulation—?"

Relief washed through Maddox. Without a doubt, he spoke to the real Valerie Noonan.

"Home in on this comm-signal, Lieutenant," Maddox said. "The enemy has captured the flitter, so you mustn't use its coordinates. In fact, I want you to be ready to obliterate anything that isn't me."

"Sir?" she asked.

"How close are you to the surface?"

"Less than two minutes, sir," she said.

Maddox glanced right and left to see if the scout could land here. Yes, this could work. He knew boarding *Geronimo* was far from victory, but it would be a good start to leaving the Loki System. Should he try to find the flitter afterward, destroying it to obliterate its onboard computer? Likely, they had no time for such ventures. The *Saint Petersburg* in orbit changed all the equations. How long would it take the enemy to try the flitter's computer, to find the security clearance that would allow landing craft to ignore the orbital platforms? Given the New Man on their side—they probably already knew about the code.

Leaving the comm-unit on for Valerie, Maddox faced Dana Rich. "Listen to me, Doctor. We're about to leave Loki Prime."

"Meta goes with me," Dana said.

Maddox's gaze flickered to the cavewoman. With her superior strength, Meta could be a problem aboard ship. He wasn't sure he could take that risk.

"She's from the Rouen Colony," Dana said. "They're miners, and they're a clever bunch. Meta is an engineer. She can fix anything you give her."

"Fine," Maddox said, even as he still considered his options.

"Another thing—" Dana said.

"Shut up and listen," Maddox told her. "Once we're aboard, you're going to have to figure out a way to hack into a space beacon."

"Do you have any idea what you're asking?"

"I do indeed, Doctor. You're a computer genius, a hacker and a tech thief. This is your area of specialty."

Dana's dark eyes seemed to glow with resentment. Even so, she gave a curt nod.

"Another thing," Maddox said. "On the ship, you'll both wear security anklets. It will be on a probationary basis until I can trust you."

"I see the ship!" Keith shouted, pointing past the tallest tree.

Before Maddox could look, his comm-unit beeped a warning. Lifting it to his mouth, he asked, "Lieutenant?"

"There are people coming your way," Valerie said, "a lot of them."

"Right," Maddox said. "I want you to land…one hundred meters from my position. Crush whatever you have too to get down."

"Those are some big trees, sir."

"You can squeeze in," he said.

"Those people I talked about," Valerie said, "they're coming fast, sir."

164

"Use the cannons on them, Lieutenant. The weapons are there for a reason."

"Roger, sir," Valerie said, sounding grim.

As a shadow passed overhead, Maddox looked up at the scout. He'd never seen anything so beautiful. They were actually going to leave Loki Prime.

The antigravity pods hummed. Then the twin cannons spat shells. Explosions, crashing trees and screams told Maddox how near the mob was—almost on top of them. He was thankful for the thick foliage slowing the mob. Seconds later, the cannon firing stopped, and the scout came down.

"You," Maddox said, pointing his gun at Meta. "Help the sergeant."

Splintering sounds and a thud shook the ground. A hatch opened. The comm-unit squawked, and Lieutenant Noonan said, "I'm down, sir. Let's go."

Maddox needed no more urging than that.

-21-

The first people broke through foliage as Keith scrambled through a boarding hatch. Meta helped Sergeant Riker, and Dana staggered after them. Maddox brought up the rear.

The Loki Prime criminals shouted for them to stop, like lost souls in Hell screaming for a reprieve. The desperate cries chilled Maddox. He glanced back. Men and women were equally red-faced with their mouths opened as wide as possible. Several aimed flintlocks, firing. Puffs of smoke appeared. Wooden pellets rattled against *Geronimo's* outer skin.

Meta pushed Riker ahead of her, clambering in after him. Dana rushed to the hatch, diving through. Maddox came in next. A pellet followed, ricocheting around the hall but thankfully striking no one.

Maddox would have shut the hatch, but he had other worries.

Meta whirled around with determination etched on her wide face. What she meant to do was anyone's guess. Before she could reach Maddox, Sergeant Riker's bionic arm yanked her back, causing her to stumble.

Under normal circumstances, Maddox might have grinned. The shouting in the distance sounded like those outside Noah's Ark demanding a berth when the rains first began.

"We're in," the captain said over the comm-unit. "Get us out of here, Lieutenant."

Ship engines whined and antigravity pods hummed. With a lurch, *Geronimo* lifted.

"Get on your stomachs!" Maddox shouted, aiming his gun at Meta and indicating Dana with his chin.

166

They hesitated for a half-second. Then, Dana complied and Meta followed suit. Maddox reached out, catching the hatch. The ship was already twenty feet up and climbing. People stared at them, imploring with raised arms. Men and women begged for the ship to return and take them off Loki Prime.

Feeling like a scoundrel but desperately glad to be aboard the scout, Maddox shut the hatch with a *clang*. He turned the wheel and wanted to relax. He couldn't, though. There was too much to do still.

Upon entering the ship, Keith had stumbled away and now brought him security anklets. Maddox programmed each, snapping one on Dana's ankle and another on Meta's. It was a simple system. For now, the bulky anklet would shock the wearer if she approached the control or engine room too closely.

"Ensign," he told Keith. "Go pilot the ship. Have the lieutenant plot a course that will avoid the destroyer. If she doesn't know *Saint Petersburg's* location, tell her to find it in a hurry."

The ace ran down the corridor.

"You," he told Meta, "in there. If you want to, use the shower. Soon enough, we'll run you through medical and rid you of Loki germs."

Meta climbed to her feet and went into the head. Maddox closed the hatch behind her.

"Help him and follow me," he told Dana.

The doctor guided Sergeant Riker to medical. Maddox took him afterward and hooked the sergeant to the robo-doctor.

"You should let me examine him," Dana said.

Maddox looked up. "I didn't realize you were that kind of doctor."

"I'm full of surprises."

Maddox thought about it and nodded.

Dana approached the control panel. She examined the readout, and she tapped in commands. Hypos hissed, dosing the sergeant with antibiotics.

"He's going to be here a few days," Dana said. "Loki organisms are incredibly resistant to treatment."

"Is he all right for the moment?" Maddox asked.

"He should be, although I'd like to check up on him in a half-hour."

167

"We may not have the luxury," Maddox said. "You're coming with me to the control room."

Dana pointed at her anklet.

"I have a temporary override code," he said, tapping it in to his control unit. "There, we're set."

They exited medical and walked down the corridor. Her anklet beeped, flashing a warning red, and she stopped short. Maddox rechecked his unit. He must have been more exhausted than he realized, as he'd made a mistake.

"There," he said. "I fixed it." A green light appeared on her anklet.

Dana gave him an indecipherable glance before opening the hatch. An argument was in progress between Valerie and Keith. The ace sat in the pilot's chair. The lieutenant tapped her instruments, studying data.

"Enough!" Maddox said, entering behind Dana. "What's the problem?"

"*Saint Petersburg* is upstairs above us," Keith said. "Valerie is saying to race around the world down here. I say we lift and go just under the high cloud cover. There's too much air density down here to travel fast enough. That means we'll crawl, and even though the destroyer has to cover more territory, they'll match us."

Inhaling, Valerie likely made ready to explain her view.

"We don't have time," Maddox told the lieutenant. To Keith, he said, "Take us up."

"Sir," Valerie said, sounding indignant.

"Didn't you just hear me?" Maddox asked her. "We don't have time for discussions. You," he told Dana, "go there." He indicated his regular spot. "That's where you're going to do your magic."

The doctor sat down and began to familiarize herself with the controls.

Maddox wanted to slide down onto his butt and close his eyes. Now was the time to concentrate, though. Clearly, he faced the most dangerous opponent of his life, the New Man.

"Here's the situation," Maddox told Valerie. "At least two New Men are down on the surface. One's dead. I believe they came down from the *Saint Petersburg*."

"What?" the lieutenant asked. "That's incredible. You can't be serious."

"You must have monitored an orbital firing two missiles," Maddox said.

Lieutenant Noonan nodded.

"The missiles struck a Star Watch shuttle on the ground," Maddox said. "The personnel tortured criminals to find her," he said, jerking a thumb at Dana. "The New Men were on the *Saint Petersburg*. What that means is that we have to win this little game of cat and mouse with the destroyer. I'm betting the New Man on the surface has found my clearance code in the flitter. That means they can mask themselves from the orbitals just as we're doing. That's good news for them and us."

"I don't see how it's good for us," Valerie said.

"Don't you see?" Maddox asked. "The *Saint Petersburg* will likely send another shuttle down to pick up the New Man. That will allow us time to flee."

"Even if that's true," Valerie said, "don't you think the monitor's crew knows something here is wrong?"

"Forget about them for now," Maddox said. "They're far away at the chthonian planet. Do you have a fix on the *Saint Petersburg*?"

"Yes," Valerie said.

"Are we cloaked?" Maddox asked.

"No, sir," Valerie said. "The cloak isn't any good in an atmosphere. The destroyer must know where we are."

"Compared to us," Dana said, speaking up, "the destroyer has the high ground. They'll just shoot us down."

"Yes," Maddox said, sarcastically. "You make a brilliant point. But I want you to concentrate on the space-beacon hacking. Let us handle this end."

"She's Doctor Dana Rich?" Valerie asked.

"Correct," Maddox said.

"I'm glad to make your acquaintance," Valerie said. "I'm—"

"Stow the welcoming committee routine," Maddox shouted. "Fixate on the destroyer and how to outmaneuver it."

"Do you charm everyone, mister?" Dana asked him.

Maddox glowered at her. Doctor Rich turned back to the instrument panel.

The scout rose rapidly as the planetary surface receded. Soon the jungle trees merged back into a vast green carpet. It was impossible to tell the mountain peaks: the abode to human bacterium living on the spore-infested nodes of existence.

The thought once again caused Maddox to feel the intense relief from escaping the jungle world and its ruthless germs. No doubt, once this was all over, Star Watch Intelligence would demand a detailed report on life on Loki Prime. If people wanted criminals to suffer for their crimes, the judicial arm had picked the perfect planet for it.

"Sir," Valerie said. "A destroyer shuttle is dropping to the surface."

"This is it," Maddox said. "My guess is the destroyer will wait to pick up the New Man and my flitter. It's our chance to make a run into space away from the *Saint Petersburg*."

"What if you're wrong?" Dana asked. "Why don't they have the shuttle pick up the New Man and wait in orbit? The destroyer can hunt us down and come back for it later."

"No," Maddox said. "Lieutenant Noonan made an excellent point a few minute ago. It's possible the SWS monitor at the Class 1 tramline entrance will have detected the shuttles. If not, the Star Watch commander out there is sure to detect the missiles or beams."

"What beams?" Dana asked.

"The ones the destroyer will use on us to obliterate our scout. If *Saint Petersburg* shows its attacking someone on Loki Prime, the monitor will have to investigate. That means the destroyer will have to flee the system. Despite their superiority at tactics, even a New Man-captained destroyer can't beat an SWS monitor. What that means is the destroyer will first have to pick up the shuttle before it chases us, because if they want to escape the star system, they won't have time later to come back to pick up the shuttle and the stranded New Man."

"Sounding confident about a thing doesn't make it true," Dana said. "You're guessing, and you could be wrong."

"Fair enough," Maddox said. "I've noted your displeasure with my decision." He turned to Valerie. "Show me the destroyer's position relative to us."

The lieutenant put it on her screen. The destroyer paced them overhead. *Saint Petersburg* had come down to Low Loki Orbit.

"Let's open it up," Maddox told Ensign Maker. "We need velocity."

170

"The atmosphere will make it difficult for us, Captain," Keith said.

"I know," Maddox said. "It's going to get hot in here. Unfortunately, I don't see any other way to do this."

"Aye-aye, Captain," Keith said, who began to tap his panel.

The minutes passed as Ensign Maker increased velocity. They reached Mach 10, 11, 12. Soon, they flew at Mach 18. It wouldn't take much longer to reach escape velocity. The ship's air-conditioning systems already hummed. The vessel shook as air turbulence struck it.

"Captain, a missile is heading down at us from the *Saint Petersburg*. Correction," Valerie said, "two missiles."

"Slave the combat equipment to me, love," Keith said. "I know exactly what to do."

Valerie glanced at Maddox.

"Do it," the captain said.

"We don't want to launch chaff right away," Keith said. "This is a heat-seeking missile, but I expect radar lock-on from the *Saint Petersburg*. They should be able to guide the missile to us. We'll make them think we're doing something different than what we're really going to do."

"What are we doing?" Valerie asked.

"Putting your life into my hands," Keith said. "It isn't misplaced."

Several minutes passed.

"The missiles are closing fast," Valerie shouted. "They're Talos Seven class, variant E 3."

"This is perfect," Keith said. He slapped a control. "Grab your seats ladies, and gentlemen, sir."

Maddox watched the lieutenant's screen. Chaff flittered out from the rear of the scout. Then, *Geronimo* swiveled, turning one hundred and eighty degrees so they faced the approaching missiles. The ship began to buck and wave as it flew backward.

"Couldn't do this without the antigravity pods," Keith muttered. "Hang on, love."

Despite the missiles' speed, they swerved around the chaff. It seemed as if the ace had used the silvery particles as a make-shift shield.

Clever, Maddox thought.

171

"Now I have you," Keith muttered. He pressed the trigger controls. Shells sped at the two bogeys. One Talos Seven variant E-3 missile disintegrated in midair. A second later, the other exploded, making a black cloud in the air.

"This will get rough!" Keith shouted.

The scout swiveled again, facing forward, and the missile's air concussion struck the craft. The control room tipped to the side as the scout descended.

"Come on, lass, dance for your daddy-boy." The ace's fingers roved over his controls as everything shook.

Maddox had to clench his jaws to stop his teeth from rattling against each other.

Incredibly, *Geronimo* straightened and the shaking stopped. The scout soon rose to its former height.

Ensign Maker slapped his chest, hooting with delight. "I own you, you crawly mothers. I'm the king of the hill."

Silently, Maddox agreed with the pilot's assessment. The man knew his trade.

As *Geronimo* continued its way around the world, Doctor Rich worked feverishly at her controls. "I never thought I'd get to do this again," she said in a voice choked with emotion.

The control room was meant for three. With four, it was crowded. So Maddox stood near the hatch, grabbing it during the violent maneuvering. "It's time," he said. "Lieutenant, hail *Archangel*."

"We'll never get through the space beacons if we do that," Valerie told him.

"I said hail them," Maddox said. "That doesn't mean I plan to speak with anyone."

"Sir?" asked Valerie.

Dana looked up from her panel, facing him. "You think there are more New Men aboard the destroyer?"

"Would the New Man commander go down to Loki Prime's surface if he didn't have backup on the destroyer?" Maddox asked.

"If I were the destroyer's commander," Dana said, "I wouldn't go onto Loki Prime under any conditions."

"You also don't believe you can do anything you want," Maddox said. "I believe they do. Anyway, that two New Men went down to

172

the surface indicates to me that more stayed up with the *Saint Petersburg*."

"Why would that matter to us so that we're now hailing *Archangel*?" Valerie asked.

"It isn't always what we do that matters," Maddox told the lieutenant. "Sometimes what counts is what the enemy *thinks* we're doing. Of course, as Doctor Rich has implied, I'm predicating this on the belief that there are New Men aboard *Saint Petersburg*."

"Sir," Valerie said. "*Archangel* acknowledges our signal."

"Send them a random message," Maddox said. "Use nonsense words."

Lieutenant Noonan gave him a blank look.

"Recite an old nursery rhythm," Maddox said. "We know it's nonsense, but maybe the New Men aboard *Saint Petersburg* will believe it's a clever code. I'm sure they're monitoring our radio. They won't be able to crack our meaningless message—what they think is a cryptogram—and that might trouble them enough into making a wrong choice."

Doctor Rich appeared thoughtful as she studied Maddox. Finally, she said, "You're attempting to use their intelligence against them. You're a subtle man, Captain."

"Don't sing my praises yet," Maddox said. "Wait until we've made it."

Thirty seconds passed, a minute. The scout continued to shiver as the engines complained.

"The turbulence is stressing the ship's structures, sir," Keith said. "I recommend—"

"Sir!" Valerie shouted. "The destroyer has slowed down. It appears to be making a turn."

"Can you spy the lifting shuttle?" Maddox asked.

"Negative," Valerie said. "It's over the horizon in relation to us."

"Pour it on, Ensign," Maddox said. "Push it. This is our sole opportunity to break out into space."

"You guessed right, sir," Valerie said. "You outfoxed the destroyer's commander."

"We're prolonging our existence," Maddox said. "That means we get to play phase two." He glanced at the lieutenant's board. The destroyer was completing the turn. The commander up there must have decided to pick up the shuttle as fast as he could. Then he

173

would use the *Saint Petersburg's* speed to try to catch the scout. Of that, Maddox had little doubt.

Thirty more seconds passed.

"Now," Maddox said. "Take us through the clouds and head for space, Ensign."

"Aye-aye, Captain, sir," Keith said. "I'm going to show these blimey crawlies what we can do."

***

Geronimo reached space at a calculated spot. They were in line-of-sight of *Archangel*, which maintained its distant post near the Class 1 tramline jump-point entrance and the chthonian planet. Loki Prime now shielded them from the destroyer, although that wouldn't last for long. The bulkheads no longer shuddered, and the scout seemed unhurt from its time in the atmosphere.

"We have clear running ahead of us," Keith said.

"Engage the cloaking device," Maddox said.

Valerie complied, although she said, "It won't work at peak efficiency while the engines are pouring exhaust from our port."

"The cloak will still make it harder for *Archangel* to tell what we are," Maddox said. "We're not going to give them long to see us, though. Set a course for the Class 3 tramline, Lieutenant. Ensign, we're going to use the Loki Prime. Take us behind it in relation to *Archangel*."

"Won't that bring us into a line-of-sight with *Saint Petersburg*?" Valerie asked.

"It will," Maddox said. "How much battery charge do we have?"

"Fifteen percent," Valerie said. "The batteries began charging again when I turned on the engines. But—"

"Fifteen percent is less than I like," Maddox said, interrupting her. "Ensign, give us full power. Open it up. Then, at my command, you will cut power and go to batteries to energize the cloaking device."

"We can use the cloak with the fusion engines powering them," Valerie said. "It's the hot exhaust out of the port that will give us away."

"This close to the destroyer," Maddox said, "we'll stick to battery power. They might be able to detect the fusion engines."

"We'll barely be crawling through space," Valerie pointed out.

174

"Yes, while cloaked," Maddox said, "and hidden from *Archangel* and *Saint Petersburg* both."

"That will allow the destroyer to tell the monitor's commander whatever he wants," Valerie said.

"Exactly," Maddox said. "We want a quiet playing field. If two of us try to tell the monitor our varying stories, *Archangel's* commander might put the drone field onto combat alert."

"He might do it anyway," Valerie said. "In fact, I'd say that's his most probable course."

Maddox took his time answering. His lungs felt bubbly, which he took to mean the lowlander spores continued to mutate. His immune system was likely stronger than Keith's or the sergeant's, but it wasn't tougher than the planet's bacterium. Soon, now, he'd have to go through the robo-doctor.

Finally, he said, "All life is a risk, Lieutenant. We have to play the hand we're dealt, not the one we'd like."

The engines began to strain as they headed out of Low Loki Prime Orbit at full throttle. Keith had already aimed the ship toward the distant Class 3 tramline.

"Now," Maddox ordered. "Cut the engines and coast."

Using Loki Prime as a shield, they hid from the distant monitor. The Star Watch commander out there might link to the space beacons, but at this point, it was unlikely the scout would show on their sensors either. As he'd said, all life was a risk.

With passive sensors, the lieutenant's screen showed the shuttle entering the destroyer's docking bay.

"In less than twenty-one hours," Valerie said, "the one satellite-beacon is going to make its report to the monitor. Then it won't matter what the destroyer has explained to *Archangel's* commander."

Maddox heard the lieutenant, and he silently agreed with her. Heaviness pulled at his eyelids. He forced them wider. He had plenty to do still. For one thing, he needed to get Meta settled. Then, he had to decide how he was going to convince Doctor Rich to join the expedition to the finish.

-22-

Sometime later, Meta stretched out on a bunk staring up at a bulkhead. It had been a long time since she'd been able to lie down without worrying about Temple Savants sneaking up on her to attempt rape or worse. That had been the official name of their tribe.

Life on Loki Prime had been a nightmare, one she'd endured for four awful years. She could still hardly believe this was happening.

It had been several hours since she'd boarded the SWS Scout *Geronimo*. Captain Maddox had installed her in these quarters, telling her the anklet would give her increasingly stronger shocks if she set foot outside the compartment. He had changed the rules of his agreement, confining her here. Meta had expected nothing less.

Even so, the man kept surprising her. Few people outside of the Rouen Colony had ever bested her in hand-to-hand combat. Dana had twisted the truth when she'd told Maddox that she—Meta—was an engineer. Everyone in the Rouen Colony was an engineer, just as, in the preindustrial past, most people had been farmers.

Meta's real specialty was fighting—not as a soldier, but as a bodyguard, enforcement agent and assassin. She had trained many years for her attempt against Baron Chabot. He'd owned the contract to the Rouen Colony.

The heavy G mining world could have doubled as a prison planet. During her time there, indentured colonists had slaved eighteen-hour shifts running the diggers. Because of the grueling gravity, the work wore people down at astonishing rates. The history of her planet and people went back to Baron Chabot's grandmother. To aid in producing greater quotas of ore, the grandmother had

176

decided on human modifications: making stronger workers through genetic alterations for endurance under extreme conditions.

The Rouen Colony was located in an independent star system. Such genetic alteration was against the laws of the Windsor League and the Commonwealth. In any case, Meta had trained in secret. The mine coordinator had believed she had a greater chance of success than others would due to her beauty.

From her childhood on, Meta had drilled in clandestine affairs. The endless memory courses, weapons training, stealth, security procedures, she knew it all. Finally, when she'd turned eighteen, Meta had boarded a packet to the baron's regular gravity world. It had taken her three humiliating years before she gained access to his castle as a maid. Then one night, Meta had slipped into the baron's quarters and throttled him to death in his bed. His eyes had opened long enough to gape at her for his final seconds of life.

Instead of fierce elation at his inert form, she'd felt sick at her deed. It had been her first kill. Staggering through the empty, enemy halls, she had found herself in the kitchens. At that point, she realized many security cameras had recorded her passage. Escaping the baron's planet had proved hard. Worse, the political assassination failed to produce the desired effect. Instead of freeing the people of the Rouen Colony, the baron's heir had passed stricter laws—and he'd placed a fantastic reward on Meta's head.

Pirates hijacked the liner where she'd stowed away. They had uncovered her presence, and it would have been deadly for her to remain on the liner once the pirates left. It had been one of the baron's luxury cruisers. So, she joined the pirates long enough for them to enter a Commonwealth system, where a Star Watch patrol captured the ship.

The authorities sentenced her to Loki Prime along with the rest of the pirate crew. Temple Savants reached her drop pod before anyone else did. The first thug tried to throw her down to start a rape train. He was the second person she killed. The Temple Savant boss had been impressed. Meta had slain the rapist with a single punch to the head. The boss made her his bodyguard and lover. The man had disgusted her, but better to deal with one than fifty at a time.

A year ago, Doctor Dana Rich landed on Loki Prime, and things began to change soon thereafter. Dana had taught the Temple Savants things, improved on their weapons and compound defenses.

177

Then, she poisoned the boss one night. Meta was the only one who knew. Dana took the pig's place. She made Meta her bodyguard, and that's all she had to do.

Captain Maddox was right about one thing. Everyone on Loki Prime dreamed of getting off. It comprised a good third of their conversations and plans. The hard truth that all of them knew was that none of them would ever leave the horror world.

As she stretched out on the bunk, Meta grinned with delight. Her skin was clean and felt fresh for the first time in years. Maddox had let the medical station inject her with antibiotics. Soon, the germs and spores crawling inside her would be dead, and she would feel like her old self again. She didn't think Maddox would be able to outfight her then, not as he had on the planet.

Meta's grin widened. She'd seen him eyeing her. Oh yes, she knew that look. Her teachers had taught her to use such things to her advantage. She had been a pirate once before—

No, forget about piracy. This time, once I own the scout, I'll go legitimate. Maybe I'll head to a Windsor League planet, start my own security agency.

Putting her hands behind her head, Meta wondered if Captain Maddox had spoken the truth about the New Men. The two golden-skinned men walking off the shuttle—

Thinking about what had happened on the surface, she shuddered.

Meta had never met people like them. Their eyes had been harder than stone. Handsome like devils, they had remorseless attitudes. Maddox had guessed right about them. The Star Watch Intelligence captain seemed to do that a lot. The golden-skinned men had gathered the nearest Temple Savants. One fool tried to knife the shuttle leader. The golden-skinned man had caught his wrist and broken it easily. Then, he'd grabbed the offender's throat and squeezed, crackling the neck bones as the knifeman gurgled to his death.

Five Temple Savants had bellowed with outrage, charging. The second New Man had drawn a gun faster than Maddox could have done. Before anyone realized it, five Temple Savants lay dead on the ground with smoking holes in their foreheads.

"You act like beasts," one of the New Men said. "So we will treat you as beasts."

178

The torturing began soon thereafter. If the orbital missiles hadn't struck, Meta was certain the golden-skinned devils would have slaughtered the entire tribe.

Had more of their kind truly invaded the Oikumene? Were the New Men as unstoppable as Maddox said? By her actions, Dana didn't believe it. Meta also knew that Dana Rich considered herself the smartest person alive. For over a year, Meta had seen the truth of that. She wondered if Captain Maddox realized just whom he'd taken aboard his scout.

There came a rap at the hatch.

Meta sat upright. "Wait," she said. "Let me get dressed."

"I'll give you thirty seconds," Maddox said.

Meta had shed the fur bikini some time ago, dropping the pieces into a disposal unit. She now put on a bra and panties, pulled on pants and buttoned a blouse. It was a Star Watch uniform for a rating. On impulse, she pulled on socks and slipped her feet into shoes. Lastly, she checked herself before a mirror. Hmm, she pulled out a string and let her long dark hair cascade to her shoulders. Picking up a brush, she combed her hair.

"Meta?" Maddox called. "Are you presentable?"

She considered jumping him when he entered, knocking him out. But why make the attempt so soon? It would be better to regain her full health before striking. Until then, she would lull the man. Despite his cunning, that should be easy enough. He was young, and she had seen the way he looked at her when he thought she wouldn't notice.

Sitting on the edge of her cot, she said, "Enter."

The hatch opened and Maddox ducked in. He had his gun hand on the butt of his weapon. The pistol was in its holster. When he saw her on the bunk, he removed his hand and snapped the flap shut.

"It looks as if you've made the adjustment to ship life easily enough," he said.

"What's the situation?" Meta asked. "Has Dana cracked into the space beacon's software?"

"Not yet," he said.

"How long do I have to wear this?" she asked, pointing at the anklet.

"That depends," he said.

Meta raised an eyebrow, and she forced herself to smile at him.

Maddox smiled back.

Men were so simple. Her teachers had taught her that.

"Meta, I'll get straight to the point. I'd like your impressions about the New Men."

His direction surprised her. "I'm not sure I know what you mean?" she said.

"You watched them in person. You observed the way they moved and talked. What did you think about them?"

Meta hadn't expected this. Usually, a man would strike up a casual conversation, trying to get to know her so he could make his moves. Maddox struck her as all business. Did he think she didn't know what he thought about her in his heart?

"I want your impressions because the Star Watch has scant information about the New Men," Maddox explained. "The invaders seem to have penetrated deep into the Commonwealth government, and yet we've never caught one of their operatives."

"Too bad you couldn't capture the destroyer then. It's full of people who have fraternized with New Men."

I doubt that's the case," Maddox said. "I suspect the invaders have compartmentalized life aboard the destroyer. But that's neither here nor there. What were your impressions about them?"

If this is what it took to lull the captain, so be it. "The New Men are decisive," Meta said. "They act without hesitation, as if they know exactly what they're doing at all times. A Temple Savant tried to assassinate one."

"Who?" Maddox asked.

She explained the tribal name and told him what had happened upon the shuttle's landing. Since Maddox kept asking, she told him about the five-person charge and execution by the other New Man, and she detailed how the invader had called them "beasts."

"Interesting and telling about their attitude concerning regular people," Maddox said. "Now give me your take."

"Could you be more specific?" Meta asked.

"You've given me raw data. I want your assessment of them. What do you feel here?" Maddox asked, tapping his chest.

"Haven't thought too about it much," she admitted. Unconsciously sticking out her lower lip, Meta began to ponder the captain's question. She shrugged shortly. "They're tough, really tough, and they struck me as men who will do anything to succeed.

A lot of people think they have what it takes to win." She shook her head. "Most people are wrong. They have scruples. Things they would never do. Most people get scared too. Those two—they didn't have any problem torturing, killing, whatever they needed. Yes. Now that I'm thinking about it, they treated us as something lower. They acted superior—arrogantly, but without the stupidity most arrogant people have."

"You've had a lot of contact with arrogant people?" Maddox asked.

"You mean besides on Loki Prime?" she asked.

Maddox nodded.

"You'd better believe it. Starting with the foremen on the Rouen Colony—" Meta stopped talking. How much should she give away concerning her past? Despite his youth, the captain was clever. He didn't need to know too much about her.

"You were saying?" Maddox prodded.

Meta shrugged.

Maddox seemed to shift tactics. It was a subtle thing, but observable to with someone of her training.

"Aren't you grateful that I took you off Loki Prime?" he asked.

"Of course I am." She smiled again to show him just how grateful.

"Then help me with this. I'm trying to stop the worst menace to ever hit the Commonwealth."

"So you keep telling us."

"Why would I lie to you?" Maddox asked.

"Since I know so little about you," she said, "I have no idea. I can think of plenty of reasons, though."

"Don't you trust your instincts?" Maddox asked.

Meta most certainly did. She had become an excellent judge of character. In her line of work, it had been critical. She nodded.

"What do your instincts tell you about me?" Maddox asked.

She frowned, wondering where the man was trying to take this.

Maddox crossed his arms, leaning against a bulkhead, waiting.

"You're sure of yourself," Meta said. "Is that what you want to hear?" All men were egotists, so she knew that he did.

He said nothing, just grinned at her.

That upset her enough that she wanted to give him a rude gesture and tell him a Rouen Colony curse. Instead, she studied the lean man. There couldn't be an ounce of fat on his frame. Did he have denser muscles just as she did? How could he have beaten her in hand-to-hand combat before? She remembered his strength but more his speed. Some of his determination leaked through his eyes, she noticed. This one would go through a force screen by sheer willpower to get to his prize. She reconsidered his actions on Loki Prime. He had faced overwhelming obstacles and had overcome them all.

"You have a purpose," she said. "No. You're driven." Her eyebrows rose in surprise. "Something haunts you."

The grin remained, but the force drained from it. For a moment, Maddox seemed uncomfortable. Then the discomfort vanished, as if rejected by the owner.

"Why are you asking me about yourself?" she said.

"You've had the rare privilege of meeting the New Men and surviving to tell of it. Lieutenant Noonan did likewise, facing them as part of a Star Watch battle group. Three enemy cruisers annihilated the substantially larger Star Watch force."

"Why should I care?" Meta asked.

"What if the New Man spoke truthfully down there?" Maddox said. "What if they think of regular humans as beasts? Not only that, but they have the firepower to take us down and then wipe us out as a species."

"Why would they 'wipe us out?' What's their gain in that?"

"Don't know," Maddox said. "I simply find it curious that once the New Men conquer a star system, no one hears anything from the captured planets again. What are the invaders doing to the population that they want to hide?"

"You think these New Men are *exterminating* the populations?" Meta asked.

"I think these highly dangerous invaders have far too many advantages over my tribe—the Star Watch. I think we need an equalizer, especially if my guesses about them are correct. Think about that for a minute. If I'm right about them, that could impact you personally much sooner than you'd like."

"You're trying to scare me," Meta said. "Okay, I'm shaking. So, why don't you get to your point?"

"You don't scare easily, and that might be bad for you."

"I don't know how," Meta said.

"Suppose you're getting ready to drink a cup of poison," Maddox said, "and someone tells you about it. All you do is shrug. You're not afraid of poison. Well, after drinking the cup, you die. In that instance, it would have been wise to be frightened of the cup."

"I already told you I was scared."

"Here's my point. We need your strength, Meta, your mechanical skills. I want you to join us of your own free will and convince Doctor Rich to do the same thing."

"To find this ancient starship you talked about?" she asked.

"Exactly," he said. "I'm not hiding my intentions."

Really? Then down there on the planet why did you look at me the way you did? Yes, you are *hiding* some *of your intentions, Captain.*

"I haven't convinced you," he said. "Therefore, you should think about this: You owe me your life, Meta."

She bristled.

"I took you off Loki Prime," he said.

"As part of our deal," she said. "You got off too."

"It doesn't matter why I did it. No one was ever going to free you from a lifetime of horror down there. I did. Me, gallant Captain Maddox. Now, you need to pay me back by helping this mission succeed."

She scowled. Did he really only want her help getting the lost ship?

"Think about it," he said. "You have some free time in here, I mean. Use it wisely." With that, Maddox straightened and took his leave.

After the hatch shut, Meta stared at it. Finally, she lay back down. As the man said, she had some serious thinking to do.

-23-

Captain Maddox raised his head, realizing his chin had been resting on his chest. He must have fallen asleep as he sat in the pilot's chair. Then, he recalled why he'd opened his eyes. Doctor Rich had spoken elatedly.

He swiveled around on his seat. Dana and he were the only ones in the control room. Why hadn't she tried for his gun, seeing as he'd fallen asleep? There were two possibilities. The first, she didn't think he really slept, or she feared he'd wake up before she could subdue him. The second, she had become so engrossed in her work that she hadn't noticed him sleeping. He was more inclined toward the second view.

"What is it?" Maddox asked.

Dana didn't respond. She sat at her station, her fingers flying over the controls. She chortled quietly, almost evilly, to herself.

Maddox stood, approaching her. Still, she didn't notice him. He had no idea what the screen meant. Lines of code flashed before his eyes.

"Doctor!" he said.

Her shoulders stiffened. She looked up and then back at him.

"What's happening?" he asked.

"Exactly what you asked for," she said. "I'm inside the satellite-beacon's master menu. I've just shut down its comm-links."

Maddox checked a chronometer. In twelve hours, the beacon would have informed the monitor. Dana had worked even faster than he'd expected.

"You did it then?" he asked.

184

She turned back to her panel and continued to tap.

"What are you doing?" he asked.

"I'm guessing you're going to want the beacon to fire up some drones for us," Dana said. "We need to knock out the destroyer, right?"

Maddox stepped to Lieutenant Noonan's station. Valerie was getting some well-deserved rest. At speed, the destroyer was accelerating toward the system's gas giant in its Jupiter-like orbit. That was nearly eight hundred thousand kilometers away. The Class 3 Laumer-Point was near the gas giant. No doubt, the destroyer raced there to block their exit from the star system.

There were three jump points in this star system: the Class 1 near the chthonian planet, the rock core orbiting closest to the sun. There was the Class 3 by the distant gas giant. And there was an unstable Laumer-Point situated between Loki Prime and the gas giant, about where the Solar System's astcroid belt would be.

Unstable tramlines were dangerous to use. Sliding down an unstable wormhole was like running between giant, chomping teeth. The tramline could contort, crushing the starship in it. That happened one out of every three to five times, depending on the instability of the tramline. It made using such a route a game of Venusian Roulette.

When the *Saint Petersburg* first accelerated away from Loki Prime toward the outer system, Maddox had finally felt the situation was safe enough to turn the fusion engines back on. They hadn't used the regular thrust, but turned on the gravity wave generator—and began recharging the batteries. Just as before, the gravity waves had shaken *Geronimo* for its short duration, but each time it had given them a little more velocity.

Ensign Maker had complained about the process. The pilot had been right, too. At this rate, it would take the scout weeks of drifting to reach the gas giant and the Class 3 entry point.

In the control room, Maddox grunted.

This time, Dana noticed. "What is it?" she asked.

Pointing at the lieutenant's view screen, Maddox said, "*Archangel* has just begun heavy acceleration away from its position near the chthonian planet."

The massive round starship would take time to build a descent velocity. It was like watching an elephant starting to move, knowing it would trot and then lumber at speed.

Dana got up and checked the screen for herself. The starship had an immensely long exhaust tail, making it easy to spot. She traded glances with Maddox. "Why do you think the monitor is doing that?" she asked.

Maddox checked something on the lieutenant's board. "Hmm, it's like I thought. There's been a lot of radio traffic between the destroyer and the monitor."

"Do you think they've been talking about us?" Dana asked.

"Maybe."

"Maybe *Archangel* is coming to help *Saint Petersburg* search for us," Dana suggested.

"Seems unlikely they'd leave the Class 1 Laumer-Point unguarded," Maddox said. "But let's say it's true. Why haven't the one hundred satellite-beacons gone to high alert? If both the monitor and the destroyer are searching for us, that would be the best move."

Maddox glanced at the screen. One hundred dark, automated satellite-beacons orbited between the chthonian planet and halfway to the gas giant. Maybe a thousand drones orbited in the same zone. The scout passed through a belt of sleeping missiles. At any time, one of them might activate and accelerate at them.

Dana laughed with what sounded like relief.

Maddox frowned at her.

"You're right," Dana said. "That's what the monitor commander would do: put the space beacons onto high alert. Where is *Archangel* headed?"

Maddox fiddled with the board. "Given their present heading, it looks as if they're chasing the *Saint Petersburg*. Seems crazy, though," he said, "the huge monitor will never catch a sleek runner like the destroyer."

Dana clapped her hands together. "The New Men on the destroyer must have overplayed their hand. They made the monitor commander suspicious." She frowned. "That means my computer hacking went for nothing. I've been wasting time."

"You're jumping to conclusions. We don't know what's going on."

186

"Now that I'm in the space beacon," Dana said, "do you want me to—?"

Maddox's instruments blared a warning.

"What is it?" Dana shouted.

With his guts twisting, Maddox told her, "*Archangel* must have just sent a high pulse signal. Satellite- beacons are switching to combat alert."

"So they *are* joining forces against us," Dana said.

"I don't think so."

"But you just told me that's what the monitor commander would do if they leagued together."

"You're right. I said that," Maddox admitted. "But the beacons nearest Loki Prime should have gone onto combat alert then. That was our last known position, right? That's not happening. Instead, the automated satellites nearest the *Saint Petersburg* are switching to a combat setting. Why just there, I wonder?"

"Oh. Yes. That is different."

Maddox checked for further data before glancing at Doctor Rich. "The monitor's commander must have upped the game. I bet he's threatening the destroyer with annihilation from the drone-field."

"That might be less of a threat than you think," Dana said.

"Why? What haven't you told me?"

Her dark eyes become hooded. She seemed to be weighing something in her mind. "I suppose you'll find out sooner or later. The beacons and drones are over fifteen years out of date, at least. I suspect the computer programs are pretty ancient too."

"Okay..." he said.

"Hacking into the beacon was child's play. If I can do it, some genius New Man shouldn't have any problem neutralizing the minefield."

"Maybe," Maddox said. "Old weapons can kill just like new ones. Besides, the fact that the monitor commander is heading for the destroyer shows me the New Men aren't invincible. They can make mistakes. Remember, we beat them on Loki Prime."

"We did not," Dana said. "That's wishful thinking, something I thought you were above. I'll have to reevaluate my opinion about you."

Maddox snorted softly.

Dana turned away from the screen and faced him. "The truth is we barely managed to escape from one New Man and his assault-rifle ally."

"That's what I just said," Maddox told her. "We beat them."

"Beating them means we would have captured the invader for interrogation."

"Wrong," Maddox said. "He attempted to impose his will on us. We thwarted his will and imposed our own."

"You mean your will, which was capturing me."

"Freeing you," Maddox said. "I *freed* you from captivity."

"Mister," Dana asked, "do you take me for an idiot?"

"The opposite," Maddox said. "Your quick suppression of the space beacon proves we need you."

"As I told you," Dana said. "The auto-beacon and its program were old. Your pilot probably could have done it if he put his mind to it." She yawned. "I'm exhausted. I've been working on this ever since we boarded. The stims I took are finally wearing off. I need sleep."

Maddox took out his control unit out. "Very well. I'll escort you to your quarters."

Dana waited a half-beat before nodding. Then she headed for the hatch and Maddox followed.

He knew she plotted against them. It was obvious, and she was cunning, maybe more than he was. How could he convince her to join the mission? Without her knowledge and hacking skills, they were never going to gain entrance into the alien sentinel. There had to be a way to sway her, but he was at a loss as to what it might be.

***

Space battles within a star system's vast expanse were often long-term affairs that went on for days instead of hours. AIs, computers and combat techs measured velocities, acceleration rates, beam ranges, cones of firing probabilities and braking speeds. The situation often became a chess game between professionals. Many times, the losing crew knew hours ahead of time that they were going to die as death remorselessly closed in on them.

As Captain Maddox, the lieutenant and the ensign watched from the control room—with the scout inching toward its Laumer-Point

188

near the gas giant—they had a front row seat to the engagement between the monitor and the destroyer.

Archangel's commander had put the satellite-beacons on high alert. The next step would be targeting the destroyer with the nearest drones. It seemed that *Archangel's* commander would have to know without a doubt that the destroyer had turned rogue before actively trying to annihilate the vessel. That decision wouldn't be made lightly.

Maddox dearly wanted to know what the monitor's commander knew. He would have to break radio silence and come into the open to ask, though. It was very probable the monitor commander would not believe him. The greater mission was too important for Maddox to risk coming out of the dark.

"Why is the destroyer still heading for our jump-point near the gas giant?" Valerie asked. The lieutenant had taken a long-deserved nap and appeared refreshed. "The *Saint Petersburg* can't use that wormhole."

Maddox had been wondering the same thing. Given the monitor's new actions, the destroyer should have already headed for a different Laumer-Point to attempt to escape the star system. He didn't like the mystery.

"What do your sensors show?" Maddox asked.

"Nothing extraordinary," Valerie said. "Ah. The monitor is sending a message to *Saint Petersburg*."

"Isn't there any way we can tap into it?" Keith asked. He'd napped too. It had made his eyes puffier and him crankier.

Neither Maddox nor Valerie answered the ensign.

"Well?" Keith asked. "Can't we listen in?"

"Not unless we want to use active systems," Maddox told him. "That would probably give us away. It's better for us to remain hidden."

"Jolly good," Keith said shortly, in a grumpy voice. He stood. "I'm hungry. Anyone care to join me?"

Maddox's stomach grumbled. He could use a break. Besides, a few minutes away couldn't hurt. "Sure," he said. "Let's go."

They exited the control room and moved down the corridor to the galley, a small area with a table and benches. Maddox picked a freeze-dried packet of tuna salad. Keith picked hamburger patties with broccoli.

They used a microwave to cook each. Halfway through the meal, Valerie spoke through the intercom.

"You ought to get back here, Captain. Things have just turned interesting."

Grabbing the plastic, Maddox hurried to the control room, wolfing down the rest of the tuna salad as he went. He hadn't realized until he started eating just how hungry he'd been.

As he entered the chamber, Valerie said, "*Archangel* turned the satellite-beacons hot. Drones are coming alive out there. They're easy to spot with their exhausts pouring behind them."

Maddox shoveled the last bite into his mouth, tossing the plastic into a disposal unit. As he chewed, he sat down at his station.

"No!" Valerie said, watching her board. "I can't believe this."

"What's happening?" Maddox asked.

"The destroyer—it has sent a message of its own to the space beacons near *Archangel*. It's turned those drones against the monitor. Captain, it looks as if the New Men have hacked the system better than Dana could have done."

Maddox went cold inside, and the tuna salad in his stomach felt as if it turned to lead. Here was another example of the enemy's superiority.

They watched, and the minutes stretched into an hour, then three hours.

The various drones kept accelerating at their targets—it took time to move those distances. Space battles were long-term affairs. Many drones raced at *Archangel*, just as many sped at *Saint Petersburg*. Then drones began to detonate, even though they were far from their respective targets. Soon, everywhere throughout the Loki System, drone warheads bloomed into incandescent brilliance.

"What's going on, love?" Keith asked Valerie.

"If I had to guess," the lieutenant said, "both the monitor and the destroyer have sent self-destruct messages to the drones. They leveled the playing field. They also turned this place into a radioactive wasteland with EMP pulses everywhere."

Maddox sat up. "That's blinding sensors, yes?"

"Of course," Valerie said. "It's difficult to look through nuclear fireballs or the intense radiation they spew in all directions. It's like throwing down a stellar blanket, at least until the radiation dies down."

190

"Ensign," Maddox said. "Get ready to engage the fusion thrusters."

Valerie nodded sagely. "They've given us temporary cover," she said. "For a little while at least, it will be hard to see much of anything. I like your idea, Captain."

"Engage," said Maddox.

Keith tapped the controls, and the *Geronimo* built up velocity.

***

Twenty-four hours later, the situation had drastically changed for the better for *Geronimo*.

"We're getting out of here," Maddox told Valerie and Keith.

He'd let Dana and Meta stew in their respective quarters. They called when they needed to use the facilities. Maddox always stood guard at those times. Sergeant Riker was still in medical. Dana had checked him three different times. Maddox had stood guard then, too.

"Like I told you," Dana had said about Riker, "those Loki germs are tough. It was touch and go there for a while."

"What?" Maddox asked. He hadn't known that.

"I didn't want to tell you. Figured you would think I'm gaming things. Anyway, your man is going to pull through. Leave him here another three days, though."

As Maddox sat in the control room, he grinned as he thought about their situation.

Saint Petersburg moved like a comet for the unstable Laumer-Point. It looked as if the New Man wanted to gamble with a bad wormhole. That was fine with Maddox. *Archangel* headed for exactly the same point. Four heavy missiles lead the way, barreling at extreme velocity for the destroyer.

"Want to place bets if the destroyer makes it or not?" Keith asked.

"Oh," Maddox said. "They'll make it to the Laumer-Point. Whether they survive the jump or not is the question."

"Those missiles say otherwise," Keith told him.

"Seemingly," Maddox said, "seemingly. I think the New Man will have an ace or two to pull out of his sleeve."

Valerie looked up from her instrument panel. She'd been tapping it for some time. "I have news I don't think you're going to like."

Maddox swiveled around to face her.

"The unstable Laumer-Point will bring the *Saint Petersburg* to Sigma Gamma Seven," Valerie said.

Maddox shrugged. "Is that supposed to be significant?"

"I think so," Valerie said. "That's two jumps away from where our Class 3 tramline will bring us."

"We'll be gone from there before they show up," Maddox said.

"Good," she said.

Maddox sat back, thinking about that. Could the New Man over there know what Valerie had just told him about the various routes? Yes, of course, he did. Was the New Man trying to use the *Saint Petersburg's* speed against the *Geronimo*? He would race the destroyer through jump routes, trying to work to the system they would enter from Loki. Hmm…The destroyer *had* beaten them to the Loki System.

"Speed," Maddox muttered. "Ensign, we're going to accelerate."

"That could blow our cloak," Valerie said. "The EMP pulses have long ago faded. We'd be in the open."

"Look at the ranges between us and the two starships," Maddox said, shaking his head. "Their beams can't possibly reach us at these distances. We're hundreds of millions kilometers too far. No missiles will have time to accelerate fast enough before we're gone. If the destroyer is trying to catch us later by speeding to the other Laumer-Points, we need to use speed now and outdistance them."

"I don't like it," Valerie said.

"I'm open to your reasons as to why not," Maddox said.

Lieutenant Noonan looked uncomfortable. "Sir, the New Men outfought von Gunther's battle group in the Pan System."

"The destroyer lacks those advanced weapons."

"I wasn't finished, sir," Valerie said. "They also outthought us. I'm wondering if the New Man is doing that here."

"No," Maddox said. "We outthought him."

"Don't you think he's going to know our reaction to his using the unstable Laumer-Point?"

"He has to use that entry point," Maddox said. "There's no other way for him to escape the monitor."

"Maybe he could outmaneuver the monitor and race to the Class 1 point near the chthonian planet near the star," Keith said, chiming in.

"If that's a wiser choice," Maddox said, "he would already be doing it. No. This time, I think we're granting them too much cunning. Ensign, head for our Laumer-Point at maximum acceleration. We want to leave the Loki System as fast as possible."

Keith glanced at Valerie. Then he said, "Aye-aye, Captain, sir. I'm engaging thrusters—now."

***

The *Saint Petersburg* must have laid invisible mines behind itself as it braked for the unstable Laumer-Point. As the heavy missiles neared, the mines began to detonate, revealing themselves and annihilating two of the monitor's missiles. *Saint Petersburg's* counter-rockets took care of the third missile, while the destroyer's lasers demolished the last one.

"Those are new types of mines I haven't seen before," Valerie said. "I wonder if they're a New Man invention."

The *Geronimo* had accelerated for a time and now braked hard. They neared the Class 3 tramline. The other two spaceships were hundreds of millions of kilometers away.

"That's a good question," Maddox said. Suddenly, a queasy feeling bit into him. "Lieutenant, start searching this area for cloaked mines."

"Sir?" Valerie asked.

"The *Saint Petersburg* spent some time here," Maddox said. "I wondered about that before. Could they have been carefully placing such mines to catch us before we leave?"

For the next twenty minutes, Lieutenant Noonan searched diligently. Finally she announced, "I think we're safe, sir.

It took another half hour until they reached the Laumer-Point.

Maddox opened inter-ship channels. "We did it. We're about to leave the Loki System. Get ready to jump."

Ensign Maker maneuvered the scout for the entry point. "Engaging the Laumer Drive," he said.

A loud whine started, and the Laumer-Point became visible to their instruments. The scout headed for the wormhole.

At the same time, a hidden device flared with high acceleration. Had it detected the Laumer Drive? Had it waited until the last possible moment? Whatever the truth, the device rapidly closed with *Geronimo*.

"Sir," Valerie said, "I'm detecting a fast approaching object."

The object exploded with the same power as the mines that had destroyed several heavy missiles earlier.

The scout buckled as interior lights began to flash. Bulkheads groaned. Then the stricken SWS Scout *Geronimo* entered the Laumer-Point, barreling down the wormhole. It was anyone's guess as to whether the ship would survive the stresses of jump to reach the exit point intact.

-24-

Lieutenant Noonan felt bone tired, worse than any exercise during her Space Academy days. For fifteen hours, she'd worked beside Meta as they attempted to repair damage to the engines in order to make them workable again.

It was worse outside the ship. Ensign Maker knew more about space welding than Maddox would any day. The two wore vacc-suits and magnetic boots, working feverishly.

The hidden mine had nearly destroyed the scout. Upon their exit from the Laumer-Point, the captain had made a fast decision, freeing Meta on a probationary basis. Would he have done the same for Doctor Rich?

Injured in the explosion, Dana was in medical, in a coma, the robo-doctor straining to keep her alive. The mine had changed many things. If they couldn't repair the scout in time, the destroyer might show up and that would be the end of the mission and likely their lives.

None of them believed the unstable wormhole had destroyed the *Saint Petersburg*. They weren't going to get away that easily.

"Hand me the drill," Meta said.

Valerie plucked it off an emergency Velcro-pad. Not only were the engines offline, the antigravity pods refused to function.

The *Geronimo* was a mess. Even so, no one had asked the fundamental question. Did this scrub the mission? Captain Maddox would never agree to that. Valerie had begun to wonder if he was completely...sane wasn't the right word. The man was logical and rational to a fault. Earlier, Meta had said something that *drove* Maddox. Perhaps that was a more accurate description.

Yes, Valerie thought, *he* is *driven. He's compelled to compete against these New Men. Is he wrong to do so? If we fail, what combination of Star Watch ships can defeat the enemy's advanced cruisers?*

The drill *whirred* as Meta took off a plate. The woman from the Rouen Colony worked tirelessly. Meta wasn't only strong; she had stamina. What had really surprised Valerie was that Meta hadn't been interested in studying the tech manuals.

For some time now, Valerie had been worrying about that, debating with herself. Despite the loss of his legs, and that he'd been a combat vet, her father had loved playing the piano. It had been the most incongruous thing about him. He'd pushed her to study books in order to get an education. About music, though, for himself, he'd had other ideas. He played by ear, by feel and instinct. Give him notes, and he uselessly pounded the keys. Let him listen, and he produced a musical miracle.

Meta was like that with the engine. Given that they lacked many of the needed spare parts, that was probably a good thing.

With a sleeve, Valerie wiped her eyes. She'd have to tell Maddox about her find. Meta's engineering talents might be priceless aboard the ancient sentinel.

If we ever reach the alien star system that is, Valerie thought.

Meta looked up. "Do we have a proton coupler?"

"No."

Scowling, Meta said, "You didn't even check your reader list."

"Don't have to," Valerie said. "I already have it memorized."

"We need a proton coupler," Meta said.

"I'm sure you're right, but we don't have one."

Meta bent her head in thought. "Okay. I know what might work. There's a chance it will blow the engine, though."

"Wait a minute. We should think this through then."

"No," Meta said. "That isn't how you repair something fast."

"Who said anything about fast?" Valerie asked. "We have to do it *right*."

"I thought you told me you went through the Space Academy," Meta said.

196

If someone else had asked her that, Valerie might have bristled. She knew Meta didn't mean anything derogatory by the statement.

"I don't understand what you're getting at," Valerie said.

"In your academy training days, I bet you had to practice emergency repairs. But you've never really needed those repairs done or you'd be dead."

Valerie thought back to the Pan System Battle.

"On the Rouen Colony," Meta was saying, "we had to repair broken machinery on the double. If we didn't, we lost credits and likely lost several meals. We learned to fix things fast, and well. The combination meant food on the table. Here, if we fail, it's our life."

That made sense. Desperation changed the rules, and it demanded a level head. Valerie decided she would always remain levelheaded no matter what the situation. No one was going to outperform her, not even Meta.

"I approve your idea," Valerie said. "Let's try it."

Meta disappeared as she ducked down, and the repairs continued at their accelerated pace.

***

Thirty-six hours after exiting the Laumer-Point into this barren system, an alarm blared. Valerie dragged herself out of bed. According to the clock, she'd slept for four hours, but she was still exhausted.

Her hands shook, and her left shoulder hurt every time she moved it.

Someone knocked on the hatch.

"What?" she shouted.

The hatch creaked open. At that point, Valerie recalled that Sergeant Riker had repaired an antigravity pod. The scout had one-half gravity. It was much better than zero-gravity.

Sergeant Riker poked his head in. "The captain asked me to help you in the engine room today."

"Fine," Valerie said. "How's Doctor Rich? Is there any improvement?"

The sergeant's gaze flickered elsewhere, almost as if he was embarrassed about something. "She's alive," he muttered.

"So there isn't any improvement?"

As he took a deeper breath, the sergeant shook his head.

Valerie didn't know why, but his answer bothered her. The old man was polite enough, but at times, it seemed he was simply an extension of Captain Maddox.

"You do know that Doctor Rich saved your life," she said.

"I'm following procedures," Riker said, a little too defensively.

"You have to do more than that," Valerie said.

"Can you suggest what that is?"

His answer made Valerie pause, and it surprised her to have said something like doing more than following procedures. Maybe these past days watching Meta had taught her a new approach to problems.

"I'm quite capable of handling emergency medics," the sergeant said. "Comas... That's out of hands. We must let the robo-doctor proceed according to schedule."

"Whatever," Valerie said. "Let's go. Meta probably needs our help."

They exited her quarters, and she turned toward the engine room. Riker caught her elbow. Valerie spun around, staring at him.

The sergeant seemed serene now. "You must eat first."

"I don't have time. *We* don't have time."

"No. You need your wits about you. Remember, Lieutenant, Meta is a cunning individual. There's a reason she was on Loki Prime. We mustn't forget that."

Valerie rubbed her eyes. The sergeant had a point. Captain Maddox was unorthodox and selected unorthodox people. She Valerie knew how to follow orders and do things the Star Watch way. She suspected Sergeant Riker was the same way. People like them needed to stick together.

"Let's get chow," she said.

Afterward, they headed to the engine room.

Several hours later, Riker yawned. "I'm taking a break," he said.

The lieutenant glanced at his bloodshot eye. The old man turned away, staggering as he departed. He was a tough old bird, but he didn't have their youthful energy. Was he even the right individual for such a daunting mission as this?

Valerie moved nearer Meta, who had grease stains on her coveralls and a burn across her left cheek. She'd gotten that earlier. Normal lighting had returned, which made repairs easier. Meta stepped away from what she'd been doing and sank onto a stool. Valerie leaned against a control panel.

It had almost been four days since they'd left the Loki System. Just how close was the destroyer to reaching them?

"We're mobile to a degree," Meta said. It meant the fusion plant was working somewhat. "Since the scout has some power, I'd like to take a break to see Dana."

Valerie almost said yes. Instead, she pondered the request. Meta was tough as well as handy with repairs. Something about the two G miner troubled Valerie, though. She hadn't been able to pinpoint her qualms before this. Now it came to her. Meta felt a lot like one of the Detroit gang members she used to encounter.

"What was it like on the Rouen Colony?" Valerie asked.

The questioned seemed to catch Meta off-guard. Her features closed down, and her shoulders tensed. Then Meta laughed. It wasn't a happy sound, but bitter. "Why do you want to know?"

The days of working together and her present exhaustion loosened Valerie's tongue. She began telling Meta something about her childhood in Detroit. Once she started talking, the words poured out of her. Maybe it was the way Meta nodded in understanding. The woman sympathized, seemed to have gone through similar troubles. Valerie had never met someone who could experientially understand her.

After a time, Meta related a few details about the Rouen Colony: the harsh rules and that everyone had legally belonged to the Chabot family as property.

"You were slaves?" Valerie asked.

"Effectively," Meta said.

"That's awful!"

Meta cocked her head as if assessing Valerie's words. After a few seconds, she smiled.

The smile shocked Valerie. She realized it was the first time the woman had truly smiled while aboard the *Geronimo*. Despite her growing sympathy for Meta, it reminded Valerie how dangerous the woman was. Those other smiles—*Did she use those to lull us?*

"Meta, I hope this doesn't make you angry, but I'm going to call Captain Maddox. I want his permission for us to see Doctor Rich."

"Does he control you, then?" Meta asked sarcastically.

"He's the commanding officer. I belong to Star Watch. A little over a month ago, I captained an escort. When I gave an order, I

199

expected my people to follow it. If I demand something from others, I should be willing to give it myself."

"We've worked hard to save the scout," Meta said. "That has created a bond of friendship between us. Friends help each other."

"I agree. But this is a military vessel of the Star Watch. We have rules to govern our behavior."

"Rules to limit you," Meta said.

"No," Valerie said. "The rules give us strength because we know we can trust each other. In that way, we can work together in order to accomplish a greater goal. The New Men have invaded, Meta. We have to stop them. Look what they did to your friend."

"I don't know what they did," Meta said. "I haven't seen Dana since the mine attack."

Valerie took out a comm-unit, switching it on with her thumb. "Captain Maddox," she said.

"Yes, Lieutenant," he said. He was outside helping Keith weld.

"I would like permission to take Meta into medical so she can see Doctor Rich."

There was a pause until Maddox asked, "Is there a reason for this?"

"Kindness for one thing," Valerie said, "for another as a reward for a job well done. The engine will work, to an extent."

"May I remind you, Lieutenant, that Meta is dangerous?"

"Ah, sir," Valerie said, looking up at Meta. "She can hear you."

"Do you have a reason for this request you're not sharing with me?" Maddox asked.

"Yes, sir."

"Very well, you may take her. But I want Sergeant Riker to join you."

"Thank you, sir."

"You're welcome, lieutenant" he said. "And thank you, Meta, for helping repair the engine."

Meta stared at the comm-unit, making Valerie wonder what the woman was really thinking.

***

Together with Meta, Valerie approached the robo-doctor. Sergeant Riker stood near the hatch, with a stunner in his regular hand.

This and the control room had been the two chambers sealed from Meta.

As Dana Rich lay prone, a metal dish sat over her skull. She'd received deep gashes there, as well as a broken arm, ribs and leg. In a parody of normalcy, as if she heard them, her brown features shifted into a grimace.

"She's in pain," Meta said. "You must give her more painkillers."

"In time," Riker said. "The robo-doctor is watching her now. It knows what to do."

Meta looked back to sneer at him. "What does a machine know? She's in pain. You must help her."

"Have you thought that maybe the robo-doctor has analyzed that it will help her wake from the coma faster if she feels pain?" Riker asked.

"I can't believe you'd say that," Meta told him.

Valerie put a restraining hand on Meta's right arm. The Rouen Colony woman looked up sharply. Valerie took her hand away.

"Sorry," the lieutenant said.

"No..." Meta said, after a moment. "I've...I've been on Loki Prime four long years. They were nasty and brutal years. It's... It's hard to remember how normal people react."

"You've been under pressure far longer than that," Valerie said. "Your concern for Doctor Rich—it's good she has a friend like you."

Meta stared at Valerie, finally nodding. The two of them turned to study Doctor Rich. Finally, Meta's shoulders sagged. It was the first sign she'd shown of being tired.

"I'm exhausted, Valerie. I'm sick of..." Meta trailed off, waving her hand. "All my life, I've lived under other people's rules. I don't remember the last time I did something for myself. Dana...she's a hard woman. She's ambitious and driven like your captain. She's angry at the universe."

Valerie wondered if she might also be angry at life. That would mean she had something in common with Doctor Rich.

"I'm tired of being trapped by situations," Meta said. "There's something else, too. I don't know if I've ever shared this with anyone. Vengeance doesn't relieve you of pain like you think it should. Instead, it twists your heart with bitterness. This past week,

201

I've had a lot more time to think than I normally would. With these repairs…I do some of my best thinking while working…"

Valerie nodded sympathetically.

"What I'm saying is that I don't want anything more to do with wars and conquest, with knives and assassination. I thought I'd help Dana achieve her vengeance. But now, I'd rather slip away to somewhere quiet."

"The New Men aren't going away, Meta. They've infiltrated the Commonwealth. They're attacking the Oikumene. Oh, it's probably just the first stage so far. Yet that means the war will likely last a long, long time."

"A lifetime?" asked Meta.

"Do you mean your lifetime, as the war won't reach you while you're alive?"

"That's perceptive. Yes. That's exactly what I mean."

Valerie first pretended to think about it. Then she faced Meta. "What good is that, really? I mean slipping away and building a life for yourself knowing that it's all built with cards that will soon tumble away? I want to build a better world, to give my children more than I had."

"You want to have children?" Meta asked.

"Someday."

"You'd bring them into this evil universe?"

"Someone has to fight the good fight," Valerie said, "to keep the human race alive."

Meta pursed her lips. Then she took several steps closer, putting a hand on Dana's arm. On the table, the doctor's grimace lessened.

"She feels you," Valerie said. "Maybe she can hear us."

"Dana," Meta said. "*Can* you hear me?"

Nothing happened.

"Dana," Meta said. "Would it be better to find this alien starship as Maddox wants or to…do what we planned?"

Valerie would have liked to know what those plans were. She didn't want to interrupt the moment, though. Was Meta really considering helping them? Did it make a difference that Dana Rich was in a coma? Did…

Valerie's mouth opened in shock. She turned to stare at Sergeant Riker. He met her look with innocence. Had Captain Maddox believed he could turn Meta their way without Doctor Rich always giving her negative opinion? In other words, had Maddox prolonged the injuries and kept Dana in a drugged coma?

Valerie hoped Maddox wasn't that ruthless.

Riker looked away.

Valerie wasn't sure, but a guilty look seemed to come over the old man.

"Do you think she'll survive her injuries?" Meta asked.

Valerie groped for the right words. She couldn't dare tell Meta her suspicions. Finally, she said, "I think the odds are good."

Meta nodded and turned back to the unconscious doctor.

"That's long enough," Riker said. His voice was softer than before. "It's time to go," he added.

Meta nodded before heading for the hatch. "Thank you," she told Valerie. "I appreciate this."

"You're welcome," Valerie said. "Maybe we should get back to work."

Meta said nothing more as she exited the medical room.

-25-

Captain Maddox sat down in the control room. Fatigue made his eyelids heavy. For the last few days, he'd been berating himself for failing to see the ploy with the hidden mine. Looking back, it was obvious why the enemy had been near the Class 3 Laumer-Point.

Well, he couldn't help that now. In this new star system, they limped toward the next Laumer-Point, hoping to leave before the destroyer appeared by working its way here through other jump routes. Had the enemy made it through the unstable point? *Saint Petersburg's* destruction would be a great stroke of luck.

We could use some of that about now. He would have shaken his head, but Lieutenant Noonan might notice. She piloted the scout. Ensign Maker slept, while Riker guarded Meta as she continued to effect repairs to the engine and propulsion systems.

Maddox knew the importance of appearing confident. *Never let them see you sweat.* That intimidated opponents and bolstered allies. Right about now, his crew needed all the encouragement they could get.

Lieutenant Noonan took the moment to swivel around and clear her throat. Her intentness alerted Maddox.

"Captain, do I have permission to speak off the record?" she asked.

"Please," he said.

"Sir...I'm not sure how to say this."

He waited, feeling as if it might be better if she didn't.

"Just how serious are Doctor Rich's injuries?" Valerie asked.

"She's recovering," answered Maddox.

While watching him closely, Valerie asked, "Do you believe she'll come out of the coma?"

"The robo-doctor gives that a high percentage."

Valerie licked her lips. "Sir...did you drug her?"

"Of course not," Maddox said.

Valerie brightened for just a moment. Then obvious suspicion furrowed her brow. "The robo-doctor administered the dosages, isn't that what you mean?"

He didn't squirm. That wouldn't do. Instead, he nodded.

"Dana Rich is in an induced coma, isn't she, sir?"

"No," Maddox said.

"No?"

He came to a swift decision. "Lieutenant, speaking precisely, she isn't in a coma at all. By your questions and manner, I suspect you realize I decided to...*inhibit* her consciousness for a time."

"Because she's too dangerous awake?" Valerie asked.

"I agree Dana Rich is dangerous, but that wasn't the totality of my reasoning."

"You're trying to win Meta over to our quest, aren't you, sir?"

The lieutenant's perception surprised Maddox. She had guessed that with hardly any clues to work on. He nodded as an answer.

"Your methods are devious, sir."

"I suppose one could make that argument," he said.

"That isn't the way to convince someone we're trustable."

"You're correct," Maddox said.

"But..." Valerie said. "You're going to suggest that our mission means we must do whatever is necessary to achieve our goal."

Maddox waited. There were times when it was wiser to let a person argue a point with herself. The lieutenant knew what would convince her better than he did.

"I can't say I approve, sir."

"If it's any consolation," he said, "neither do I."

"I find that hard to believe," Valerie said.

"Lieutenant, it's a given that you and I will never do anything as important with our lives than to complete this mission. Without the sentinel, do you think Star Watch can defeat the New Men?"

"We don't have enough information to make a perfect guess," Valerie said.

"You're hedging," Maddox said. "What we do know tells us we can't match their cruisers, their advanced weaponry. Three of their ships took out a double-strength battle group."

"I understand your logic," Valerie said, "and I'm not saying you don't have a point. It's just that I hate to practice deceit on people we're hoping to trust with our lives. If Doctor Rich ever discovers what you did…"

"I'm telling you this in strictest confidence," Maddox said.

"Yes, sir," Valerie said.

A red light began to blink on his screen. Seeing it, a cold feeling worked through Maddox. "Our discussion is over," he said. He adjusted controls, using passive sensors. A ship had just entered the star system from a different Laumer-Point than the one they had used to get here. The computer analyzed the data and—

"An SWS destroyer has just appeared at a distant jump point," Maddox informed her. A few seconds later, he added, "It's the *Saint Petersburg.*" He stood. "Take your station and engage the cloaking device."

"The cloak is damaged," Valerie said. "Maybe if we waited to employ it, waited until their Jump Lag wore off—"

"No," Maddox said. "It's too risky to cut it too fine. We don't know how quickly New Men recover from Jump Lag—quicker than us, you once said. Maybe they brought computer systems with them that recover faster than ours do from jump. We have to fade away now and reach our next tramline in secret."

Valerie stood, moving from piloting to her controls.

Maddox shifted as well, calling Keith on the ship's intercom.

"Will they try to follow us all the way to the alien star system?" Valerie asked.

"That would be bad," Maddox said. "How is the cloaking device responding?"

"Do you hear the clicking noise?"

Maddox listened. He could hear it, and he told Valerie so.

"The cloaking device is straining, sir. I don't know how long our jury-rigging is going to work. We need a dockyard and a major overhaul. The mine hurt us, sir, worse than I think you want to admit."

"It's not how good our ship is but if we can beat the other fellow across the finish line."

The clicking noises increased.

Maddox swore under his breath. The hatch opened and the sleepy-eyed ace entered. "Explain the situation to him, Lieutenant. Keep us cloaked at all costs. Ensign, at your judgment, engage the gravity generator to build our velocity."

Keith paused, rubbing his eyes, taking his time digesting the order. Finally, he said, "I'm not sure the scout can withstand more of that kind of stress, Captain, sir."

"I imagine we're going to find out," Maddox told him.

"The cloaking device, sir—" Valerie said.

"I'll tell Meta to keep it operational," Maddox said.

"Do you know which Laumer-Point I'm supposed to aim us toward once we jump into the next system?" Valerie asked.

Unfortunately, Maddox did not. A prolonged reading of Professor Ludendorff's notes had convinced him the text was encrypted. Dana might understand the script, but so far, Maddox knew he didn't.

"I'm off to see if I can answer your question," Maddox said.

"You're going to wake Doctor Rich?" Valerie asked.

"Precisely," Maddox answered. "Wish me luck on convincing her to stay with us to the end."

"Luck," Valerie said.

Maddox exited the control room.

***

Sitting on a chair, the captain waited with his legs crossed as Doctor Rich slowly regained consciousness.

Maddox had time to ponder his situation. Down on the prison planet, what had the appearance of the New Men truly meant? He kept replaying the incident on Loki Prime. The golden-skinned invader had dodged his gunshots. That was incredible. Only by anticipating the man had Maddox been able to shoot him to the ground. Could a regular man have done as well as him?

That's what I'm really asking, isn't it? Am I a normal man, or do I have their blood in me? Was my mother a breeder for the New Men? Suppose she was. What does that mean for me?

The idea of genetically altering humans was repugnant to most people. Making replicas such as clones also made people uneasy. The Clone Laws were there to halt the practice, and yet some rich folk on Earth bought clones from planets outside the Commonwealth.

Did the New Men have feelings of racial superiority? Back before interstellar travel, Earth had fought world wars concerning such matters. The Eugenics War of the Twentieth Century had destroyed the nation attempting to fashion a master race. Had that horror now come to the Oikumene? If he and his crew failed to acquire the alien sentinel, would the Star Watch go down in defeat against the invincible cruisers?

Maddox scowled. The New Man on Loki had fired into the undergrowth, unerringly hitting his targets. That had been uncanny. The man's running speed was faster than Maddox could have sprinted. He also happened to know that he ran much faster than others could.

Maybe this is my mission in life. I'm alive to halt a monstrous racial war. Yes, I drugged Doctor Rich. I did it to keep her out of the way for a time. The mine almost finished us. We had to fix the scout before the destroyer came and demolished us. The Saint Petersburg *may annihilate us anyway. I drugged the doctor because it's harder for one person to resist others mentally when they're on their own. According to Valerie, Meta has come closer to our way of thinking. We need her.*

On the table, Dana smacked her lips. Even though her eyes remained closed, she reached up and began to rub her face.

Even more than Meta, Maddox thought, *we need this unpredictable woman. Without her, the operation is likely doomed to failure. How can I convince her to help us? Do I dare try to trick her? Maybe it's better to lay my cards face-up. What will sway Dana Rich? What should I base my appeal on? You're supposed to be a smart operator, Captain. What would appeal to me if I were in her shoes?*

Yes. That was the question. Know yourself and you could know others.

"What...what happened to me?" Dana whispered in a dry voice.

Maddox held his breath. *Here we go.* Then, he stood and approached her with a glass of water.

Dana struggled to a sitting position. Although noticing it at first, she ignored the tumbler in his hand. First glancing around, she asked, "How long have I been here?"

He gave her the number in days.

Gingerly, Dana touched the back of her head. She gave him a suspicious glance as he explained how she'd been knocked unconscious and into a coma.

When he finished, she said, "I haven't been in a coma. The signs are wrong. The truth is you drugged me."

"The robo-doctor gave you medicine," Maddox said.

"You know what I mean. By your decision, you put me under. I want to know why you did it."

"Here," Maddox said, pushing the water forward.

He could see in her eyes that she wanted to slap the glass away. Finally, she snatched the tumbler, spilling liquid. He wondered if she would fling it in his face. No. She sipped. Finally, she drank the glass dry. Then, she let the container slide from her fingers to bounce off the deck.

"What's the situation with the scout?" she asked. "The engine sounds different."

Ignoring the glass, he told her about their repairs, and how the *Saint Petersburg* was in the same star system with them.

Her eyes darted from side to side thoughtfully. When her orbs came to a rest, she said, "Okay. The destroyer is hunting us. Isn't that what you're saying?"

"It is," Maddox agreed.

"I could have helped with the repairs," Dana said. "I can do more than Meta."

"I believe you. The thing is, Doctor, it's easier to trust Meta than to trust you."

Her eyes widened until understanding fired in her pupils. "Oh, I see. You're trying to win her over to your cause. With me out of the way, you could persuade her more easily. Yes. I understand now."

"And?" Maddox said.

"What do you mean, 'and?'"

"Aren't you going to tell me that my trickery won't work?"

"I don't engage in useless comments," Dana said. "Of course your skullduggery could work. It's a common enough tactic, building camaraderie under extreme conditions. Meta hungers for friends. She's a lonely person."

"You aren't?"

Dana smiled as a predator might. "If I thought about it, I might have time for loneliness. Your trouble, Captain, is that you ponder things too much. You're much more transparent than you realize."

"Oh?"

"How is it that your people chose you to try to beat the New Men?" she asked.

Tension bubbled in his chest. "Could you explain your statement?" he asked.

"I don't have to. Your reaction tells me I struck a nerve. Let me tell you something about your operation. Your plan to gain the sentinel is futile. It won't work."

"Doctor Ludendorff believed it could work," Maddox said.

Dana made a dismissive gesture. "Ludendorff is a hopeless romantic. Yes, the man is brilliant. I concede that much. Frankly, that's part of his problem. His brilliance blinds him to what can and can't be done. Most of his life, he's been doing things everyone told him was impossible. Thus, when he finally came to an impossible situation—I'm talking about the alien star system—he was too puffed up to realize we all would have died if I hadn't acted quickly enough getting us out of there."

"Why exactly is gaining the sentinel impossible?"

"You're a smart man, Captain. At least, you seem capable enough. It should be elementary to figure out the reason."

"Why don't you tell me," Maddox suggested.

Dana looked at him as if he'd become simple-minded. "Ludendorff estimated the alien war to have taken place nearly six thousand years ago. Knowing the man, he's probably right. Let me ask you something. Can you imagine how long ago that was? Oh, I understand that you think you can. You can't, though, not really. The timeframe contains all of humanity's recorded history, everything. The sentinel is impossibly old, yet it is still dangerous. Don't you think others throughout the centuries tried to tame it as you're hoping to do?"

"I have no idea," Maddox said. "By the articles I've read, the aliens vanished long ago. Maybe this is the first attempt since their disappearance."

"Even if you're right, the sentinel would be too different for us to use. Its controls are likely based on incomprehensible alien realities, at least as we think of them."

210

"Wouldn't rational minds think alike?" Maddox asked. "For instance, aliens must have used the same mathematics we have."

"Clearly, you've read Ludendorff's notes," Dana said. "He spoke as you do. No! I reject the concept out of hand. Different races from different worlds would think and act inconceivably different from us."

"Then how do we defeat the New Men's star cruisers?" Maddox asked.

"Not my job," Dana said.

"We—meaning you as well—are presently hunted by a New Man."

"Correction, *you're* hunted by a Star Watch destroyer. I'm beginning to suspect your entire story, Captain. I think you have a completely different agenda in mind, one you're refusing to tell us."

"No," Maddox said. "That doesn't fly. You saw the New Men down on the planet. You witnessed them and you know they're incredibly dangerous to us. They have several edges over regular humans, not least of which is that they know us but we know very little about them. Tell me, Doctor. What must I do to convince you to aid us?"

"Nothing," she said, "because I'm never going to help you in the way you want. It's death to go back."

"At least show us how to get to the alien star system. I'll drop you off before we reach it."

"Forget it," she said. "Firstly, I don't trust you. You drugged me, Captain. You lack a sense of decency. Secondly, if you want to go there, you have Ludendorff's notes. Read them and use them."

Maddox stared into her eyes, feeling like a deer watching a wolf panting under a tree. "I believe the professor wrote in code," he said.

An eyebrow lifted. "So, you're more intelligent than I've given you credit for. Yes, the professor was a maniac about security. He put everything he wrote into an inscrutable cipher."

"I'm sure you could crack it," Maddox said.

"That goes without saying. He was smart. I'm smarter."

Maddox pursed his lips. "I must say, Doctor. You're a difficult person to like."

"All you mean is that I'm not doing what you want. As you can see, I'm too wise to fall for your ploys."

"Nevertheless, you are in the same predicament as us. You're in the same craft. The New Men are hunting for us, meaning they're also hunting for you. What will you do as they close in? You must come to your senses before they trap us, and you, for good."

"You forget," Dana said. "I was on Loki Prime, more trapped than anywhere in the universe. Yet, I escaped."

Maddox could have pointed out that he was the one who had taken her off the planet. Instead, he shifted directions because he realized that an appeal to her better nature wasn't going to work. Doctor Rich was proud. She was ambitious, and she obviously looked down on others. She was hyper-intelligent. That must have meant a childhood full of loneliness. Maddox knew something about that.

He now snorted softly.

She bristled.

Seeing her reaction, he changed tactics. He would needle her, after all. "You didn't escape from Loki Prime," Maddox said. "I did that, taking you with me. Don't you realize I won't always be there to save your ugly hide from the New Men?"

"Ha!" she said. "Nice try. I'm not as sensitive or as vain as you seem to think. Let me tell you something. You need me. I don't need you."

"If I have to," Maddox said, "I will decipher Ludendorff's notes on my own and take us to the alien system."

"Once you're there," Dana asked, "how will you trick the sentinel into letting you board?"

Maddox shrugged as if it would be child's play.

"You do know that you're racing to your destruction," she said.

"Possibly," he said. "I'm also taking you with me."

"You'll have to drop me off first."

"Under normal circumstances I'd be happy to oblige. I'm afraid with the destroyer on our tail that I cannot."

"That's madness," Dana said. "You've already admitted the scout is limping along. They have a fully functional machine. You will not shake them. The only rational choice is to return to a Star Watch shipyard and effect repairs."

"In this you are correct," Maddox said. "I am irrational and will stubbornly attempt the mission no matter how poor the odds are of succeeding."

She squinted at him. "You're bluffing."

"Did I try to bluff the New Man on Loki?"

"No…" she said. "You shot him, but he still got away."

Maddox wanted to shout with frustration, pick up his chair and hurl it at her. What would it take to convince this stubborn genius?

"Look at it this way," said Maddox. "The destroyer isn't going to give up. That means we'll barely stay ahead of them. Whatever else I do, I'll take the scout into the Beyond. Without your help, I'll make mistakes deciphering the professor's notes. That means a longer journey than otherwise. The longer this trip takes, the greater chance that I slip up and they catch us. That personally affects you, Doctor."

She lay back down and stared up at the ceiling. "At least I get to live longer this way—your proposed zigzag journey through the Beyond. Once we reach the alien system, our lives will be measured in hours, not decades."

"I know what you're thinking," Maddox said. "Let me assure you, Doctor, you won't hijack my vessel."

She didn't answer.

"If it's in my best interests," Maddox said, "I can always give you the same drugs as before, put you back to sleep."

"True enough, you can," she said, "but you won't."

"If I don't, you'll be spending a lot of time alone locked in your quarters."

"We'll see how well Meta does with that," Dana said.

Frustration seethed through Maddox. He realized she wasn't going to budge now. That meant he'd have to start reading Ludendorff's notes again. He couldn't believe freeing Doctor Rich had actually hindered their mission instead of aiding it. The scout wouldn't be in this poor condition if he hadn't gone down to Loki Prime.

"You know you'll never decipher the professor's notes," she said. "You lack the brainpower. Thus, this mission is doomed to failure."

"I don't understand why you're aiding the New Men, Doctor."

"I'm not aiding them. I already told you once. I hate the Commonwealth of Planets and think even less of the Windsor League and the Wahhabi Caliphate. Let the New Men make a clean sweep of it. In time, I'm going to get a starship of my own. Then, I'm heading far, far away, Captain. So you see, your threat of heading even deeper into the Beyond is no threat at all, but a boon for my plans. By all means, take us far away from your precious Commonwealth and its oh so high and mighty Star Watch. Good riddance to them all."

Silently, Maddox admitted defeat. "Very well, you've convinced me. Let me help you to your new quarters."

"I can walk on my own," she said. With that, she struggled off the robo-doctor and limped for the hatch.

Maddox followed, knowing he'd have to keep a sharp eye on her, or despite his best efforts, she would hijack the vessel.

-26-

The deadly game of tag begun with the *Saint Petersburg* in Earth orbit and taken to the Loki System now entered its most frustrating phase for Captain Maddox.

With its head start, the *Geronimo* slipped from the barren star system. For a day—twenty-three hours to be precise—it seemed they had finally shaken off the destroyer. Instead, as the scout neared the next Laumer-Point, the *Saint Petersburg* entered the same star system. After two hours of active sensor sweeps, the destroyer accelerated hard for the jump point the scout neared.

"Since the mine-attack, our cloaking device no longer functions one hundred percent," Valerie said. "They must be able to see us."

Maddox stood in the control room, staring at the lieutenant's view-screen. The *Saint Petersburg* aimed at them like an arrow, if six hundred million kilometers away. He hated the New Man over there, and he hoped the commander's ribs hurt where he'd shot him on Loki Prime.

The scout's engine worked after a fashion. The gravity generator shook the wounded scout too much when employed. The cloaking device—as the lieutenant suggested was still less than perfect.

"Drop the cloak," Maddox said.

"What if the destroyer's crew just guessed right?" Valerie asked. "If we appear now, that will let them know exactly what to look for next time."

Maddox didn't think so, but it was possible the lieutenant was right. He put his hands behind his back, squeezing his fingers into fists. This was different than his normal spying mission. Given a situation like this on Earth, he would...

Maddox shook his head. To win this time, he had to accept that his choices could produce defeat. He had to *think*, and he had to accept responsibility. If Valerie had a better idea than he did, he should use it. Captaining a starship, even a small one like the scout, was an art. It was conceivable he still had much to learn in this area.

"Maintain the cloak," he said.

Now it was Keith's turn. "If we remain cloaked, the destroyer is going to catch up," the pilot said. "We have to move as fast as we can, and we don't dare use the gravity generator until further repairs have strengthened the scout's structures."

"Understood," said Maddox. "Stay cloaked, but put the fusion thruster online."

"If we do that," Valerie said, "they'll certainly see us."

"Nevertheless, we will risk it," Maddox said. "Ensign Maker is correct. They're heading for us, even if they can't see us. We must keep as far ahead of them as we can, staying out of missile and beam range."

Geronimo accelerated. Several hours later, the ship entered the Laumer-Point at speed. Without the destroyer in the new star system—at least for a time—Maddox ordered the lieutenant to let the cloak drop.

During this time, Meta, Valerie, Keith and Sergeant Riker continued to effect repairs the best they could. Doctor Dana Rich stayed locked in her quarters. Meta constantly asked to see her. Maddox refused every request.

The captain's normal calm deserted him when he was alone in his quarters. He read Professor Ludendorff's notes again and again, stalking back and forth in his chamber in frustration and then returning to his computer to retype the words, hoping to see something new. He tried old encryptions and finally ran the notes through the computer. Nothing made sense.

"Deeper into the Beyond," Maddox ordered. "The alien star system is out there, so that's where we'll head."

Always—sometimes just minutes before they jumped—the destroyer appeared in the star system, *pinging* its sensors off the cloaked scout.

Maddox had Riker read the notes. The sergeant shrugged afterward. The old man had no ideas. Keith read the notes and laughed when asked if he saw a code embedded there. Valerie didn't laugh, but she didn't have any ideas, either. Meta pondered the words. She tried hard but came up with nothing.

After the tenth jump, Maddox lay on his bunk, staring at the ceiling. They had just used a small Class 3 wormhole. The destroyer would have to work around, using larger jump points to reach this star system. If the scout proved fast enough, they could leave this system before the *Saint Petersburg* appeared to resume the chase.

To Maddox's amazement, they made the jump, a second one too—several days later—and the *Saint Petersburg* still hadn't showed up.

"We did it," Valerie said in the control room. "We've shaken the hunter. Now, we can think about a space-dock and extended repairs."

There were grins all around. Then an alarm rang. Maddox, Keith and Valerie bent over their controls. The lieutenant found it first. She looked up, stricken.

Maddox noticed her features. He sat up, asking, "You found the *Saint Petersburg*?"

The lieutenant shook her head. "Worse," she whispered, "it's much, much worse." She pointed at her view-screen. "I'm looking at a New Men star cruiser. I'd recognize that triangular shape anywhere. The same model annihilated von Gunther's fleet. How it found us, I don't know, but it's here."

An icy sensation spread through Maddox's chest. "I think I know what happened. They've widened the search, using more vessels. Maybe they've figured out what we're after or they knew all along. They're not about to let us reach the alien star system."

Instead of swearing, Captain Maddox drummed his fingers on the console. He stood and pointed at Valerie. "Map out an escape route—don't worry where it takes us in relation to the Oikumene. Shoot us through five star systems in quick succession. Oh, and use as many Class 3 wormholes as possible, making sure each Laumer-Point is as near to the next one as possible."

"Excuse me, sir," she said. "I'm not sure what you're driving at."

"We're going to try to shake *all* of them," Maddox said. "Bam, bam, bam," he said, clapping his hands each time. "We jump, jump,

jump before they appear to get a fix on us. If they have several vessels chasing us, we have to shake them all off."

"How are they coordinating with each other in the various star systems?" Valerie asked.

There wasn't a hyper-communications system in existence as far as Maddox knew. Messages traveled as fast as starships could carry them and no faster.

"I wish I knew," Maddox said. "They're being clever. That means we have to pull every rabbit out of the hat we can. Now get to work."

"Where are you going, sir?" the lieutenant asked.

"I have a new argument to present to the doctor," he said. "Wish me luck."

"Not this time," Valerie said.

Maddox was already headed for the hatch. He halted and glanced at her.

"This time, we need something stronger," Valerie said. "I'm going to pray."

"Ah," Maddox said. Then he hurried for the corridor.

***

Maddox didn't bother knocking. He simply opened the hatch and stepped through.

Doctor Rich sat up in bed, scanning a reader. She gave him a bored look then went back to reading.

He closed the hatch and locked it. Meta had tried to enter once when he'd done something like this before. He didn't want that happening again.

Maddox pulled up a chair, sat down and began to wait. After fifteen minutes, he realized Dana Rich would never speak first. Part of him wanted to get up and leave.

Don't be absurd, he told himself. *Winning a stubbornness contest with the doctor means nothing. Gaining the alien sentinel to defeat the New Men is the only measurement of victory.*

"I have news," he said.

He saw the fingers holding the reader tighten slightly. Slowly, she lowered the device to her lap. Maddox had the feeling she'd been waiting anxiously for him to talk. Maybe it had been hard on her to outwait him. If he'd stalled just a little longer…

"I'm reading an interesting chapter," she said. "So I hope you can get to the point and leave me in peace."

She's bluffing. She must desperately want to talk. Even a tough bird like her will crack over time. She's smart, but she's not immune to the same defects and needs we all possess.

"Of course," he said. "I'll be brief. A star cruiser had taken up the chase."

"You mean one of the New Men's special cruisers?" she asked.

"Precisely," Maddox said.

"And you've rushed to tell me this for what reason?"

"I would have thought it obvious."

"My wits have atrophied since you've locked me in," Dana said. "Why don't you explain the reason to me?"

"It's simple enough. The destroyer lost our trail. Now one of the star cruisers has taken up the slack. Possibly, it indicates the New Men's starship has always been there."

"Hmm, possibly," Dana agreed.

"There might be more star cruisers."

"I wouldn't doubt it," she said.

"I believe that proves the New Men's agents in Star Watch have divined our objective or known it for quite some time."

"I'm still not following you," Dana said. "Why tell me any of this?"

"Don't you see? The New Men must believe that our objective is possible. If it were impossible, why use important cruisers to trail a scout?"

With her brow furrowed, Dana glanced back down at her reader. A smile worked its way onto her mouth as she looked back up. "I can see how you reached your conclusion. That they're following us doesn't make the impossible any more feasible. Instead, it proves the New Men are less a menace than you've painted them."

"Why is that?" Maddox asked.

"The sentinel is beyond anyone. So, the New Men are as capable as we are of making misjudgments."

"What if you're wrong about this?" he asked.

"I'm not wrong," Dana said. "Remember, I've been to the alien system. You haven't, and neither have the New Men."

Maddox watched her. Did she really believe what she said, or was she angling for something he couldn't see yet?

"Even if you're right," he said, "the New Men are closing in on us."

"Then you must outfox them, Captain. That means you should leave me in peace while you do your job. Please, go. Your insistence wearies me."

Nodding slowly, Maddox dared to asked, "What happened to you, Doctor? Why are you so bitter?"

"Do you jest?" she asked. "Isn't it obvious that my bitterness, as you put it, is caused by the powers that spurned my efforts and dropped me onto Loki Prime?"

"One of those powers also rescued you."

Her dark features hardened. "Go away, Captain Maddox. Your presence annoys me."

Reluctantly, he stood. He wanted to know the right words to unlock her heart. It seemed frozen on some bitter memory, some slight she refused to forget. Seeking those words, his mouth moved and his right arm rose as he made a forlorn gesture. Finally, silently admitting defeat once more, Captain Maddox retreated from her quarters.

***

By a combination of luck and hard work, the *Geronimo* easily beat the star cruiser to the tramline. Pushing the scout to its limit, they made five jumps in quick succession. They hopped from system to system. On the third jump, they raced away from Nemesis System frigates. The ships demanded identification, launching missiles after the scout refused all requests. Using an unstable wormhole, *Geronimo* barely slipped away. It saved them from the missiles, and it seemed to lengthen their lead over their adversaries.

Meta and Valerie worked overtime on the struggling engine. Keith helped them, and Sergeant Riker spelled the other two in order to keep an eye on an unflagging Meta. The Rouen Colony woman kept the scout running more than any other two of them combined.

All too often, Maddox sat hunched in his quarters, rereading the professor's notes over and over. Even when his eyelids drooped, he forced himself to read, to think, to read some more.

The captain shuddered and awoke with a yell. Sweat slicked his face, and his heart pounded. He could only remember pieces of the dream, but it horrified him—a woman on the run had carried him in her womb.

"Mother?" he whispered.

Maddox squeezed his eyes shut. He'd never known his real mother, or his father, for that matter. Who had they been? What kind of people exactly? Would they have been proud of what he was trying to do, or would they have laughed at him?

My father—

Maddox's head snapped upright. His eyes shined. He grabbed the professor's notes and began to read for what felt like the one hundred and first time. What if "sun" meant "comet" and "asteroid" meant "star system?" That would mean—

He jumped to his feet and turned on the computer. With the notes in one hand, he tapped in the coordinates on the computer and finally deciphered Ludendorff's record of his visit to the alien star system. An hour later, Maddox had a chart leading into the Beyond. The departure point would be the Nine Whiskey Star System.

He pulled up a star chart and found they were four jumps from there. Afterward, he slumped in his chair with his gaze blurred. Could this be it? Had he truly broken the code that would bring them to the most legendarily haunted region in space?

There's only one way to find out. He downloaded the information, sending it to Valerie's computer in the control room. Then he hurried there to tell them the good news.

***

The next three weeks left the crew exhausted as they worked overtime keeping the scout running. *Geronimo* had left the Oikumene far behind. They ranged deeper and deeper into unknown territory. The *Saint Petersburg* and the New Men star cruiser had both shown up again, but the *Geronimo* had managed to shake them off.

Maddox imagined the New Men spreading a net after each jump the scout made out of their sight. There were only so many routes to choose from. Each enemy starship must head for a different point. Then, the enemy used their sensors in each newly-entered star system to search for the *Geronimo*.

How are they coordinating the moves between ships in different star systems? That's what baffled Maddox. The only method he knew was actually sending other ships as messengers. Whatever the New Men were doing, though, was working.

"Do you think they're letting us run ahead of them on purpose," Lieutenant Noonan asked one day.

"Maybe," Maddox admitted.

They sat in the galley, Meta, Valerie and him eating freeze-dried pork chops. The favorite meals were vanishing from the menu selections. Soon, only the skipped meals would remain. After those vanished, there wouldn't be anything left to eat but dried fruit and nuts.

Maddox cut his pork chop, popping a piece of meat into his mouth, chewing. It lacked salt. He picked up a shaker and added granules.

"That's no good for you," Meta said.

"You like your meat without salt?" Maddox asked.

"I'm not like you," she said. "You eat for pleasure. I eat to sustain myself."

Maddox indicated himself. "Do I look as if I eat for pleasure?"

Her gaze flickered over him. "I've wanted to ask you this for a while," she said. "Why are you so thin?"

"Lean," he said. "I'm not thin but lean."

Meta bristled. "Are you saying I'm fat?"

After examining the full-figured woman in her rating uniform, Maddox shook his head. "Not fat at all," he said. "I'd call you pleasing, easy on the eyes."

Meta blushed at this uncharacteristic remark.

Lieutenant Noonan noticed and frowned at Maddox. "Captain, please, we're eating."

As if nothing had happened, he cut another slice of pork chop, chewing in silence.

"I want to get back to my point," Valerie said. "If we're leading the New Men to the alien star system, maybe we should turn back and try again later. If the enemy gains the sentinel, the New Men will become even more invincible than before."

Maddox raised his head. He stood, took his plastic dish and paused long enough to tell Valerie, "That's a brilliant idea, Lieutenant."

"What did I say?"

"I'll tell you later if it works."

222

With that, Maddox hurried from the galley, gulping down the rest of his pork chop. He tossed the plastic into a disposal unit. After washing his hands, he stopped before Dana Rich's hatch. Should he just barge right in?

Instead of doing so, he rapped his knuckles against metal. There had to be a better way to do this. This was a starship, for Heaven's sake. Knocking on metal didn't make much sense.

"Who is it?" Dana asked in a muffled voice.

"Captain Maddox," he said.

After a short pause, she said, "Go away."

He turned the wheel, opened the hatch and failed to spy the doctor.

"Do I have to gas your room?" he asked.

"No," she said, from the wall beside the hatch. She moved toward her bed, becoming visible, tossing a lamp so it hit her sheets.

She'd been hidden from sight, ready to whack him over the head as he entered her quarters. Warily, Maddox stepped within.

Dana thumped down upon her bed. He pulled up a chair, sitting down.

"I'm weary of our arrangement," she said. "I'm going stir crazy. In the name of decency, you must change the situation."

"I have a proposal to make," Maddox told her.

"I won't join you in your mad venture. That hasn't changed."

"You know we're nearing the alien star system right? I cracked the professor's encryption some time ago."

"So you say," Dana told him. "When we're there, you can let me know. Oh, how about this, just before we jump into said system, tell me."

"Of course," he said. "Look, this is…" He squinted at her. "Why did you ask me to tell you just before we get there?"

"No particular reason," she said offhandedly.

"You're—" He was going to say, "lying," but decided on greater tact. "I'll keep your request in mind," he finished.

She nodded indifferently. "What's your proposal then?"

"The New Men are following us. Whether they mean to capture the sentinel, I don't know. Let us suppose you're right: no one can board the alien vessel. Okay. We'll use the sentinel to set up an ambush."

"Meaning what?" she asked.

"We'll lead the New Men to the alien starship. It's automated, you say."

"Correct," agreed Dana.

"Fine," he said. "We lead them there and it destroys the hunters for us."

"How does that help us?" she asked.

"That should be easy to understand. They're following us, and I don't think they'll quit until they have us. This stops them, and it gets rid of one or more of their elite star cruisers. Afterward, we're free to return home. You get your pardon and I have the honor of destroying however many enemy cruisers the sentinel annihilates."

Dana studied him, and finally, she laughed. "Nice try, Captain. I almost believed you."

"Well, whether you believe me or not that's my plan as of now. We're almost to the second-to-last star system."

Doctor Dana Rich expelled a lungful of air. "Are you serious?" she asked. "You've actually taken us that far into the Beyond?"

"Correct. Now, what do you want to tell me?"

"I have no idea what you're talking about," she said.

Maddox sat perfectly still. Scout duty was hard work. The ship was too small and they'd rubbed elbows too long. Normal Patrol scout crews were carefully chosen for their abilities to get along and to handle the cramped quarters for extended periods. Maddox doubted any of them were constitutionally suited for the small craft. Thus, he forced himself to sit quietly as he studied the doctor anew, instead of jumping up and pacing.

He envisioned Dana Rich, as she'd been the first few days after she awoke. Since then, the woman had become tenser. More than that, she seemed frightened. But because of her pride, she tried to hide it.

"Fine," he said abruptly, standing. "If you have nothing else to say—" He started for the hatch.

"Wait," she whispered.

Maddox turned around.

Doctor Rich stared at her hands. She breathed heavily, causing her breasts to rise and fall rapidly. She was older than either Valerie or Meta, but she was beautiful in an exotic way.

She raised her head, and a tic twitched under her right eye. "You're a monomaniac, Captain. I can't believe you've brought us

224

so far out into the Beyond. The dangers out there..." She shook her head. "It doesn't matter. This next jump, well, the one into the alien system, must be done exactly how I say. If you don't do it like that, we'll die."

"Why is that?" Maddox asked.

"Does the scout have a deflector shield?"

"You know it doesn't," he said.

"Then the minute you exit the jump point into the alien star system, you and everyone else aboard the *Geronimo* dies."

"Because the sentinel will attack us?" asked Maddox.

"Not at all," Dana said. "The alien star system will do the killing."

"Can you elaborate?"

Once more, the doctor stared at her hands and began to speak in a low voice. The reason shocked Maddox. Without the good doctor's insight—if she were right—the alien system would indeed destroy the scout. The question had changed, then. Did they have enough time to get ready to enter the alien system the doctor's way before the star cruiser or the destroyer found and annihilated them?

-27-

The constellations had changed drastically since Maddox had begun the mission on Earth over three months ago. In a straight line, they were well over three hundred light-years from the Solar System.

The scout had entered this system at high velocity and accelerated. Now, several days later, they approached the other end, decelerating for some time already.

The system possessed an A spectral class star. That made it a bluish-white furnace with a mean surface temperature of 8000 K. Three terrestrial planets made up the inner system, each about twice the size of Earth. The first two had molten surfaces like Mercury. The last resembled a giant dust-blown Mars.

The lone outer system planet—the one they approached—was unique, at least as seen during their travels. It was a brown dwarf with twenty-one times Jupiter's mass, making it gargantuan. The dwarf was a substellar object, meaning that despite its size, it lacked the mass to sustain hydrogen-1 fusion reactions in its core. Instead, the planet fused deuterium in the center. This was a T spectral type dwarf and was magenta to the eye rather than brown.

The massive planet was over four billion kilometers from the star, the reason for the longer travel time. The dwarf had moons, the largest similar in size to Saturn's Titan. The T dwarf also possessed highly elliptical orbiting comets, which thickened in the region near an unstable wormhole.

This system possessed two Laumer-Points: the one they'd entered near the third planet in the inner range and the one they approached out in the comet field.

"I'm still not picking anything up yet," Valerie said. She sat at her station, engaging all the ship's sensors. She had been targeting comets since exiting the Laumer-Point.

"It has to be out there," Maddox said. "The doctor told me so."

Valerie muttered under her breath. After days of fruitless searching, it seemed she'd reached her limit. She straightened and swiveled around.

"Ensign," she said, "Could you give us a moment."

Keith sat at the pilot controls. He glanced from her to Maddox. "What do you want me to do?" he asked.

"Aren't you hungry?" Valerie asked him.

"Have you seen the menu choices lately?" Keith asked. "If I'd tried to serve that stuff in my bar, the patrons would have stoned me."

"Ensign!" she said.

Keith sat back, and it seemed he was about to go into his Scottish routine.

"Go head," Maddox told him. "Grab some chow. Give us a few minutes."

"Aye-aye, Captain, sir," Keith said. He marched out of the control room, banging the hatch louder than usual behind him.

The moment the hatch closed, Valerie said, "Permission to speak—"

"Yes, yes," Maddox said, with a wave of his hand. She was obviously strained, and so was he. "Please tell me what's troubling you."

"Sir, meaning no disrespect... Is it possible Doctor Rich lied to you?"

"The thought has crossed my mind," Maddox admitted.

"This may be her attempt—"

A beep sounded from her board, interrupting Valerie's speech.

Maddox's stomach tightened. He knew what the sound meant. For weeks, this had happened with increasing regularity.

"It's *Saint Petersburg*," Valerie said, studying her panel. As she spoke, the lieutenant engaged the cloaking device. A loud thrum told them all they needed to know about the device's condition. "We can't keep this up much longer, sir."

Maddox silently agreed. If it could last for just another day... This was supposed to be the end of the line for them. One more jump would bring them to the sentinel-haunted star system. Doctor Rich had told him a song and dance about how to get into the alien system intact. Could it really be true?

"You do realize that we won't be able to follow the doctor's suggestion now," Valerie said. "We can't, not with the destroyer in the system."

Slowly, Maddox stood and his features stiffened. The past weeks had eaten away at his reserve. The endless chase, the running away again—

"Use the passive sensors only," Maddox said. "Keep searching for the comet. Instruct Meta to babysit the cloaking device. We can't let the destroyer see us this time, not a smidge or wattage of power to give away our location."

"I'm not sure I can do that, sir. The *Saint Petersburg's* crew has gotten better at their craft."

"True. But you've also gotten better, Lieutenant. We've both become experts at this cat and mouse game."

Valerie paused before asking, "Captain, why do you think Doctor Rich still refuses to help us one hundred percent?"

A hard smile pasted itself onto his face. "That's a good question. I'm about to discover the answer."

Like a tiger, Maddox stalked out of the control room. Keith lounged against a bulkhead. Jerking a thumb at the open hatch, Maddox said, "I'm done. You can go back."

A possibly sarcastic reply died on Keith's lips. He nodded before moving out of the captain's way.

Maddox hardly noticed. He marched to the doctor's hatch and swung it open. Letting it stay ajar, he climbed into her quarters.

The doctor was in the middle of doing push-ups and she mustn't have heard him enter.

"You must decide," Maddox told her.

Her head swiveled sharply toward him. A brief twitch of her face was the only indication she'd been surprised. The doctor jumped to her feet. Perspiration dotted her brown skin.

He opened his mouth. This was it. He wouldn't accept anything less than total assistance.

Panting, she held up a hand. "I'll save you time, Captain. Your sensors haven't found the equipment because it's buried too deep under the ice. Ludendorff was a tricky man, and he suffered from a persecution complex. It served him well on most occasions. Ah," she added, after searching his face. "I take it the New Men are in the system with us."

Maddox was too angry to reply verbally, nodding instead.

"You're in something of a dilemma, then," Dana said. "Therefore, I believe I'll finally play my strongest card."

"Meaning what?" he asked in a thick voice.

Dana's gaze darted behind him.

Maddox could feel the threat to his rear. In a flash of understanding, it struck him what was about to happen. The strain of the monotonous weeks had taken their toll on his concentration. The voyage had been out of his comfort zone. It had told on him, making him reckless and causing him to miss otherwise obvious clues. It appeared as if Doctor Rich had finally outmaneuvered him.

With a twist of his neck, Maddox looked behind. Standing in the hatchway, Meta held a stunner aimed at his back. He expected to see a triumphant smile. Instead, worried concentration marred her beauty.

Meta motioned with the stunner. Maddox raised his hands.

"Oh, I like this, I really do," Dana told him. "Yes, I find it rewarding to see a difficult task through to completion. Don't you find that to be the case, Captain?"

He watched her gloat.

"What do you propose?" Maddox asked.

"A new arrangement," Dana said. "You are hereby demoted to wretched piece of Star Watch scum. I am confining you to these quarters. I, on the other hand, am accepting a promotion to ship's captain. What do you think?"

Maddox turned, putting his back to Doctor Rich to face Meta. "You know we're in danger," he told the Rouen Colony woman. "You've seen the New Men hunting us. Humanity desperately needs the sentinel."

"Please," Meta told him, "no more talking, Captain."

Staring into her eyes, Maddox said, "I freed you from the prison planet."

"I don't want to do this," Meta said. "You have to believe me."

"Then don't do it," Maddox said. "Make the right decision."

As her eyes tightened, Meta pressed the trigger.

The blast struck Maddox in the chest. He strove to remain conscious but felt himself falling...falling...

I've just lost control of my ship.

***

Maddox groaned. His head was pounding. The taste of sand made his mouth incredibly dry. He unglued his eyes, and he realized someone had been shaking him and calling his name.

"Sir, I wish you'd wake up."

"Riker?" whispered Maddox, with his eyes still closed.

"Ah, that's good, sir. He's coming around," Riker called. "You were out for some time, sir."

Maddox forced himself to open his eyes. Blurriness made his stomach heave, and he almost threw up.

"Easy, sir, take it easy."

"Did Dana and Meta put you in here with me?"

"Ha-ha!" Riker laughed. "Not an old hound like me, sir. Not on your life. I think I know what happened. You're not used to grubbing it, sir. But me, you see, I'm a sergeant. Someone is always telling me to do this or do that. It's hardened me to privation, it has."

Maddox rubbed his forehead. "Where's Doctor Rich? Where's the scout?"

"I'll start with the last question first, sir," Riker said. "The scout has moved beyond the T dwarf and is headed for the thickest clot of the comet field. The lieutenant doesn't believe anyone over there on the destroyer has seen us yet. I believe Meta is examining the vacc-suits and powerdrill. Once we land, she plans to go outside and dig for Professor Ludendorff's hidden engines and atomic fuel."

That didn't sound right. Meta the traitor was still running free in his ship? "What are you talking about?" Maddox whispered.

"Well, sir," Riker said. "As I was trying to tell you, I'm an old space hound. I also happen to be a very suspicious man. I've been watching. This one old eye sees pretty good, sir."

"I'm sure that's true, but would you please get to the point."

"Sometimes, I even see quicker than a genius. That's how I spotted the Tojo bodysuit back in France, remember?"

"Yes," Maddox said wearily. "That was an excellent piece of deduction. Now would you kindly get to the bloody point, Sergeant?"

"Don't go straining yourself, sir. You're still weak from the stunner blast. I'm still finding it hard to believe Meta did that. Not that she got the drop on you, but that she actually pulled the trigger. I think we should punish her, but maybe a reward is more in keeping with her latest action."

Maddox closed his eyes. His sergeant had gained a coup over him. The man wouldn't go on like this otherwise. Riker liked to boast even as he pretended not to.

"Do you want to hear what happened, sir?" Riker asked.

"I'd be delighted." Maddox opened his eyes again and found that the blurriness had departed. He lay in Dana's abandoned room, on her cot.

"Well, sir, I peeked out of my quarters, and I saw Meta and Doctor Rich come out of hers. Meta looked crestfallen. The doctor strutted like a gambler pulling in a hard-won pot. In a beeline, she headed for the control room. Not to put too fine of a point on it, sir, I stepped out of my room. I stunned Meta first. It took a strong blast to bring the lady down. Then I aimed at Doctor Rich. Well, first I blasted the gun in her grip so it clattered onto the deck. She cradled her hand as if she wanted to scream with agony. She didn't scream though, not her. No, sir, that woman can talk faster than you can run. She told me all sorts of gibberish, threatening and promising all in one breath. It made me smile inside."

"I can imagine," Maddox said. He noticed that Riker was smiling openly now.

"I didn't get fancy. Well, the hand-stunning was a trick shot like you might have done. After that, no sir, no more fancy pants with a dame who had outsmarted Captain Maddox. I knew she was too dangerous for an old codger like me. So I just shot her with the stunner, and I did it again as she lay on the deck, in case she was faking."

"You didn't harm her, did you?" Maddox asked, worried he'd lost the doctor.

"Ah, that's what I love about you, sir. You're so solicitous about your enemies that you forget to ask how your boon companions are feeling."

"Let us rectify that, Sergeant," Maddox said. "How are you feeling?"

"Good, sir, very good indeed," Riker said.

"Splendid. It does my heart good to know it. I have a few questions, though. Do you believe you can answer them quickly?"

"I do indeed, sir."

"How did you, or we, the crew, discover which comet held the professor's secret supply of spare engines and fuel?"

"Meta told us—that was her positive action I've been trying to tell you about. The guilt of shooting you loosened her tongue. She's decided to pitch in with us all the way, after all. It seems she and the doctor had been communicating in secret for the past few weeks. Ain't that interesting, sir."

Maddox said nothing.

"At the moment, Doctor Rich is on the robo-doctor. I used the computer and found the formula to an old-style truth serum. It's an underhanded way to do this, I know, and beneath us to—"

"What did you say?" Maddox asked, interrupting.

"Truth serum, sir," Riker said. "I read up on the computer how to make the right formula."

Maddox closed his eyes. He'd been a fool and overlooked an obvious solution. It galled him, but not as much as letting Meta knock him unconscious. He knew that becoming overconfident was a problem with him. This time, he'd paid for it with a headache and wounded pride. Thank God for a good man like Sergeant Riker to back him up.

With his eyes closed, Maddox said, "I congratulate on you on your cunning and forcefulness, Sergeant. You have single-handedly saved the expedition and possibly humanity as well."

"Keep talking, sir. I like the sound of this."

Even though it hurt his head, Maddox grinned. He opened his eyes once more and swung his legs off the cot. Dizziness threatened. He heaved up to his feet nonetheless.

"To work, Sergeant," Maddox said.

"We're already working, sir. I think you should rest a little longer."

"No. Everyone must pitch in. We lost the luxury of time a while ago."

As if to punctuate his thoughts, Ensign Maker looked into the room. "Captain, sir, you'd better come to the bridge. I mean the control room. According to Lieutenant Noonan, the destroyer has increased its acceleration above its safety limit maximum."

232

-28-

Keith followed an unsteady Captain Maddox to the control room.

Upon entering, the captain stopped and stared. Keith climbed through the hatch after him. Meta sat in the captain's usual spot. Maddox looked straight at her.

Lieutenant Noonan swiveled around. She didn't bother with the captain, but gave Keith a meaningful glance. He nodded and headed for the pilot's chair. Once he'd strapped in and assessed his board, Keith turned and found the captain still glaring at Meta.

Finally, the former Rouen Colony miner dropped her gaze. She gave her head a quick shake. It made her long hair cascade behind her.

"I don't expect you to understand...sir," Meta said in her pleasant voice.

Keith never got tired of studying her, the way she walked or listening to her talk. It defined logic that she'd captured him on Loki Prime, had manhandled him, in fact.

Would you call what she'd done woman*handling me? Sure, a few bodybuilding women can bench press more than I can, but to just push me around so easily...*

The crazy part was that he still recalled her grip, the way her breasts had mashed against his back while she'd forced him through the jungle. What would she be like in the sack?

"I lived on Loki Prime for four terrible years," Meta quietly explained to Maddox. "Living there changes you. Well, maybe not *you*, but it did me. Dana...she saved me from some grim predators. I owed her, Captain."

"I understand that part," Maddox said.

"I shouldn't have shot you."

"No," he said.

"To pay for my…action, I've decided to help you more directly," Meta said.

"You decided this after Sergeant Riker shot the doctor?"

"I did," Meta admitted. "I don't expect you to trust me now."

"You're wise to realize that," Maddox said.

Lieutenant Noonan cleared her throat.

Maddox tore his gaze from Meta. "What is it?" he asked the lieutenant.

Valerie pointed at her view-screen. "I think you ought to look at this, sir."

In two strides, Maddox reached her station. He squinted as he examined her screen. "They're moving fast."

Keith craned his neck to get a look. The destroyer had accelerated from its Laumer-Point in the inner system, heading out here. Now, the *Saint Petersburg's* exhaust had lengthened farther behind itself then any of them had ever seen before.

Why are they coming so fast all of a sudden? Keith wondered.

The *Geronimo* had traveled to the edge of the outer system, past the T dwarf and its many moons. They'd reached the system's back comet cloud. There were a lot of them out here. An unstable Laumer-Point waited even farther out. According to the professor's star chart, that tramline would take them into the alien star system.

"We're over three billion kilometers from the *Saint Petersburg,*" Valerie said. "Even at their velocity, it's going to take the destroyer a couple of days to reach here."

"I can see that," Maddox said.

"I still don't think we should use our fusion thruster," Valerie said. "We're cloaked, drifting at our present velocity. Before the *Saint Petersburg* entered the system, we braked with the fusion engine. We still need to slow down even more."

"We can use the gravity generator," the captain said.

Keith winced. He hated the way dumping gravity waves shook the ship. The *Geronimo* had taken far too much stress throughout the voyage. He was afraid they might shake something permanently loose. If they did, no one was coming to rescue them. This was deep into the Beyond. They were so on their own it wasn't funny.

Rubbing his hands together, Keith knew fear and excited elation in the pit of his stomach. This was the reason for existence: doing the crazy thing. They'd been waiting for this moment for months of travel.

"We can hide from the *Saint Petersburg*," Valerie told Maddox. "Any of those comets would make an excellent spot. After landing, we shut down almost everything and become a dark object. Of course, it would be even better to land on the right comet."

"Which one is that?" asked Maddox. "It could take years of searching to find Professor Ludendorff's stash."

"That's where my apology comes in," Meta said.

The captain straightened, regarding her. "You can tell us which one it is?"

"From hints Dana dropped," Meta said. "Yes, I think I know which comet. I only have one request."

Maddox said nothing.

"When all is said and done," Meta told him, "you spare the doctor."

Keith wondered what the captain was thinking. The man was proud, and Dana and Meta had beaten him. Slowly, Captain Maddox nodded.

Drawing a deep breath, Meta told the lieutenant the needed coordinates.

"Ensign Maker," the captain said. "We will use the gravity generator to continue deceleration. Then, you will land the scout on the comet."

"With our wounded generator," Keith said, "that won't be easy."

"Are you capable of the task?" the captain asked.

"Oh, yes, Captain, sir," Keith said, puffing out his chest. "It's the reason I was born."

Maddox grinned. Keith liked that about the man. He could be a stuffed shirt and then change into a cunning devil.

"I'm glad to hear it," the captain said. "Lieutenant, plot the exact course. Then we'll see if our scout can slip onto the comet without the *Saint Petersburg* noticing."

***

235

Later, after the second use of the gravity generator, Keith flexed his fingers. He sat with a straight back in the pilot's chair. His focus was glued to the flight screen.

For the umpteenth time this trip, he wished he were in a strikefighter. Piloting wasn't as enjoyable locked in the same room with everyone else. To float alone among the stars while popping his head next to the fighter's canopy was far more freeing.

Keith double-checked the scout's velocity and its relation to the approaching comet. Behind them, one hundred million kilometers away bulked the massive T dwarf. Its pull affected them more because the ship dumped gravity waves. If he'd maneuvered with the thruster...

Keith cracked his knuckles. "Ready, sir?" he asked.

"Take us down, Ensign," Maddox told him.

Grinning from ear to ear because he felt nervous, Keith began to use the gravity generator with greater flexibility and control than he'd done before. "A bit at a time, sir," Keith explained.

The ace eased the *Geronimo* lower toward the comet, which traveled around the T dwarf in a giant elliptical orbit instead of around the system's star. The comet was a dirty snowball, composed of ice, rock and bits of miscellaneous debris. For its size, the thing didn't have a lot of weight. What he didn't want to do was land so hard it cracked the snowball. Even worse would be to break it into pieces as if hit by a billiard ball. That would be a dead giveaway to the destroyer where the scout had gone.

"Easy does it," Maddox told him.

"No worries, sir," Keith said. "This will be a piece of fluff." He didn't feel that in his gut, but why let them know. This was his specialty. He would see them through.

"Baby, baby, baby," Keith whispered under this breath. "Now we're going to see." He applied more power.

The gravity generator shook the ship. Metal groaned.

"Let up on the generator!" Lieutenant Noonan shouted.

Keith did no such thing. This was the final approach. His panel shook before him. The gravity generator clacked with strain. It could break any second, and maybe the smart thing to do would be to let it rest. He kept it running.

"Ensign!" shouted Maddox.

The generator began to make even worse screeching sounds. Keith winced. His chest erupted with fear. If the gravity generator blew up—the game would be over. The others kept shouting at him. He ignored their pleas. This was just like strikefighter combat. The man with bigger balls won these. He continued to use the overburdened generator, dumping more gravity waves.

"Sir!" Valerie pleaded with Maddox.

Keith studied the approach. They still came down too hard. He tapped his board. The overburdened generator roared with complaint. The entire scout shook. So did Keith as he sat in his chair. He refused to stop, though. Either the generator lasted or—

The *Geronimo* gently settled onto the snowball. A few ice particles broke off and drifted into space. That wasn't good. But the comet held, and they had survived the landing.

With another tap on the board, Keith turned off the gravity generator. It whined down the scales, at last going silent before it stopped running. The ace waited in his chair for his nerves to settle. Finally, he looked around and laughed heartily to show them he was the pilot extraordinaire.

"Nothing to it, Chaps," Keith said. "It was a lovely piece of fluff, just like I told you it would be."

***

They were down. Now they waited on the comet as the destroyer crossed the star system.

For Keith, the waiting proved harder than the landing. Having something to do kept his thoughts from lingering on the staggering odds that always seemed to climb higher against them.

Just like the others, Ensign Maker's nerves had frayed throughout the past months of run, endless repair, hide and slip away down another wormhole. It didn't help that they did this in a battered scout. The *Saint Petersburg* or the star cruiser always found them again. It was maddening and debilitating to shipboard morale.

Keith wore a vacc-suit as he jumped out of *Geronimo's* hatch. The stars blazed around him as he glided onto the dirty-white surface. He turned back, viewing his home for the last three months. He'd always had a good eye, able to tell where he'd welded, where the dents mashed inward and which hull parts were good.

237

I can't believe I gave up my pub for this. I must have been out of my bloody mind. We're never going to survive the alien system. The idea of using the comet as a sheath—pure rotgut arrogance is what it is.

He faced forward and began to glide across the surface. Keith had a knack for this. He was well aware that if he jumped too high, he would reach the comet's escape velocity and float away. It was like ice-skating, something he used to do a lot of as a kid. He'd played hockey for a time. His small size meant he'd been a target for the bruisers trying to check him into the boards. His skating speed and slap shots had won more than one game for the team.

He glided, feeling free as he never could cramped within the scout. Everyone was getting on one another's nerves. Seeing the same faces every day, smelling the recycled air and eating the freeze-dried crap—

I need a drink.

In his helmet, Keith licked chapped lips. A good brew would help. Even better, would be a shot of Scotch sliding down his gullet.

I wonder where the captain hid it.

Keith had been good for longer than he believed he could. By the Rood, he hadn't been this sober ever since Danny-boy's...

Keith licked his lips one more time. He didn't want to recall his brother's death. Oh, yes, he had taken the captain's evil pills for a time. If he drank, he'd likely puke out his guts. Well, he would if he'd continued to pop the little traitor capsules every several days. Starting a week ago, he'd flushed the pills down the toilet. He remembered the captain's threat. The baton smashing the bottle—

That was a dirty trick. He had a scar on the back of his right hand because of it. *Will one drink make any difference?*

In his heart, Keith suspected it would. He'd given the captain his word. The blighter had helped him remain sober. The abyss—

Don't be melodramatic, Keith, my boy. What abyss? That's pure tommyrot.

He knew that wasn't true, but he wanted to lie to himself. Despite the cramped quarters aboard *Geronimo*, he'd felt alive these past weeks. It had been like that at Tau Ceti. The threat, the excitement, the pressures fed his sense of adventure. He'd saved the crew a time or two. That had been the best part of all.

I haven't lost anything flying a craft.

In his helmet, Keith grinned. He glided over a ridge and saw a red flare out there. It was time to go to work.

He reached Meta with her jackhammer. She was almost indistinguishable in her silver vacc-suit. She'd made a huge hole already. Frozen down at the bottom was supposed to be Professor Ludendorff's cache: engines and fuel.

They had short-speakers between them to communicate. He hailed her. She lifted a gloved hand to acknowledge him. Afterward, she pointed at the second item, a spacetorch.

Keith went to it, clicking it on. In seconds, he had a hot tongue of flame on the end. He put the blue flame against the ice, burning it away. He helped her uncover the cache. The *Saint Petersburg* was coming fast. He didn't see how they could possibly make the comet-sheath ready in time.

One more drink for old time's sake. The captain can't deny that if we're about to die because we couldn't push our lead far enough. I tried. The least I can do is go out with style.

Yes, he'd have to start looking for the bottles. The captain was cunning, but Keith bet he could beat him if they both piloted strikefighters. The captain might know how to hide whiskey, but Keith trusted his nose and instincts. Of course, he didn't want to let the crew down, but the nearing destroyer—didn't that change the equation?

Bloody yes it does.

Meta raised her head. "What was that?" she asked. The words crackled over his headphones.

"Down there, love," he said, pointing. "Do you want me to start there?"

She considered it and finally nodded, and the work continued.

***

Two days later, the destroyer began to slow its tremendous velocity. The *Saint Petersburg* neared the massive T dwarf. At its speed, it would soon reach back here among the comet cloud.

Meta and Keith had sent up passive sensors on the star-side of the comet, linking it by cables to the "hidden" *Geronimo*. The scout rested on the other side of the comet as the approaching *Saint Petersburg*.

As the ensign sat in the control room, he watched Valerie's viewscreen. The destroyer was easily visible with its intense burn.

"Why are they slowing near the planet?" Valerie asked.

The two of them were alone in the control room.

"They don't want to enter the next Laumer-Point the way we have," Keith said. "It's not considered safe going through a jump point too fast."

Valerie looked up at him.

"Did I say something wrong?" he asked.

"I know the procedures," she said. "I'm the one who's been suggesting we take a more cautious approach through the tramlines."

"Right you are," he said. "I'm just nervous, love, talking too much. That destroyer—do you think it can sniff us out?"

She'd returned to studying her screen. "I don't like this waiting game any more than you do."

Keith made a soft sound. More than ever, he wanted a drink. Waiting was the worst. "There's no reason they should know we're hiding back here," he said.

"There's no way they should have been able to follow us this far into the Beyond either," Valerie said. "Yet, they have."

"Do you think there's an emitter aboard we haven't been able to find? Do you think it's been helping them track us?"

"No," Valerie said. "We've gone through the ship too many times. If there were an emitter, we would have found it by now."

They waited and watched the destroyer slow down enough to lock into the T dwarf's orbit. The day passed as *Saint Petersburg* circled the brown dwarf twice, their sensors washing the system with electronics. Finally, the destroyer escaped the planet's orbit and headed for the unstable Laumer-Point beyond the comet.

In the control room, Keith kept watch with Valerie and sometimes with Maddox or Sergeant Riker. The crew endured.

"Maybe they'll go through the wormhole for us," Keith said.

Captain Maddox was in the control room. He didn't say a word.

Later, Keith stood in the corridor, trying to psyche himself up to go into the captain's quarters. He told himself that he no longer needed the drink. It had become the principle of the thing. Finally, he stalked off to his quarters to play another game of Solitaire.

The destroyer finally reached the unstable Laumer-Point, nosing around the area. After several hours, the *Saint Petersburg* accelerated, heading back toward the T dwarf.

The destroyer passed their comet by two hundred thousand kilometers. Keith felt as if he stopped breathing. The enemy ship didn't decelerate nor did it fire its lasers at them. The destroyer kept a steady velocity as it neared the T dwarf. Then, its exhaust tail lengthened as *Saint Petersburg* accelerated back toward the distant star over four billion kilometers away. The other Laumer-Point was there in the inner system.

As tensions eased throughout the scout, Captain Maddox called a meeting. Dana was still laid out in medical. She was the only one to miss the get-together.

Keith sat down in the wardroom. Meta, Valerie, Sergeant Riker and the captain all entered, taking their places.

Keith kept thinking about those bottles of beautiful Scotch. They had to be in the captain's quarters. Given Maddox's methods and distrust, it would be difficult to break in and search—difficult and possibly dangerous. That had helped to dampen the thirst for a time. Now it had returned stronger than ever. Keith debated pleading illness, leaving the meeting and then hurrying to the man's room.

If they found him, though, how could he live with himself? He had some of his old pride again. He'd saved the team more than once. To throw that all away—

I wish I could get drunk in secret. Then I could come back better than ever. I'm due for a drink. It's killing me to say sober.

Captain Maddox cleared his throat.

Keith decided to worry about whiskey later. He didn't like the captain's rigid features. Ever since Dana's attempted mutiny, Maddox had seemed tenser than ever. Even his skin seem to stretch tighter across his cheekbones.

The waiting is getting to him just like the rest of us. I guess he's human after all.

"It's time to make a decision," Maddox said. "I'm uncertain about the correct choice. The destroyer's latest behavior troubles me."

"This is different for you," Valerie said.

"How so?" asked Maddox.

"You usually just snap out orders without explaining the situation."

Keith watched Maddox. The captain's skin tightened a little more for a moment. Then he smiled. It was an infectious thing. The man was part highhandedness and part mischievous prankster. So far, his extreme effectiveness had carried him through whatever trouble the captain managed to bring upon himself.

"Lieutenant," Maddox said. "I have a confession to make."

Keith felt it. Everyone perked up. What was the captain going to tell them?

"I am a spy by trade," Maddox said. "Commanding a starship is new. I've been learning the craft as I go. I've felt lately that I should trust my crew more. That doesn't come easily. It's my nature and training to distrust. I must thank you for bearing with me."

Valerie laughed. "Well, I'll be, sir. Yes, thank you."

Keith got it. That was the best apology any of them were going to get for some of the man's imperious actions throughout the past months. Lieutenant Noonan had recognized it was an apology. At that moment, Keith had what he considered as an unworthy thought. Had Maddox just said those things because he meant them, or had the man said them to help put the lieutenant at ease?

"In any case," Maddox said, "the point of the meeting is the *Saint Petersburg's* latest actions. I'm referring to its orbit around the T dwarf and its slow approach and time spent at the unstable Laumer-Point. Why didn't the destroyer jump through the point into the next system to see if we were there?"

"That would have solved our problems," Valerie said.

"Nothing is going to be easy," Maddox said. "We must remember that."

"I have an idea," Meta said, "about the destroyer, I mean."

"We're listening," Maddox told her.

"They must be able to directly trail our passage," Meta said. "Maybe they sense our exhaust particles even after we've passed through an area."

"I've wondered the same thing," Valerie said. "But if you're right about that, they would have trailed us to the comet."

"Not necessarily," Keith said. "We used the gravity generator at the end. It doesn't leave particles to trace."

Valerie tapped her head with the flat of her hand. "That's right. But I have a different theory. Instead of tracking, I wonder if they have a device that can tell if a Laumer-Point has just been opened or not."

"Ah," Maddox said. "That might explain their behavior. If that's true, they'll know we entered the star system, and that we haven't left yet."

"If the destroyer jumps elsewhere from the inner system tramline," Valerie said, "that will trash the theory. But if they stay in this star system—they'll soon be out here again hunting for us."

Maddox scanned the others' faces. "It's time to bury the *Geronimo*."

"The destroyer might spot us doing that," Valerie said.

"They're returning to the inner system," Maddox said. "Now is the time to make a cave. Afterward, we seal up and make a run for it."

"We'll be crawling with the comet surrounding us," Valerie said.

"I know," the captain said. "But I'm convinced this is our last opportunity. If anyone has a different suggestion, now is the time to make it."

Keith swallowed with a parched throat. He desperately wanted a drink. He wanted to make an excuse, leave and ransack the captain's quarters. They owed him. Yet...he also wanted to stay sober. The abyss of drunkenness was real, and he wanted to stay far away from it.

Feeling worthless and dirty, the ensign raised a hand.

"Yes?" asked Maddox.

"Sir," Keith whispered, knowing he had to confess. "I want a drink so badly I'm ready to do anything for it. I stopped taking the pills some time ago."

The wardroom turned silent.

Maddox eyed him. Keith hated the look. He felt like dirt, knowing he'd let them down. Finally, the captain stood. "Come with me, Ensign."

Feeling like a whipped cur, with his gaze downcast, Keith followed the captain. The man headed straight for his quarters. Shuffling his feet, Keith entered the Spartan room.

243

Maddox went to a drawer and pulled it open. He picked up a bottle of Scotch, pried out the cork and brought it to a small table. With a clunk, Maddox set the bottle onto the surface.

"Come here, Ensign, have a drink, if you wish."

Keith swallowed and shuffled nearer. The desire for drink pulsated through him. Why was the captain doing this? Did Maddox wish to humiliate him even more? Did it matter why the man did what he did? Keith reached for the bottle, expecting Maddox to swat his hand away. The captain did no such thing. The man watched coldly.

Trembling with desire, raising the bottle to his lips, Keith could smell the beautiful whiskey. He expected a last warning. It never came.

With a cry of horror, Keith lifted the bottle above his head and hurled it down. The thing smashed against the deck. Glass flew everywhere and Scotch rained.

"No," Keith said, hanging his head. "I can't drink. I want to, sir. You have no idea how much. But I can't let any of you down."

When no words came, Keith looked up. Maddox still watched him, but it was no longer with cold indifference. The captain put a hand on Keith's shoulder and patted it twice.

"I'm proud of you, Ensign. Now tell me. What should I do with the other bottles?"

"Pour them down the disposal unit, sir," Keith said in a thick voice. "Please, get rid of them. I-I want to remain on your team."

Maddox smiled with approval in his eyes. "Come," he said. "Let's finish our briefing. With a man like you in my crew, we're either going to beat the New Men, or they're going to know they've been in the fight of their lives."

Keith squared his shoulders. "Yes, sir, Captain, sir," he said, saluting crisply.

-29-

Captain Maddox watched from outside the scout as he stood on the comet. Ensign Maker maneuvered the *Geronimo* into the vast cavern he and Meta had carved out of the dirty ice-ball.

It had been two days since the meeting in the wardroom. Since then, the crew had fixed the professor's engines to the outer comet and positioned the fuel for consumption. Only once the scout was embedded within and the entrance frozen over would they pilot the comet to the unstable Laumer-Point.

Despite their best efforts, the destroyer must have detected something suspicious. Before reaching the inner star system, the *Saint Petersburg* had braked hard. After the vessel came to a halt, it started accelerating for the outer, unstable Laumer-Point.

Valerie wondered why the destroyer hadn't gone toward the inner system at full acceleration to circle the star and whip back out here.

"They're doing it faster this way," Maddox had told her.

"Yes, but the fuel consumption is enormous the way they did it."

"The obvious conclusion is that speed is more important to them than fuel. Perhaps the star cruiser, when it shows up, gives the destroyer more fusion isotopes as needed."

As he stood on the comet, Maddox recalled the conversation. If—

The comet shuddered beneath his vacc-boots. The captain staggered in slow motion. The gravity here was negligible. A moment later, Maddox's earphones hissed.

"I'm down," Keith said. "We're going to begin icing the landing gear to the comet.

Maddox jumped, floating toward the torch. It was time to begin sealing the cavern and the *Geronimo* inside it.

***

Everything was hooked to the control room panels. Maddox took his spot and watched Keith and Valerie take theirs.

"Once we start," Valerie said. "They'll know exactly where we are."

Maddox understood. This was the final lap to the alien star system. The comet had to beat the destroyer to the Laumer-Point. Nothing else mattered.

"Ready?" Maddox asked Keith.

The ace nodded.

"Engage thrusters," Maddox said. "Engage every one of them. We're blasting full throttle until we've made it, or we're dead."

Keith tapped his board.

Watching his screen, Maddox saw the engines glow orange. Each of them was frozen into the ice at the "back" of the comet. The orange color intensified. Then blue fusion exhaust burst out. The tails quickly grew. Soon, they stretched far behind the comet. The thrusters pushed the mass of ice, snow, rock and *Geronimo* core.

Soon, the stellar object broke out of its ancient orbit around the T dwarf. Very slowly, it began to head toward the unstable Laumer-Point. It didn't have far to travel, a few hundred thousand kilometers. That was nothing compared to the destroyer's three billion, four hundred thousand.

"We need more velocity," Valerie said. "At this rate, the destroyer will catch us."

Maddox couldn't contain himself. He stood and shook his arms, willing the nervous tingling to stop. They were doing the impossible. After endless weeks upon weeks—

"Keep pouring it out," he told Keith.

"Don't worry about me, sir. I'm gunning the engines. The comet's mass is too much, though. It may be ice, but there's so bloody much of it that we're not going to accelerate fast enough. Ah, I have an idea. We edge the *Geronimo* closer to the exit so its thrusters stick out of the back. We add our thrust to the other engines."

"Not a bad idea for gaining greater velocity," Maddox said. "But if we do that, we'll never survive the other side. The only way we're going to exit the wormhole and live to finish our task is if the comet takes the brunt of the heat for us."

"You really believe it's going to be that way, sir?" Keith asked.

"Oh, yes."

***

The acceleration continued for another day. The professor's engines held, and Keith managed to eke a bit more thrust from them. It gave them slightly more velocity, possibly changing the endgame a day from now.

Compared to how far they had to travel to reach this place, the last lap was gallingly short. The comet's mass was both their bane and their approaching salvation.

Maddox paced inside his quarters. His stomach fluttered with anticipation. He had three distinct fears. First, he dreaded the possibility of the *Saint Petersburg* catching them before they reached the unstable Laumer-Point. If the destroyer reached them too soon, the twin laser batteries could possibly dig through the ice-shield to bite into the *Geronimo*. Second, while buried under millions of tons of ice and snow, could the scout's Laumer Drive open the wormhole entrance? Supposing it could, would the voyage down the unstable tramline annihilate them with random flux instability? Third, could they survive the red star on the other side?

That was the reason for the ice-shield. According to the professor, the unstable tramline was the only way into or out-of the haunted star system. The extinct race must have possessed incredible deflector shields or maybe they used millions of tons of rock as protection. The alien system had a red giant for a star. Once, it must have been a regular G glass star like Sol. Now, it was an M class star.

The star had used up the hydrogen fuel in the core, so the thermonuclear reactions had ceased there. That had begun a long process. From a 1-solar mass star, it had become a red giant with 1000 solar luminosities with a surface temperature about 3000 K and

100 solar radii. The Sun at this stage would engulf Mercury in its photosphere, or outer layer.

The red giant in the alien star system had grown over the only known Laumer-Point. That meant, once a starship exited the tramline, it would be in the star's photosphere. If the *Geronimo* exited normally, the star would crisp it in seconds.

The plan called for the comet taking the star's blasts. At their speed—if the calculations were correct—they would only be in the photosphere for a brief amount of time. Still, even for many hundreds of thousands of kilometers beyond the star, they would need the comet to absorb the hellish heat and radiation.

Maddox paced in one direction, turned sharply and paced in the other. If even *one* of the three fears came true, the mission would fail. They would be dead, and humanity would never gain its balancing starship.

He snorted to himself. Even if they beat all three worries, they still had to deal with the killer sentinel. They had to find a way aboard—and then they had to figure out how to make the ancient starship work for them.

Maddox shook his head. If they passed all those tests, could they take the alien vessel out of the star system into the wide universe?

The *Geronimo* had almost reached the goal, yet the imponderables seemed to expand before him.

Although he hated to admit it, Maddox realized he'd just have to wait for the answer.

I'm unsuited for starship command. The need to do, to act, is too strong in me. The waiting game and dispassionately playing each move—I want to get this over with one way or another.

***

Time crawled as the comet-vessel headed for the unstable Laumer-Point. The engines thrust, and hourly Maddox expected one of them to give out.

Behind them, the *Saint Petersburg* came at maximum drive, building greater velocity with each second. It launched two missiles, which accelerated even faster.

"Those are going to hit, sir," Valerie told Maddox in the control chamber.

Maddox stared at her screen. They had expected the move. At his orders, they had previously dismantled the scout's two cannons, freezing them and their autoloaders on the back of the comet.

"When the time comes," Maddox said, "Ensign Maker will have to shoot down the missiles."

Valerie gave him an unreadable look.

More time passed. The destroyer rapidly closed the distance. The two missiles zoomed toward destiny.

Finally, Maddox ordered Keith to his station.

The ace flexed his fingers. "I have this," he told them. "They're coming so fast there's no way they can maneuver out of the way of my shells."

With the primitive targeting system they'd frozen into the comet, Ensign Maker selected the lead missile. He began long-distance firing.

At thirty thousand kilometers from the comet, he struck the hardened nosecone. It should have shredded the warhead, but the thing held together. At twenty-one thousand kilometers, Keith nailed it again. The missile and its warhead died.

"I told you!" Keith shouted.

The last missile bored in. It had better ECM, and Keith failed to lock onto it. The shells sped past it as the missile kept coming.

"Blimey cocker," Keith hissed under his breath. "I ain't missing this close."

Before he could hit it, at nine thousand kilometers from target, the warhead ignited. The EMP blast and heat did its trick. All but one comet-frozen engine malfunctioned and kept spewing exhaust.

"Shutdown the last engine," Maddox said. "We don't want to skew our entrance trajectory."

The comet no longer accelerated, but drifted at its present velocity for the approaching Laumer-Point. Behind them, crossing the plane of the brown dwarf, *Saint Petersburg* made its last run. The destroyer traveled at high velocity. It would reach the Laumer-Point at almost the same instant as the comet.

"Sir," Valerie said. "We're being hailed."

Maddox massaged his chest, taking his seat. He debated with himself for all of three seconds. Decision made, he clicked on the comm equipment, letting his features appear to the other side. What did it matter now?

His screen showed the inflexible face of a New Man. The eyes were like swirling black ink, the skin like golden ivory. Gigantic haughtiness faced him.

"I know you," Maddox said, thinking to recognize the face. He'd had a momentary glimpse on the prison planet's surface and would never forget the man.

Despite the words, the enemy's masklike features never changed.

"I beat you on Loki Prime," Maddox said. "I shot you to the ground and took your weapon. I've kept it as a memento in my trophy case."

"You have failed," the New Man said.

The deep voice shocked Maddox. It was so utterly controlled and confident. He envied the New Man that.

The other cocked his head and seemed to peer through the screen with greater interest. "I detect an anomaly. You are not like them."

"What's he mean?" Keith whispered.

Lieutenant Noonan shushed the pilot, tapping her index finger against her lips.

Maddox sat frozen in his chair. He yearned for the New Man to elaborate. Was he a failed experiment? Had they used his mother as a breeder, putting their *exalted* seed into her womb?

Am I like them? Maddox wondered.

"Surrender," the New Man said. "There is no need for you to die."

"Why would you care?" Maddox asked.

"You have information I would like to confirm."

Maddox mulled that over. The New Man hadn't said, "You have information I need." Instead, the haughty New Man wished to *confirm* a thing.

"What's your name?" Maddox asked.

The New Man frowned. "You young presumptuous pup of the Star Watch, you have insulted me for the last time."

"What insult? I just asked you your name."

The New Man stiffened before he said, "Know that your mission will die with you, Captain Maddox."

Maddox's eyes widened with surprise.

"We always know more about our targets than we need to understand. Thus, I know you and your inefficient crew." The New Man leaned closer. The black eyes seemed to burn with passion.

"You were always doomed to fail, Captain. It was inevitable. We have arrived to halt the madness of your species' chaotic inconsistencies. You should surrender to us as gods coming in judgment. Homo Sapiens' era of rutting and ugliness will finally cease."

"Are you saying you're no longer human?" Maddox asked.

"Your conceit is ill-reasoned," the New Man said. "Homo Sapiens have risen little higher than the brute beasts around them. Perhaps you have something more personally compared to the common ruck of your Orion Arm herd. I would like to examine your DNA to discover what this difference is, but it is a small matter. We of the Race have arrived at genetic perfection. That makes us human. You and your ilk are something lower on the evolutionary scale."

"Yet we can communicate," Maddox said, "which disproves your theory."

"How you strive to reason like a man. It is pitiful to watch. Attend my words, Captain Maddox. A cow lows to let its master know it is hungry. A farmer shouts to guide the cow to the waiting grain. They communicate, but they are far from equal. Can you grasp the point?"

"I do," Maddox said. "Your arrogance will destroy you."

"I see a half-beast wishing to ape humanity. You practice what you conceive as self-awareness. We of the Race are true to ourselves—what you perceive as arrogance."

"Did you call me to gloat?" Maddox asked.

"How you struggle to understand me. To you, I am *Per Lomax*. Know then that I have degraded myself to give you an opportunity to surrender and save your genes for study. I also require Professor Ludendorff's notes. Do this, and live. Refuse, and go into an eternity of oblivion, never to know again."

"You don't believe in an afterlife?" Maddox asked.

"Show me the evidence you've complied of such a state."

"Humanity's sacred books all teach this," Maddox told the New Man.

"Do not speak to me of the cries of a terrified subspecies. The Race is humanity. Our books do not speak of pale illusions needed to soften the realities of existence."

"Per Lomax is like calling you master?" Maddox asked.

"As I said earlier, you are a grade above the others of your herd. Bravo, you can see to a limited degree. Now, the moment is upon you, Captain Maddox of the Star Watch. Surrender or die. You will not have another opportunity."

With his heart pounding, Maddox put the comm on mute. He turned to the others. "How much time until we reach the Laumer-Point?"

"Ten minutes," Valerie said. "We don't even know if the scout's Laumer Drive can activate the tramline through all this ice."

"Lasers!" shouted Keith. "*Saint Petersburg* is firing."

"Blow off the first engine," Maddox said.

With a forefinger, Keith stabbed his board. The great mass of the comet meant that down here no one felt the explosion that ripped away the engine, hurling it behind them.

On the screen, Maddox watched an engine tumble from the comet. At the same time, the twin lasers stabbed into the ice, burning deeper and deeper.

The lasers boiled ice into water and vapor. As the lasers kept digging, they boiled away more and more. Finally, that created a cloud. The cloud dissipated some of the lasers' strength. Unfortunately, the temporary situation wouldn't last.

"According to my calculations," Valerie said, "the lasers are going to dig through to us. Once the beams reach the scout's hull, the game will be up."

Maddox knew that. He waited as the tumbling engine continued away from them and toward the approaching destroyer. The distances were too great between the vessels to make much of a difference. The captain waited for the engine to be far enough away from the comet.

During the wait, the lasers sliced through the ice and past the hidden scout. The attack lasted long enough for the beams to reach the other side of the comet, stabbing through.

"The destroyer is retargeting," Valerie said. "They must know they missed us with the first shot."

Beaming once again, the lasers tried another area of the comet.

"Now," Maddox told Keith. "Send the signal."

The pilot did just that.

Seconds later, the engine with its atomic pile went critical, creating a thermonuclear fireball. That blocked the beams. The ice protected them from the EMP wash and the heat and radiation expanding back to them.

"The destroyer's deflector shields snapped on," Valerie said.

"Blow the next engine," Maddox said. "We'll try this again."

Per Lomax of the Race refused to let the trick play out a second time. He used the destroyer's beams to melt the next engine before the atomic pile could go critical.

"It's no good," Valerie said, her eyes so wide the whites showed as she stared at him.

"Wrong," Maddox told her. "While the destroyer's beams struck the engine, they weren't needling through the comet. Ensign, blow off the next engine."

For the next several minutes, the comet detached engine after engine. The *Saint Petersburg* destroyed them one at a time, beaming into the comet between intervals.

"The Laumer-Point is approaching," Valerie shouted.

"I can hear you just fine, Lieutenant," Maddox said in a calm voice.

She cast him a harried look but nodded. "Yes, sir," she said in a more controlled voice.

"Activate the Laumer Drive," Maddox told Keith.

"Aye-aye, Captain, sir."

They watched the board, watched—

"It's not activating," Valerie groaned. Then a green light flashed. "Wait! The Laumer-Point is opening, Captain."

Maddox grinned fiercely. "Get ready for jump," he said.

"The lasers," Keith said. "They're digging straight for the scout this time."

Maddox glanced at his board. He knew the lasers wouldn't make it in time. "We're going in, people."

"Will we make it through the red giant's photosphere?" Valerie asked.

"That," Maddox said, "is the question of the hour."

-30-

The comet with *Geronimo* embedded within shot down the wormhole. Flashing through the non-liner medium, the mass of ice, snow, rock and other debris exited the unstable tramline as an intact whole. It appeared inside the outer edge a red giant's photosphere.

Immediately, the 3000 K of heat began transforming ice to water to steam and then down to its component particles.

The scout's antigravity-pods screamed, screeched and soon smoked with complaint. The considerably lessened comet erupted out of the star's surface like a bullet through a wall, speeding away. The heat continued to dissolve the comet, but at a lesser rate. Intense radiation struck the icy surface. Less of it reached the centrally placed scout, and the special hull blocked most of the deadly rays. Still, too many rads penetrated their bodies. Provided the crew survived the next few minutes, each of them would have to take heavy dosages of anti-rad medicine.

The minutes passed, and the ancient ice boiled away into vapor, leaving a great misty trail. The star's gravity began to slow their velocity. Fortunately, they had built up to quite a speed before shooting through the Laumer-Point.

Ten minutes after entering the alien star system—if this was truly it—Maddox said, "We're going to make it."

Lieutenant Noonan swiveled around. She kept blinking. Finally, she smiled so hard it seemed as if it would crack her face open. She began to scream with laughter.

Ensign Maker joined in, gales of pent-up terror erupting as he howled with joy.

254

Maddox felt the maddening elation grip him as well. It bubbled, threatening release. Finally, he swallowed it down. Turning his head, he waited, letting the other two enjoy their well-earned moment of relief.

They were here, heading away from the red giant. What would the ancient star system show them? He was eager to find out.

Now comes the hard part. I have to convince Doctor Rich to help us. Either that, or I have to drug her with truth serum and see if I can get useful data out of her.

***

Like a newborn chick, *Geronimo* burst out of the shell of what remained of the comet. It was a sick scout in too many ways. Most of the crew suffered from the radiation treatments.

Maddox felt the effects the least. Meta was in a similar condition. Riker and Doctor Rich were the sickest.

The Star Watch spaceship was in poor repair. The gravity generator had become inoperable. The antigravity pods limped along, and the cloaking device refused to respond. They lacked ship's cannons of any kind. They didn't even have a missile or a mine to their name.

"We made it to the star system," Maddox said, "but we're in no condition to do anything."

He sat beside Lieutenant Noonan as she wheezed on the robo-doctor.

"What's it..." she coughed weakly. "What's it like out here?" she whispered.

Maddox used a portable holo-unit. With a control, he clicked it on. The box hummed and an image of the star system spread out before them. Valerie raised her head, examining it.

Maddox did likewise. It was surreal. Little red dots showed the position of drifting space hulks, wrecks from an ancient war. Humanity might have fought with chariots at that time, the charioteers hurling javelins at each other. There wasn't a mere thousand or ten thousand wrecks. It was more like fifty thousand drifting hulks.

"Incredible," Valerie whispered. "It's a graveyard of starships."

Maddox nodded. Fifty thousand odd spaceships drifting from a war fought so long ago that all memory of the reasons had vanished with the alien races. Had it been two alien species fighting each other? Maybe it had been two subspecies like the New Men and old humanity struggling for dominance and existence.

From one end of the star system to the other, the hulks drifted, orbiting the monstrous red giant.

"Where are the planets?" Valerie asked.

"The professor's notes told the truth," Maddox said. "There're aren't any planets left, just thickened asteroid globules showing what once must have been worlds."

"No gas giants either?" she asked.

"Gases in thick profusion and nickel-iron asteroids," Maddox said, "but not planets. Whatever weapons the aliens used, planet busters seem to be among them."

Valerie tore her gaze from the holoimage to stare at Maddox. "Is there any sign of the sentinel?"

The captain felt a growing numbness in his heart. He shook his head.

"What? You mean there never was one?" Valerie asked.

"If it's here, the sentinel is hidden."

"Sneaking up on us?" she asked.

Maddox stared at her. "I don't like to think of that."

Swallowing audibly, Valerie asked, "Is there any sign the *Saint Petersburg* followed us down the wormhole?"

"None," Maddox said. "If they did, the red giant's photosphere overloaded their deflector shields and annihilated the destroyer."

"If there's no sentinel…" Valerie said.

Just then, the scout's interior alarms rang. The ship's intercom came online. Ensign Maker spoke between bouts of coughing. "Ladies and gentlemen, we have company. The alien sentinel is barreling straight for our ship."

***

"We're back to square one," Maddox said. "Now, you're in the fire with us, Doctor. If you want to live, you're going to have to help us board the alien ship."

Dana Rich lay in her cot in her former quarters. She wheezed with phlegm lodged in her lungs. She was sick with fever, but the robo-doctor had given her a seventy percent chance of recovery.

With red eyes, Dana chuckled throatily. "I'm sick of disappointment, Captain. I don't like defeat either. Your sergeant broke something inside me when he used the stunner on its high setting. It makes me feel good watching you suffer with anxiety."

"You have a fever," he said. "Provided we survive the sentinel, you will recover."

"I don't think you're hearing me. I don't want to get better."

"To spite me?" he asked.

"Maybe you are hearing me after all," Dana said.

"Doctor, the sentinel is coming fast." Maddox pointed at the holoimage.

The sentinel was big, and it generated powerful deflector shields. The alien starship had two broad disc-shaped areas and it bristled with weaponry. It had already blasted the *Geronimo* with harsh sensor sweeps.

"Do you have any final words, Captain?" Dana asked. "Our end is fast approaching."

"You used to have fire, Doctor. Are the New Men that much better than you that you're afraid to try to compete against them?"

She gave him a weary smile. "I enjoy watching you flail, seeking to find a way to unlock me. You have no idea. Maybe I should prolong your agony. Send your sergeant here. Let me stun him as many times as he stunned me. Then I'll tell you what you must do."

Maddox rose from his stool. Putting his hands behind his back, he began to pace. He didn't know how to proceed. He wouldn't sell out his people. He wouldn't hand over his authority. Was his life over then?

Halting, he peered at Doctor Rich. She'd propped up onto one elbow with a smile on her face. She watched him with avid delight.

"I need your help," he told her. "I've said that from the beginning."

"You think that's what I want to hear?"

They stared at each other. He saw pride. He saw a wounded person, a genius and someone incredibly bitter.

I'm about to die. The sentinel will swat us out of existence. What does such a lonely, bitter person want to hear? Does she hate me because Riker and I defeated her?

257

Maddox moved to the stool. Picking it up, he set it just before her cot. He sat and put a hand on her arm. She jerked away, scowling at him.

"I'm different," Maddox said. "My mother escaped from the Beyond to the Oikumene. I have some of the qualities of the New Men. I fear that half of me belongs to them."

The scowl eased from her features. She looked at him with interest. "You're the spawn of a New Man?"

"I don't know. It's possible. I want to capture one of them and test his DNA, matching it against mine."

"Do the others realize this about you?" Dana asked.

Maddox shook his head.

"You think knowing this about you will sway me?" she scoffed.

"I have no idea," he said. "I felt like telling you, like telling someone."

"Why?"

"If we succeed, think of the enjoyment you could gain by holding that over me."

Dana Rich blinked several times. "I'm not your friend, Captain."

"I don't think you have any friends, Doctor."

"You're right!" she snarled. "I'm alone. We're all alone."

With the outburst, bitterness seemed to flow from her as if from a broken dam. Hate twisted her features. Her eyes radiated something profoundly troubling. She panted, and she worked her mouth with silent rage.

Maddox watched the performance. This woman had been deeply hurt. The amount of suffering awed him.

Finally, her features grew less rigid and twisted. The intensity pouring from her became normal anger. The pants turned to wheezing for air as her lungs bubbled with phlegm. She coughed for a long time before finally closing her eyes.

In time, her breathing evened out.

Maddox rose silently from the stool. He had no more ideas about what to do. With a leaden step, he moved toward the hatch.

"I'll do it," she said behind him.

Maddox turned, surprised at what he heard.

"It has nothing to do with you or your silly secret. This has everything to do with me. I'm Doctor Dana Rich, and I'm going to give humanity its fighting shot at your uncles."

"What do you need?" Maddox said.

"Help me up to medical. I'll dial the robo-doctor and give myself the needed shots. Then, you and I are going to the control room. Let us see if I have the magic you're looking for."

Captain Maddox didn't like it.

In medical, Doctor Rich had injected herself with massive doses of stimulants. Her eyes burned with feverish intensity. Now, she sat in the control room, her fingers blurring across a computer console.

The woman didn't talk. She hunched over her board, twitching instead of moving. Muttered comments drifted from her, but no one knew what she said.

This lasted for hours. During this time, the sentinel approached in what seemed like serene majesty. The starship didn't seem to be in any hurry. Where could the scout go? Yet, how did the sentinel know they were trapped?

Maddox must have asked Valerie the question.

Doctor Rich quit tapping. She straightened and swiveled around. "What did you say?" she asked.

With a helpless gesture, Maddox said, "How does the sentinel know we can't escape the star system?"

"It has no idea," Dana said.

"Then why doesn't it rush after us?" Maddox asked.

Dana's eyelids flickered several times. It made it seem as if her brain flipped the question hundreds of times in several seconds, attempting to decipher the answer.

"Why are you bothering me with your nonsense?" Dana asked angrily. "I'm trying to work. Your chatter disrupts my thought process. Worse, your inane ideas clutter my mind with trivia. Leave, please. Let me work in peace."

Maddox inclined his head. Without glancing at Valerie—the lieutenant would know what to do if the doctor went berserk—he left the control room, softly closing the hatch behind him. Under different circumstances, the doctor's behavior might have bothered him. He recognized a genius at work, though. They could be inordinately touchy.

Riker and Keith slept, exhausted from days of effort. Noises came out of the engine room. Meta must be tinkering. On impulse, Maddox headed there.

Most of the journey, he'd avoid the Rouen Colony woman. She troubled him because he enjoyed the sound of her voice too much. He enjoyed her face, the eyes especially, and he fully appreciated her womanly form. That did not change the troubling fact that she had stunned him several days ago.

Ducking his head, Maddox entered the large compartment. Meta wore coveralls with a Star Watch logo on the upper front pocket. She had a belt of jangling tools around her waist.

From where she worked, Meta gave him a half-glance. She wore a hat with a protruding bill. The long hair was tucked out of sight. The burn on her cheek had almost healed. Despite it, Maddox found it difficult to tear his eyes from her features.

With a magnetic wrench, she tightened a fitting. Lowering the tool, she faced him. "Is something wrong, Captain?"

He shook his head.

"Why the stare-down?" Meta asked.

"Procedure," he said.

"I don't understand."

"Time has compressed my energy toward a single goal," he said. "Now, Doctor Rich attempts to create a tech spell against the approaching monster. My presence hindered her, so she asked me to leave. I now find myself with a surfeit of time on my hands."

"How about you use regular words," she said.

"I like what I see," he said.

Meta smiled, and that surprised Maddox. The smile lasted less than a second, though. Then it seemed as if she caught herself and forced a frown into place.

With a decisive nod of her head, Meta hooked the magnetic wrench onto her belt. With a swift unlatching, she removed the belt and set it on a panel.

261

"Don't you know it's impolite to stare?" she asked.

"So stop looking at me," he told her.

"I mean *you* staring at *me*."

"Ah," he said.

Meta bristled. "Do you know something? On the planet—I mean Loki Prime. You beat me because I'd been infected with a million spores and germs. It weakened me. Now, I'm stronger and quicker."

"I see."

"If we sparred again, you would lose."

Maddox glanced at the ceiling. In his mind's eye, he kept seeing her momentary smile. The past few months had moved with startling speed. He'd been so busy with the prize that he'd forgotten about life, his in particular. He finally admitted it to himself. He liked Meta and the smile showed she liked him. She was beautiful, but it was more than that. She was different from regular people. He felt an affinity for her, and he liked her bluntness.

He looked at her again, letting his eyes lock with hers.

Her head swayed a fraction. Perhaps not even realizing she did it, she buttoned her coveralls all the way closed. The top two had been undone.

"Would you like to freshen up?" he asked.

"What for?" she said.

"To look more presentable," he said.

"How dare you say that?"

"Ah."

Her chin lifted. "You're a conceited ass, Captain. You think far too much of yourself."

"In that case, you should be pleased. I'm thinking of you right now," and he took a step closer.

"It's time we retested our sparing skills," Meta told him.

"You're right," Maddox said. "I've been contemplating a new hold. I call it, 'a hug.'"

Meta rushed him and threw a right cross at his chin. Maddox caught her fist with his hand. If she had been a woman from a 1 G world, he could have twisted her arm into a submission hold. With Meta that proved impossible. Using her considerable strength, she shoved the hand, and he staggered back, forced to relinquish his grip.

"You're quick as a snake," Meta said, "and you're stronger than you look. Why is that?"

"Lack of cigarettes," Maddox said. "And I train daily. Now, it's my turn to ask something. Why do you have a hair-trigger temper?"

"That's your fault. I don't care for your cockiness, the way you come in here and start—"

Maddox moved then, and he was fast. He darted close, touched her chin with his fingers and brushed his lips against hers. Anticipating her reaction, he shifted his head, sidestepping away from a delayed swing.

After fanning air, Meta touched her lips and stared at the floor. Finally, she looked up. "Don't ever try that again."

Maddox said nothing.

"If you do," she said, "you won't like what happens."

Like an old-style courtier, Maddox made a flourish with his hand and bowed at the waist. Straightening, he said, "Good day, Meta. Please, carry on."

Afterward, he headed for the hatch. He expected her to call out. It didn't happen. Instead, before he could duck his head and exit into the corridor, he heard her bang a tool against a bulkhead.

Maddox sighed. With the sentinel coming, the odds of them getting out alive were no good. Shouldn't they enjoy what could be their last moments of life? It seemed that Meta didn't think so.

***

Twenty hours later, Maddox inclined his head to Doctor Rich. Everyone met in the wardroom. Valerie had whispered to him earlier that Dana had worked herself to exhaustion at the computer.

The doctor sat at the other end of the table. She had dark circles under her eyes, and the flesh on her face seemed to sag. Maddox knew she'd taken another massive dosage of stimulants. According to Valerie, the doctor had admitted to her that she—Dana—knew a special mixture to goad her mind to furious outbursts of activity. Clearly, the witch's brew of chemicals cost the owner.

Maddox looked around the table. Meta wouldn't meet his gaze. The Rouen Colony woman had her arms crossed before her breasts. She seemed intent on letting everyone know that she was ignoring the captain. Maddox found himself more intrigued with her than ever.

Let the chase begin.

No. He didn't have time to indulge now. That would be for later when they won.

Keith Maker grinned. Sergeant Riker kept kneading his one good eye. The old man had just woken up. Valerie sat straight, seeming the perfect Star Watch officer in her crisp uniform.

The others wore their uniforms, but they didn't keep them as sharp as Lieutenant Noonan did hers. Maddox decided his uniform could use pressing. These past weeks, he'd become too lax about dress codes.

Doctor Rich cleared her throat, giving him a meaningful glance.

"Doctor," Maddox said. "You've been hard at work. Would you like to discuss your findings with us?"

"Thank you, Captain Maddox," Dana said. "You are correct. These past hours, I have reanalyzed the alien sentinel. During our voyage into the Beyond over the last three months I have been replaying in my mind many of the arguments I had with Professor Ludendorff. He was a frightfully intelligent person, with stunning insights. Without him, our original expedition would never have reached this strange system. We spent weeks studying various wrecks. We also analyzed rubble, searching for technical or civilizational clues, anything to help us understand the sentinel. Near the end of our stay, the professor believed he had found the ticket."

Dana shook her head. "I rebelled at the professor's idea. It seemed like a suicide mission. Convincing several key crewmembers, we took over the professor's ship and escaped the star system. Eventually, he regained control. As I said, Ludendorff was the opposite of the absent-minded professor. He was brilliant with theoretical ideas and their practical application. I should have foreseen that and marooned him somewhere. Eventually, that's what he did to me."

Doctor Rich sighed. "In any case, I have probed the approaching sentinel. I wish I could tell you I've discovered something new and amazing. That is not the case. I am down to trying the professor's plan, as I can think of no other way to gaining entrance onto the sentinel. At this point, I don't see any other way of surviving the killing machine."

"What is this method?" Maddox asked.

"It will sound ridiculous, I'm sure. It still sounds that way to me. Yet I would rather take a risk attempting to survive than wait idly for death to claim us. Thus, it is either the professor's plan or nothing."

"What's his idea, love?" Keith asked.

Doctor Rich gave the pilot a cold glance. Afterward, she cleared her throat and regarded Maddox. "Part of me wishes to hate you, Captain. If you hadn't come down to Loki Prime, none of this would be happening to me. But you did come, and I am off that Godforsaken world with its horrible spores. Now, Death comes for us. And I am propelled to try Ludendorff's crazy scheme. I'm sure that somewhere the professor senses this and smiles."

Raising her voice, Dana said, "You always were far too smug to like, Professor. Yet I say, good luck with whatever thing you are presently trying to achieve."

Maddox wondered if this uncharacteristic flowery speech was an effect of the stimulants Doctor Rich had taken.

Dana glanced around the table. "This is the plan," she said. "We will set the scout on autopilot. It will approach the sentinel. Likely, we will see some interesting form of destruction."

"What kind of silly plan is that?" Keith asked, snapping his fingers. "Phtt, so ends our expedition?"

"I said put the scout on autopilot," Dana said. "All of us will leave before *Geronimo* is destroyed."

"Where are we going to be?" Keith asked. "Floating in space watching the bloody fireworks?"

Doctor Rich raised her eyebrows. "You're sharper than you look, Ensign."

"What?" Keith shouted. "You're serious?"

"As I said, it is a harebrained scheme. Professor Ludendorff claimed it would work, given the right adjustments on our part. That's what I've been working on for the last fifteen hours. I've been trying to remember what sequence he said will succeed."

"Your plan calls for us to spacewalk off *Geronimo* and send the scout to its doom against the sentinel?" Maddox asked.

Doctor Rich didn't seem to hear the question. She stared at a bulkhead. Maddox wondered if she'd fallen into a trance.

Suddenly, she began to speak in a soft voice. "We had a death on our expedition. A crewmember named Hassan died while we were in the alien star system. We gave him all the trappings of a Muslim burial—the man had been a renegade of the Wahhabi sect. Then we set him adrift in the system as if we were at sea on Earth. The sentinel hurried to investigate. It even launched a small vessel, which scooped up our dead friend. The shuttle returned to the sentinel."

"With the body?" asked Maddox.

"The professor thought so," Dana said.

"Do you, or he, have any thoughts as to why it did that?" Maddox asked.

"Ludendorff had many ideas," Dana said. "The one he finally fixated upon was the sentinel wishing to dissect the individual for study."

"Why did the professor pick that idea in particular?" Maddox asked.

"I wondered the same thing," Dana said. "Why not as reasonably believe the sentinel tried to save one of its own species? Suppose the computer, or whatever the aliens used in lieu of one, finally malfunctioned. It tried to save the corpse, believing that it was really trying to save one of its own, bringing it to the ship for resuscitation. The starship is old. One would suspect failing systems. The marvel is that the vessel runs at all."

Keith shifted in his seat. "I don't know about the rest of you, but if the sentinel is picking us up to run tests, I think it will have a way to subdue those it catches."

"Very good, Ensign," Dana said. "I pointed out the same thing to the professor. He assured me he would figure something out when the time came."

"Did he tell you what the something was?" Maddox asked.

"No."

Maddox grew uncomfortable. "What's your plan for our defeating this possible subduing agent?"

Dana fixed her bloodshot eyes on him. "I did a lot of pondering. I finally realized the solution." She pointed at him. "You're going to defeat the subduing agent, Captain Maddox. You have guns and a fighting crew. As I said, I'm also hoping that after six thousand years something over there has fallen apart. If not, the subduing agent will likely defeat us."

"If your hope is true," Maddox said, "—that the ancient starship has fallen apart—it may not be much help to us against the New Men."

266

"First things first," Dana said. "We're not on the starship yet. Now you know my plan for getting us aboard. Are you willing to attempt it?"

Maddox sat back. She was right. It was a crazy plan. "One thing bothers me," he said. "Back on Earth, Brigadier O'Hara spoke about needing people with the right brain patterns. She said the professor had spoken about it."

"I don't recall that," Dana said.

"Then why did the brigadier and the Lord High Admiral say that?" Maddox asked. "Cook had me gather the people I did due to those supposed patterns."

"I have no idea," Dana said. "Maybe it was subterfuge on their part, something to throw off the enemy if they learned of it."

Maddox doubted that. It would have to remain a mystery for now. "I'm willing to attempt your plan, Doctor, or the professor's plan as you say. What about the rest of you."

One by one, the others agreed that any attempt was better than none.

"Then we'd better hurry," said Dana. "The sentinel will be here soon enough."

-32-

Captain Maddox floated outside the scout, staring in grim anticipation. The plan had sounded saner sitting in the wardroom. Out here, doubts began to assail him.

The entire venture had been a desperate gamble from the beginning. The operation showed the Star Watch's—humanity's— weakness against the genetic marvels, the so-called New Men.

He kept wondering what group had fled the Oikumene to travel into the Beyond to create *better* men and women. If Star Watch knew the answer, it might help unravel the mystery. It might reveal a weakness in the supermen. What had Per Lomax told him? The New Men came as gods in judgment of old-style humanity.

Growing progressively sleepier, Maddox blinked in an effort to remain awake. If the enemy were gods, he had to become a godslayer. This lunatic plan of acting as corpses had to work.

Ever so slowly, Maddox turned his head. The others drifted nearby in their vacc-suits. Dana had explained it. She would override the robo-doctor, injecting them with a hibernating drug, simulating death. Each of them wore a medikit around their waist. When something attempted to peel off his spacesuit, the medikit would inject the wearer with stimulants.

Maddox's final hibernating injection would come soon. He had taken stage one aboard the *Geronimo*. Afterward, he had carted the comatose people into the outer bay. Opening the hatch, Maddox let decompression eject the crew in a tumbling mass. With a thruster-pack, he glided into the void after them. He'd gathered the sleeping crew, bringing them to a central area.

Now, Maddox watched *Geronimo* drifting away. The red giant blazed its fierce starlight, casting the system in a red nimbus.

Under the computer's guidance, the scout came alive. Its thruster port glowed orange and then red. A moment later, blue exhaust poured out for several seconds. That shoved the Patrol scout toward the ancient vessel.

Maddox watched sleepily, imagining that *Geronimo* went to investigate the prize. Ah, what was this? His eyes blinked rapidly. Another light flared into existence, one farther away. The dot of light grew, and so did a pinpoint object.

In time, a chill swept through Maddox. He saw it then: the ancient sentinel. It was coming, growing in size.

A hoarse chuckle reverberated inside his helmet. The annihilator came to investigate the foreign objects. What would the alien starship do to the scout and then to them as *corpses*?

A purple beam slashed through the void. The tip touched *Geronimo*. In a flash of destruction, the scout exploded as metal rained in all directions. Water, coolants, bedding material, electronics and computer pieces all flashed into the void as tiny hot objects. Like that, their workhorse, their home these past months, was gone.

Did the scout travel far enough away from us? Are we safe from the blast radius?

Maddox tried to turn his head to see what had happened to the others. The muscles in his neck refused his mental commands. The medikit must have already given him the stage two injection. His eyelids were becoming too heavy to keep open.

Time blurred for Maddox even as he fought to remain awake to see what would happen.

Oh! What was this?

Maddox saw a vast shape gliding through the interstellar night. Blue lights dotted the vessel, showing the twin disc areas.

It's here. The sentinel has come to investigate. Does the starship wonder about our so-called corpses?

The giant warship slowed. A section in one of the large discs slid open. Light poured from it. Then something thin slid out. An alien shuttle—if that's what it was—began to nose toward them.

Maddox strove to stay awake to see this marvel, but he was losing the fight. What would the alien craft do to them? He almost

269

overrode the medikit to give him the stim now. An instinct warned him that would be a deadly idea.

I'll trust the geniuses, Professor Ludendorff and Doctor Rich. I hope they guessed right. I'm too young to die. I want to live. I want to defeat the New Men...

***

Maddox's eyelids flickered. He felt groggy despite the apprehension weighing on his chest.

Why am I feeling so—?

With a start, he realized he'd heard a scream of pure agony. That's what had focused his lazy thoughts. It sounded like Doctor Rich.

Maddox strove to open his eyes, to wake up. Another scream put goosebumps on his arms. By a sleepy force of will, he lifted his eyelids as if they were lead shutters. The sight horrified him.

Doctor Rich lay on a lumpy upright pad with tubes stuck in her body. Blood surged through the tubes. He guessed the life essences pumped out of her body.

Maddox made a croaking noise of outrage. The blood pumped into a container that was rapidly filling.

Even as he watched, thin flexible cables attached themselves to Doctor Rich. They jolted her with electricity or something similar. She screamed once more. Blue webs of energy snaked across her body, making her arch upward. A hat of some kind sat on her head. Cables led from it to a pulsating bank on the nearest wall. No, on the wall was a mass of what looked like alien flesh with quivering nodes and more cables or tentacles slowly waving in the air.

With an inarticulate bellow, Maddox strove to move his arms. He could not. A cool portion of his mind forced him to look down. Crisscrossing bands of alien material strapped him in place.

A fierce and feminine roar of determination caused Maddox to look to his left. Meta strained against the bands holding her down. Her muscles were rigid with strain with veins popping up from her skin. Then, one after another, the bands around her body snapped off.

"Free me!" Maddox shouted. "Get me out of here!"

Like a wild beast, Meta leaped to him. By her floating movement, it was clear she was weightless. Meta crashed against his

270

pad, her knees striking his chest, knocking the wind out of him. As he gasped to breathe in the smoky atmosphere, she intertwined her fingers around a thick band across his pectorals. With a heave of strength, she ripped it loose. She did it again and again, tearing off the other bands, freeing him.

As Maddox sucked down air, the most bloodcurdling scream of all erupted from Dana Rich.

In a fluid motion, acting with lethal rage, Maddox drew his gun. He fired bullet after bullet into the pulsating half-alive proto-flesh on the wall, the one in charge of all those tubes. Meta did the same thing. Each shot blasted its noise against his ears. Each slug exploded chunks of flesh from the alien mass. Vile jets of steam hissed from the flesh. The thin cables that had electrified Dana flew off her cot and began to thrash back and forth.

"Keep shooting!" Maddox shouted. He leaped at Doctor Rich, sailing toward her. A tentacle-like cable slashed toward his face. He caught it, and the thing struggled with him.

Audibly panting, Meta reloaded her gun and continued to fire into the main mass. The smell of gunpowder had grown thick in the chamber.

The tentacle in Maddox's grip flailed with less power than before.

"Empty every bullet you have into it!" Maddox shouted.

"No," Dana moaned. "Don't do that. You'll kill us if you do."

Maddox's focus snapped onto the doctor. Her eyes were wide and staring. Drool spilled from her mouth.

"I'm so tired," Dana said. "It's taken too much of my blood."

"Why did it do that?" Maddox asked.

"To feed," Dana said. "It's hungry, very hungry."

A feeling of loathing came over Maddox. With a manic grasp, he tore the cap off the doctor's head. He ripped tiny leads from it attached to her scalp, and blood drifted in the air. Then he pulled the larger leads off her flesh, freeing her from the proto-flesh. In the zero gravity, he manhandled her away from the torturing pad.

Blood oozed from her many wounds, floating away from her in tiny globules.

"Quick," Maddox said in a loud voice. "Help me save her."

Perhaps sensing his intent, Meta holstered her smoking gun. Together with Maddox, they applied bandages to the many wounds.

Once the bleeding stopped, Maddox ordered Meta to free the others. They watched with openmouthed horror and drooling sleepiness.

The Rouen Colony woman applied her strength yet again, freeing each of the crew from their restraints.

"The doctor's too pale," Valerie said. "We have to use our medikits."

Maddox nodded for her to proceed. Valerie used a higher function on her kit. She gave the doctor a direct blood transfusion. It turned out Sergeant Riker had the same blood type. So, he also gave Dana a transfusion.

The room stank of alien stenches, gunpowder and blood. More vapors and a dark oozing substance extruded from the fleshy mass on the wall that seemed to operate the torture chamber.

Maddox looked around. He couldn't spy any hatches out of here.

"What do we do now?" Keith asked as he panted.

"Good question," Maddox said.

Dana's eyelids flickered until she finally focused on him. "I know what to do," she whispered.

"We're listening," Maddox said.

"The…the creature communicated with me," Dana said. "It's so terribly lonely."

"You can tell us all about that later," Maddox said. "For now, I want to know if we're on the shuttle or in the starship."

Dana frowned at the question.

Maddox explained to her what he'd seen before passing out.

"Oh, yes, the shuttle," Dana said. "I see what you mean. We're on it or in it. The creature is too afraid to move into the sentinel. It's been waiting for reinforcements."

"What do you mean?" Keith asked with his eyes wide and wild. "You're telling us this…*creature* has waited for reinforcements for six thousand years?"

Dana nodded weakly.

Maddox felt cold inside as ruthlessness and despair battled within him. "Is the alien ship filled with these life forms?" he asked, indicting the quivering flesh.

Dana stared at him. "Do you mean the ship or shuttle?"

"The starship," Maddox said, "our goal."

"No, I don't think so," Dana said. "This one invaded the sentinel or was part of a combat group. It was or is a medical creature."

"How do you know any of this?" Maddox asked.

Gingerly, Dana touched the bandages on her scalp. "It communicated directly with my brain. You should have left those in place."

"It was draining your blood!" Maddox shouted.

Dana shuddered.

"Is that thing—" Maddox jerked his thumb at the mass of alien-flesh beginning to ooze off the wall—"flying the shuttle?"

"I don't think so," Dana said. "I have the feeling the sentinel is flying it. The creature merely intercepts those the starship tries to rescue."

Maddox fought for calm. "How do we get out of this room?"

Dana frowned as she looked around. Finally, she pointed at the barely quivering flesh. "We have to peel that thing off," she said. "The hatch is behind it."

"We'd better put our vacc-suits back on," Sergeant Riker said. The suits lay scattered on the deck. "We don't know what's in the rest of the shuttle, if it has more air we can breathe."

Maddox glanced at his aide. The sergeant looked shaken, and the man gripped his arm where the medikit had drawn blood.

"Good idea," Maddox told him. "Let's suit up, people. We're alive, and it appears we might have the freedom of the shuttle. Now is the time to make the most of it."

***

Peeling away the shuddering warm flesh might have been too difficult without their suits on. The hatch was smaller than those on the scout, but it was large enough for them to squeeze through.

What looked like crusted slime coated the deck plates. It crackled as their boots crunched over it.

"We can call them the *slime aliens*," Keith said over his short-speaker.

"Are there more of them aboard the shuttle?" Meta asked Dana.

The doctor shook her helmet. She wheezed over the headphones. Meta and Valerie helped her along the short corridor.

"No," Dana whispered. "Use the other hatch."

Maddox released his grip on the one and forced the other. It opened into a narrow control room with a triangular window in front.

He and the others piled into the chamber. What might have been tentacle slot buttons on a panel glowed with various colors.

Maddox glanced back at Dana.

Meta helped the doctor forward. Dana examined the lights on the panel. "I don't know, maybe."

"Maybe what?" asked Keith.

No one answered him. Everyone was too busy staring through the triangular window, watching the growing starship.

"It looks as if we headed for that bay," Valerie said, pointing at the bigger vessel.

Silently, Maddox agreed with her. First the medical flesh creature and now the narrow control slots on the panel—he was glad humanity hadn't encountered alien life before this. The New Men were different enough. What would communication be like with a sentient squid alien?

"Are there more of the wall creatures on the starship?" Keith asked.

"I don't think you understand," Dana told him. "The creature had a single function as a medical machine."

"It wasn't truly alive then?" Maddox said.

"Oh, it was," Dana said, "which is interesting."

"No," Valerie said. "It's disgusting."

"You only say that because it's different," Dana told her.

"Exactly," Valerie agreed, "too different. The thing was eating you alive."

"It didn't want to," Dana said. "It hungered, yet it tried to communicate with me. It taught me whatever I asked it."

"How could you ask if it was an alien?" Maddox said.

"That certainly compounded the problem," Dana said. "Direct thoughts helped." She grew quiet. "The loneliness of the creature staggered me. I felt sorry for it. Over the centuries, the creature has fed off the others like it to sustain itself."

"Disgusting," Valerie repeated.

Dana turned on her. "You're a Star Watch officer. You're trained to explore the universe and understand things that are different."

"Sorry," Valerie said, who didn't sound apologetic at all. "Blood-sucking alien vampires don't count."

"You must look past your primitive emotional responses," Dana said. "It was alive. It thought, and it had survived the ages until now."

"You have a point, Doctor," Maddox said. "I'm hoping your brief time linked with it has given you enough information for us to take over the sentinel."

"I'm afraid I have bad news for you," Dana said. "I'm just remembering now what the medical creature told me. The starship has defenders. That's why the creature has stayed in the shuttle, searching for fighters of its kind to overpower the defenders and take over the vessel. Then it can return to its homeworld."

"Where is that?" Maddox asked.

"It doesn't know," Dana said. "It was a simple medical creature. I think over the centuries—due to need—it started thinking. That's what slowed its reactions against you. In the old days, it would have subdued you after the first shot. While you were busy firing, I communicated with it, pleading for your lives. It listened long enough for you to kill it, and for that I will always feel badly."

Like the others, Dana had watched the approaching starship even as she spoke. Now she turned around to face Maddox. "You may have killed the only true alien mankind will ever find. That should give you pause for reflection."

Maddox grunted. He didn't care one bit about medical creatures from six thousand years ago. He wanted this starship, and he needed it now.

"Let's get ready," Maddox said.

"We're going to attack the alien defenders head-on?" Sergeant Riker asked him.

"I don't see what else we can do," Maddox said. "We didn't come all this way to wait in the shuttle. After we dock, we're going to storm the sentinel."

-33-

Through the window, they watched their ship enter a hangar bay. Other narrow shuttles waited down below on a lit deck. Then their craft descended. Soon, it made loud metallic sounds as vast cylinders of compressed air hissed outside the shuttle's hull. The entire craft shuddered until magnetic locks attached to the vessel and the vibrations stopped.

"We're in," Maddox said.

As if on cue, their vacc-boots clanked down onto the deck. Each of them had been floating above the floor.

"We have gravity," Keith said. "Is that good or bad, do you think?"

"Only one way to find out," Maddox said. Although he wore a spacesuit, he readied an assault rifle he'd brought from the *Geronimo*. The others checked theirs. After everyone nodded, he led the group to the outer hatch. Dana had shown them where it was.

The pit of Maddox's stomach twisted as nervous tension oozed through his arms and made his fingers burn. He glanced back one last time to see if everyone was ready.

"This is it," Maddox said. "We're Star Watch officers and personnel."

"Not all of us," Meta said.

"As of now, you are," Maddox told her. "And I don't mean an honorary member. The Lord High Admiral gave me the authority to draft whomever I wanted. Do you agree?"

Meta nodded, saying. "I do."

"Then repeat after me," Maddox said. He administered the oath, and she swore to uphold it.

"Doctor Rich?" Maddox asked.

"Forget about your rituals," Dana said. "Let's get on with this."

"No," Maddox said. "This isn't only for you. It lets the rest of us know you're with us."

"I'm standing here, aren't I?"

"You must also be with us in spirit," Maddox said. "We must be a team or we're never going to succeed. We have to be able to rely on each other."

"This is military gibberish," Dana said.

"We want you to belong with us, Doctor. Will you take the Star Watch oath? Will you fight with every fiber of your being to help us defeat the New Men?"

"Your ringing platitudes mean nothing to me," Dana said stubbornly. "I am an island unto myself."

"Wrong," Maddox told her. "The others gave you their blood to keep you alive. You're aiding us with your exceptional intellect."

Dana glanced at the others. "Is this true? Do you want me to join your war party in spirit and in truth?"

"I do," Meta said.

"And I," Valerie said.

"Sure, love," Keith said. "Let it be all for one and one for all."

"The old musketeer slogan," Dana said. "That is quaint. What about you, Sergeant Riker, you shot me with your stunner? Do you want me in the Star Watch?"

"An old dog like me in an alien starship on the edge of nowhere would like all the allies he can get," Riker said. "I want you to join up, Doctor. We need you with us all the way."

Maddox was surprised at Dana's reaction. As the gruff sergeant spoke, the doctor turned away. She didn't speak, but her helmet went up and down in a nod.

"Administer the oath," Meta told Maddox.

Clearing his throat, Maddox did just that. In a quiet whisper, Doctor Dana Rich took the Star Watch vow, finally joining the team.

Only then did Captain Maddox approach the hatch. He unlocked it and swung it open into the alien hangar bay.

A few interior lights gleamed overhead. From here at least, the other shuttles appeared to be intact. He climbed down, stepping onto the alien sentinel. After a long journey, it was difficult to believe he had gotten this far. A grin split his features. A laugh bubbled.

Twisting around, he saw the hangar bay door they'd entered sliding shut, sealing them from the stars.

"Nothing," Lieutenant Noonan said in a hoarse voice. "I don't see any movement. Where are these defenders?"

"Fan out," Maddox said. "Look everywhere. Lieutenant, do you have your motion detector out?"

"Like I said, sir, I don't see a thing. I meant on my detector."

Like mice in a deserted castle, the Star Watch team began to cross the hangar bay deck. They passed other shuttles. Nothing moved. No dust stirred. Scrawled across the floor in various places were alien numbers or words.

"I see a hatch, sir," Riker said. "Do you suppose the defenders are waiting on the other side?"

Maddox hefted his repeater. What would ancient, alien space marines be like after six thousand years? "This is it, people. If we're going to control the starship, we have to defeat them."

His stomach twisted with anticipation. The closer they neared the hatch, the tighter his guts became. Turning, he pointed at each member in turn, showing each person where he wanted him or her to stand. Only then, did he take the final step toward the hatch. Finding his mouth bone dry, Maddox shifted his stance. He gripped his repeater one-armed and swung the hatch open with the other.

Valerie shouted, and she fired several rounds. His helmet muffled the noise of the sounds even as the bullets burned past Maddox into the giant corridor.

"Stop shooting!" Maddox shouted. "They're dead. Look! They're all long dead."

He stared into a brightly lit wide curving corridor. The sight shocked him. Monstrous skeletons of nine-foot... The captain squinted. They were big pincer-creatures with steel-shod claws. Each skeleton gripped what appeared to be a hacked-apart fighting robot. Instead of humanlike arms, the robots had segmented metallic tentacles with grippers on the ends. Littered among the dead combatants were serrated blades, oddly shaped rifles, tubes, possibly grenades and...

"What is that?" Valerie asked. She'd moved up beside him by the hatch. Her gloved finger pointed at a crusty substance covering most of the corridor decking.

The lieutenant's words coming out of Maddox's headphones caused him to start. He took a sharp breath and stepped into the corridor. The bottom of his vacc-boots crunched upon the crusted substance, causing it to burst into powder.

The others followed him, observing similar reactions.

"Slime," Sergeant Riker declared. "This brittle stuff must have been slime once. Did the skeleton things crawl like slugs?"

"Sick," Valerie said, "sick and disgusting."

Maddox studied the corridor, looking for clues about the battle that had taken place here. The bulkheads bore scotch marks and had holes in places. He accidentally kicked a tube, which rattled and bounced down the corridor, coming to rest against a skeleton's skull. The struck bone disintegrated into dust, sending up a puff that slowly drifted onto the deck.

"Was this the defenders' last stand?" Keith asked.

"I'm not interested in that," Meta declared. "Where are the other defenders? The medical creature in the shuttle told us some still live or function."

Maddox halted, and with greater intensity, he stared down the corridor. The littered deck went on as far as he could see. He told himself to think.

"If the starship's defenders had survived the last battle," he said, "wouldn't they have cleaned up this mess?"

"That's an interesting question," Dana said. "Yes, I believe you're correct. By this—" a sweep of a hand indicated the dead— "it shows us nothing alive or functioning remains on the starship."

"That isn't what the medical creature told you," Valerie pointed out.

"Let me ponder the implications of that," Dana said.

As if they were on a battlefield, the team moved down the corridor in a staggered formation. Their weapons aimed here and there. Vacc-boots continued to crunch the ancient slime and occasionally caused a skeleton to burst apart into dust. The lights burned from the ceiling, providing illumination.

"I'm beginning to think that Doctor Rich is right," Valerie said. "The ship is deserted."

"Why the dichotomy?" Dana asked. "The medical creature painted a different picture of what we would find. I wonder if the last time it tried to board, the fight was still in progress. Yes. It might have tried once, maybe twice, and then it *knew* the hopelessness of entering the sentinel. After communicating with it, I sensed it wasn't a curious creature, but lonely and frightened, as I've said before." The doctor shook her helmet. "For six thousand years, the medical creature sought a way out of its predicament, refusing to try the only thing that would work: making another attempt to enter the sentinel."

"Do you know this to be true," Maddox asked, "or is this conjecture on your part?"

"Maybe a little of both," Dana admitted.

They continued down the curving hallway. The skeletons of dead aliens and broken combat robots thickened in places and thinned in others. It appeared as if the battle had taken place along the entire breadth of this giant corridor, at least.

"I wonder how big the ship is," Riker said later.

"I've been a fool," Valerie said. "I've been so worried about these fabled defenders that I haven't thought of anything else." She adjusted her boxlike motion-detecting device. It made clicking sounds.

Maddox's spine tightened. What did the noise indicate?

Lieutenant Noonan laughed, looking up. "I have good news. The ship's atmosphere is breathable, although its carbon dioxide content is higher than I like. The bad news is that it's far too cold to take into our lungs. We have to figure out a way to heat the air before we can take off our vacc-suits."

"We'd better find a way to do that quickly," Meta said. "Our oxygen tanks won't last forever."

They had brought extra tanks, but Maddox knew she was right.

"Even if we can breathe their air," Keith complained, "we're going to starve to death unless the aliens ate the same foods we do."

Not only had they taken extra tanks, but each person had stuffed their suit with frozen food packets. Maddox figured they could eat rationed servings for another two weeks. After that, they would begin starving. Losing the scout could well prove deadly to their future survival.

For the next several hours, they explored the giant starship, walking from one end to the other. They found that it was three times the size of an SWS *Gettysburg*-class battleship, the largest Star Watch combat vessel.

Everywhere, broken fighting 'bots lay entwined with alien pincer skeletons. Clearly, it had been an epic boarding battle fought without quarter to the death.

"If you hadn't linked with the medical creature," Valerie told Dana, "we wouldn't know who invaded and who had defended."

As they began to retrace their steps, Maddox shouldered his repeater. The others had already put away theirs. It didn't seem anything remotely alive had survived the many centuries. The starship was in effect empty, a Flying Dutchman of the space ways.

During the sweep back, they explored side hatches, possible weapon storage rooms and finally found the engine area. It was vast, with more of the dead on the floor and crusted slime on the plates.

Big broad metal-colored cylinders hummed with energy. Blue electrical currents flowed between the narrow structures on top of the cylinders. What might have been control panels to the side showed a bewildering set of Christmas lights that blinked in undecipherable sequences.

"Here is the evidence," Meta said with awe in her voice. "The engines are running. Do you know how incredible that is?"

"Are they a type of fusion reactor?" asked Maddox.

"No," Dana said. "That wouldn't be my guess."

"What would be?" asked Maddox.

"Antimatter," the doctor declared.

"Do you agree, Meta?" asked Maddox.

"That's far above my pay grade, Captain," the Rouen Colony woman said.

"Supposing we can figure out how to control the vessel," Keith said. "How do we *fix* the starship if she takes hits? The Commonwealth doesn't have antimatter technology."

"First things first," Dana said.

"We've just gotten our first break," Valerie chimed in. She was studying her device. "The air is breathable *and* warm enough here for us to take off our helmets. I think the engines heat this spot."

Inside his helmet, Maddox exhaled sharply. He was the leader. He would test the lieutenant's theory in order to make sure it was safe for the others. Reaching up to remove his helmet, he found Meta holding his arm, keeping him from it.

281

"Just a minute," the Rouen Colony woman told him.

Maddox raised an eyebrow.

"Meta is right," Dana said. "We must practice caution. Don't do anything hasty, Captain. We're on an alien vessel, a running starship from an era six thousand years ago. It's reasonable to expect odd dangers. We must think through each of our steps before we try them."

"You have a point," Maddox said. "But if some of the basics don't work, we're dead anyway. This is one of them." He shook off Meta's restraining hand and twisted his helmet. Air hissed as he pulled off the metal. The pressure was greater in their suits than in the ship.

Maddox sniffed experimentally. The alien odors made him scowl. The chamber stank, although there was the smell of ozone mixed in that he didn't mind. He drew a lungful through his nose, held it and exhaled. Then, he glanced at the others staring at him.

One part of Maddox wanted to drop onto the deck as if stricken. This would be the perfect moment for a joke. He refrained from that, however, smiling instead to show them everything was okay. "Let me breathe this stuff for a while. Then another of you can try it. Until then, you can watch me eat."

He chose a packet of frozen hamburger patties. His rumbling stomach made no protest. Ripping open the fiber, he began to chew the cold hard particles.

A moment later, he heard popping noises and hisses of air as several of the others removed their helmets. Soon, the sound of chewing interrupted their search and thoughts.

Maddox had tasted better, but this was one of his most satisfying meals. He'd been ravenous.

Shortly thereafter, they began exploring again. They had to find the bridge, and then see if there was some way to figure out how to operate the starship.

***

It proved strange. The sentinel possessed large curving corridors that could have handled elephants. Then there was a spider web of tubular links so small Maddox's shoulders brushed both sides as he negotiated one.

"Did the aliens have various sized individuals?" Dana asked.

"The small tubes give me claustrophobia," Keith said.

They searched for hours, and found no evidence of a bridge or a living soul onboard.

"Now we know for a fact the vessel is fully automated," Valerie said.

They were back in the antimatter engine chamber, breathing the tainted atmosphere.

"I keep thinking I'm forgetting something," Dana said. "I'm so tired, though. It's making it hard to deliberate."

"You do look strained," Meta told her.

Dana rubbed her eyes, saying, "Believe me, I feel it."

"Go to sleep and regain your energy," Meta said. "You've been through a lot today. We'll keep watch."

Dana shed the rest of her vacc-suit and wadded up an extra shirt, using it as a pillow. She closed her eyes and soon began to snore softly.

Unlimbering the repeater, Maddox took the first watch. The others, following Dana's example, faded into slumber. The endless hours of preparation, the shuttle horror and searching through the monstrous vessel had tired everyone out.

After watching the others fall asleep, Maddox suppressed a yawn. His limbs ached with fatigue. His turn would come soon enough. Rubbing his arms, he looked around. On impulse, he approached one of the cylinders towering over him, listening to its constant *thrum*. Had the mixing of matter with antimatter taken place throughout the six thousand years? How had Professor Ludendorff come to his conclusion of the exact passage of time? Ha. What could this starship really do anyway? Would it be a match for the New Men? Maybe their advanced beams would cut this vessel down to size just as it had done to Admiral von Gunther's battle group.

There were many imponderables, he realized.

Maddox turned back to his crew laid out on the floor. They'd shoved the skeletons and robots aside and brushed away the crusted slime. Gray decking showed there now. It vibrated slightly from the engines.

The captain walked back and forth to keep awake. After all this time, he had actually done it. Well, they all had. What a disparate crew: Lieutenant Noonan, Ensign Maker, Sergeant Riker, Meta and Doctor Rich. They had found the haunted star system and boarded the ancient vessel just as Brigadier O'Hara had planned. It had been a team effort, and what had it gained them and gained humanity?

So far, we haven't helped the Commonwealth of Planets in the slightest. We have to get this relic back to Earth. Our best scientists will have to go over the artifact and see what new technologies we can reverse engineer from it.

Maddox became thoughtful. That wasn't going to happen unless they could make this thing run under their control. Even then, it would be an iffy proposition. Could the ship enter the star's photosphere to use the tramline? Did this craft have a Laumer Drive or something equal to one?

Stretching his back, Maddox wondered if—

He stiffened with alarm. Something small and bright darted to his right. Whirling to face it, he aimed the heavy repeater at…

A blinking spot on the deck the size of his hand slowly moved toward him. With sick fascination, he watched it near. Fear bubbled and a panicked shout nearly erupted. Horror crawled up his back—the starship wasn't empty after all.

He looked up at the ceiling, but couldn't spot an aperture pouring out the light. At the last moment, he heard a scape of metal against metal from behind. Maddox began to turn. Mist hissed into his face, some of which he breathed. He caught a glimpse of a metallic construct, a robot, with a nozzle aimed in his face. The mist had come from it. Maddox finally held his breath, but it was too late. The chamber spun.

Maddox attempted to pull the trigger of his assault weapon. That was beyond him now. He toppled toward the alien robot. His second to last thought was that the robot had used the light to distract him long enough for it to sneak up on him. That implied intelligence and cunning.

Does the robot run the starship?

Before he could drum up an answer, Captain Maddox lost consciousness.

-34-

By slow degrees, the captain's awareness returned. He found himself deposited upon what might have been a piece of alien reclining furniture.

The last few minutes before he went unconscious bloomed upon his memory. Maddox didn't panic. That wouldn't help him. This was the time for maximum calm.

He opened his eyes and sat up. The chair was too big for him, but that hardly mattered. A swivel of his head one way and then the other showed him he was in a round chamber. What seemed like control panels lined the circular room. Lights flickered on those panels, and they had the tentacle slots.

He searched in vain for the robot that had incapacitated him. Wisely, the thing had taken his gun.

"Hello," Maddox said. "Can you hear me?"

Silence greeted him.

He tried to stand, but found himself too groggy to get his limbs working properly. With a sigh, he sank back against the chair. First squeezing his eyes shut, he opened them and carefully examined the chamber. It seemed like the starship's bridge. No skeletons littered the floor. No torn robots lay about strewn here and there. The deck gleamed. No slime had ever stained this area.

"What's the point of this?" Maddox asked.

A hissing noise alerted him. To his left, the air shimmered and then crackled strangely. Once more, panic threatened. He swallowed, waiting, watching the crackling air.

Slowly, it solidified into a shape, but lines in the thing—like bad reception—made it fuzzy and blurry.

Is that a holoimage?

With this puzzle galvanizing him, Maddox struggled to his feet. Swaying, wondering if this is what it felt like to be drunk, he approached the hazy image. Gathering his resolve, Maddox passed his hand through it.

Yes, it's a holoimage or the alien equivalent of one.

The haziness of the thing became fractionally more distinct. It showed something vaguely humanoid. Was that accurate or did his mind play tricks on him? The shape didn't appear to have tentacles of any kind.

Then, distinct alien words sounded from it.

Maddox yelped and staggered back, crashing against the chair.

The sounds vibrated once more, and they definitely seemed to come from the hazy thing that he'd first thought a holoimage.

Is it an alien ghost?

Maddox's head twitched in the negative. This wasn't the time to be superstitious. Besides, the idea terrified him. He didn't want to deal with something like that.

"Hello," he said.

Around the chamber, slots opened in various bulkheads. Out of each popped a small radar-like dish. They aimed central antenna at him.

Maddox wanted to dodge, but he played a hunch, standing still. Light at the end of each antenna told him the dishes had activated. Heat struck his head. It intensified. Finally, he cried out, ducked away and rubbed his scalp where it hurt.

The lights on the antenna dimmed, and the dishes moved, aiming at his head again. The heat returned, although not as hot as before. Maddox felt lightheaded. Then vertigo struck. He clutched his stomach and threw up what remained of his meal, leaving a stain on the otherwise clean deck.

The radar dishes with their antenna retreated into the bulkheads and the slots slid shut.

The hazy image before him solidified into a replica of himself. Is this what Brigadier O'Hara had meant by needing the right brain patterns? The Iron Lady would only have learned that through

Professor Ludendorff. Why hadn't Dana known about that? Could the doctor be lying about not knowing?

"Captain Maddox," the holo-replica said, the mouth moving in an approximation of speech. "Welcome to the bridge of Starship *Victory.*"

The unreality of the moment made it difficult for Maddox to think. Was he dreaming? Had a robot really sprayed a knockout drug in his face? Maybe the strain of these past months and the dire need caused him to hallucinate. He so wanted to understand the ship that he had invented this scenario.

"Are my words unclear?" the holoimage asked.

"No," Maddox managed to croak.

"Are you unwell?"

Did it hurt to play along with his delusion? Maddox shrugged. It would probably be okay. "I'm disoriented," he told the thing.

"A moment while I translate your words. Oh. I see. You are recovering from the effects of the drugging."

"Yes," Maddox said. He wasn't sure he could take much more of this. "Tell me. Are you real?"

"Please, define your question."

"Am I hearing your words?" Maddox said.

"That is an odd question. Now that the Cognitive Analyzer is offline, I cannot sense your thoughts. Therefore, how can I know whether you hear or not? That you answer me implies that you do hear."

Maddox rubbed his forehead. Could this be a hallucination? He was beginning to think not. "Are you *really* speaking to me?" he asked.

"The answer is obvious," the thing said. "Yes. I speak."

Maddox swallowed hard. If he did hallucinate, nothing mattered anyway. He was going over the edge, then. If this was real, he should attempt to figure out what was going on. Therefore, logically, he would act as if this was truly happening. Deciding to go with this helped settle his fears.

"A few minutes ago," Maddox said, "you aimed devices at my head that made me vomit."

"The Cognitive Analyzer," the holoimage said. "It was a necessary procedure. Until now, I haven't understood your language. I have been listening to your group as you wandered throughout the

287

vessel. My curiosity index finally overrode my security codes. Thus, I have acted, brought you here and analyzed your brain patterns and synapses. Because I am the ultimate in computing, my core deciphered your language and studied your memories. I must admit that I find your conclusions preposterous."

"Which conclusions specifically are you referring to?" Maddox asked.

"That I have lived in this state for six thousand years. I find the length of time passage beyond reason and therefore preposterous."

Maddox blinked rapidly, struggling to maintain his calm. "Ah…who are *you* exactly?"

"Isn't it obvious? I am the engrams of *Victory's* last commander."

Maddox shook his head. "I'm afraid I don't understand that."

"You should. I tested and measured your brain. You have sufficient mental capacity and technical savvy to understand the meaning of my words."

"You're a computer recording of the old commander?" Maddox asked. "Is that what you're saying?"

"There you are. You see. You did it. Yes. In your parlance, I, the former commander of Starship *Victory*, imprinted the primary AI with my personality."

"So you *are* a ghost," Maddox said, "a technical apparition."

"Let me think about that." The holoimage froze. Seconds later, it moved again as it said, "Yes. I suppose I am a wraith, at least in a manner of speaking."

"Why have you brought me here? Are you angry with us for boarding your ship?"

The replica looked away and froze once more. Then the holoimage shivered as if a glitch ran through it. A moment later, the sharpness of visual definitions departed. The hazy lines and indistinct shape returned. It moved again, but Maddox could no longer tell where the ghost looked.

"Six thousand years," it said. "That is too long for *Victory's* AI. If your time references are correct, I have exceeded the starship's limit by several factors. I am beginning to believe that my race has vanished. Your word *extinct* likely says it best. I think…I think I will turn *Victory* into a funeral pyre. Let us finish with a thermonuclear bang."

288

"Ah," Maddox said, "I wish you wouldn't do that."

"You strive for life, is that it?"

"I do."

"It is a vain wish," the holoimage said. "Take me, for instance. I have survived longer than anyone has. Yet what will it achieve me? Nothing. Survival is futility."

"You mustn't have always believed that," Maddox said. "Clearly, you once fought to save your people."

"I did, and I failed. They are all dead. Your boarding has reactivated the AI's core to full capacity. I'm not sure how long I slumbered. Six thousand years…that seems impossible. In any case, because of the power of my computing, I can reach these conclusions in seconds instead of hours or days of contemplation. These moments of full and careful reasoning have cleared my thinking. I realize now that my life lacked meaning. It did nothing to prolong the existence of my species. This is a nihilistic belief, I admit, against my imprinting codes. And yet—"

"You haven't failed," Maddox said.

The fuzziness of the image grew worse. "You have just made a false statement."

"I haven't. I can see why you think that—" Maddox stopped speaking as inspiration struck. First clearing his throat, he said, "Really, your outlook all depends on your definitions."

"I find that a curious statement. Explain what you mean."

"Your enemy was evil," said Maddox. "Was he not?"

"Give me a moment. Your concept of evil—oh, yes, the Swarm were antilife, a parody of strength, if you will."

Maddox wondered if the translations of alien thoughts into human words were perfect. He doubted it. Frankly, that they could communicate at all was a miracle.

Forget about that. Win the AI to your side. You have to outthink it. Keep talking.

"Ah…" Maddox said. "Like your ancient enemy, the New Men also represent tyranny. In a sense, you and I fight similar foes. Therefore, I believe you have survived the ages for a reason."

"That would be good to believe. Your statement, however, is verifiably false. My people are gone. Therefore, I failed and hence, my life had no meaning."

"No, no," Maddox said, "*life* is the issue, not its particular variant. You have remained in order to help the Commonwealth of Planets defeat the New Men. In this way—"

"No!" the holoimage declared. "You are quite wrong. I analyzed your brain patterns, remember? I know that the New Men are alive like you. They are not antilife, but a superior human subspecies."

"They carry the seeds of death and destruction in them," Maddox said. "They wish to annihilate everything that isn't them."

"This is a supposition only. It is not a fact."

"The indicators point in that direction," Maddox said. "They conquer in order to exterminate others. We attempt to defend our homes. We are for life, and they are for death."

"Perhaps you have a point. I'm unclear on several matters. Yet, even if what you say is true, what is any of that to me?"

"Why, it's a reason to exist," Maddox said. "You survived six thousand long years in order to help a thinking breathing species to halt evil. Consider the odds of our successfully reaching this star system and boarding *Victory*."

"In your terms," the holoimage said, "it is something of a miracle."

"Precisely," Maddox said. "And you are part of the great miracle."

"That is an interesting thesis. I certainly enjoy it better than the nihilism of meaninglessness. Yet I must inform you that my circuits, or the functions of the AI, are nearing their limit. I may not exist in an existential sense for much longer."

"Teach me about *Victory*," Maddox said. "Let me carry on in your grand tradition."

"She is an old starship," the holoimage said, as if not hearing the captain's words. "I doubt she can function to full capacity. I'm not sure I can bear the thought of that."

"In any capacity she will help us," Maddox said.

"That is not precisely true."

"No, no," Maddox said, shaking his head. "You are the last and mightiest starship of your race. To voluntarily admit defeat is cowardly."

"Surely, you do not accuse me of timidity. That is a baseless assertion. In fact, I resent it. I fought valiantly to the very end. Once I realized the Swarm's spores had infested *Victory*, I as the living commander did the only thing possible. You may call it suicide, but it certainly was anything but that. I allowed the AI to elevate me into Deified status."

"When you say that," Maddox asked, "do you mean your engrams imprinted upon the AI?"

"Humans are an inferior species, to be sure. I've already tried to speak in a way so you could understand. I have lived through the ages, hunting the ancient enemy, ready to reengage in battle when needed. Now, I find myself weary. I believe ship functions have deteriorated to a greater extent than I had imagined. Your successful penetration of my vessel shows that."

"What about the dead intruders strewn throughout the ship?"

"They were a last mad gamble," the holoimage said. "The Swarm failed to subdue me. We, or I, held to the end and annihilated their last ships so they couldn't infest other star systems."

"They destroyed all your worlds then?"

The holoimage froze as if thinking. When it revived, it said, "Yes, yes, our worlds are smashed wrecks. Clearly, I have outlived my usefulness. With the extinction of my race, it is time for me personally to enter eternity."

"Before you go," Maddox said, "you must teach me how to run *Victory*."

"Surely, you jest. None but I will control the greatest starship of the ages. Do you believe I will relinquish command so easily? I have already shown you and the universe the great lengths I will go to hold my post. None shall say I gave up."

Maddox began to wonder if the AI had become unbalanced. Wouldn't a man go insane if he were trapped for six thousand years? What did it really mean to say that the commander's engrams were imprinted on the AI?

"What is this?" the holoimage asked with anger. "You brought others with you? Now I see your scheme. This is baseless trickery, Captain Maddox. You plotted all this, sensing I would want to communicate after all this time. Admit I'm right."

"I have no idea what you're talking about now," Maddox said.

"Look then, foul sentient. Know that you and your allies have not caught me unawares. Even as you and I speak, I am busy watching the void."

The holoimage pointed at a large screen. It activated, showing the red giant star.

"I still don't understand you," Maddox said. "What about the star am I supposed to see?"

The holoimage seemed to glance at the screen. "My mistake," it said. "Observe now."

Maddox took several steps closer, and the star leaped closer in view as the holoimage showed him greater magnification. Maddox saw the burning photosphere. Then three dark pinpricks burst out of the star. They each shimmered blackly. As the three objects traveled away from the star's surface, the darkness faded to lighter colors.

"What are those?" Maddox asked.

"It should be obvious," the holoimage said. "The vessels have powerful deflector shields. Those shields protected them from the star's energies and heat. With the intensities drained away from them, the shields are now reverting to their normal color."

Finally, Captain Maddox understood. "The New Men used the wormhole," he whispered.

"Your allies, you mean," the holoimage accused.

"Not so," Maddox said. "They are my hunters, seeking me, seeking you now. They are the new antilife, the new Swarm. They will batter down *Victory's* shields, if the starship possesses them."

"It does if I will it," the holoimage said.

"Yes," Maddox said. "They will batter down your shields and no doubt send boarders. The New Men have come to capture you and your ship."

"Never!" the holoimage said. "I will self-destruct before that happens."

Maddox thought quickly. He'd detected vanity in the being. He needed to play off that.

"Yes," Maddox said. "You are exceedingly wise to self-immolate yourself."

"I know that I am wise. What I wonder is how a foolish creature like you has come to the right conclusion about me?"

"That's easy," Maddox said. "After six thousand years of depreciation, *Victory* has become weak. It could never defeat three star cruisers. Do you know three of those craft annihilated Admiral von Gunther's strengthened battle group?"

"You think that *Victory* is weak?" the holoimage asked.

"Of course," Maddox said. "By your own admission—"

"Three star cruisers *dare* to approach me?" the holoimage asked, interrupting the captain.

Maddox waited a half-second, thinking how to say this. "They are the New Men I spoke about earlier, the new Swarm, if you will. They dare to face anyone they want because *none* has been able to defeat them. I believe they plan to turn this star system into a shrine, dedicating it to their own greatness."

The holoimage began to flicker as if thinking. Finally, it said in a strange voice, "If that is so—that they dare to take what is holy to me and profane it—then they shall die. Prepare yourself, Captain Maddox. After six thousand of your years, *Victory* is about to engage in momentous battle."

-35-

Maddox retreated to the odd-shaped chair. The lights in the panels around him began to twinkle as they engaged. Engine noises—at least, he assumed they were engines—*thrummed* with increased power. The deck under his feet vibrated.

"I wonder if I might be of assistance," Maddox said.

"In what way?" the holoimage asked.

"There are those in my crew who have fought the New Men before. Perhaps you should bring them here to give you information as needed."

"Yes. I approve. I will send my robot for them."

"I wonder if that's wise?" Maddox asked. "They might attack the robot."

"For what reason would they attack?" the holoimage asked. "The robot means them no harm."

"You and I know that. They don't."

"No. If they harm my peaceful robot, they will die in penalty. Now, you must desist from speech. I am planning my attack sequence."

"Naturally," Maddox said, "I'm excited to watch and learn from your actions. However, I suggest you hail my crew using intra-ship communications. At least guide Lieutenant Noonan here."

The holoimage lifted what might have been an arm, pointing at a blinking screen. "Go there. Speak to them. I remember now that living organisms should be in acceleration couches in case the antigravity systems are destroyed."

294

Maddox hurried to the panel. "Doctor Rich," he said. "Can you hear me?" No one responded. Maddox looked up. "Is there a malfunction to the system?"

"No," the holoimage said. "In response to your voice, your crew approaches an AI receptacle."

Maddox waited, and the blinking screen shimmered. Then he stared at Doctor Rich, who wore her helmet.

"Captain Maddox?" she asked. "You're alive? Why did you sneak away while we slept?"

"I'm in the *Victory's* bridge," Maddox told her.

"That's the name of the starship?" she asked.

"Precisely," Maddox said. "I am speaking with the *Victory's* illustrious commander. In the past, he imprinted his engrams onto the ship's AI. As to why I'm here, as you slept, he sent his robot to escort me here to him."

Dana's eyes widened, first with shock and then with seeming understanding.

"The New Men have appeared in the system, using the tramline just as we did," Maddox said. "They have three star cruisers. We are about to go into battle with them. The AI has suggested that Lieutenant Noonan come to the bridge. She's faced the cruisers before. The rest of you will head to acceleration couches. Is that clear?"

"Yes, Captain," Dana said. "Can I speak to the AI?"

Maddox glanced at the holoimage.

"No," the fuzzy image said. "I have analyzed your brain patterns. Translating them was costly enough already. I do not care to analyze another's. I'm also no longer inclined to let your lieutenant onto my bridge."

"Oh," Maddox said. "That's too bad. I suggest—"

The holoimage raised a hazy hand. "I do not care to discuss it, either."

Maddox chewed the inside of his cheek, thinking fast. He glanced sidelong at the screen. Dana still stood at an AI receptacle, obviously listening. He decided to go with the flow, hoping the AI was too busy with its computations to worry about turning off the link.

"You're right, of course," Maddox said loudly. "You don't need Lieutenant Noonan's assistance. The others of my crew will await your coming victory."

"I have scanned the enemy star cruisers," the holoimage said. "They possess powerful deflector screens. What weaponry do they have?"

"Your scanners can't penetrate their shields to find out?"

"That is correct, Captain."

"Their beams sliced through Star Watch shields of some of our best vessels."

"Do you know the composition of those deflectors?" the holoimage asked.

"We use an electromagnetic field," Maddox said.

"I see," the holoimage said. "Compared to that, I have an advanced deflector shield. Their beams might or might not be as effective against it as it was against your people's ships. That means the strength of the New Men's beam is an unknown factor. Captain Maddox, we may have a fight on our hands."

"Can you defeat them?" Maddox asked.

"I have insufficient data to make a proper assessment. We once possessed the greatest weaponry, and we had developed the most advanced civilization. Reason points to my present superiority. Yet that isn't a given. Battle will determine the outcome."

"They have three to one odds," Maddox said.

"In ship numbers you are correct but not in tonnage," the holoimage said. "They barely match me in that regard. Ah…they attempt communication."

"I just had a thought," Maddox said.

"Yes?"

"Tactical surprise might benefit us."

"That is logical," the holoimage said, "as surprise is a force multiplier. Therefore, you are correct. What do you suggest?"

"Let them address me as *Victory's* captain. They will believe I've just boarded the ship and couldn't possibly understand all the alien systems. The New Men believe themselves superior to regular humans, such as me."

"I scanned your brain, Captain. I am aware of the situation."

"My point," Maddox said, "is to lull them into a false sense of security. Then, once we engage in battle, your brilliant tactics might well dull their reaction times, giving us a greater margin for victory."

The holoimage froze for several seconds before moving again. "That is well-reasoned. Yes. Go to your...left. Do you see the blinking screen there?"

"I do," Maddox said.

"You will receive a visual link with the alien caller."

Maddox didn't have long to wait. The same being appeared as he'd seen earlier on *Geronimo's* screen. The New Man had golden skin, inky eyes and masklike perfection.

"Captain Maddox," the New Man said, "well, well, well."

"Per Lomax?" asked Maddox.

The faintest of smiles appeared on the New Man's lips. "That is correct."

Irritated, Maddox said, "I use the name simply as a point of reference. Whatever meaning you supply to the name, I do not."

"You are resourceful, Captain. I admit to surprise at seeing you in the relic."

Out of the corner of his eye, Maddox noted the holoimage turning to him. He hoped the AI didn't speak.

"Not only have you reached the alien vessel," Per Lomax said, "but you have restarted the engines. Our scanners indicate energized weaponry. Do you mean to attempt to fight us?"

"Not if we can come to an understanding," Maddox said.

"Ah," the AI said softly behind him. "You plot deception. That is interesting. I had not expected such guile from a lowly life-form such as you."

Maddox had become thoroughly tired of everyone thinking humans were idiots. Still, he held back a retort and concentrated on the situation. Winning the battle wasn't half as important as getting *Victory* to Earth. The Star Watch needed this vessel for future engagements with the enemy.

"You wish to surrender?" Per Lomax asked.

"Surely, you can offer me more than that," Maddox said. "I have a valuable commodity in this starship."

"Do you truly think you can dupe me?" Per Lomax asked. "Your deceit fools no one but yourself. We will defeat the relic and

297

possibly capture you. If you wish to forgo lengthy torture, surrender now."

"Your negotiating strategy lacks subtlety," Maddox said.

"Do you negotiate with ants? No. You spray them, eliminating the problem. I realize you will not surrender to me. Your previous action proves this. Therefore, we shall engage in battle." Per Lomax glanced at something below him. "You have less than two hours of life remaining—unless you brake and flee away from us. Then you may have three hours left. Good-bye, Captain Maddox."

"Wait!" he said.

The New Man stared at him.

The words stuck in Maddox's throat. He wanted to ask the man if he was like them. Yet he felt Per Lomax would laugh at best. He also remembered that Dana and the others listened in on the open channel. The thought he was part New Man shamed him deeply.

"It is nothing," Maddox said.

"You are a troubled creature," Per Lomax said, "yet you a have a spark of genius in you. I speak compared to the common ruck of your kind. If you compare yourself to me, it is like a candle versus the sun. The hour of your extinction approaches. Prepare for non-existence."

The screen went blank.

"He is an arrogant sentient," the holoimage said.

"Yes," Maddox said.

"He also happens to be correct."

"Oh?"

"We will engage in battle in less than two of your hours."

***

Victory increased velocity as it approached the three star cruisers. They fanned out so the edges of their shields brushed against each other. The red giant blazed behind the three vessels. The battle would take place within the inner system. Various ancient wrecks drifted between the enemy and *Victory*, debris from the long lost war.

Time passed as the vessels closed. None of the combatants launched drones or missiles.

Maddox sat in silent contemplation. This was a pregnant moment. He wished there was some way he could inform Brigadier

298

O'Hara he'd made it. To have reached the impossible goal and never let her know…it galled Maddox. He also wanted to know who he was. If by some quirk he wasn't part New Man, then what was he? Where would his mother have fled from in the Beyond?

Who is my father? A man should know.

"Do you feel anything?" Maddox asked.

The holoimage had remained perfectly still like a photograph. Now the fuzziness returned. Did that mean the AI's *intelligence* animated it again, and it hadn't before?

Maddox wasn't sure why it would matter either way, but he couldn't help himself. Until he died, he would struggle with every fiber, looking for any advantage he could. This was *his* moment in the universe, his time in the ring for humanity. To come this far and lose the engagement no! Failure was out of the question, and yet, it was all too likely.

Three enemy ships had destroyed a strengthened Star Watch battle group lead by a veteran admiral. Who was he to think he could do better than von Gunther had?

"I'm Captain Maddox of the Star Watch," he told himself.

"I know who you are," the holoimage said.

Maddox smiled.

"Why are you speaking as you do with your lips twitching…oh, yes, yes, I remember now. Blood and flesh creatures such as you have synapse trouble. How do you say it? Nervous? You are nervous before the beginning of a battle. I almost envy you the feeling."

"Almost?" asked Maddox.

"I have been deified, advanced to a higher plane of existence. I am no longer troubled by my former biology and physiology. Yet, in a sense, I miss those days of…"

You've trapped yourself in the soulless hell of a computer, Maddox thought. Yet that wasn't logical, was it? If the personified AI didn't have emotions, it couldn't feel its loneliness.

"Nervous or not," Maddox said, "I'm glad to enter combat with you."

"Does that imply you think you're going to help me?" the holoimage asked.

"Only in the sense of offering a suggestion or insight," Maddox said. Could AI's be touchy? This one seemed to be.

"It is too bad," the holoimage said. "As you spoke, I assessed my weaponry. The disruptor no longer functions. With it, I could have swept these three vessels out of existence. I do not have use of the gyro destabilizer either."

"What do you have?" Maddox asked.

"The neutron beam," the holoimage said. "It is my most primitive weapon. Yet it did well enough against the Swarm. These New Men will not survive it, I'm sure."

Maddox wondered about the ancient battle. "How many star systems did you control before the Swarm attacked?"

"This system," the holoimage said.

"You hadn't colonized other systems?"

"We had not yet used our newly discovered star drive. *Victory* was an experimental model, the first of its kind. Perhaps I should have attempted faster than light travel, but it doesn't matter now."

"By star drive," Maddox asked, "you mean the wormhole, right?"

"Wormhole?" the holoimage asked.

"The one that begins in your star's photosphere," Maddox said.

"I have no idea what you're babbling about now," the holoimage said.

Maddox ingested the information. Could the alien not know about tramlines and Laumer-Points? It seemed inconceivable.

"Ah," the captain said, "didn't the Swarm burst out of the sun as these star cruisers just did?"

"Of course not," the holoimage said. "For over one hundred years, we watched the Swarm advance toward our star system. Their massed fleet came at sub-light speed, heading straight for us. In their arrogance, they made no attempt to hide their approach."

"Wait a minute," Maddox said. "Let me get this straight. The Swarm didn't use tramlines?"

"What are these tramlines you keep speaking about?" the holoimage asked.

"They're wormholes, the means we used to enter your star system. How do you think we got here?"

"I've had enough of your senseless chattering," the holoimage said. "The enemy is energizing his weapons. Can it be his beams have a greater range than ours?"

300

Maddox crouched over his screen, watching the void. As he did, three rays of light speared from the three enemy starships. The captain stopped breathing. Would *Victory's* deflector shields hold?

Yes! Before the lances of light touched *Victory*, a shimmering substance halted them. The three beams poured energy against the ancient vessel's shield. The rays turned that area red. As the enemy continued to beam, the color darkened, and the area grew larger and larger as the shield attempted to dissipate the energy.

"This is unbelievable," the holoimage said. "Their beam range astounds me. The Swarm possessed nothing like this. Neither did we possess such long-ranged weaponry."

Maddox gritted his teeth and balled his fists tight. The New Men continued to beam *Victory's* shield. The starship began to tremble. It didn't come from the strain against the shield. Rather, the antimatter engines whined so Maddox could hear the sound from the bridge. The *thrumming* engines shook the panels.

"The star cruisers are slowing down," the holoimage said. "No. I need to close the distance faster. If only I had use of my primary weapons. I would smash these gadflies then."

"How much longer will it take until we're in neutron beam range?" Maddox shouted.

"No!" the holoimage groaned. "This isn't possible."

Maddox saw it on his screen. A beam speared through the blackened shield. The ray sped for the ancient starship and boiled against hull plating. Armor grew red hot. The beam dug deeper, deeper—

"I am overriding the safety precautions," the holoimage said. "There. That should fix it."

A fierce high-pitched whine grew louder. The entire bridge shook harder than ever. The holoimage became dimmer, his words harder to hear.

On the screen, the enemy ray no longer melted outer armor. The deflector shield was no longer black, either. It had turned back to a brown color, with the three hellish beams trying to batter it back down.

"In a few more minutes we'll be in range," the holoimage whispered.

With pent up frustration, Maddox struck a panel. The alien shield was obviously better than anything the Commonwealth of Planets had. With even that improved technology, the lost vessel would immeasurably help the Star Watch against the New Men. How could he get the starship home was the question.

With their heavy laser beams, Star Watch battleships could have already been hammering the enemy. This short-range alien neutron weapon—

Maddox sat up, blinking rapidly. *How daft do I have to be? The AI spoke about a star drive. He doesn't mean wormholes either.* Could the aliens have discovered a *different* way to go faster than light?

An explosion shook the room. The motion threw Maddox out of his seat to sprawl onto the deck. He looked up from his spot.

"Did the antimatter engines blow up?" he asked.

"This is incredible," the holoimage whispered. "One of the neutron chargers exploded. I've taken interior damage. The shield—"

Maddox scrambled to his feet, rushing to the screen. On it, he witnessed three savage beams digging into the vessel's hull armor. *Victory's* deflector shield had disappeared. Pieces of starship melted away in great globular clumps.

"Do something!" Maddox shouted.

"Yes, I will attack now," the holoimage said. "In dying, I will strike a fearful blow."

A supercharged purple beam lanced out of the starship. It struck the nearest star cruiser. The alien beam boiled against the enemy screen. First, the shield turned red, then brown and then black. Afterward, the neutron beam speared against the cruiser.

"Yes!" Maddox shouted. "Yes. Yes."

Star cruiser armor blew apart as the neutron beam dug into the enemy vessel. This was fantastic. The New Men weren't invincible after all.

"I must attempt the hyper-drive," the holoimage said. "Otherwise, the enemy will annihilate the greatest starship in history."

For a terrible moment, intense vertigo overcame Maddox. His eyesight failed him. He heard roaring sounds. It felt as if he left his body and exotic colors swirled around him. Then everything became quiet. It felt as if he floated in space. The next second, the roaring in his ears and a brilliant flash caused his senses to overload. He felt

302

himself thrashing on the deck and shouting incoherently. Then, every color seemed to fly inward toward him—and normalcy returned to the bridge. It left Maddox blinking and panting on the floor. With strangely rusted muscles, he turned to the holoimage.

"What happened?"

The holoimage had frozen. It said nothing.

Painfully, Maddox climbed to his feet and checked his screen. No beams burned into *Victory*. He saw the void with its distant stars, and something seemed very wrong. He frowned, trying to figure out what the something was. Then he realized that he no longer saw the red giant.

What does that mean?

Ah, Maddox noticed that he still saw the red nimbus. They were still in the alien star system. Yes, he noticed several wrecks. Yet the red light seemed to come from the wrong direction, from the opposite direction as before.

"It worked," the holoimage said.

The captain whirled around. The thing was hardly visible, but it moved. "What worked?" Maddox asked.

"The hyper-drive was a success," the holoimage said, "although extremely limited in range."

"We jumped?"

"I suppose that is the correct way to describe it," the holoimage whispered. "We were there, and now we're here on the other side of the star. The others are hunting for us with their sensors. If they move to a new position so we're no longer hidden by the star, they will no doubt find us soon enough."

"Hyper-drive," Maddox said. "You can jump without having to use a wormhole. Why, this is fantastic."

"Why do you say so?" the holoimage asked.

"You can escape the New Men. Let's go. Let's jump to a different star system right now."

"No," the holoimage said. "You are incorrect in your assessment for several reasons. Firstly, I will not abandon my home system to these primitive invaders. Secondly, the hyper-drive was badly damaged in its limited use just now. Remember, I said it was experimental in nature. The star drive has become inoperative. Instead, I will use my last robot to effect what repairs I can to ship damage. Then I shall finish the fight with these arrogant whelps."

"I hate to say this," Maddox said, "but I don't think you can defeat the three star cruisers with the weaponry you have at hand."

"Perhaps not," the holoimage admitted. "But I cannot conceive of a better way to cease existence than fighting for what I love."

"But—" Maddox said.

"Prepare for the final encounter, Captain. *Victory* is heading back toward the star, seeing if we cannot surprise the enemy."

-36-

Maddox took several steps toward the holoimage and stiffened into parade ground attention. He snapped off the best salute of his life.

"What is the meaning of your action?" the holoimage asked.

"I formally request permission to offer my full services to you, sir," Maddox said. "Not only that, but I will give you the complete use of my trained technical team to help with ship repairs."

"Please, Captain, it is obvious that you indulge in theatrics."

"Not so," Maddox said. "I hate my enemy as much as you must have hated the Swarm."

"You mean me as the once physical commander, I take it," the holoimage said.

"Exactly."

"Yes. I do dimly recall an emotional aspect to the conflict. It was both upsetting and pleasing."

"Then you must understand that I will do anything I can to destroy the New Men."

"Why, yes. I do understand. Hmm, a technical team, you said."

"You probed my brain," Maddox said. "You know that I have an excellent engineer in Meta of the Rouen Colony. Not only that, but I have the full use of Doctor Dana Rich. She is a genius and can do anything required of her."

"I seem to recall you had trouble with Doctor Rich."

"You're right, of course," Maddox said. "I did have trouble. Now, she has sworn a Star Watch oath. She will do exactly as I command. Since our desires are the same—to inflict as much

305

damage as we can against the New Men—let me return to my team. Through me, you can tell us what to do. We will repair more of the starship than your robot could do on its own. That will allow you to give a better account of yourself."

"I am heading straight for the enemy, Captain. We won't have time for such repairs."

"Then I suggest you take the time," Maddox said. "You've waited six thousand years. What are a few more hours in order to achieve lasting glory?"

"You fail to perceive my goal. I am attempting a death ride, oblivion in the most honorable fashion possible."

"Honor demands we destroy as many of them as we can," Maddox said.

The holoimage froze.

Maddox waited. A desperate gamble had formed in his mind. First, he needed to get back to the others. Could he trick the AI? It struck him as doubtful. Yet, if he could…what bag of marvels did the ancient starship possess? It hadn't surprised him that the ship was in a state of disrepair or that many of its weapons systems buckled under the strain of battle. If they could escape the star system and return to Earth…

The holoimage moved. "There," it said, pointing a barely visible arm. "Go through that door until you come to a red-marked hatch. Your team waits by the AI receptacle."

Maddox noticed a new hatch where a bank of machinery had been. Had the AI been hiding the exit with a holoimage? Whatever the case, for his plan to work, he needed to buy time.

"You must give us a few hours to help your robot repair failed systems," the captain said.

"It seems senseless. The New Men are busy searching for us even now. Yet, maybe you can clear out the damage in my neutron charger. I will give you one hour. Then, I will attack from over the star's top. It is my best chance of gaining nearness to them so I can rake them with the full power of my beams."

"Since we are under combat conditions, I will hurry," Maddox said.

"Go," the holoimage said. "Time is critical."

Maddox couldn't agree more. Lowering his head, he sprinted for the exit.

***

Lieutenant Noonan picked herself off the decking. They had huddled around the open screen, listening to the dialogue between Maddox and someone they couldn't hear.

Sergeant Riker had suggested the captain had taken leave of his senses. Dana had told him not to be ridiculous. If Captain Maddox had gone crazy, how had he figured out where the bridge was and how to use the ship's systems?

With great interest, Doctor Rich had listened to Maddox's one-sided conversation. As Dana groaned from the floor, holding her head, she sat up.

"What happened?" Meta asked.

"We're still alive," Dana said. "The engines don't sound as strained now. The decking isn't shivering, as it was earlier, either. I think there's been a pause in the battle."

"Listen," Valerie said. "No sounds are coming out of the screen."

Just then, something unseen opened. Valerie perked up, hearing panted breathing. The ancient starship frightened her. The halls of alien dead, of entwined corpses, intensified the feeling until dread had come to fill her.

"Someone's coming," Valerie whispered. She checked her assault rifle. Capture was out of the question. She didn't want to end her life on a torture pad as Dana almost had on the shuttle. Planning to sell her life as dearly as possible, Valerie aimed down the corridor and was the first to see Captain Maddox. The man sprinted without his vacc-suit and his eyes looked wild.

"Don't shoot!" Dana shouted.

Valerie lowered her weapon. She could see Maddox had been through hell. Well, they all had. Maybe they looked as unsteady to him as he did to her.

He stopped before them with sweat glistening on his face. "Listen carefully," Maddox panted. "We have one chance to do this, so there're can't be any mistakes."

"Do what?" Dana asked.

"Gather round," Maddox said. "This is going to sound crazy, but it's all true."

He told them what he'd been doing. It did sound insane. It also made sense. Valerie couldn't see how Maddox could have figured out how to use the alien vessel otherwise.

"It seems to have figured out a way to talk to you by reading your mind's electrical pathways," Dana said.

"Whatever," Maddox whispered. "The point is the AI has a death wish. Maybe that has fixated its thinking. We have to…" the captain didn't finish his thought, but he gave them a long, meaningful glance.

"I understand," Dana said, with her eyes wide and staring.

Valerie figured that maybe she did too. Clearly, they had to hijack the starship from the AI. But they couldn't do it too soon, or the New Men's star cruisers would destroy *Victory*.

"Does that make sense?" Maddox asked.

"It does," Dana said.

"I have to go back and talk the AI into a jump attack," Maddox said. "That means we have to repair the neutron charger *and* the star drive."

"How much time do we have?" Dana asked.

"He said one hour."

"You do know that what you suggest is impossible for us to accomplish?" Dana said.

"I don't know anything of the kind," the captain said. "We're rolling the dice for everything and looking for snake eyes. Now, let's go to work."

Valerie saw the doctor and Meta stare with disbelief at the captain. That wasn't going to help. "Yes, sir," Valerie said. "We're going to do our best or die trying, Captain."

Maddox grinned at her. "The Lord High Admiral picked the right navigator when he sent you, Lieutenant. It has been my distinct pleasure serving with you."

Valerie saluted. "The pleasure has been all mine, sir." She stepped up and thrust out her hand. He gripped it, shaking.

Then, Captain Maddox solemnly shook each of their hands. "If I don't see you again—" He looked down, staring at the floor. Looking back up, his smile seemed forced. "Humanity doesn't know it, but they're counting on us. I've seen what this starship can do. With it, the Commonwealth has a chance. Star Watch might well defend our homes and go on to attack the New Men and end their

308

menace forever. First, though, we have to win here. I know each of you will do your best, and then go beyond that to do what must be done for victory." He took a deep breath before adding, "Speechmaking time is over. Now, it's time for action."

With that, Captain Maddox spun around and walked away. After three steps, he lowered his head and took off sprinting.

Valerie felt a lump in her throat. She nodded to herself. This hour was why she'd pushed through her suffering in Greater Detroit to win a spot in the Space Academy. This moment was why she'd climbed into the escape pod and survived the New Men when all her comrades had died in battle in the Pan System.

A robot on treads wheeled into sight. It was an ugly thing and stopped short. With a mechanical tentacle, it beckoned them.

Valerie swallowed and turned to the others. "We have a job to do. Doctor. You'd better use your intellect for all it's worth. Our lives and the lives of humanity back home are resting on it."

Dana stared at her. "No pressure, Lieutenant?"

"Wrong," Valerie said. "All the pressure in the galaxy is on you now. I'm wondering if you have what it takes to surmount it."

Doctor Rich's eyes seemed to burn for a moment. Then she nodded, beginning to head for the robot. "We shall shortly find out," Dana said.

Captain Maddox reentered the bridge. The holoimage had vanished. With a shrug, Maddox went to his former station and studied the screen. The red giant looked bigger. That meant the ship continued to head toward it.

A crackle of sound caused Maddox to turn. The holoimage solidified into existence. It still looked hazy and indistinct although it maintained a humanoid shape. Maddox wondered what the aliens had looked like. Did they have tentacles or had they been manlike?

"I am disappointed with you, Captain," the holoimage said.

Maddox kept his features even. He wondered if the AI measured his heart rate and other telltale signs. The captain had training in that area, having used biofeedback to keep himself calmer than others could do in these situations.

"I ran back here as fast as I could," Maddox said.

"Do not try your subterfuge tactics on me. I have already implied that I know about your plan."

"Could you be more specific?" Maddox asked.

"I don't need to be."

"I agree that this is your ship," Maddox said. "We are guests here, beholden to you. We will follow whatever rules you decide to enforce."

"You are quibbling," the holoimage said. "Stop it at once."

"If I have offended you, I am sorry."

"*Captain*," the holoimage warned.

Maddox decided to wait.

"You huddled together with your crewmembers," the holoimage finally said. "You whispered so my sensors couldn't pick up what you told your people. My probability factors indicate you plotted munity against me."

"Ah," Maddox said, acting as if he was relieved. "I realize now what happened. There's been a terrible misunderstanding. I whispered because…"

"Yes. You did so why?"

"It's rather embarrassing to tell you in particular," Maddox said, hanging his head.

"This isn't the time for your games, Captain. Speak to me at once. Admit that you're plotting against me."

"It's not what you think. You see, I've had difficulty with my crew. At times, they've flouted my authority. This is my first stint in a warship as a captain. Surely, you recall my troubles with them. Your mind probe earlier should have picked that up."

"Yes," the holoimage admitted. "I do recall something of the sort."

"What adds to my embarrassment is that you're the greatest starship commander in history. You do realize that, don't you?"

"I do indeed," the holoimage said.

"You're making this hard for me." Maddox looked stricken as he blurted, "Don't you realize I wish to look good in your presence? This is my final battle, my reason for existence. I can help humanity by doing as much damage to the antilife New Men as I can. That means my crew needs to excel. I don't want them to embarrass me in front of you."

The holoimage froze. When it moved again, it said, "You may not believe this, but I had not considered that."

"Then let me tell you again," Maddox said, "I feel awful if my whispering has offended you. Ever since learning who you are, I've strained to impress you."

"Interesting," the holoimage said. "Perhaps I've misjudged your species. You have more refinement than I believed you capable of having. You can recognize greatness in others. Even among my people, that was a rare quality."

"Please, Commander, let my crew aid you in repairing the starship. We can help fix the neutron charger, any shield generator and star drive damage, and AI memory cores as you would like."

311

"Memory cores?" the holoimage asked, sounding suspicious again. "Why there?"

"I've begun to suspect you might be missing some of your tactical programs."

"How dare you say that?" the holoimage said. "What possibility makes you pronounce such a baseless thing?"

"Why, logical deduction proves this must be the case. You are the greatest starship commander in history. That is the first given. Yet the cruisers managed to inflict damage onto *Victory*. What's even worse is that I suspect they hurt you more than you hurt them. The only conceivable reason for this is that your AI has fallen below its optimum operating levels."

"I see," the holoimage said. "Interesting. I cannot fault your reasoning. Yes, I should have swatted the cruisers out of existence. Originally, I concluded the lack of the disrupter ray or the gyro destabilizer was the cause for my failure to annihilate. Now, I sense it may be a less than optimal computing function. Hmm, I *have* detected a malfunction or two in my cognitive capacity, blockages in thought."

Maddox waited quietly.

"What I don't understand is why, at this point, we should repair the star drive," the holoimage said. "That makes no sense. I am not going to attempt to flee the intruders."

"On the contrary," Maddox said. "I thought the reason why was obvious—as a military ploy."

"You're being evasive. I demand that you explain your meaning."

"Certainly," Maddox said. "The tactic seems elementary to me. I believe any Star Watch officer would realize how valuable the mini-jump was. We could use the red giant as a shield against the cruisers, only attacking when it's to our advantage. Naturally, you would place a beacon or two at the star's edges—in relation to your enemies. In that way, you could fix their precise location. At the right moment, using the jump, you move through or bypass the star to appear beside an enemy cruiser. As soon as possible, you energize the short-range neutron beam, smashing an enemy shield and destroying the vessel. Before the others can react, you jump away out of range back behind the shielding red giant."

"That is a brilliant strategy," the holoimage said.

"You are most kind to say so," Maddox said. "It shows true magnanimity on your part. I wonder if that's a portion of your greatness, to shower praise where it's due. Of course, I hasten to add that I realize you would have thought of the ploy before I did if your AI core had been operating at peak efficiency."

"Yes, yes," the holoimage said. "That goes without saying. I *would* have thought of it. That means my cores must be damaged."

Maddox waited.

"I think I *will* have your Doctor Rich look over my computing core. It is…wrong that I am below peak…what was the word?"

"Efficiency," Maddox said.

"Yes, that," the holoimage said.

"Consider it done," Maddox said. "I will inform the doctor via a screen."

"Yes, good," the holoimage said. "Now, as to the other matters, here is what we shall do afterward…"

***

Time passed as the robot and crew repaired what damage they could. Finally, hours later, the holoimage reappeared on the bridge.

"An enemy sensor has located us," the AI said.

Maddox noticed the holoimage was sharper than ever. It was shorter than he was, with thicker shoulders and thin dangling arms. It wore what looked like a jumpsuit with red tags on the chest, perhaps to symbolize his rank. The holoimage had thick, silvery matted hair and extremely deep-set eyes. The alien was far more humanoid than he'd realized. Why did the control panels have tentacle slots then?

"What are the star cruisers doing exactly?" Maddox asked.

"Heading closer to the red giant," the holoimage said.

"It's as I feared. Per Lomax and his brethren are clever. After replaying what happened earlier, they must realize you have an intrasystem jump capability. Perhaps they have anticipated our next tactic. I think you must attack this instant before they refine their strategies."

The holoimage studied him. Maddox could tell because of the greater clarity. The AI must be able to see or sense through the image's eyes.

313

"Yes, I understand your reasoning," the holoimage said. "With my re-linked cores operating together, I have—well, never mind about that. Prepare for jump."

Through his screen, Maddox informed the others they were about to attack.

A minute later, a terrible whine began from somewhere deep in the ship. The vertigo returned. Maddox felt all the same sensations as last time.

I'm heading back into combat. This is it. Do or die against the New Men.

The quietness of jump felt strange. Then, light and colors flowed into him as before. Sounds and smells overburdened his senses. Maddox slumped onto the deck, panting as drool spilled from his mouth. Then he realized the engines thrummed and the deck vibrated horribly.

"Error, error," the holoimage said. "We have committed an error."

"What's wrong?" Maddox shouted, dragging himself to a sitting position.

"They were ready for us," the holoimage said. "You were right in believing they anticipated the tactic. We have committed an error. Their rays are burning through the shield. There, one beam has burst through."

Maddox staggered to the screen as the starship shook. An enemy beam chewed against *Victory's* cherry-red hull armor.

"Fire into their guts!" shouted Maddox. "Use the neutron beam. Destroy one of them, at least. Let them know they've been in a fight."

As the starship shook, its purple beam struck an enemy shield. It might have been Maddox's imagination, but the shimmering held longer than last time. The enemy's deflector became red as neutron energy blasted against it. Far too slowly, the shield became brown, the color spreading outward. Then, the central area turned black. Finally, the purple neutron beam punched through the shield, smashed hull armor and tore into the star cruiser.

"Breach!" the holoimage shouted.

At first, Maddox thought the AI meant against the enemy.

314

"*Victory* has a hull breach," the holoimage said. "The New Men are destroying my beautiful ship. If only I had my old weapons systems. Then they would have known. Then they—"

On Maddox's screen, a terrific explosion turned everything stark white. The captain threw his arms before his eyes. When he looked again, he saw expanding debris where an enemy star cruiser had been. Armor, laser fluids, flesh, decking, food concentrates, water, all kinds of material expanded in a mass. Some hit the next star cruiser's shield, frying into energy, halted from moving farther.

"Hit!" shouted Maddox. "You hit and destroyed one of them. The fight's not over yet."

***

At that precise moment, in a different part of the starship, Lieutenant Noonan caught Doctor Rich's wink.

The two of them were in a critical AI nexus area. Bulkhead plates lay strewn on the deck. Earlier, Dana had used her implements to attach loosened cables and alien *radiant* connectives. The AI had shown the doctor specialty tools to work on the parts. Not only listening to the explanations—through Maddox doing the interpreting—the doctor had studied the machine with her critical, professional eye. A so-called "encryption" pad lay in plain sight. The AI had instructed Maddox, who had told the doctor how to use it. Dana had whispered earlier to Valerie that the pad was the central override board to the entire AI system.

Horrible sounds now echoed in the starship. Explosions shook the nexus area and metal crumpled nearby that they couldn't see.

The wink was Valerie's prearranged signal to act. The Star Watch lieutenant unlimbered her heavy assault rifle. While wearing her vacc-suit, she leveled the weapon at the nearby robot. It was a squat rounded thing that moved on treads and possessed six mechanical tentacles. It stood a little taller than her and must have weighed three times as much.

"Here goes," Valerie whispered to herself. She pulled the trigger. Bullets hosed from the assault rifle as the weapon bucked in her hands. The first few shots ricocheted off the robot. What kind of metal did it have, anyway?

Instead of worrying about that, the lieutenant focused on hitting the same surface area. Gritting her teeth, she kept firing.

Doctor Rich swiveled around, leaving what she'd been doing. Instead, she began typing on the encryption pad, her fingers blurring as she attempted to override the ancient computer.

The robot waved its many tentacles. The treads clanked, and the squat machine headed at Dana Rich. It looked as if the robot intended to ram the doctor against a bulkhead.

Inside her helmet, Valerie shouted, moving between the robot and Dana. Kneeling, Valerie ripped out the expended magazine and shoved in another. The robot loomed before her. She held the muzzle centimeters from its skin and let the rifle tremble in her hands. Bullets smashed through dented outer armor. They sparked inside the electrical guts. Yet still the robot's treads carried it closer.

Then, Valerie released the rifle as she began to roar and rave. Pushing with her feet, she collided with the thing so hard her teeth jarred together with a *click*. She shoved as her vacc-boots kept moving, straining against the robot. Mechanical tentacles struck her helmet and whipped against her shoulders. Her cries changed to those of pain. A last convulsive effort gave her more strength. She toppled the robot and rolled free of it. With sweat dripping into her eyes, she scrambled to the assault rifle lying on the deck. She jammed in a new magazine. As the robot's treads spun and the tentacles attempted to right itself, she shoved the muzzle through a torn area. Valerie pulled the trigger, pumping slugs into the undying robot. Finally, smoke billowed from the thing. Flames flickered, and the robot's efforts weakened until it no longer mattered.

Exhausted, Lieutenant Noonan staggered away from the alien machine, crashing onto her butt as she panted. She didn't know if they had won or lost, but she sure as heck felt as if she'd done her part.

***

On the starship's bridge, the holoimage raged at Captain Maddox. "You traitor! You lied to me. Your people are attempting to gain control over my AI core. I will drop the deflector shield and let both enemy beams strike the ship into oblivion."

"Wait!" Maddox said. "They aren't supposed to be doing that. My crew is attacking you?"

"What?" the holoimage asked. "They're doing this against your orders?"

"Of course," Maddox said, trying to gain time for whatever the others were attempting. "I have too much respect for you to do anything other than serve you. Strengthen the deflector shield. Use everything you can against the New Men while I stop my team from hurting you."

"No. It's too late for all of us. Can't you hear the interior destruction?"

Maddox heard something, all right, as explosions shook the starship.

At that moment, several things occurred at once. The holoimage faded away. As it did, vertigo struck Maddox again. He couldn't tell which way was up or down, right or left. It felt as if he was frozen in time. Expectantly, he waited for colors to smash against him and normalcy to return. It felt as if they jumped again. The *frozenness* stretched longer and longer.

Finally, with great effort, Maddox turned his head. He realized that he no longer heard the enemy beams destroying interior ship's systems and bulkheads.

Are we in hyperspace? Did Dana take over the starship's AI and force it to jump? What's going on?

Slowly, Maddox inhaled. As he blinked, he felt his eyelashes intertwine with each other. Time seemed to have slowed an immeasurable amount.

I have to see what's wrong.

He began to turn around. It seemed to go on forever and ever. Finally, he rose from his seated position. Then, the riot of colors flooded his senses. A roaring sound invaded his hearing, and his nose seemed clogged with scents. He bellowed, and his descending foot slid out from under him. With a thump, he crashed against the deck, laying there panting in bewilderment.

What just happened? Are we still in battle?

He listened, but he didn't hear anything telltale. Maddox closed his eyes, exhausted. *I can't just lay here. I have to see what happened.*

Captain Maddox struggled to his feet. The screen showed him the void of space. He couldn't see the red giant star or the enemy cruisers. No wrecks drifted outside and no planetary rubble showed what used to be worlds.

Did we just jump then, as I first suspected? How far did we go?

317

A laugh escaped his lips. Maddox was certain they were no longer in battle or in the alien star system. He pressed his lips together, containing the laughter. It was time to figure out if they had just won or lost.

-38-

It turned out they had won…after a fashion, Maddox decided.

A day after the battle, *Victory* drifted in the void three light years from the alien star system. The vessel wasn't near another star, but in the middle of nowhere. The craft had made the jump in one large bound.

The red giant blazed its light, the brightest object in the darkness.

The alien ship had taken severe damage from the star cruisers. Entire sections of the vessel were off limits because they were smashed wreckage now open to space. Perhaps one third of the craft lacked an atmosphere because the stellar vacuum drifted through it. In certain places, the crew had to take large detours to get from one point to another.

Still, they had survived the encounter with the New Men. No more fires raged or energy dissipated in the starship. They had fully acquired *Victory*, and they were in no immediate danger of destruction. Those were the good points. The bad troubled Maddox and severely depressed the crew. They had a two-week supply of food, at best. Dana had found a water supply, so they wouldn't die of dehydration. The star drive needed repair before it could work again. Once it began working—if they ever reached that point—they weren't sure they could keep it functional for long. They lacked a Laumer Drive, so they couldn't use the regular tramlines. Earth was three hundred light years away. With *Victory's* present star drive, they wouldn't remotely reach the Oikumene, never mind the Commonwealth of Planets or Earth, before the drive failed for good. And, without this ship in the Star Watch's possession, nothing

319

Maddox and the others had done out here mattered in a grand strategic sense.

"There's only one way we're going to survive more than a few weeks," Dana said. "We have to repair the ship."

They met in a chamber with low chairs and what they used for a table. It was warm in here, so they didn't have to wear their vacc-suits. That was good, because the last tanks only had a half-supply of air left.

"Okay," Keith said, as he twirled what looked like a key ring, "we need to fix stuff. What do we try to repair first?"

"That's easy," Dana said, "the star drive. Without it, we're trapped in the void with no way of changing our fate."

Valerie set a tube she'd been fiddling with onto the table. "I'm still worried about the AI. You told us before it isn't dead. You just cut it off from the ship's controls."

Doctor Rich nodded. "That's right. It's alive and likely brooding, if such a thing is possible."

"The AI must know of ways to bypass what you did," Valerie said. "Maybe it's secretly working to regain control of its ship."

"No. I don't think so," Dana said. "Think of the AI as a genie, and we've corked its bottle. It's not getting out unless we first pry out the stopper."

Maddox cleared his throat. "We must work under the assumption the AI will remain inoperative for a time. In that way, Doctor Rich is correct. Our primary goal is to fix the star drive. That will be your department, Doctor and Meta. I'm giving you Keith and Riker as helpers."

The sergeant sat morosely in a corner. His bionic hand opened and closed with faint *whirring* sounds. Meta also seemed despondent, with her elbows on the table and her eyes staring and distant.

First glancing at Meta and then looking back at the captain, Dana said, "I'd also like Valerie's help."

"No," Maddox said. "Lieutenant Noonan will help me. Once we figure out how to use the ship's sensors, we're going to scour space for a clue as to where we should go next. We're deep in the Beyond. That doesn't necessarily mean a lack of humans. We're going to search for planetary industrial signs. If nothing else, if we find such a system, we can go there and fill our food stores. At best, we'll also gain technical help to effect fuller repairs. I suspect we'll only fix everything at a Star Watch dockyard."

"Trying to bargain for repairs in a human-run star system out here in the Beyond would be dangerous," Dana said. "The starship is a fantastic prize. It has alien technology that includes a new beam, a better shield and a completely new star drive that bypasses tramlines. Whoever captures the ship will be tremendously wealthy. Greed motivates people do to nasty things."

Maddox took his time answering. Did he detect avarice in the doctor's eyes? He didn't want to believe it. She had taken the Star Watch oath. Would she hold to it? Or would Doctor Rich think of it as some lesser superstition she'd taken to build morale at the most critical juncture of the trip? Without Dana, none of this would have been possible. Maddox didn't want her for an opponent again. He needed her to remain one hundred percent on the team.

"I'm not speaking about riches for myself," Dana said, "if that's what you're thinking."

"Of course not," Maddox said.

"I'm merely saying we have to worry about hijackers if we enter a technologically advanced star system. There's something else, too. People in the past fled into the Beyond for a reason. Usually, the emigrants were odd in some way. Those oddities might trip us up if we go into their star system."

"There are dangers all around us," Maddox agreed, "but we have a deadly warship. People will trifle with us at their peril."

"The starship has sustained heavy and obvious damage," Dana said. "We're limited in what we can do, and people are going to know it. That's provided we can even get the star drive working again."

"And that we can find such a technologically advanced star system somewhere close by," Valerie added.

"Nevertheless," Maddox said, "we have the neutron beam and a sturdy shield. We can fight whoever thinks to cheat us."

"Once we repair the deflector generators, you'll have a shield again," Dana said. "I don't even know if any of the other ship's systems are repairable. The star drive has taken all my thoughts and energy. We have to restore it *now*."

"Agreed," said Maddox. "That's why you'll continue attacking the problem with Meta, Keith and Riker helping you."

Both Maddox and Dana glanced at Meta.

The former two G miner continued to stare forlornly at a distant and unseen point.

"Meta," Dana said softly. "Is anything the matter?"

Slowly, Meta turned her head. She no longer had her hair bound up. It now swept forward, partially hiding her features. From what Maddox could see, her eyes were red-rimmed and puffy.

"We're stranded in the void," Meta said. "We're fast running out of food. My metabolism runs hotter than ordinary. I'll starve long before anyone else does."

Maddox had wondered the same thing about himself.

"You can't give up now," Dana told her. "We're closer to winning everything than ever before."

Meta made a soft sound. "Do you know how long I've been hearing that? Try all of my life. Every time I win, I land in something worse. I thought the prison planet was the height of despair. Wrong. It's being in a starship that can't jump, with food and hope quickly dwindling into nothing."

"No, no," Dana said, obviously pumping heartiness into her voice. "We have a window of opportunity. This is the time to use it. You have strength and wits. We can eat for a little while longer. During that time, let's work like demons and fix what we can. If we fail, well, we can worry about it as our stomachs shrivel into nothing. Until then, I'll fight with all my strength against the universe. I'm not going to let it beat me. And if it does, well, it will know that it has been in the fight of its life."

Meta turned weary eyes onto Doctor Rich. "I realize that's one of your strengths. You refuse to quit. You're remorseless and never say die. I'm finally seeing that every victory lands me in a worse position. Can't you understand how demoralizing that is?"

"Bah!" Dana said, chopping a hand through the air. "I can't accept defeatism from you of all people. Do you remember all those monotonous months on Loki Prime? You were the most stalwart Temple Savant of the lot. Your positive attitude was more valuable than your mechanical shrewdness and strength. It's the person who keeps trying that eventually wins."

Meta sighed wistfully.

Looking away, Maddox realized something he hadn't suspected before. Dana needed Meta. Maybe the Rouen Colony woman was the only real friend Dana Rich had ever had. The doctor needed someone who believed in her. That was interesting. As their leader, he couldn't afford to let any of them wallow in despair. How could he help snap Meta out of her depression?

Hmm. They required the woman's skills now, not at some later date. Ah. He knew how to snap her out of her despair. He'd already laid the groundwork with her. Their situation meant he needed to use whatever would work quickest.

Turning back to the others, Maddox reached across the table and put a hand over one of Meta's.

She looked up sharply, staring at him.

"I wish you'd come with me," he said. "There's something I need to talk to you about."

"Where do you want to go?" Meta asked in a lifeless voice.

"Outside," he said, removing his hand and standing. For several seconds, he didn't think she would respond further.

Finally, with a heave, Meta stood.

"This way," he said, motioning with his head. As he headed for the hatch, Captain Maddox didn't wonder what he was going to do or say. For months, he'd fought to reach the alien starship. Now, the thing was in his possession. That was phenomenal. Not only that, but he'd faced three star cruisers, destroyed one and lived to tell about it. Now, he had to get this relic back to Earth. They would need Meta for that.

Behind him, Meta closed the hatch.

Maddox kept walking down the corridor. He used a well-worn path, avoiding any crusted slime. When they stepped on the ancient substance, it put noxious fumes in the air. He walked until they turned a corner and the hatch was out of sight.

"Where are you headed?" Meta finally asked.

Even with his back to her, he heard the difference in her voice. She sounded exasperated instead of hopeless. His present action seemed to have stirred a tiny amount of anger in her. Good. He needed the anger to leverage her out of the depression.

"Captain Maddox," Meta said. "I'm not walking any farther until you tell me what this is about."

He turned around, facing her. "I don't understand you," he said.

"That isn't surprising. I don't think you understand anyone."

He grinned in order to exasperate her.

323

"You find that amusing, do you?" she asked.

"You're beautiful," he told her.

Meta shook her head, making her dark hair swish back and forth. "No. You'd better not try any more of your tricks. If you do, I'm going to break an arm."

"That's better than quitting and moping."

"Oh, I see," she said. "You think you can perk me up with your witty ways. Well, it won't work."

He was sure it would. Stepping closer to irritate her, he said, "That's exactly what I think."

She watched him warily and raised her hands as if ready to enter a combat stance.

Maddox's grin widened.

"Don't try it," Meta warned.

Maddox moved in, and Meta thrust a knee at this groin. He blocked with his leg but the crash of her knee against his thigh caused him to stagger back.

Meta laughed as Maddox regained his balance. "I warned you," she said, and there was humor in her eyes.

"You did warn me," he said. "Yet, that's why I asked you to come out here."

"For me to thrash you?" she asked.

"No," he said, "to show you the power of persistence." He moved at her again. Once more, she thrust a knee at his groin. He slipped to the side so her strike failed to connect. That caused Meta to lose her balance. She stumbled as he moved back, catching her in his embrace. For a moment, Maddox held her in his arms. It was time for the final provocation. He bent his head, kissing her.

The Rouen Colony woman melted into his embrace. She gripped him, giving him a rib-shifting hug.

"Are you sure about this, Captain Maddox?" Meta whispered, staring into his eyes.

He almost lost his breath from her hug. And he wondered to himself why he had chosen this tactic. With his considerable strength, he hugged her back. Then, he bent his head again and kissed her longer than before. This time, she returned it as the power of her hug lessened to something tolerable.

"Meta," he whispered.

"Captain Maddox," she said back.

324

He liked the sound of her voice. He liked the feel of her against him even better.

After a time, he released her. She also let go of him and swept her fingers through her hair. This hadn't proceeded quite as he'd expected.

"In the end," she told him, "we can't win. You know that, right?"

He raised an eyebrow.

"That's why I let you do what you just did," she said. "It's only fair that I tell you, Captain. I took a vow long before this. My past won't allow me the kind of emotional attachment you're craving."

"Me?" asked Maddox.

Meta nodded sadly. "I am what I am. That can't ever change. You think you're so clever, but in this arena, I understand you better than you understand me."

Maddox said nothing.

"I was an assassin," she said, "and I did whatever I had to in order to succeed for my world."

Maddox still said nothing.

"In case you haven't noticed," Meta told him, "I'm not a nice person. I'm a killer with a pretty face. You're...a unique man. I could learn to like you too much. That won't do."

He frowned at her.

"I don't want to be hurt, you see. You're the kind of man who unintentionally hurts women. I've had to armor myself for the things I've done. To let a man like you past the armor would destroy me. Of course, I'm already destroyed, but you don't want to hear about that. None of this matters, though, because we're doomed to die out here."

Maddox scratched his cheek. Meta was unusual, and she kept herself emotionally separate from others. Is that why she despaired now?

"You understand what I'm saying, don't you?" Meta asked.

Maddox shook his head.

"You're lying," Meta said softly. "You think you don't have to pay the bitter price of your power, your unusual abilities. In this, I see more clearly than you do."

"Let me ask you a question," Maddox said.

"Yes?"

325

"If we're doomed, as you say, why not strive with every fiber in you to defeat the night? Why go quietly down to death? Let's fight oblivion together. Let's fight to live longer and do more than simply quit. If you admit defeat, the game is already up. If you strive, well, who knows, maybe we'll produce another wonder."

Meta turned away.

Maddox waited. Would she respond to the challenge?

"Yes," Meta said finally, looking up. "Let's try." She shrugged. "What do we have to lose?"

-39-

Two days later on the bridge, Lieutenant Noonan sat back in frustration. She had spent the last forty-eight hours trying to figure out how to use some of the instrument panels in order to scan the nearest star systems.

Captain Maddox used a thin metal rod to press tentacle-slot controls. He had become more cautious since accidentally locking them in here and draining the atmosphere a day ago. At the last moment, he'd figured out how to reverse what he'd done.

"Sir," Valerie said.

Maddox looked up. His features had become even gaunter than usual, with the beginning of circles around his eyes.

"We have to be realistic," Valerie said. "I'm not going to figure out these instruments before our food runs out. Sure, we can keep going as we starve, but I don't think we'll use our wits very well by that point."

"Defeatism isn't going to solve the problem," he said in an irritated voice.

"I'm not admitting defeat," Valerie told him. "I'm saying we're going about this the wrong way."

"I'd be delighted to hear your suggestion for a more productive avenue."

"You're not going to like it," she said.

"That doesn't matter. If it works, at this point, that's all that counts."

"I agree with you there," Valerie said. "In my opinion, we have to reactivate the AI. It can communicate with you and it can make

327

the ship do what it wants. Given our limited window of opportunity, I don't see any other way than semi-reactivating the AI and using it like a rider uses the reins on a horse."

Maddox frowned. "You want to give control of the vessel back to the AI?" he asked.

"First, we have to dumb it down," Valerie said. "Or, we have to change its coding so it listens to our orders instead of thinking it can make the commands."

Maddox snorted. "That would be immeasurably more difficult than learning how to use the ship's sensors ourselves."

"Maybe you're right if you mean for someone like me," Valerie said, "but not for Doctor Rich. She could figure out how to do what I'm suggesting"

"That's preposterous," Maddox said.

"I have to disagree with you, sir. There's something uncanny about Dana. She has a sixth sense about these things. As you've said before, she's a genius."

Maddox flipped his thin control rod into the air, catching it. "Do you trust her?" he asked suddenly.

"Dana? Of course, I trust her. She doesn't want to die any more than you do."

"That's not what I mean. Can we trust her to stick with the team, with following my orders? What's your gut feeling?"

"I don't know," Valerie admitted. "That's a good question. She has issues. That's for sure."

"Has she said anything to you about her past?" Maddox asked.

"No," Valerie said. "If you want to know that you should ask Meta."

"I think not," Maddox said.

"Even if we can't fully trust Dana, we should still try it my way," Valerie said. "The present way…isn't going to work for us."

Maddox put his hands behind his back and began to pace. He was quiet for a time. Finally, he said, "We have the starship. We just don't know how to run it. Soon, we're out of food. Even if we can jump, we're going to need a margin for error, food to last for a time. Yes, you're right, Lieutenant. We must shake the dice one more time. You must talk with Meta and sound her out about Dana. I'll go see the doctor and find out what she thinks about reactivating the AI."

Captain Maddox spoke with Doctor Rich. They wandered through the mammoth engine area. Fortunately, the star cruisers' rays hadn't touched the antimatter cylinders.

The broken combat robots and skeletal pincer-creatures no longer littered the deck here. Keith and Riker had cleared them away a day ago.

Dana nodded as Maddox explained the situation to her. "I've come to a similar conclusion," she said. "We have to open the stopper just enough to let the genie's intellect come out but not its power."

"Do you think it can be done?"

"Oh, certainly it *can*," Dana said. "That isn't the question."

"What is?"

"Whether or not *I* can do it," she said. "Then, we must broach the heart of the matter of what's really troubling you."

"I didn't know there was something else," Maddox said.

Dana smiled. Her teeth seemed so much whiter than any of theirs because her skin was darker. "Now, you're lying to me. It's something I notice you do easily and do quite well, I might add."

"I wouldn't call it lying, specifically," he said.

"I realize you wouldn't," Dana said. "You're in Star Watch Intelligence. In the end, you're a spymaster more than you're a starship captain. Disinformation—lying—is your stock in trade."

"Why the sudden flattery?" Maddox asked, dryly.

Dana nodded. "I suppose it's my turn to make a confession. I understand you'd like to know whether I'm trustworthy or not for the long haul back home."

Maddox wondered if Valerie had already talked to Meta about this, and if the Rouen Colony miner had come to the doctor.

"How much do you know about my past?" Dana asked.

"Could you be more specific?"

"You know I went on an expedition with Professor Ludendorff. What do you know about me after that?"

"Simply that you were a clone thief," Maddox said. He figured why let her know what he already knew from the Star Watch Intelligence files.

"Your vaunted Star Watch didn't give you any more specifics than that?" she asked.

Of course, they had, but his instincts led him to hedge his bets. "Nothing more than that you once engaged in espionage against the Social Syndicate of the Rigel System. I also know you're a computer expert."

"Much more than a mere *expert*," Dana said. "I excel with any form of electrical system or device."

"I'll willingly grant you that. According to your dossier, you were the heart of the attack against the ruling syndic. How and why you made these attacks—" Maddox shook his head. "You're right. My brief concerning you was too light, with too many unanswered questions."

"It's as I suspected." Dana compressed her lips together before asking, "What do you know about the Rigel Social Syndicate?"

"Very little," Maddox admitted. "I know they're part of the Commonwealth of Planets, if troublesome members."

The Commonwealth was a loose, large union of sovereign systems with the Star Watch as its protective and space-enforcement arm. A few of the systems, such as the Rigel Social Syndicate, only gave nominal allegiance.

"The Social Syndicate controls several star systems," Dana said. "Their navy keenly patrols its various tramlines. They also happen to quarrel incessantly with Brahma."

Dana studied her hands before looking up. "I was born in Bombay, India on Earth, but at an early age I emigrated to Brahma. As the name indicates, former inhabitants of India colonized the Brahma System. Our planetary religion is an accelerated form of Hinduism. That's unimportant to my story, as I'm an agnostic." The doctor shrugged. "I believe something made all this—the universe, I mean—but I have no idea who or what combination of super-powered beings did it."

"Fair enough," Maddox said.

"The social contract, as preached by the syndic and his cronies, has little appeal to those of Brahma," Dana said. "Our planet engages in high tech production and sales. We're a single star system with perhaps three hundred million inhabitants. The Social Syndicate dwarfs us in territory and population. In these sorts of things, it doesn't pay to be weak or small."

"No," Maddox said.

"Still," Dana said, "we had a solid navy and fought with zeal. From time to time, however, syndicate raiders slipped into our system, kidnapping men and women for various rich people's sex objects. Sometimes there were acts of technological piracy as well. It grew worse several years ago, and our hegemon—the name of our ruler—decided it was time for more vigorous defensive action. The Star Watch had failed to act decisively enough, no doubt wishing to keep the peace with the syndic. Instead of embroiling our systems in war and possibly bringing a Star Watch blockage on us and killing trade, we decided the Social Syndicate needed a civil war to split it apart."

"Ah," Maddox said, intrigued.

"The situation was something you might have excelled at," Dana said. "It was a spymaster's affair. How much do you know about the Social Syndicate philosophy?"

"Almost nothing," Maddox admitted.

"The key facet to understand for my story is that there are two major branches of thought. The first is known as the Maxim school of thought while the second is the Limited. I won't go into the philosophical differences between them. To an outsider they might not seem important. To many Social Syndicates, they are critical. The Rigel rulers and military are Maxim in belief. That being said, not all the Syndicate's subjects adhere to those doctrines."

"And..." Maddox said.

Dana grinned. "You wish me to get to the point. Very well, my task was to infiltrate certain clone centers. I was part of the team that planned to break into the most heavily guarded sanctuary in the Oikumene: that is, the syndic's personnel clone garden, where his clones and those of his immediate cronies lived. Our idea was simple and elegant.

"I cracked the security codes, and we herded the poor clones into a waiting spaceship. With them, we fled to a secret center in the stars. The Brahman secret service wasn't nice. They wanted to stop a war, after all. You can understand that, I'm sure."

"Yes," Maddox said.

"The clones underwent intensive retraining," Dana said.

"Brainwashing, you mean," Maddox said.

331

"I prefer my term. In any case, instead of the Maxim beliefs, the clones become Limited in outlook. After a certain length of time, the Brahman secret service released the first clones back onto Rigel."

"I think I can guess the rest," Maddox said. "The clones gathered a following and started a political rebellion."

"That's right," Dana said. "It was the germ of a possible civil war. It didn't get that far. But it gave the syndic's people a headache they most certainly didn't want."

"So what happened next?"

"The hegemon sent representatives to the syndic and they signed a non-aggression treaty. The Rigel Navy would from now on help patrol the tramlines leading to our star system. That was the overt wording. The secret clause was very clear. The syndic would make certain that no more raiders kidnapped or pirated our people."

"What about the other clones you'd stolen and continued to *retrain*?"

"You have to ask?" Dana said. "You're in Intelligence. You should know what we did."

"The Star Watch doesn't play quite so rough as those on Brahma," Maddox said.

"About that, I don't believe you for a moment," Dana said. "Anyway, the other clones continue to live in seclusion. That's in case the syndic changes his mind about us. They're the Sword of Damocles permanently hanging over his head."

Maddox knew the ancient Greek legend of Damocles. A man had complained to a king about how wonderful life was for the ruler because of the power he wielded. The king let his friend live like a monarch for a day. The only caveat was the man had a sword that dangled by a thread above his head. If the thread snapped…that would obviously end the good life. And that was the punch line of the tale, the Sword of Damocles. The king told the man he had power, but he always had to fear the assassin's knife.

"You tell an interesting story," Maddox said. "I fail to see, though, what it has to do with our current situation."

"That's because I'm not finished. Not so long ago, the Star Watch stopped a Brahman ship. The problem for me was despite the treaty between Brahma and Rigel, the syndic had declared me a criminal. And that's how the Star Watch officers treated me. I happened to be on the vessel they stopped."

"Wait a minute," Maddox said. "I don't understand. Didn't you belong to the Brahman secret service?"

Dana shook her head. "I've never been much of a joiner. I'd worked as an independent contractor. The syndic's people were ruthless. They saw the loophole and used it. The Brahman secret service had paid me well, but they didn't use any back channels to help me with the Star Watch. So, I hate them as much as the Star Watch for what happened next."

"What did happen?" Maddox asked.

Dana blinked several times before sighing. "It would have been worse if the Star Watch handed me over to the syndic. A clause in Star Watch rules didn't permit them to give me to a judicial system that has the death penalty. That was something, I suppose. Instead, the oh-so noble Star Watch held a kangaroo court. Afterward, they dropped me onto Loki Prime, where they intended I rot forever."

"Until they sent me to come and get you," Maddox said.

"Because you needed my skills," Dana said.

Maddox clasped his hands behind his back. He nodded solemnly. "I can understand your anger. You helped your people, and they turned their back on you. Yes, that is ingratitude of the worst sort. I wonder, though, have you ever thought about the clones?"

"What about them?"

"You set them up for failure. You must have realized they never had a chance. The syndic's hitmen would eventually find them. They were ciphers in the game of nations."

"Your point is what, exactly?" Dana asked.

"The very thing you hold against the Star Watch, you did to the clones."

"You're saying I'm not a nice person?"

"*I'm* not a nice person," Maddox said. "You and I cut corners. But we get things done. That's why the brigadier chose me and told me to get you."

"Are you saying we're no different than the New Men?"

"No," Maddox said. "I'm not saying that at all. I suppose our end-goals are what matters."

"The ends justify the means?" Dana asked.

"The New Men are attacking the Oikumene with all its various faults," Maddox said. "We have peaceful worlds and those like the Social Syndicate with its illegal clones. None of that matters to the

New Men. It would appear they plan to exterminate us or install a master-slave relationship of them over all of us. To protect your people, you played dirty with the Social Syndicate. The clones were caught in the middle. I'm not saying you did right by them, but it's not as bad as what the New Men plan to do with us."

"The clones originally lived to supply body-parts to the Social Syndicate leadership as they aged," Dana said. "I helped give the clones something more."

"That's one way to look at it." Maddox brightened. "Maybe that's how you should think about the Star Watch."

"They didn't give me something more," Dana said. 'They stuck me on Loki Prime."

"No. They gave you life instead of death. That's what the syndic would have done to you. Then, the head of the Star Watch sent me to come and get you. I took you off Loki Prime. What I really want to know is if you're going to remain on my side for the long haul."

"Even if I tell you I am, will you trust me completely?"

"I think you already know the answer," Maddox said. "I'm a spymaster before I'm a starship captain. Maybe if we hang together long enough, I'll become more of a captain than a spymaster, and then I'll trust you implicitly."

Dana snorted. "Okay. Fair enough, Captain. Yes. I'm going to fulfill my oath, at least long enough for me to pull you out of your own Loki Prime. Then we'll be even."

"I'll accept that," Maddox said. "Let's shake on it."

Doctor Rich thrust out her right hand. They shook, and then they got to work on the AI system.

-40-

Sergeant Treggason Riker paused as he walked through a cleared corridor toward the bridge. The starship's jump alarm had just sounded.

Riker knelt and then decided his old joints could use all the rest he could give them. He sat down on the deck. A second later, the combination of jump sensations, then quiet and finally, disorienting colors and noises slammed down on his head. He hated jumping, but he was fiercely glad the doctor, Meta and the indomitable Captain Maddox had restarted the AI and convinced it to pilot the starship for a time.

Unlike Lieutenant Noonan, the sergeant didn't care *how* they managed such a feat. He had learned a long time ago not to question Captain Maddox.

With the jump completed—the others would need time to recalibrate a host of things before they jumped again—Riker climbed to his feet. His left knee popped and pain flared. Ever since Loki Prime, he'd never quite been the same. That had been a screw-up all right: dropped onto the worst prison planet in the Commonwealth. Only Maddox's flair for doing the impossible had saved his old hide.

As the sergeant limped for the bridge, Riker recalled the first time he'd seen Maddox do the incredible. They had stalked a supposed cat thief, a veritable spider of a man. Interestingly, they had nailed the suspect at a Nerva laboratory.

The sergeant knew himself to be very old school. An Intelligence operative solved cases through diligence, hard work and asking endless questions and data searches. Eventually, somewhere, the criminal made a mistake. Often, that mistake was bragging about his deed to the wrong person.

That person was usually his girlfriend. It was a tried and true fact. The thief knew the importance of silence, so he kept his mouth shut for weeks, maybe even months. Finally, though, he had to tell someone. He'd committed a fantastic heist, and no one knew how splendid he was. So, one day, the thief would set his girl on his knee and say, "Honey, what I'm about to tell you has to stay just between you and me."

"Of course," she always said, "I won't tell a soul, darling."

"I'll have to kill you if you do," the thief would often say.

"Cross my heart and hope to die if I squeak a word, my love."

Satisfied with the reply, the thief would tell his woman exactly what he'd done. She'd laugh with delight, hug him and they would go to the bedroom and seal their love for each other.

Time would pass, and the woman would simmer with pride about her man. Finally, her pride would boil over. She'd pull aside her best friend, and say, "You can't tell anyone what I'm about to tell you. It will mean my man's death if you speak a word about this."

"You can count on me," the girlfriend would say. "I won't tell anyone, not even my husband."

Satisfied, the woman would explain her man's daring exploit.

The new informant would keep the secret for maybe an entire day. Finally, at night, she'd turn on her pillow and whisper, "You should hear what I know. It's too bad I promised never to tell anyone."

"What is it?" the husband would ask sleepily.

"I can't say."

"Come on. You have me curious. Tell me already."

"Do you promise never to tell anyone?"

"Yeah, yeah, I promise already," the husband would say. He'd hear the story, be duly impressed at the daring and tell his buddies at work about it the next day.

Finally, with his ear to the ground, asking his questions and making data searches, Riker would hear a tidbit. Over the course of several days of footwork and questioning, he'd follow the story to its source. Then, they would catch the thief because the man had to tell someone about his feat.

That was old school Intelligence work, and Captain Maddox knew very little about it. The lean man with his unnatural quickness and athletic prowess must consider himself a lion or leopard in disguise.

Riker recalled that time in the Nerva laboratory at night in the Black Forest in Germany. Maddox had a theory the cat thief would strike that night, and he'd been right. They had chased the man through the building. The thief had raced to a window with his climbing gear still on. Using suction cups, the thief had scaled away outside on the wall.

Maddox sprinted to the window. Riker remembered his lungs aching as he ran to keep up. That hadn't compared to the astonishment he felt as the captain climbed out the window and began scaling after the thief.

Oh, yes, Riker remembered. He raced to the window and stuck his head and shoulders out. First, he looked down, and didn't see anything in the flooded lights there, five stories away. A trickle of grit struck the back of his head. He looked up, and Riker remembered his mouth dropping open in amazement. Maddox scaled the brick building using his fingers and toes. The captain must have believed himself half-lizard. Riker had thought so at the time.

Anyway, despite the ache in his lungs, Riker raced for the stairs leading to the roof. He clumped up them and burst through the door. The cat thief lay dead by his rotors, shot through the back by Captain Maddox. The Star Watch officer had barely made it in time as the thief tried to fly away, but Maddox had caught him through an act of bizarre daring.

That's when Riker had known Maddox wasn't normal. Maybe he should have asked for a transfer right then.

The old man shrugged as he continued down the starship corridor. The officers running the Star Watch had certainly picked the right agent for the task of reaching the alien vessel. Now, they were going to try to get this machine home again. The New Men needed stopping. Riker wasn't sure the starship would be enough, not after all the things he'd seen. The New Men were a race of Captain Maddox's plus. How could humanity keep such a group down?

"Sergeant on the bridge," Riker said.

Lieutenant Noonan turned from where she sat. The lass smiled at him. "Come in, Sergeant. Please, come in."

Riker did. He liked Valerie and appreciated the way she did things by the book. The lieutenant didn't toss outlandish surprises in your face the way a soldier would heave grenades. Maddox was always exploding one wild maneuver after another at him.

It's a wonder I'm still alive. Imagine, dropped onto Loki Prime and canoeing for my life from crazy-eyed prisoners.

Riker still had nightmares about that, waking up coughing and spluttering.

"Is the starship still on course?" Riker asked.

"Come stand here," Valerie said, indicating a spot near her viewscreen.

He did, and he enjoyed the scent of her perfume. The lieutenant put on just enough. She also kept her uniform crisp and military. Riker did the same thing with his uniform. He liked things orderly.

"Do you see that star there?" Valerie asked. She used a thin metal rod to point at the screen. The tip tapped a yellowish object surrounded by a cluster of other stars.

"I see it," Riker told her.

"The AI sensed radiation and other background indicators that would seem to mean an advanced society. I've been checking for radio waves. Personally, I think I've found what we're looking for. The captain hopes I'm right, but he hasn't admitted I am."

"Are you right?" Riker asked. "I mean really?"

"I'd give myself an eighty-five percent probability," Valerie said.

"Why doesn't the captain agree, then?"

"That's what I want to know," Valerie said. "You've been with him the longest. I was hoping you could tell me."

Riker thought about that. He began piecing together past events. A thought dawned on him. "You know, there's something about the New Men that troubles the captain."

"The New Men trouble me," Valerie said.

"It's more than their superiority—" Riker snapped the finger of his regular hand. He never snapped his bionic fingers. Even after all this time, he was careful with the bionic hand. He had accidently petted a dog too hard once, and the poor creature had yelped with

338

pain, running away with its tail between its legs. After that, Riker was cautious with the bionic arm and hand.

"What were you saying?" Valerie asked.

Riker hesitated. He almost said, "I'm going to tell you a secret, but you have to promise never to say a word of this to anyone else." He knew that Valerie would never be able to keep it secret. In time, she would tell someone. If a man wanted to keep something quiet, he couldn't tell anyone.

"It's nothing," Riker said.

Valerie looked up at him. "Sergeant, please, I can keep my mouth shut."

He remained silent.

"You aren't going to tell me, are you?"

"No. I'm afraid not," Riker said.

She smiled at him. "You're a good man, Sergeant. Captain Maddox is lucky to have you."

"You should tell him that."

"I will."

"Glad to hear it," Riker said, and he chuckled softly.

They both watched the stars for a time.

"Do you think we'll make it the star system?" Riker asked.

"It's fifteen light years away," Valerie said. "That's five more jumps. We're not going to try anything higher than three light years at a time just now. So yes, we should reach there in two or three days."

"That's not leaving us much food in the storeroom."

"No," Valerie said quietly.

"Do you trust the AI?"

Lieutenant Noonan shook her head. "I most certainly do not. But it's teaching us the ship systems. I can already perform most of my duties on my own. Soon, we can turn it off for good."

Riker was glad to hear it. He continued studying the stars. Three more days at the most, if this ancient vessel held together, and they would be in a new star system. What would it hold? Would the sentients there be human, and would they have the needed tools to help effect greater repairs to the starship? He hoped so.

They had to get this vessel home before the Great Space War started with the New Men. Would the enemy hold back long enough? Would Captain Maddox bring them home through sheer force of will?

"We've made it this far," Riker said.

"What's that?" Valerie asked.

"We've made it this far, Lieutenant. We've done the hard work. Now we're like a horse out in the pasture, racing to get home again."

"Well," Valerie said. "In my opinion, we can't do it fast enough. Now, if you'd find a place to sit, Sergeant. I'm going to sound the jump alarm."

He hurried to an alien chair.

"Are you ready?" Lieutenant Noonan asked.

"Yes, ma'am," Riker said.

Valerie sounded the alarm. A few moments later, they began the next jump.

***

Captain Maddox's stomach growled as he stood on the bridge. He was hungry and gaunt. Like Meta, his metabolism burned too hot.

He studied the screen. The G class star waited three light years away, one more jump. They hadn't detected any spacecraft in the system—not that he'd expected to. Starships were too small and quick to see from such a vast distance. The fourth planet of the star showed industrial technology but no radio waves. Could they be human emigrants from the Oikumene who had fallen back into barbarism? Had they forgotten how to make radios? It was beginning to look that way.

Exhaling, Maddox glanced at the diminutive hologram on the panel beside the screen. It showed the alien commander from six thousand years ago, who looked human enough with his silvery matted hair and dangling arms. They still hadn't gotten an answer for the tentacle-like control slots. The holoimage of the former commander didn't look up at him, ever. Was that significant? Maddox hoped not but felt it must be.

Dana had successfully enslaved the AI, which remained coded to his voice. None of the others could understand the holoimage when it spoke. That must have to do with the original brain scan. They hadn't figured out how to replicate that, and the holoimage seemed to have forgotten what he'd done earlier.

Lieutenant Noonan sat at her scanning station. Doctor Rich remained in the AI nexus. Meta, with Riker and Keith as helpers, tried to fix the main deflector shield generator. It refused to cooperate. That meant the starship had no screens, just its shredded hull armor. They had a single neutron cannon, which so far had proven to be enough.

"We can't face a star cruiser again," Dana had told him.

"Do you think they're waiting for us?" Maddox had asked.

"I think the New Men don't give up easily. They must realize we escaped the alien system and how we did it. Yes, I think they're hunting for us. We must be ready for the worst. They're out there somewhere."

Maddox's stomach growled loud enough so Lieutenant Noonan looked up. When their eyes met, she looked away.

"Food," she said.

"I feel like a desperate predator ready to tackle a bull elephant for lunch," Maddox said. "We may have to figure out how to use one of the shuttles and take it down onto the fourth planet."

"I volunteer to go," Valerie said.

"I believe I'll be the one going down onto the planet," Maddox said.

The lieutenant looked up, shocked. "Sir, you can't leave the ship now. You're too valuable. No one else can speak with…it," she said, using her chin to jut at the tiny holoimage.

The thing gave her a fervent glance.

"Sir," Valerie said, "I think it knows what we're—"

"Lieutenant!" Maddox said, interrupting her. "Whatever you were going to say, don't."

She grew pale, nodding quickly. "I'm sorry, sir. The thing gives me the creeps. It listens to us much too—"

"Lieutenant," Maddox said, "*desist* your line of reasoning."

"Yes, sir," she said.

"We're about to jump," he said. "We must be ready for anything. Think about that."

Valerie waited before saying, "This next jump is exciting and terrifying at the same time."

With his hunger, Maddox found it difficult to concentrate on anything but food. He'd finished the last of his rations. He could commandeer someone else's, but he didn't feel right doing so. If this

341

star system failed to provide them with food…nothing else mattered anyway.

"Inform the others we're about to make the jump," Maddox said.

Valerie opened intra-ship channels and told the crew to prepare for the next use of the star drive. Then she got up, moving to a different station. There, using the thin rod to tap slot-controls, the lieutenant made the last jump to the new system.

-41-

The ancient starship *Victory* slid toward the fourth planet of the system.

The G class star was eight percent larger than Sol. It had a similar luminosity and ten planets. The inner system contained four of those planets; the outer had five gas giants and a Pluto-like world. There were no asteroid belts or visible comets.

"Well?" Maddox asked.

"No artificial satellites orbit the fourth planet, sir," Valerie said. "It has two small moons, which we already knew."

"Yes, I see those," Maddox said.

"The industrial index shows that the greatest concentration is on the approaching continent, sir, the one shaped like an octagon."

The starship was several hundred thousand kilometers from the fourth planet, about the distance of the Moon from Earth. It was a blue-green world similar to Terra. The octagonal-shaped landmass facing them radiated the most industrial signs.

"I'm detecting nuclear power," Valerie said, sounding surprised.

"Good. What about radio waves?"

"Nothing," Valerie said. "I have no indication they know we're out here."

"That seems strange," Maddox said.

"I agree, sir."

"Well, we need food. Start calculating an orbital entry above the planet."

"Sir?" the lieutenant asked.

Maddox glanced at her, and then he remembered himself. He wasn't on the *Geronimo*. This was *Victory*. "Sorry, Lieutenant," he said. "Old habits die hard." The captain thereupon gave his orders to the holoimage.

The starship shuddered as the vessel's engines applied power, slowing the mighty craft so it could soon enter planetary orbit.

"We made it," Valerie said. "We're really here. I can hardly wait to see what kind of foodstuffs they have."

"Yes," Maddox said absently. "We're here."

"Is something wrong, sir?"

"I wish our new starship had the instruments to sense the system's Laumer-Points. How many tramlines run into this star system? How do they link with the others? Are the beings down there men or some new alien species?"

"We'll know some of the answers soon enough, sir."

A half-hour passed and the planet loomed before them.

"Oh-oh," Valerie said, as she studied her board.

The words sent a shudder down Maddox's spine. "What's wrong? What are you sensing?"

"There was something and now there's nothing," Valerie said quietly. She used her rod to stab controls. "If I were on the *Geronimo*, I'd know how to replay what I just picked up."

"What—"

"It came from the nearest moon," Valerie said, "the one swinging toward us."

"Computer," Maddox said to the holoimage. That's what he'd taken to calling it. "Did you pick up those readings?"

"I did," the tiny image told him.

"What was it?"

"A broadcaster," it said.

"Where did it broadcast?" Maddox asked.

"Toward the inner planets," the holoimage told him.

"What—"

"Sir," Valerie said, with horror in her voice. "Look! That has to be the *Saint Petersburg*. I'd recognized its shape anywhere."

Maddox stepped toward her screen. He saw the familiar shape. The SWS destroyer used the smallest moon, accelerating as it swung around it. The warship sped at them. It would appear the enemy vessel had been using the moon to hide from them.

"Its laser batteries are charging," Valerie said. "Do they mean to try to take us down, sir?"

Maddox stared at the screen. Despite his hunger and the shriveled state of his stomach, his mind now moved at lightning speed. If the destroyer raced at them...*it* must have sent the broadcast signal toward the inner planets. That implied reinforcements, which in turn likely meant at least one star cruiser. If two enemy vessels were in this system, it stood to reason the New Men—maybe Per Lomax in particular—had deduced *Victory's* state of ill repair. That would indicate the New Men had studied the nearby planets and made a calculated ambush site: where the alien starship would go. Either that was the case or the enemy had tracking systems able to cross light-years. That seemed improbable. Therefore, the New Men's heightened intellect had probably reasoned out what their best chance of success would be against the ancient starship.

In these precious seconds of lightning thought, Maddox realized humanity indeed faced its gravest challenge. These beings were supermen in every way.

"What are we going to do, sir?" Valerie asked. "We can't enter planetary orbit now. The *Saint Petersburg* will destroy us. If there's a star cruiser nearby—"

"We must replenish our food stocks," Maddox said.

"Not at the cost of our lives, sir."

Maddox blinked once, twice, three times before he laughed.

"We'll have to jump far away, sir," Valerie said. "I don't see what else we can do."

"Negative," Maddox told her. "The enemy has just made his greatest mistake."

"Sir?" asked Valerie.

"Computer," Maddox told the holoimage. "Can you focus the neutron beam into a tighter ray?"

The image didn't answer.

"Computer, I have asked you a question. Can you tighten the neutron beam?"

"I can," it said at last.

"What are you planning, sir?" Valerie asked.

"Sit tight, Lieutenant. Tell the others to do the same thing. We're going to attempt fast maneuvers. Computer, you will reverse course

345

and head for the nearby ship. Target its engines first and take them out. Then retarget its laser batteries and destroy them. On no account must you annihilate the vessel itself."

"The *Saint Petersburg* has a deflector shield, sir," Valerie said.

Maddox scowled in irritation. "Kindly shut up, Lieutenant, and let me think. I have to do this right the first time. There must be a star cruiser accelerating for us, maybe two. We cannot face them and survive."

The starship shuddered as the AI began to follow Maddox's orders. The heavy braking almost caught the captain by surprise. He stumbled, grabbed a panel and thrust himself into a seat.

The antimatter engines whined, and the anti-gravity systems made thumping noises. *Victory* no longer headed for a fourth-planet low orbit, but slowed until it stopped and began moving toward the moon and the approaching destroyer.

"Enemy beams have reached the outer hull," the AI said.

"This is the tricky bit," Maddox said. "We have to sustain a little more damage to win everything. Take out the destroyer's engines."

"They are not yet in range," the AI said.

"Then get us in range, pronto!" Maddox said.

Now began an uneven contest. The *Saint Petersburg's* lasers were not those of a battleship or even a cruiser. Still, they were lasers, and by slow degrees the twin beams turned the outer hull red and then molten. Too soon, the lasers began chewing inside the starship.

"I know you want me to shut up, sir," Valerie said. "But we're taking damage. Sergeant Riker just radioed and said the beams are near the antimatter engines."

Maddox nodded, accepting the report. He tapped a fist against a panel. "Come on," he whispered.

Explosions shook the ship.

"Sir," Valerie said, looking up in alarm.

Maddox licked his lips.

"We are in beam range," the holoimage informed him.

"Fire!" Maddox shouted. "Destroy their laser batteries first. Then take out the engines."

In a thin line, the purple neutron beam touched *Saint Petersburg's* deflector shield.

346

"Full power," Maddox said. "Knock down the shield. Then focus the ray for sniper shots."

The heavy neutron beam blasted the destroyer's shield. The enemy's electromagnetic screen overloaded and went down all around the ship. At that instant, the AI refocused the beam, and it obliterated the enemy's lasers."

Maddox snarled with glee.

The neutron beam retargeted, and it killed the destroyer's engine port.

"Tell Ensign Maker to race to the bridge," Maddox ordered. "I'm going to need his expertise."

"The destroyer is firing its point defense cannons," Valerie said.

Maddox ordered the AI to take those out, too, and it did in short order.

By the time Ensign Maker staggered onto the bridge, *Saint Petersburg's* escape pods ejected from the ship. The personnel were fleeing.

"That's all the proof we need a star cruiser is in the vicinity," Maddox said. "Those people must be sure it will pick them up. Ensign, come here. You're going to tell me exactly what to do. Lieutenant," he said, turning to Valerie. "Tell Riker and Meta to suit up and grab their assault rifles. They're going to form my boarding party."

"Ah…yes, sir," Valerie said, sounding perplexed, "at once."

Maddox nodded, concentrating on the destroyer. *One thing at a time*, he told himself. *I have to do this before the star cruiser gets into range and forces us to jump.*

***

Saint Petersburg's escape pods headed away for deeper space. The empty destroyer raced for its collision with the fourth planet, fated no doubt to burn up in the atmosphere.

Captain Maddox had other plans for the hijacked Star Watch vessel. Under Keith's guidance, he ordered the AI onto an exact course. Halfway through the complex maneuver, *Victory's* sensors picked up a star cruiser's fast approach. It had hidden behind the third planet and now accelerated for them. Did that imply the New Men's sensors had seen the starship coming before the last jump? It would seem so, and that had grave implications for the coming war.

Victory raced in a long curving loop with the *Saint Petersburg* as its central pivoting point. The destroyer streaked past, heading for the planet. Finally, the starship completed the turning maneuver, aiming at the nearby world and following the empty craft.

"Now," Maddox said, striking a panel with his fist. "Give it everything."

Using full thrust, *Victory* sought to reach the destroyer before the Star Watch vessel hit the atmosphere. Both ships were perilously near the looming blue-green world. Every minute caused more of the planet to fill up the view-screen. Soon, the world would blot out all the stars.

"We're not going to be able to brake in time," Valerie said.

"You're correct," Maddox said. "Therefore, you will prepare for jump."

"Sir?" the lieutenant asked.

"Remember the red giant? We jumped right through it. We must have entered hyperspace when we jumped, and the red giant wasn't there. That's what we're going to do here, jump before we reach the planet's atmosphere."

Ensign Maker laughed with delight. "I love it, sir. It's a brilliant plan."

Maddox grinned as he kept his eyes on the screen. The starship began overtaking the *Saint Petersburg*. Still, this was cutting it much too finely.

"Sir," Valerie said. "The star cruiser is hailing us."

With a long stride, Maddox stood behind her chair. "Put him on," he said.

A moment later, Per Lomax stared at Maddox. The New Man maintained his haughty poise. Then, if it was possible, the enemy commander straightened even more.

"The present encounter between us means nothing in the larger scheme of our conquest," Per Lomax informed the captain.

"Oh no, of course not," Maddox said, sarcastically.

Per Lomax stiffened. "You would do well to remember this, Captain. My coming retribution will be hard and exacting."

"I have an idea," Maddox said. "Let us reason together. You hunted me once and failed. In fact, you're still carrying a scar from the bullet that knocked you to the ground on Loki Prime. If you take those factors—"

348

"You fail to realize how wrong you are," Per Lomax said, interrupting. "I have no scar. Our bodies are many times more efficient than yours are. We heal perfectly. No. For you, the game is over, as you are already dead. In your case, you simply lack the sense to know it. Good-bye, Captain Maddox. In futility you struggled against me, and now you have failed as it was fated to occur."

The burning question about his origins rose to Maddox's lips again. He shook his head, refusing to ask the New Man. Maybe they would meet again someday. Maddox tapped Valerie on the shoulder. She cut the connection.

The captain returned to his station. The holoimage looked up at him. The simulacrum's eyes seemed to gaze with intensity.

"The star cruiser has almost reached its outer beam range in relation to us," the holoimage informed him.

"We can't do anything about that," Maddox said. "So I want you to ignore the cruiser for now."

"Noted," the holoimage said.

Keith shook Maddox's shoulder. Once the ace had his attention, the younger man told him the next maneuver.

The destroyer headed for the atmosphere. At the same time, the starship's main bay doors opened. Like a Great White shark, it came behind the destroyer. Instead of jaws, Keith Maker used *Victory's* open bay as a maw.

"We have to do this exactly," Keith said, with his eyes fixed on the view-screen.

Maddox related the ace's instructions to the AI.

While traveling at great speed, the starship scooped up the destroyer, seeming to swallow it whole. Because *Victory* moved faster, *Saint Petersburg* smashed against parked alien shuttles and interior bulkheads. The entire starship trembled violently from the collision.

Maddox shook in his chair, waiting for the outcome. Were they dead? Was Per Lomax right? No! The destroyer finally came to a halt inside the starship. The shaking and metallic screeching stopped.

"Close the bay doors," Maddox told the AI.

Without giving anyone a warning, Valerie pressed the jump button. *Victory* shook even more as it entered the planet's upper atmosphere. A million kilometers away, the cruiser fired its main beam. Each act was all for naught—because the starship jumped once again. It bypassed the fourth planet. The beam slashed empty space, sizzling into the atmosphere. And *Victory* left the star system three light years behind.

They hadn't touched down for food. Neither had they found any spare parts on the planet.

"What we do have," Maddox said, after the jump ended, "is an SWS starship under our control. We're going to raid its stores, use its tools and hook up its star charts. Best of all, we're going to use the destroyer's Laumer Drive to open wormholes for us. People, I have good news, it looks like we're going to get home after all."

-42-

Three light years away from the fourth planet, and in the void, Captain Maddox led the boarding team. Sergeant Riker and Meta headed for the main docking bay with him.

It would have been better if they had powered armor. Instead, they wore vacc-suits and cradled assault rifles. Escape pods had jettisoned from the *Saint Petersburg*. Yet, who knew if everyone had gotten away? Maybe the New Men had a surprise for them in the battered destroyer.

"Ready?" Maddox radioed the others.

"Yes, sir," Riker said.

Maddox turned around. After a moment, Meta nodded.

A few more steps took them to the main hatch. There were raised dents in the metallic entry, a slew of pimples. Maddox's stomach squeezed with hunger and worry. What would they find?

He tapped the controls, but the hatch refused to open. Maddox tried it again, but nothing happened.

"Let me look at it," Meta said.

Maddox moved aside. The Rouen Colony woman set her rifle against a bulkhead, unhooked a tool from her belt and worked off the panel. She began fiddling with the circuits. Ten minutes later, the hatch finally slid open.

Smoke drifted out of the darkness. Sparking lights appeared in the distance.

Maddox switched on his HUD imaging. The sight shocked him. It was worse than he'd expected.

A vast field of destruction spread out before him. Smashed alien shuttles, ripped-up decking and torn bulkheads made the gigantic chamber a twisted, metallic maze. Sparks and burning cables created a thick, drifting haze everywhere. Surely, the starship couldn't take much more damage. It was amazing the vessel was still functioning at all.

"Look," Riker radioed, pointing into the distance.

On the other side of the docking bay, the *Saint Petersburg* lay on its side, a smoldering wreck. Huge chunks of the destroyer lay strewn about the bay.

"It's a jungle, sir," Riker said.

Maddox nodded.

"We'll have to move carefully," Meta said. "Many of those pieces will have sharp edges that could slice through our vacc-suits and then us."

That was a good point.

The sergeant glanced at his assault rifle. "Don't see that anyone in the destroyer could have survived the crash, sir."

"Maybe," Meta radioed. "We should be ready for anything, though."

"Agreed," said Maddox. "Let's get started."

He led the way, his boots crunching over debris. For the next hour, they wound their way past the wreckage, often having to turn around and try a different path.

Maddox wondered if they should try to temporarily shut off gravity, but decided against it because of all the junk that could start floating.

Finally, they reached the sideways-lying destroyer.

"How are we going to get inside, sir?" Riker asked. "I doubt we're going to find a usable hatch."

"We won't get in by talking," Maddox said, irritably. His stomach clenched with the need for food. It had been too long since he'd eaten.

They began searching for a way in, but there didn't seem to be one. In the end, Meta climbed onto the destroyer. She used dented hull planting as a makeshift ladder, scaling it like a gymnast.

"Do you see anything?" Maddox radioed.

"I think I can force this metal," Meta said from the top.

"No," Maddox said. "Find some other way. I don't want you to cut yourself."

The sound of screeching hull planting told him Meta hadn't listened to the order. She was going in.

Riker glanced at him.

Maddox shrugged. Maybe Meta had the right idea. He wanted to reach the galley and see what there was to eat. He was famished.

"Let's start climbing and see what she found," Maddox said.

When the captain was halfway up the *Saint Petersburg's* side, Meta radioed. "I'm inside the ship."

"Wait for us," Maddox said. "We want to search it together."

"I don't see why," she said. "Your sergeant is right. No one's alive in here. Besides, I suspect they all used the escape pods."

"At this point, there's no need to take risks," Maddox said. "If anyone is in there, we need to tackle him as a team."

"All right," Meta said. "I'll wait."

Several minutes later, Maddox reached her former position on the hull. He eased through the torn plating, landing inside a corridor beside her. Riker dropped down after him.

Maddox wasn't sure what he expected to find. The *Saint Petersburg* had been under New Men control for quite some time.

He clutched his assault rifle as the three of them filed down the corridor. Electrical smoke drifted everywhere. He imagined there had been fires. Maybe one still raged. Most of the time, he watched his feet. Otherwise, he kept tripping over ripped decking or debris on what they used as the floor. As he walked through the *Saint Petersburg*, an eerie feeling possessed him. The New Men had been here. Would the arrangements inside the ship give him greater clues as to their enemy's nature?

Soon, they reached a dead end, with the corridor ahead pinched shut.

"We'll have to backtrack," Maddox said.

Meta tried to peer past the crushed bulkheads to the other side. Her visor remained glued there for twenty seconds. Finally, she faced them.

"It's worse in here than in the docking bay," Meta said. "If we're going to search everywhere, I'll need a cutting torch."

Maddox's stomach growled. He wanted to force his way to the galley now. What good would it do him, though, if he cut himself on

353

the sharp metal edges? Bleeding to death due to an accident seemed like a foolish way to die, especially after all they'd been through. He could wait to eat a little while longer.

"What if they sabotaged the galley?" Sergeant Riker asked. He was obviously worried about the same thing as the rest of them. "What if there isn't any food left?"

"What if our legs fall off?" Meta asked him testily. "You worry too much."

Maddox almost told her that was her problem, but he held his tongue. "We need a cutting torch," he said.

Riker sighed into his microphone. "I'm too old for all this back and forth, sir."

"You can wait here if you like," Maddox said.

"Thank you, sir. I'll do that."

"Let's get your equipment," Maddox told Meta.

She didn't reply, merely turned around and headed back the way she had come.

After a second, Maddox followed her.

***

They worked hard inside the *Saint Petersburg*, slowly opening up all the corridors and searching the various chambers and quarters. Soon, it became clear no New Men or traitorous Star Watch personnel remained aboard the destroyer dead or alive. At that point, Maddox summoned the rest of the crew to help.

As he bent metal or cut new openings, the captain examined the interior. He didn't find anything out of the ordinary. It simply looked like a smashed Star Watch vessel. He was disappointed not to gain any new information about the New Men.

Six and a half hours after entering the *Saint Petersburg*, Meta and he forced their way into the galley.

The Rouen Colony woman knelt, cutting the final opening with her blue flame.

Maddox couldn't ignore his gnawing hunger and the worry in the back of his mind. Maybe a fire had destroyed all the stored food. If the destroyer's galley failed them—

Standing, Meta removed her thumb from the switch. The flame disappeared. She shoved her shoulder against the plate. The metal toppled into the galley.

Maddox peered into the gloom. The place was in shambles.

"Watch the hot edges," Meta warned, pointing at the glowing entrance. Then, she stepped through.

Maddox did likewise, striding to a selector switch. They were all smashed. The heat unit had also been demolished. Swallowing with a dry throat, Maddox went to a locker. Gripping torn edges, he strained, but failed to move anything. Meta joined him. Together, they finally bent back the stubborn metal.

Maddox blinked several times and laughed with exhausted relief. "Food," he said. The packages were intact. He tore one open and saw dried peas, potatoes and frozen pork. They were going to have enough to eat.

"Let's take these," Meta said, with her arms already full of packages.

It reminded Maddox that Meta had a high metabolism just as he did. "Agreed," he said. Then, he studied the packages, picking tacos and rice.

As he started back, his mouth watered. It had been days already since he'd eaten. This was going to be glorious.

***

Twenty-two hours later, Maddox stood on the destroyer's bridge with Doctor Rich. With nutrients in his system, he felt good again. They would have enough to eat for months now. Hopefully, they could return to Earth before they ran out of food a second time.

In a different chamber, Meta, Riker and Keith worked on the *Saint Petersburg's* Laumer Drive, trying to fix the damage. They would need the drive to get home using the tramlines. Meta had told him she could repair the destruction. He hoped she was right. Like all the important ship's systems, it had its own armored bulkheads, which might have made the difference.

They also needed tramline star charts. *Victory* didn't possess a map of various wormhole points. Those should lie in the *Saint Petersburg's* computers.

Doctor Rich toiled at the main terminal on the bridge. Because the *Saint Petersburg* lay on its side, she worked at an odd angle, her gloved fingers tapping a panel. Suddenly, she straightened.

"Trouble?" Maddox asked.

"No!" Dana shouted. She raised a fist and smashed it against the panel. Curses flowed from her mouth. "May the Goddess of Destruction devour your guts a worm at a time."

"What's wrong?" Maddox asked.

Dana slammed her fist against the panel several more times. Finally, she swiveled around, her visor aimed at him.

"Per Lomax or one of the other New Men must have set up a self-destruct booby-trap," Dana said. "Detonations have just destroyed the *Saint Petersburg's* hard drives."

"Are you sure?" Maddox asked. He hadn't heard any explosions.

Her visor remained aimed at him.

"I see," Maddox said. She was sure. He wondered what had been on the ship's computers that the New Men hadn't wanted them to find. He doubted the enemy had done this in an anticipation of their need for the Laumer-Points and wormhole trails. The reason for the destruction hardly mattered, though.

"Without the Laumer-Point coordinates..." Dana trailed off helplessly. "The drive will help us, but we'll be like a Patrol survey team, painstakingly searching our way from one star system to another. At best, this will triple our travel time. We might be a year out here instead of months."

That would be a problem, Maddox conceded to himself. Time was one of their worst enemies.

"You should begin hunting for backup systems," he told her.

"Don't you understand the nature of our enemy yet?" Dana asked bleakly. "The New Men are thorough. If they sabotaged this, there won't be a backup system that works."

"You don't know that," he said.

"But I do," she said. "Believe me, it is a fact."

"No," Maddox said. "Let's make them work for their advantages. Let's not concede them any."

Dana cocked her head.

"We know the New Men are dangerous adversaries," Maddox said. "That doesn't mean we grant them godlike abilities and throw our hands in the air. We check everything, seeing if they *did* make a mistake. I refuse to let someone's reputation defeat me, only his actions."

"Meaning what?" Dana asked.

"That you start hunting for backups."

356

After a second of thought, she nodded. "Yes! You're right. We must try all avenues. That is the proper attitude. This…this destruction surprised me. That's all."

Maddox understood. The booby trap had surprised him, too.

Four hours later, Dana made her report as Maddox watched Meta and Riker. The others labored on the Laumer Drive.

"Did you find something the New Men overlooked?" Maddox asked the doctor.

"No," Dana said. "They destroyed every backup. The New Men didn't miss a thing. The *Saint Petersburg's* computer systems are gone."

That was bad. The Patrol arm of Star Watch sent scouts into the Beyond. The Patrol mapped the star lanes, finding out where a tramline went. It was exciting but dangerous work. Even if they got the *Saint Petersburg's* Laumer Drive working, they would have to do a lot of backtracking as they went down the wrong jump lanes, having to do their own exploring.

"Very well," Maddox said. "Why don't you help Meta? The sooner we have the Laumer Drive working again, the better."

"Of course," Dana said.

Several hours later, Maddox sat at the communal table in *Victory*, eating fish and chips. Lieutenant Noonan sat down, having chosen meatloaf.

"Good news," Valerie said.

Maddox looked up, noticing her tired eyes. Like everyone else, the lieutenant had been pushing herself hard.

"We've almost repaired the Laumer Drive," Valerie said.

"Ah," Maddox said.

The lieutenant scowled. "I thought you'd be happy to hear that."

"I am."

"No, you're not. You're glum. What's wrong, sir?"

Maddox almost shrugged. No. That wouldn't do. If the Laumer Drive worked, that was good news. It might take longer, a lot longer, to get home. But, with the drive, they could make it. Even so, he found himself telling the lieutenant the bad news.

"The New Men booby-trapped the destroyer's computers," he said.

"So?"

"We don't have any charts showing us the Laumer-Points and the destination of the various wormholes."

Valerie blinked at him. Understanding flooded her eyes. "Oh," she said.

"Indeed," he said.

The lieutenant became thoughtful. "You know, sir, in the academy, I had to memorize the tramline entry points. I've been doing the same out here. It's an automatic process with me."

Maddox sat up. "Do you think you could write that down?"

"I think so," she said.

"You must start mapping it at once."

"Let me gulp this down first," she said, indicating her meal.

"Of course, of course," he said. "What will you need?"

"Some old-fashioned pen and paper will be best. I think better that way."

Maddox laughed. This was excellent news. After the meal, he scrounged up the needed items for her.

Valerie sat at a table and began to write from memory. Over the course of several hours, she painstakingly produced a Laumer-Line star chart. First, she mapped out the Commonwealth points. Then, she began to retrace their journey into the Beyond.

By the time Meta, Riker and Doctor Rich repaired the drive, Valerie handed Maddox the finished product.

It took several starship jumps to bring them to the nearest tramline. Then, the decisive moment arrived.

Meta stayed in the destroyer, linked by radio with the bridge where Maddox and Valerie readied themselves.

Victory neared the system's known Laumer-Point. Maddox couldn't sit. Through an act of will, he kept himself from pacing.

"We're ready," Valerie radioed Meta.

"Wait a moment," Meta said. Several seconds passed. "There," she said. "Do you see it on your screen?"

Maddox looked up. So did Lieutenant Noonan. He wanted to groan. He couldn't see anything at first. Finally, a shimmering nimbus appeared.

Valerie clapped her hands. "Look at that, sir."

"I am," Maddox said quietly.

Valerie bent to her panel. "I'm seeing the Laumer-Point, Meta. The destroyer's drive works."

Meta laughed. Maddox found the sound intoxicating.

"We're going home, sir," Valerie said.

Maddox nodded. Their odds of making it had just improved. He wondered, though, if the New Men were going to let them go just like that. Yet, what could they do to stop them? *Victory* must be far ahead of the enemy star cruisers. Well, he wasn't going to worry about it now.

"Enter the wormhole," Maddox told the holoimage.

Soon, the mighty vessel applied thrust, slipping into the entry point. It was the first time the starship used a tramline.

-43-

The journey home should have been uneventful. They had a tremendous lead over the enemy star cruisers. Even better, the New Men couldn't possibly know which route they used. That made the coming situation more than troubling.

Meta continued to prove her worth as an engineer. Despite the battle damage to the ancient starship, through ceaseless work, she kept the needed systems running. Fortunately, the antimatter engines didn't require any repairs. Not even Meta could have fixed those. Everyone pitched in, helping where they could, which kept them all occupied.

The days soon merged into a week and then a month. After a month and a half, the impossible happened.

Victory moved through what Lieutenant Noonan had dubbed on her charts as the Oran System. It possessed a G class star, a large world with a carbon dioxide atmosphere, a moon and a distant asteroid belt. According to Valerie's recollection, two wormhole entrances existed here. *Victory* exited the one near the star and traveled to the other beside the world.

Everything should have been routine. Captain Maddox was on the bridge with Lieutenant Noonan watching the controls. It was the second day without the AI. Dana had suggested they turn off the alien artificial intelligence.

"Why?" Maddox had wanted to know.

"Every second we keep the AI on makes me nervous," the doctor had told Maddox. "I believe it's secretly attempting to regain control of the ship."

"Why didn't you tell me that earlier?"

"I didn't want to give you yet another worry. We needed the AI, right? Well, we don't anymore. We finally know how to run the starship by ourselves."

At Maddox's orders, Dana had disconnected the artificial intelligence. They ran the starship manually. They'd had enough practice over the last few weeks.

A soft sound alerted Maddox. He moved to a board. "What's that?" he asked.

Valerie had been studying her charts. Even after a month and a half, she kept remembering refinements. Setting the charts aside, she rose, moving to the control where Maddox pointed.

"Our instruments are tracking a spaceship," Valerie told him.

"Why didn't we see it sooner?" Maddox asked.

Valerie sat down at the controls. She hesitated a moment. Then, she began tapping buttons. Lines appeared in her forehead as she studied the data. The furrows deepened.

"What have you discovered?" Maddox asked.

"The configuration of the approaching spaceship, sir," she said. "It—" Valerie sat up, turning around. "Captain, that's a star cruiser."

"You mean a New Man vessel?" he asked.

She nodded.

"Did it use a cloaking device?" he asked.

Valerie hunched over her panel, studying it before tapping more controls.

Maddox watched the screen. Another star cruiser appeared. It moved fast out of the distant asteroid belt.

"Those can't be the same cruisers that battled us in the Beyond," he said.

"I think they are, sir."

"That's impossible."

"Captain," she said, slapping a console. "There's a third wormhole in the system."

"You can sense it with your instruments?" Maddox asked, surprised.

"No, sir," Valerie said. "It's a logical deduction. The exit point must be inside the asteroid belt. The enemy ships must have just come out of the third Laumer-Point in this system."

"That can't be right," Maddox said. "The enemy doesn't show any signs of Jump Lag."

"They're New Men, sir."

"The ships—"

"Must have configurations we lack, sir."

Thoughtfully, Maddox stroked his chin. "Maybe," he said. "Jump Lag can also be fickle."

"True," Valerie said, "but not that fickle. I think the enemy ships clearly use technology we don't have. Jump Lag doesn't seem to affect them."

As the two of them watched the screen, the cruisers increased velocity. The distances were great, but at the starship's present speed—

"We're going to have to use the star drive again," Maddox said.

"Without the AI's help, sir?"

Maddox didn't like the idea. Yet, it seemed clear that with their present speed and heading, and that of the enemy cruisers, the New Men would have a window of opportunity for long-distance firing. While Meta had repaired *some* systems, the starship wasn't in any condition for more battle.

Maddox shook his head. How had the New Men found them again? *Victory* had a great lead over the enemy vessels. Even if the New Men had faster ships, how had they known to come to this system? It was the same old reoccurring problem.

At a beep from a different panel, Valerie jumped up, moving to it. After tapping the board, she said, "We're being hailed, sir."

"Ignore it," he said. Maddox didn't want to speak with Per Lomax again. "We have to leave this system, and we should do it now."

Valerie coordinated with the others. Without the AI, it took time to ready the various systems for a star jump.

"Maybe we should turn on the AI," Maddox told Dana over the intercom.

"I don't recommend it," the doctor said. "Besides, we can do this without it."

Maddox studied the screen. The two star cruisers kept closing. The enemy commander continued to hail their ship.

"How did they find us?" Maddox asked Valerie. "The enemy can only use the wormholes. *Victory* has the tramlines and the star drive to cross over to better situated wormholes. We should have left the New Men far behind in the Beyond.

"Well," Valerie said, "the enemy cruisers must be faster than Star Watch vessels. We've been over this before, sir. I think they also have longer-ranged sensors."

Maddox thought about that. The idea of such sensors just didn't seem right. It would give the enemy too much of an advantage. Scowling, he wondered when Dana would be ready. They needed to star jump sooner rather than later.

As the minutes ticked away, Maddox pondered the implications of the enemy vessels. The cruisers continued to show remarkable powers. With ships like those at the command of men such as Per Lomax...

"I'm beginning to suspect the New Men have fewer starships than we believe," Maddox told Valerie. "Otherwise, why haven't they begun a full scale invasion of the Commonwealth?"

"I don't know," the lieutenant said.

"Consider the situation," Maddox said. "The New Men took Odin, Horace and Parthia, stopping there. It's almost as if they challenged us to come and look at what they had done."

"Why would they do that?"

"Good question," Maddox said. "Maybe they need more time to construct extra star cruisers?"

"More?" she asked.

"Enough to face our united fleet," he said. "Yes, their ships are better than ours, but perhaps we still have the numbers to swamp them in a big battle. Given sufficient time, though, they'll bring their newly built cruisers to the front."

"If that's true," Valerie said, "Star Watch should be attacking them with everything before they're ready."

Maddox glanced at the screen. What was taking Dana so long? Would they have to turn on the AI again? Why should that be a problem?

"We know they've infiltrated the Commonwealth with spies and found traitors among us," Valerie said. "Maybe they'll try to start a civil war inside us just as Dana's people once tried to do with Rigel's Social Syndicate."

He'd told the lieutenant about that.

"The New Men have found traitors and use spies, but maybe not as many as we think," Maddox said. "I've thought about Octavian Nerva. I'm not sure he was their tool."

"The evidence indicates that he is," Valerie said.

"I disagree. If the New Men were that strong—with tycoons like Octavian in their pocket—the enemy would have already have conquered us. I believe we're making some false assumptions. The New Men aren't stupid. If they haven't moved directly against our strength, there's a good reason for it."

"What reason?" Valerie asked.

"That's what I'd like to know."

A squawking sound came from the nearest panel. "We're ready on our side," Dana said.

On the screen, Maddox checked the enemy's position. The star cruisers closed fast, but it would still be several hours before they were in firing range.

"Let's do it," he told Valerie.

Together, Dana and Valerie coordinated. Then, the lieutenant engaged the star drive.

For a second, nothing happened. *Will we have to turn on the alien AI?* Then, the ship jumped, leaving the two cruisers far behind.

"We did it. We're in the clear," Maddox told Valerie after he recovered.

"Yes," Lieutenant Noonan said, "but for how long?"

***

As they journeyed through the Beyond, they kept watching for enemy cruisers. Using tramlines, *Victory* went from one star system to another.

"Can the New Men communicate with a faster-than-light system?" Maddox asked Dana.

"That would give them incredible power," the doctor said.

Maddox believed that.

After several more days, the excitement of the encounter died down. Once more, they fell into a routine.

Two weeks later, they exited the Beyond and entered the Oikumene. It should have been cause for celebration, but they'd still made sure to use wormholes that led into the system in a roundabout way, skirting the Wahhabi Caliphate in an effort to reach Commonwealth territory.

The Caliphate and the Commonwealth had issues with each other that had brought about more than one skirmish in the past. If the Wahhabi princes could get their hands on the ancient starship… No. None of the crew wanted that.

For five days, they traveled even more warily than before. In the Deneb System, their luck ran out.

Maddox and Ensign Maker were playing checkers on the bridge. It turned out that Keith was something of a prodigy at the game. He only lost two thirds of the time. Maddox couldn't believe it.

Keith frowned constantly, sitting hunched over the board. They'd played two hundred games so far. This was their two hundred and first. The ace rubbed his fingers as his hand hovered over a red piece. Finally, he stared up at Maddox.

"Before I played you," Keith said, "I hadn't lost a game in seven years. Why are you so good?"

Maddox shrugged moodily. For quite some time, he'd been wondering the same thing about the ex-strikefighter ace.

Keith's nostrils flared, and he shook his head. Something must have caught his eye then. He stiffened, sat up and stared at the screen.

Maddox noticed and gave the screen his attention as well.

Both men rose at the same time, each moving to a different panel. Blips had appeared on the screen.

"We're being hailed," Keith informed him.

"Give me a minute," Maddox said. He studied the enemy ships, waiting for the sensors to tell him more.

"That's a Wahhabi battle group," Keith said. "I'd know those shapes anywhere."

The *Scimitar*-class vessels were oblong craft with extremely long-ranged lasers. The Wahhabi navy preferred distance battles, using speed to keep their opponents from closing.

"Their commander is insistent," Keith said.

"Put him on the screen," Maddox said.

A moment later, the battle group's sheik-superior appeared on the screen. He was a dark-skinned man wearing a red turban with a large diamond in the center. He had shrewd features and thin lips.

"You are in Wahhabi space," the sheik-superior said.

"I am Captain Maddox of Star Watch."

"Can this be true?" the sheik said. "Your vessel matches no known Star Watch configuration."

"That may be—"

"Please do not interrupt me," the sheik said. "I am speaking to inform you to prepare for boarding."

"You're hours away from us," Maddox said.

"Which is why you must shut off your vessel now as we match velocities," the sheik said. "If you do not comply, we will fire to disable you. Afterward, we will claim your vessel."

"Oh," Maddox said. "I see." He bent his head as if thinking. Then, he looked up. "Yes. It will be as you wish."

Keith covered his mouth, possibly to hide a grin. At Maddox's signal, the ace turned off the sheik-superior.

"We're going to use the star drive to get away?" Keith asked.

Maddox nodded. He'd hoped to avoid something like this. He hadn't wanted to let the Wahhabi Caliphate know about the new technology. But he didn't see any way out of the situation. He couldn't let them board *Victory* and take the Commonwealth's prize.

Fifteen minutes later, the ancient starship made its second-to-last star drive jump of the trip, leaving the Caliphate's sailors far behind.

***

Twenty-eight hours later, Maddox chose pasta and Swedish meatballs, heating the packet and taking the meal to the table.

Meta sat there, polishing off freeze-dried steak and fries.

He nodded a greeting.

Her mouth tightened. Finally, she said, "I'm almost done."

He sat across from her, putting his meal and utensils on the table. "We're nearing Commonwealth space," he said.

"Good," she said.

"It appears we're going to make it to Earth."

"Uh-huh," Meta said.

"Have you given any thought to your future?"

She eyed him before shaking her head.

"In my report," Maddox said, "I'll indicate that your services were invaluable to the mission's success."

"Is that supposed to make up for the way you've treated me?"

Maddox raised an eyebrow. "I'm merely letting you know that if you wish to remain in Star Watch, I'm sure there will be a place for you."

"You think your oath meant anything?" Meta asked.

"You willingly took the oath."

"You know what I mean," she said.

"I suppose I do," Maddox said. He picked up his fork, hesitated and finally said, "You have a knack for making repairs when they're most needed. That's a rare quality."

"My services are already taken," Meta told him.

"If you mean the Rouen Colony—"

Meta stood abruptly. "It looks like I'm finished eating. If you'll excuse me, Captain Maddox?"

"Of course," he said. "Think about what I'm saying, Meta. There's a war to the death coming. You've already helped deal the New Men a critical blow."

"Save your speeches," she said. "We're not home yet. The New Men will have a few more surprises left. You and I both know that."

"Perhaps," he said.

"Enjoy your meal," Meta said. She grabbed her empty packet, tossing it into the dispenser before stalking out of the chamber.

Maddox watched her leave and wondered if she was right. Would the New Men have another play to make? Could they transmit messages faster-than-light? Or would the enemy's secret service act against them as a matter of course?

He speared the tines into the pasta, rolling the noodles around his fork and taking his first bite. The last leg of the journey was about to begin.

***

Victory entered official Commonwealth space. Two Laumer-Points later, they exited a wormhole into the Vancouver System.

It had an F class star with twelve planets and thousands of comets. They were all barren, although two of the gas giants had scoopers floating in the upper atmosphere. The biggest difference for the crew was seeing a Star Watch frigate.

"Finally," Lieutenant Noonan said, "one of our own."

"Maybe," Maddox said, as he studied the sleek craft.

Valerie had already hailed the frigate. She turned to face the captain. "Do you suspect the ship?" she asked.

"Of course," he said.

"I don't understand. What gave them away?"

"Nothing," Maddox said. "This close to the finish, I suspect everyone."

"Oh," Valerie said. "I thought you meant—"

"I know," Maddox said. "Please, they're answering."

Valerie turned back to her board and established communications with the frigate.

Soon, Maddox used the screen to speak to Commander Kris Guderian of the *Osprey*. She had short hair and a splash of freckles across her nose. She belonged to the Patrol Arm of the Star Watch, routinely making voyages into the Beyond.

"I am Captain Maddox of the Star Watch," he said. He wore his dress uniform. He'd been doing so for the last few days in anticipation of a meeting like this. "If you have your recognition codes with you…"

"Just a minute, Captain," Commander Guderian said. On the screen, she turned away, speaking quietly to someone unseen. Finally, nodding to someone else, she turned back to him. "I'm ready. Go ahead."

"What color are you presently using?" Maddox asked.

"Indigo Green," she replied.

Maddox thought a moment. *Ah, right.* "The fox is red, and the hen is purple," he said.

Guderian paused as she no doubt checked her records for the proper response. "I see," she said. "You're claiming priority clearance passage."

"Negative," Maddox said, grinning. "And nice try. You Patrol people always were a suspicious bunch. I'm claiming a Star Watch emergency, as your codebook says. You will escort us to Earth. Before we start, though, I have to know the situation with the New Men."

Commander Guderian frowned. "The last I heard, Star Watch Command is debating sending a second expedition to Odin."

"You know about the first expedition?" Maddox asked.

"I take it you've been in the Beyond for quite some time, Captain."

"Have you ever seen this type of starship before?" he asked.

"You know I haven't," she said. "When do we get started for Earth?"

"Immediately," he said. "Two enemy star cruisers have been chasing us. It's possible they might show up again."

Worry entered Commander Guderian's eyes. "Did I hear you correctly?"

"You did," Maddox said. "Two New Men star cruisers are out there, trying to close in on us. Those ships are extraordinarily fast."

"Then, how have you kept ahead of them?"

"No more questions, Commander," Maddox said. "If we can't get this starship to Earth, we've never going to win the coming war with the New Men."

***

Several days later, Maddox summoned the others for a meeting. His gut told him this wasn't finished. They had journeyed deep into the Beyond, found and captured the alien super-ship, escaped the New Men and returned to Commonwealth space. What's more, Kris Guderian was a good officer. They had even picked up more escort vessels, a second frigate, a destroyer and a missile cruiser.

Maddox explained all this as Valerie, Riker, Dana and Meta sat at the table. Pushing away from his spot, Maddox stood, putting his hands behind his back.

"We should be safe now," he said. "Yet, we've learned to expect the cunning of the New Men."

"What are suggesting?" Dana asked.

Maddox shook his head. "I don't know. My instincts tell me to beware. How deeply have the New Men infiltrated the Commonwealth and Star Watch? Commander Guderian seems solid. These other starship captains, though…"

"You don't trust the other officers?" Valerie asked.

"No," Maddox said.

"What are you suggesting we do?" Dana asked.

"That we be ready to star jump at a moment's notice," Maddox said.

The discussion went on for a time, but he'd emphasized his plan to them. Suspect everyone until he could hand off *Victory* to those at home.

***

In the New Siberia System with its radioactive moons, two SWS destroyers approached the small flotilla. Commander Kris Guderian led the pack in the *Osprey*, with the other frigate and destroyer between *Victory* and two new ships. The missile cruiser brought up the rear.

Informed about the two destroyers, Maddox sprinted to the bridge. He spoke into a comm-unit as he ran.

"Meta!" he said loudly.

"I can hear you just fine," she said over the comm. "What's wrong?"

"Are you ready for a star jump?"

"No," Meta said. "I'm relaxing."

"I need you in the engine room," Maddox said. "Is the doctor with you?"

"Why are you so upset?" Meta asked. "Valerie told us the new ships are Star Watch vessels. She asked for their recognition codes. Each captain gave them."

"I know," Maddox said. "Be ready, though."

It took a moment. Finally, Meta said, "I'm on my way."

Stowing the comm-unit, Maddox ran until he reached the bridge. Lieutenant Noonan glanced at him in surprise.

Ignoring her, Maddox went to the main screen. The two destroyers were matching velocities. He stared at the ships, wondering about their crews.

"How did they get so close before anyone noticed them?" he asked Valerie.

"Do you see all those moons?" Lieutenant Noonan asked. "The amount of radiation they're pouring interferes with our sensors. New Siberia is rich in fissionable ores, but it's no place for a colony."

Maddox's nostrils flared. He'd been getting more nervous the closer they came to Earth. The New Men weren't going to give up easily. But how could anyone near Earth know about the super-ship anyway?

"Call Guderian," he said.

Valerie patched through a call.

Soon, the freckle-faced commander greeted Maddox.

370

"This might sound odd," the captain said, "but you need to send a heavily armed boarding party to each destroyer."

Kris Guderian blinked at him. "The recognition codes—"

"Can easily be duplicated," Maddox finished.

"No, not that easily," Guderian said.

"Nevertheless, I want you to send a boarding party to each destroyer."

Kris Guderian opened her mouth, maybe to protest. Finally, she nodded. "As you wish, Captain," she said.

Afterward, Maddox watched the screen. The destroyers were too close. Something about their presence here—

"Captain," Valerie said, as she monitored her sensors. "Their weapons have just gone hot."

Maddox bared his teeth. He knew it. If he simply attacked Star Watch vessels, that might land him in terrible trouble. But if he waited for them to make the first strike…

"Use the neutron beam on them," he said.

"Sir?" Valerie asked.

"Now!" he shouted. "Target the nearest destroyer and fire! We have to get *Victory* to Earth no matter the cost."

Valerie turned pale, but she carried out his order. As the two destroyers accelerated toward them, *Victory's* ray reached out. It struck the nearest destroyer's shield, causing an overload. At the same time, enemy lasers beamed from the stricken ship at *Victory*.

Fortunately, a week ago, Dana and Meta had finally repaired the starship's deflector shield. It easily fended off the destroyer's weak lasers.

The enemy's overloaded shield collapsed. The neutron beam chewed into the hull. Seconds later, the vessel blew apart, sending hull plating spinning into the void.

The SWS missile cruiser launched at the remaining destroyer. The two frigates began to use their limited weaponry on the last ship.

"They're finished now," Valerie said.

Maddox watched the screen. One moment, the destroyer fought. The next, the traitorous vessel turned a brilliant and expanding white. Crying out, Maddox turned away from the screen, throwing an arm in front of his face.

After a moment, the intense light faded.

"What happened?" Valerie whispered.

371

"Quantum blast," Maddox said, who faced the screen again. "They must have detonated themselves."

Victory's shield turned black, threatening an overload. Soon, though, it began to dissipate the horrendous energy.

"There's an incoming message for you, sir," Valerie said. "Commander Guderian wishes to talk."

Maddox nodded absently. The attack implied that the New Men or their people on Earth already knew about the super-ship just as he had feared. How was that possible?

The screen had become hazy due to the quantum blast. Now, it began to clear as Commander Guderian came online. Shock gave her a bewildered look.

"The destroyers just committed mass suicide," she whispered.

Maddox concentrated on the moment. Guderian looked as if she needed to hear the truth.

"The New Men have deeply infiltrated the Commonwealth and now, it appears, the Star Watch," Maddox told her. "That's why I'm so careful all the time."

"If I hadn't witnessed this," Guderian said, "I never would have believed such a thing possible."

"Humanity is in a conflict like no other," Maddox said.

Guderian stared at him. The shocked expression changed into something more thoughtful. "One thing keeps bothering me. How did the destroyer captains know about you?"

The Patrol commander was sharp, maybe too sharp. "That's an excellent question," Maddox said. "I'm afraid I'm going to have to jump again."

"What do you mean *jump*?"

Maddox never explained it to Commander Guderian. "A moment," he told her. Then, he gave Valerie a nod.

The star drive took them three light years away, bringing them to a new tramline.

After they recovered, Maddox said, "We have to travel fast."

"Why not use the star drive all the way to Earth?" Valerie asked.

"I'm not sure if *Victory* can take it. Otherwise, that's what I'd do."

They were close to home, and each tramline brought them to a populated star system. It meant interrogations and a greater chance of falling into an enemy ambush.

Finally, a bit of luck helped them. In the Tau Ceti System, *Victory* came upon a battle group.

"What do we do?" Valerie asked.

Keith was on the bridge. "An entire battle group can't be under enemy control. If that were the case, the war would be over before it started."

"Captain," Valerie said. "Admiral Fletcher wishes to speak to you."

"He knows it's me?" Maddox asked, surprised.

Valerie put a hand to her ear, pushing the bud embedded there. "No, sir. He wishes to speak to our commander."

"Right," Maddox said. "Put him on." He knew that Admiral Fletcher heartily disliked him.

Soon, a big man with heavy features glared at Maddox. "You!" the admiral said, as if accusing Maddox.

"Yes, sir, it's me."

It only took a moment for Fletcher to regain his composure. "What's the meaning of this, Maddox? I have word that an enemy ship is heading for Earth for a sneak assault."

"I have no doubt of that, sir."

Fletcher grinned nastily, almost with glee. "You're an enemy agent, then?"

"No, sir, I've been working undercover for the brigadier, at the Lord High Admiral's orders."

Admiral Fletcher scowled. "Why aren't you surprised I have a message to intercept and destroy your ship?"

"Because the New Men and their agents have infiltrated our organizations," Maddox said. "Somehow, they know that I've retrieved an alien super-ship. This vessel has the technologies needed to defeat the New Men."

"You expect me to believe such trash?"

"I do indeed, sir."

"I'm going to send over a team—"

Maddox shook his head, interrupting. "I'm afraid I can't allow that, sir."

"What did you say?" Fletcher asked.

"This is a top secret mission. Agents of the New Men have already tried to destroy the ship. Now, they're attempting to use trickery to get others to do their dirty work for them."

373

"Are you trying to tell me you think I'm in league with the New Men?"

"Sir, you are too cantankerous to be one of their agents. I believe you're exactly what you appear to be: an angry admiral wishing to crush Earth's enemies."

Admiral Fletcher took his time answering. Finally, he said, "You know I don't like you, Maddox."

"I do, sir."

"I have my doubts about you."

"This I realize."

"But I don't believe you're a traitor. Very well. If Cook authorized this, I'm going to listen to your outlandish scheme. But if you're lying to me, I'm going to break you, son."

"Thank you, sir. I'm going to need an escort to Earth, traveling under combat conditions."

Fletcher seemed taken aback. "Do you have any idea what that means?"

"I know exactly what that means, sir."

Fletcher gave him a wolf's grin. "I see. I hope Cook disowns you. Until then, I'll work under the assumption you're actually doing what you're supposed to be." He turned away barking orders. Then, the admiral faced Maddox again. "Let's get started."

They did, with Admiral Fletcher's battleships taking up escort duty around *Victory*.

Each jump point took place under full combat conditions with a single caveat. A frigate went through first to warn any defenders on the other side. Afterward, high-grade thermonuclear drones went through, igniting in case any New Men were waiting by the Laumer-Point entrance on the other side.

A week later, they entered the Solar System. Four Star Watch battle groups took up station in the Oort Cloud, far away from any wormhole entrance. There, Maddox and the others finally left the alien starship.

A fast cruiser whisked them to Earth. The voyage was over. They had found the needed vessel and brought it home again. Now, the Star Watch experts planned to study it in detail, seeing if they could duplicate alien technology to the Commonwealth's advantage.

-44-

Captain Maddox felt uncomfortable striding down the hall toward Brigadier O'Hara's office. He was back in Geneva on Earth. It still seemed unreal. To have traveled so far and risked his life on an uncanny mission, and then to be home again in familiar surroundings—

Have I changed? Have I lost something? Why do I feel different?

He couldn't define it to himself. The hall seemed to press inward, crowding him. Maybe he had acquired Ensign Maker's disease. The ace loved flying in space. The Scotsman didn't seem alive unless he was gripping flight controls, attempting an impossible maneuver.

I had a deck under my feet. I commanded a starship. Is that what I want to do with the rest of my life?

Maybe he was simply feeling post-mission depression. It would leave him soon enough. He would fully decompress, rest, gain strength and soon be ready for his next assignment.

A nagging doubt lingered. Captain Maddox wondered if only a line command on a starship could scratch a new itch. The New Men gathered. Humanity had to stand together and defeat the menace, or they would succumb one by one as Odin, Horace and Parthia had fallen.

He reached the secretary's desk. The man informed him the brigadier was waiting.

"Go ahead," the secretary said.

Maddox opened the door. The Iron Lady was hunched over her synthi-wood desk, scribbling something.

"Please, sit," she said, without looking up.

Maddox moved to a chair before her desk, settling himself. He'd done this many times before. Yet, now it felt different, almost surreal. He glanced at the glass case of model starships. The feeling of unreality bit again. The room seemed to shrink, along with Brigadier O'Hara.

He concentrated on her. Her gray hair remained perfectly in place. No doubt she used hairspray. Her veined hand scratched a stylus on a pad. Abruptly, she set down the stylus and looked up at him. Her eyes were bright and alive. They seemed to swell her stature. She no longer seemed small and cramped, but an energetic spider queen busy capturing traitorous flies and enemy agents.

"Captain Maddox," she said. "You have returned. I congratulate you on a successful mission. Well done."

"Excuse me, ma'am," Maddox said. "But that seems horribly anticlimactic for an operation that might have possibly just saved humanity from the New Men."

She stared at him before saying, "Your flair for the melodramatic hasn't changed a bit, I see. Still, I suppose you have a point. I imagine you'll want the Lord High Admiral to enter, bend on his knee, grasp your hand and weep his thanks."

"That would be more in keeping with my exploit, yes, ma'am," Maddox said, grinning.

Brigadier O'Hara pursed her lips. "I would be happy to oblige you, Captain. Unfortunately, my thoughts and those of the Lord High Admiral are too dark for such joy. We have the alien wreck you brought back. I've read the reports. It's falling apart even as the experts study it."

"Yet, the wreck, as you put it, is brimming with alien technologies," Maddox said. "The improved deflector screen can withstand the New Men's beams better than Star Watch shields can. Even better, the alien neutron beam can punch holes through the enemy's deflectors. According to the AI, the starship possesses even more powerful weapon systems. The ancient vessel is a bonanza of technologies. It has a new star drive that bypasses tramlines."

"We're going to need every one of those weapons if we're to stay ahead of the New Men," O'Hara said.

Maddox grew more alert. "There's bad news, I take it."

"Yes, Captain. The New Men have been busy while you were away. This is strictly confidential. They have sent envoys to the Wahhabi Caliphate. Certain factions in the caliphate's court want to ally with the New Men. Others counsel a wait and see attitude, if there should be open war. They're considering neutrality."

"Are they mad?" Maddox asked. "The New Men are simply using divide and rule tactics to try to pick us off one by one."

"You are astute as always, Captain. The news is even worse, I'm afraid. Certain Commonwealth systems are also considering neutrality. Chief among them is Rigel's Social Syndicate."

"Don't they understand their very lives are at stake?"

"This is an interesting point," the brigadier said. "Do you have proof for such a statement?"

Maddox frowned. "I'm not sure I understand you."

"Captain, as I've said, the New Men have sent spies and envoys to many worlds. They speak soothing words, hoping to divide humanity, perhaps even gain allies among us. News of the Pan System Battle has made some people cautious toward antagonizing powerful enemies. We need proof as to what's happened on Odin, Horace and Parthia."

"With the new systems in *Victory*—"

"Ah," O'Hara said. "You can duplicate them in our ships?"

"Me? Certainly not, ma'am. I'm not an engineer."

"Reverse engineering a system takes time, Captain. Duplicating it takes even longer. We have to build new starships. Unfortunately, building an ordinary battleship normally takes three years. That's with systems everyone knows how to construct. How long will it take our shipyards to build alien weaponry that works?"

"Maybe you should repair *Victory* and use her as she is in battle."

"We are exploring all options," O'Hara said. The brigadier closed her mouth and set her hands on the desk. Lines appeared in her forehead. She smoothed those away and smiled sadly.

"I'm sorry," the Iron Lady said. "You don't deserve to hear my gloom. You have accomplished an amazing feat, Captain Maddox. I'm proud of you. With the alien starship in our hands, we have a chance against the New Men. We have hope. You've given us that. One way or another, it is going to be a monumental struggle. The New Men have exposed some of their prime assets among us in trying to destroy you when you left and then when you returned with your prize. Still, we have heavy work ahead of us. Your debriefing might take longer than you like. We have to know everything you can remember about them. We *must* find weak points that we can exploit."

"I'll do what I can, ma'am."

"I know you will, Captain. I have faith in your abilities. After the debriefing, you will leave on another dangerous mission."

"I'm not sure I'm ready to hear about it, ma'am."

"No," she said. "I suppose not."

"You know," Maddox said. "I do have a suggestion about the starship."

"Yes?"

"You must find and recruit Professor Ludendorff. Most likely, he can tease useful information from *Victory* that no one else could."

"I'll keep your suggestion in mind. Do you happen to know where we can find the professor?"

Maddox studied the brigadier. The way she asked that… "I have no idea," he said.

"Hmm…well, never mind. We'll concentrate on your debriefing. Before you go, Captain, the Lord High Admiral would like a word with you."

He nodded.

Brigadier O'Hara stood. She was a small woman. She came around the desk. Maddox stood to his feet. She held out her hand and shook his.

"Well done, Captain. I'm proud of you and very glad you made it back in one piece. Don't ever repeat this to anyone, but sending you on this hopeless mission has given me many sleepless nights. I didn't truly think you could do it."

She squeezed his fingers. Then, she released his hand and straightened her tunic. She almost seemed embarrassed. Heading to a hidden door, pressing a switch, she caused it to open. "Go down the hall and to your left. The Lord High Admiral is waiting."

Maddox blinked several times. A tightening of his chest made it impossible for him to speak. Instead, he inclined his head and then marched into the corridor. Behind him, the door shut softly.

Epilogue

After leaving *Victory* and the Oort Cloud and landing on Earth, Ensign Keith Maker went to the Star Watch London debriefing center. There, for six weeks, Intelligence experts went over what he thought of as his excruciatingly detailed recollection of the journey.

Keith underwent many tests, and he found them interesting. The truth was he liked the attention. Finally, he left the center and received official notification that Star Watch wished him to remain with the Fleet. Would he consider a bump in grade to Second Lieutenant and attending the advanced strikefighter school on Titan?

"Bloody yes, I will," Keith told the commodore who asked him. "Do you want me to be an instructor there?"

"Ah...no," the commodore said. "You'd be a student for an elite strikefighter arm we're building."

Keith frowned.

A big man with a thick chest, the commodore studied him keenly. "There something else I should tell you. The new *strikefighters* have to do with the alien starship."

"I don't understand what that means," Keith said.

"It's a new idea and it's going to take extremely individualistic and egocentric men to pilot the experimental craft."

Keith began to have an inkling what this was about. "You're talking about a new secret weapon, aren't you?"

With his thick fingers folded on his desk, the commodore said no more.

Keith had been with Maddox long enough to interpret certain signs. The commodore had just given him a hint. Star Watch wanted individualistic pilots for something fancier and more dangerous than mere strikefighters.

"I'm in, mate. I'll go to Titan."

"We thought you would," the commodore said. He opened a drawer and pulled out a single paper. "If you'll sign this, you'll be on your way."

Keith barely glanced at the official Star Watch paper. With a flourish, he put his signature on it. That evening, he left for the fighting school that would forever change his life.

***

Lieutenant Valerie Noonan went to a Star Watch debriefing center in Cleveland, Ohio. She spent four weeks there. Lord High Admiral Cook spoke to her at the end of her stay. They walked in the outer garden, tossing breadcrumbs to quack-begging ducks.

"I'm impressed with you, Captain," the Lord High Admiral said.

Valerie might have pointed out she was a lieutenant, but this was the Lord High Admiral speaking. She tossed a breadcrumb to a mallard. No. It sat wrong with her that he didn't even know her rank.

"Excuse me, sir," she said. "I'm a lieutenant not a captain."

The white-haired man smiled at her, causing deep wrinkles in his red face. "I see. You believe I'm so old that I don't know the rank of the person I'm speaking to, eh. You dare to correct me. Good. That means I'm making the right choice."

"Sir?" she asked.

"I've just given you a promotion, Captain. Congratulations," he said.

"Thank you, sir," Valerie said, shaking hands with the Lord High Admiral of Star Watch. "Uh, does this mean I get a ship of my own?"

"Not yet," Cook said. "I'm putting together an advisory team on the New Men. I want you on the team, Captain."

What Valerie wanted was her own command. She had no desire to become a staff officer.

Maybe the Lord High Admiral sensed this. "I'm going to insist on this for the moment," he told her. "There are a handful of people who have seen, spoken or listened to a New Man. You're the most responsible of those."

"Do you mean the members of our group, sir, those who have seen a New Man?"

"I do indeed," the Lord High Admiral said.

Valerie thought about that. Finally, she asked, "Will I ever get a line command again, sir?"

"That might happen sooner than you think," he said.

"Then I would be happy to join your team, sir."

"Splendid," he said. "You're leaving with me, then. I have a meeting in Geneva to attend. You'll be at my side listening. We're planning our next step against the New Men."

Captain Noonan of the Star Watch nodded, following the Lord High Admiral to a waiting armored air-car.

***

Among the group, Sergeant Riker spent the least amount of time in debriefing. He knew what the experts would want and gave concise statements.

Afterward, he headed to Geneva and a waiting Captain Maddox. There was no rest for the damned of the Star Watch Intelligence Service.

***

Doctor Rich never went to an official debriefing. She remained in the Oort Cloud, taking up residence on the SWS Battleship *Antietam*. She received notification of a pardon regarding her crimes against the Social Syndicate of Rigel. As of that moment, she wouldn't have to worry about returning to Loki Prime.

She accepted the honorary rank of colonel in the Star Watch Marines. Then she headed the A-team that worked aboard the alien starship. No one knew as much as she did about it, and Star Watch Command wanted these new technologies as soon as possible.

War was coming against the New Men. Humanity was going to need every advantage it could squeeze in.

***

Meta spent six long weeks in debriefing in the underground Leif Erickson Center in Iceland. She also received a pardon. A major offered her the chance to join Star Watch. She turned him down.

Finally, they released her. Meta flew to New York City. She planned to leave Earth for good. Before she boarded a shuttle to a waiting star liner, Captain Maddox intercepted her.

They spoke for a time. Finally, Maddox bent near as if to whisper in her ear. He kissed her lingeringly. Afterward, he asked her if she'd like to dine with him that evening.

Meta accepted his offer, and remained on Earth for a time, spending the majority of her stay with Captain Maddox. They were among the happiest weeks of her life.

The End

Made in the USA
Lexington, KY
04 April 2016